The Long December

By L Sutton Schleicher

For my dad, the original cheerleader who believed in this story
long before it existed — and for my mom, who taught me how to
bring stories to life.

Prologue

She threw the keys on the counter and followed the sound of the TV to the living room, where her mom sat, surrounded by papers.

Her breath caught, and her body stilled. She felt a chill run down her spine and leaned into the couch to catch her balance.

He was on TV, smiling confidently, flanked by an army of men in suits.

She thought about the first time she saw him. Sitting at her table in the cafeteria, headphones on, nose buried in a book. That entire lunch period, he'd never moved, never looked up from his book. Was it the books? No, it was his soft voice, his shy smile. How he unconsciously brushed his shaggy hair out of his eyes.

Then it was the way he complimented her, the way he noticed things about her. That he relished invisibility the way she did, but still managed to see right through her. How had he gone that long with no one but her even noticing him?

Everyone knew who he was now, though, and he knew it. His shaggy hair was cut and perfectly styled. He looked sharp in his suit.

One of his attorneys said, "We have no comment at this time. We are confident the facts of this case will speak for themselves and that our client will be found not guilty on all counts." Then the other gently guided him up the stairs and into the courthouse.

Andrew turned halfway up, met the camera's gaze, and smiled—confident, deliberate, practiced. The screen stilled on his smile, the same one she'd once believed was just for her.

CHAPTER 1- JITTERS

"I brought you my sweater. It will probably be cold in school." Her mom laid the gray cardigan on top of the pile of clothes Allie had just put on her dresser.

"Thanks, mom," she said absently, flipping through the pile. "Have you seen the jeans Kenzie gave me? I thought they were here on the dresser, but I can't find them anywhere."

"Well, there was a pair of jeans on the dresser, but they were all torn up. I threw them away."

"Mom!" Allie exclaimed, then rushed to the kitchen and started digging through the garbage.

"Oh, honey, stop! I already took the trash outside," Allie was heading to the back door before her mom could finish her sentence. "No, seriously, Allie, stop! I dumped the grease from dinner in there —that's why I already took it outside. Even if they weren't all torn up, they're certainly ruined now."

Allie didn't even slow down. Her mom hadn't been kidding, though. By the time she dug the jeans out of the bin, she was trying not to gag from the smell. She held the jeans up, dismayed.

"Why would you want to wear a pair of Kenzie's old hand-me-down jeans anyway? I thought you were going to wear the cute jumper dress I got you from Penny's?"

"These aren't hand-me-downs!" Allie threw the jeans in the sink and poured dish soap over them, hoping to get the grease stains out. "Kenzie spent a ton on these, even with her discount. These are Threadbare Jeans, Mom! Kenzie says these are the hottest thing this fall." Allie scrubbed furiously, barely keeping her emotions in check. Her best friend worked at Vibe Society, the place to shop if you were under 25.

As if on cue, Allie's phone chimed. She left the jeans in the sink, dried her hands, and grabbed her phone.

"We need to go over your schedule!" Her mom called as she wandered out of the room.

Kenzie: U ready?

Allie thought about the jeans soaking in the sink.

Allie: Not even close.

Kenzie: Hot lunch?

Allie: No. Mom already packed it. Idk what's in it. Don't ask.

Kenzie: Sneaks or Sandals?

Allie: Sneakers. Why?

Kenzie: No. Sandals. The ones you got at Zimmers. So Hot!!!

Allie: It's only supposed to be in the 70s tomorrow.

Kenzie: Not the temp dork. U

Allie: yeah right

Kenzie: evry1 looks hot in tbares. U didn't dry them did u? They cant go in the drier.

Allie thought guiltily about the jeans again.

Allie: All good

Kenzie:

Kenzie: Gotta go. CU in the AM

Allie sent a thumbs-up back and trudged back into the kitchen. Her mom was holding the jeans to the light and inspecting them.

"Are you sure these are new? There's not a lot of material left in some of these places." Allie had thought the same thing when Kenzie gave them to her, but she wasn't going to tell Kenzie no, especially since Kenzie had probably spent her whole paycheck to buy them.

"Well," her mom conceded, "that was quick thinking with the soap. I don't see any stains on them. I'll go throw them in the dryer for you."

"No!" Allie shouted, then blushed, "I mean, they can't go in the dryer. Look at the tag." She gently tugged them out of her mom's grip. "I'm going to go hang them in the shower. They'll be dry enough by tomorrow morning."

Her mom followed her up the stairs, reciting Allie's schedule and filling her in on everything she knew about the teachers. Angela Ellis had been a secretary at the elementary school for over a decade, and in a town as small as theirs, she had the scoop on everyone— including her eccentric AP US History teacher and her Trigonometry teacher, who'd left academia to teach high school math.

"I don't know anything about your English teacher," her mom said, sitting down on her bed and watching her review her checklist and pack her backpack. "She's new to the district and made quite an impression at in-service. I don't know exactly what Coach Horne said to her- you know how he is- but she slapped back at him and he was so stunned he went and sat back down."

"Clapped back," Allie corrected her, and packed her backpack. She paused, then turned to face her mom.

"Mom," Allie said tentatively. "Can we please change my schedule? Five AP classes?"

"Asked and answered." Allie knew she shouldn't push. That was the answer her mom gave whenever her dad's mind was made up.

"But," Allie started, then flinched when her mom interrupted.

"Allison Catherine!" Her tone was sharp— automatic. "We've been over this. You are fully capable of not just taking, but succeeding in, five AP classes." She rifled through the clothes in her closet, stopping and pulling out the pink JCPenney jumper.

"Maybe," Allie replied, pretending she didn't see it, as if ignoring it might make it disappear. "But there's a reason we had to get an exception from the district for me to take this many. I already have my language credit— I passed the AP Spanish test last year, remember? I don't even need to actually take AP French, I just need to pass the test... I'm already fluent; I just need to review the culture stuff. That was the original plan." She gave her mom her most earnest look, "And if I dropped AP Bio..."

Her mom interrupted, "Your dad has already mapped this all out. You can start college as a junior, Allie. Do you have any idea how much it costs to go to Madison?"

"About that," she said. "I could go to Whitewater..."

"You're not going to Whitewater," her mom said firmly.

"Or even MATC," Allie knew she was losing this argument. Again.

"You are not going to community college," her mom said. "Do you have any idea what your father had to do to get that exemption approved? You are perfectly capable of doing the work if you apply yourself."

* * *

Her mom sighed as Allie took the jumper from her and hung it back in the closet. A beat later, she was off again—talking about credits, testing out of classes, the same speech Allie had heard all summer.

When she was done, Allie zipped her backpack and set it by the door, then waited for her mom to notice.

"I'm sorry, sweetheart. It's late. I'll let you get to bed." Her mom kissed her on the head as she passed by.

"So let's plan on leaving at quarter after. I want you to get there early on the first day. You know, between traffic and everything…" Her voice trailed off as she watched her daughter's face transform. "What did I say?"

"You said I could ride with Kenzie this year," Allie reminded her.

"I don't remember saying that you could for sure. I remember you asked and I said I'd talk to your father."

Allie crossed her arms, trying to hold herself together. She didn't want to ride with her mom again this year. It was bad enough she wasn't even old enough to drive herself yet, but really? She was a high school junior. Even if no one knew or cared who she was, it was humiliating.

"You said it would be fine, and that you'd tell him. I already told Kenzie you said yes, and she'll be here tomorrow morning. Please don't do this, Mom. It'll be fine. Kenzie is an excellent driver."

"I'm sure she is, honey, but she's only been driving since March. That's not a very long time."

"It's almost six months, Mom! And she worked all summer. All summer, she drove between here and the mall—pretty much every day. No problems. At. All." As soon as she said it, she crossed her fingers. She shouldn't have challenged the universe like that.

"I know, I know," Her mom sighed. "But she still has her probationary license, so she isn't allowed to have you in the car with her."

"Mom!" Allie cried in exasperation. "She can have one passenger. We've gone over this. She can legally drive me to and from school. She is a good driver. You complained the whole year last year about having to leave so early so you could drop me off. Now you don't have to this year." Technically, Allie could ride the bus, but that was even less appealing.

Her mom hesitated and finally said, "We'll see how it goes this week. We don't need to let your dad know, okay?" She bent and kissed Allie on the cheek. "I just worry about you. You know you're the most precious thing I have."

"I know," Allie said and gave a resigned smile.

As soon as the door clicked shut behind her mom, Allie was on her phone.

Allie: Mom's freaking about me riding with you. No craziness in the morning.
Kenzie: But she already said it was okay
Allie: She doesn't remember it that way
Kenzie: Great.
Allie: CU
Kenzie: CU

CHAPTER 2- HOTTIES

Allie and Mrs Ellis watched at the window as Kenzie eased the battered Jeep into the driveway.

"I don't know about this," her mom hesitated. "Her car looks like it's falling apart."

Allie grabbed her backpack and reached for the front door. "It's good, Mom. She just replaced the brakes. It looks rough, but it runs great. She takes really good care of it, I promise."

Before her mom could change her mind, Allie pecked her on the cheek and ran out the door. Kenzie waved to Mrs Ellis and exhaled deeply when Allie got in the car.

"Hurry! Before she changes her mind!" Allie exclaimed, "But go really slow. Be super careful. Don't give her any reason to change her mind. Go! What are you waiting for?" Allie stared at Kenzie expectantly.

"For you to decide which personality is going to win. Am I hurrying or am I going slow?" Kenzie teased.

Allie laughed and said, "You're hurrying very carefully. But we need to go, she's still standing at the door. She'll come out here if you don't move."

Kenzie put the Jeep in reverse and backed cautiously out of the Ellis's driveway. Once they were out of Allie's neighborhood, she turned the radio up and accelerated.

She glanced at Allie, then did a double-take. "Oh my god. Are you wearing your mother's sweater?" Allie blushed. "First of all, it's not even cold. Take it off. Second of all, you're not a middle-aged secretary. You're a hottie in a Jeep with your hottie best friend. Take it off. " Kenzie laughed and teased, but Allie stiffened. Her smile vanished, replaced by something tight and unsure.

"What?" Asked Kenzie.

"Don't say things like that. You don't have to pretend that I'm hot, too. It just makes it worse." Allie turned away to watch out the window.

Kenzie turned the radio down. "Stop it, Allie. I'm not pretending. You are beautiful."

"In my own way," Allie interrupted.

"In every way," Kenzie finished. "You have the most gorgeous hair, and you don't have to do anything to it. You have the best smile of anyone I know, and you are the kindest, smartest person I know."

"And none of that translates to hot, Kenzie. You are hot now. God, the boob fairy, whoever, blessed you with C cups and perfect skin this summer. What did that lifeguard at the pool call me?"

Kenzie shifted in her seat uncomfortably.

"Two by four," Allie continued. "No bumps or curves anywhere."

"The opinion of one ignorant pool boy doesn't count," Kenzie argued, "I'm your best friend and I say you're hot, so you're hot." Allie started to speak, but Kenzie held up her hand and talked over her, "No. We're not talking about this anymore. We are two hotties in this beast of a Jeep, and we are about to conquer our junior year!"

She let out a whoop, and Allie jumped. She wanted to smile, wanted to share in her friend's enthusiasm, but Kenzie was being ridiculous. Allie knew what was coming next, and sure enough, Kenzie continued the conversation they'd had a dozen times over the summer.

"This year is going to be different, Allie. We're not going to be stuck at that table in the back of the cafeteria at lunch. We're going to get invited to parties and go to football games. We're going to have friends and go places and do things. And boys! The boys are going to notice us, and we are finally going to get boyfriends!"

Not gonna cry, not gonna cry, not gonna cry, Allie silently repeated the mantra as she stared out the window.

She willed the tears she could feel to go away. She loved Kenzie, but she did not love Kenzie's vision of their junior year. Kenzie had been her best friend since kindergarten, when she'd walked up to her and announced to the class, "This is my best friend."

All of these years, through everything they'd both been through, it had been just the two of them. Allie didn't want or need anyone else. Allie liked their Friday night tradition of popcorn and a movie. She had no interest in parties or football games, and she had zero interest in boys.

"Allie!" Kenzie snapped her fingers in front of Allie's face to get her attention. "Don't cry," her tone softened. "It's going to be a good thing, I promise."

Allie forced a smile, and Kenzie laughed. "You are the worst liar. I swear it's going to be a great year. I can feel it." She whipped the Jeep into a parking spot. "Have I ever steered you wrong?"

"The haircut you gave me in third grade?"

"Oh my god! Are you ever going to let me live that down? It was very on trend." Kenzie laughed and reached into the backseat and thrust a bag at Allie.

Allie immediately recognized the logo and shook her head. "Kenzie, I can't. You already bought me the jeans. How much did those cost?" She pushed the bag back at Kenzie, who refused to take it.

"You cannot put a price on friendship, bestie. You can, however, put a price on saving your best friend from wearing her mother's cardigan on the first day of school— and looking like she raided the lost and found in the teacher's lounge."

Allie rolled her eyes, then gasped as she pulled the sweater out of the bag. "I love this color!"

Kenzie smiled knowingly, "Technically, this fall is all about the reds... but I knew you'd love this. Earthy tones are in, too — so olive green for you. And look, it has pockets!"

"Can I pay you back for this? The jeans were already too much."

"I'll make you a deal. I get first dibs at your lunch anytime your mom packs it, and we're even."

"That's not a fair trade, and you know it!" Allie laughed.

"You say that because you have a mom that's actually home and cooks for you. Boxed Mac n Cheese is about the best I ever get from my mom now that she decided to go back to school again."

Allie pulled her lunchbox out of her backpack and ceremoniously handed it to Kenzie, "With my eternal gratitude for your wisdom and guidance. And for not letting me look like a dumpster-diving secretary."

Kenzie laughed and grabbed it greedily. Allie's phone chimed as Kenzie hopped out of the Jeep.

* * *

"My mom says have a good day," said Allie, reading the text.

"At some point, she's gonna have to cut the cord. She does know you're in high school, right?"

"I don't think she'd still be packing my lunch if she did,"

"Point," said Kenzie, reaching into the Jeep to grab her purse. "I'll stop complaining." She accidentally hit the horn as she backed out of the Jeep and jumped.

Two boys walking by turned at the sound and stared at Kenzie's bobbing backside. Allie didn't say anything, but her face said enough. Her eyes followed the boys, then dropped to the ground. She folded her arms across her chest, shoulders curling in slightly, like she was trying to disappear.

"What?" Asked Kenzie

She turned to see what Allie had been staring at and froze as the tallest one smirked.

"Who knew the view in the parking lot would be so prime on the first day of school?"

The other boy smiled appreciatively and nodded in agreement.

"Very prime."

Allie watched Kenzie blush a deep crimson before she regained her composure and turned away from them with a flick of her hair. They stood, staring, for a moment more, then walked off joking with each other about Jeeps and other things.

Allie's smile was gone as she carefully folded the sweater and returned it to the bag in the backseat. She grabbed her backpack and the grey cardigan and muttered, "Can we please just sit at our regular table for lunch?"

"Sure thing, bestie," said Kenzie, but even Allie could hear the disappointment in her voice.

CHAPTER 3- MORNING CHAOS

The warning bell rang, and Allie was already overwhelmed. First period, AP French, had been worse than she expected— not because they weren't allowed to speak any English at all, but because the teacher had a stringent no-phone policy and her mom had texted her the entire class. The buzzing in her backpack had drawn every pair of eyes in the room until she finally pulled it out, texted her mom to stop, and turned it off entirely. Just thinking about it made her shoulders tighten.

She hesitated at the door of AP Lit & Comp, debating between the few empty seats left. She recognized some of the other honors track kids, sitting in groups— their easy conversations about summer and new schedules floating through the room. She wasn't friends with any of them and didn't have anything to add, so she grabbed a seat in the front, near the wall.

The next bell rang, signaling the start of class. "Good morning and welcome to AP Lit & Comp. A couple of quick things before we dive in," said a girl who didn't look like she was old enough to be teaching, much less an AP class. She dropped stacks of papers on the first desk of each row as she talked. Allie pulled one out and passed the rest back.

"If you're here because you need an AP class for your college resume and you're looking for an easy A, this is not the class."

Allie gulped as she flipped through the syllabus.

"I'm Miss Lindstrom, and I've been teaching AP Lit and Comp and Language and Comp for almost a decade. It's my job to make you better writers and thinkers. I don't teach to the test, but my students consistently outperform the national average. Most years, I see a 70-80% pass rate, with a significant number of those getting 4's and 5's."

Allie's stomach dropped when she saw the list of essays they'd be writing. The room was completely still as everyone took in the syllabus.

"So let's start simple," she said, powering on the smartboard.

Tell me about yourself.

"This is an easy one to help you with your Common App essays. Write until the end of class… whatever you can think of. We'll edit later." She assured them they could do it, but when class ended, Allie had barely written a paragraph. She sighed and hit submit.

The science wing smelled like formaldehyde. Allie clutched the strap of her backpack, navigating the traffic in the hall until she stood in front of the door to her AP BIO class.

A paper sign was taped to the closed lab door:

Maintenance emergency- moved to Room 221.

"Of course," she murmured as her pulse spiked.

Room 221 turned out to be a conference room at the end of the math wing, and every seat was already taken. She and several other students hovered in the doorway, unsure what to do. She startled when a boy she recognized from Lit & Comp waved at her. He whispered something to the redheaded girl next to him, then stood, offering his chair as the teacher squeezed into the room, pushing metal folding chairs at the standing students.

"Grab one. Find a spot. We'll make it work," he said. Allie thanked him, grabbed a chair, and sat near the door.

The boy nodded as she plopped the chair down near the wall and mouthed, "Thanks." The teacher looked as frazzled as Allie felt.

"It's not ideal," he said, passing out stacks of papers and offering an explanation and an apology —a student in an earlier class had stuffed rubber gloves down a drain and burst a pipe in their actual lab room. "We'll get through the safety quiz and syllabus today, and hopefully we'll be back in our room tomorrow."

Allie balanced her Chromebook on her knees and logged into ClassLink again. Another syllabus. Another warning about late work and college-level expectations. Her heart raced as she clicked through the safety quiz.

When the bell finally rang, she stood too fast and had to steady herself on the chair. The boy from before gave her a quick smile as he and the redhead passed by. She almost smiled back, but he was gone before she could.

* * *

The hallway outside was chaos again- voices bouncing off lockers, bells echoing through the maze of intersecting wings. Allie focused on her breathing as she tried to navigate to her next class. She had mentally rehearsed the route from the original lab room and was thrown off and unsure of the fastest way to get there now.

The bell rang, and she practically sprinted down the hall toward the open door, fighting the familiar panic as she slipped in, head down, and took a seat.

"You must be Miss Ellis," a voice called from the back of the room. "Thank you for joining us."

She whipped her head around to see the teacher standing beside a podium, smiling.

"S...s...sorry," Allie stammered. "My bio class got moved and I got lost."

"Ah, you must be in class with Miss Pierce," he said, gesturing at the redhead from the conference room. "She's filled us in on the pipe disaster." The class laughed, and Allie tried to reassure herself that they weren't laughing at her. "Grab a syllabus from up front and try to log in to ClassLink. If you can't get logged in, just follow along and hopefully IT will have everything fixed so you can take the syllabus quiz at home tonight."

Allie breathed a sigh of relief when everything loaded instantly. Small victories.

Mr. Grant paced slowly as he walked them through the syllabus, finally focusing on the first group project.

An animated popcorn machine bounced names across the smartboard. The first two names landed together, and two boys near the back high-fived each other.

"The goal is to mix you up, get you working with people you don't know," Mr Grant laughed.

Allie's heart pounded as kernels popped, paired, and vanished. Finally, hers landed next to T. Pierce. The redhead from biology turned and offered her a friendly smile.

Before Allie could return it, the blonde next to her raised a manicured hand.

"Mr. Grant?" she said sweetly, not waiting to be called on. "Don't you think assigning partners is a little… authoritarian? I'm sure I speak for everyone when I say that you aren't respecting our autonomy or recognizing that we are capable of choosing our own partners and still getting the work done."

Allie held her breath, and the room went still. Mr. Grant scanned the room, "Well? Does Miss Walton speak for everyone?"

No one answered, and the blonde kicked the redhead under the desk, shooting her a terrifying glare.

"Okay, then," he said mildly. "Let's pop the rest."

The bell rang a minute later. Allie gathered her things, intending to introduce herself to her new partner.

As they walked past, the blonde hissed, "What the hell was that, Tea? You were supposed to have my back!"

The redhead- Tea- shrugged, not even noticing Allie waiting. "What did you want me to say?"

Allie waited until they were well ahead of her in the hall to leave the room, deciding she would say hello tomorrow in Biology.

CHAPTER 4- LUNCH FOR TWO

Allie swiped her ID and grabbed the tray. She breathed a sigh of relief when she saw Kenzie sitting at their usual table, digging through her lunch box. By the time Allie sat down, the pasta salad was almost gone.

"I wish my mom would buy these weird olives. They are so good." Kenzie smiled and popped one in her mouth.

"They're Kalamata olives," Allie reached across the table and snagged one. "They're healthy, but they have a ton of salt in them." Allie picked through her wilted salad with her fork. Kenzie noticed and sighed.

"Do you want your lunch back? I shouldn't have stolen it this morning, especially since you didn't even keep the sweater." She pushed the pasta salad across the table.

Allie pushed it back. "It's fine. This tastes fine, it just looks rough. Can you get your money back for the sweater?"

"Yeah, but I think you should keep it. Oh!" Kenzie exclaimed, "I forgot to tell you. I have to work Wednesday, so I can't drive you home."

"That's fine. I can take the bus." Allie forced a smile, thinking about the noisy, smelly school bus — and dreading the conversation with her mom.

Her mom didn't like her being home alone for too long, especially late at night. Wednesday evenings had always been their thing, Allie and Kenzie, together since forever. It gave Allie company, meant her mom didn't worry as much, and guaranteed Kenzie a hot dinner and breakfast.

Just another routine Kenzie didn't seem to mind giving up this year...

"I'm sorry. So it's a slack night for your dad?"

Allie nodded and pushed another clump of wilted lettuce to the side. "He presented last week. So it's drinks and dinner this week."

"Do they actually accomplish anything at their 'Wednesday Round Table' or is it just an excuse to charge dinner and drinks to the firm once a week?" Kenzie finished off the apples and peanut butter and pulled out a container of cheese and crackers. "I swear you get more food in one lunch than my mom makes me all week."

Allie flinched a little. It had been just Kenzie and her mom since her dad left them to start a new family when the girls were in first grade. Kenzie's mom had never really recovered.

At first, she had walked around in a daze, and she and Kenzie had moved in with Allie and her family because her husband had cleaned out all of their accounts, and she couldn't even afford rent. Then, she was angry. She was angry that he'd left and started a whole new family while she was stuck taking care of Kenzie by herself. She was angry that she had to work two jobs just to afford a dumpy apartment while her ex bought a house and drove a new car.

Then, she was on a mission. She still worked both jobs, but went back to school at night to become a nurse. Now, she was back at school to get her RN, which meant that she was home even less. Allie felt bad for Kenzie. Even if she hated how her mom hovered and interfered with everything, it was better than having a mom who acted like you didn't even exist.

Allie shrugged. "Dunno. My dad thinks he's got a chance at managing partner this year, so maybe?" Kenzie was scanning the cafeteria. When she noticed Allie had stopped talking and was watching her, she turned her attention back to her best friend.

"Sorry," she said. "I've got first period with Teagan, and she said we could sit with her and her friends, but I couldn't find her. I don't want to spend another year stuck in the corner again." She backpedaled when she saw the look on Allie's face. "Oh, Allie. Don't be like that. You know what I meant."

"Yeah," Allie pushed her salad away from her. "I get it."

They'd been having this conversation all summer, since Kenzie started working at Vibe Station and started hanging out with the people she worked with. Until this summer, it had always been just the two of them. Now, it seemed like that wasn't enough for Kenzie anymore, and Allie fought hard not to let Kenzie see how upset she was.

"It'll be fine," Kenzie assured her. "You'll love Teagan. And I've only met her friend, Trent, once but he was super cool."

Allie put Kenzie's trash on her tray and stood. "Yeah, okay. Hey, we're still doing popcorn and movie night Friday, right?"

"Is there a football game?" Kenzie wondered aloud. "If there's a game, we could go to the game and then do popcorn and movie night after, right?"

"Sure, sure," said Allie as she threw her trash away.

Not gonna cry, not gonna cry, not gonna cry...

She didn't understand why Kenzie wanted everything to change. It had always been the two of them, and it had always worked. Why did she want new friends and football games and all of that? Wasn't she enough?

CHAPTER 5- DROWNING

Allie froze in the doorway, her heart in her throat. She hated math and didn't want to take Trig this year, but that wasn't what had her rooted to the floor. The blonde from her AP Psych class was already there, laughing and tossing her hair like she was auditioning for a commercial.

Allie scanned the room for a seat as far away as possible, but most of the empty desks were orbiting the blonde's gravitational pull. A trickle of sweat slid down her temple, and still she couldn't make herself move.

Two girls jostled past and took the last seats in the back. If she didn't move now, she'd be stuck right next to her. The blonde's back was turned, so Allie slipped quietly to the opposite side of the room and sat down beside a broad-shouldered boy who looked like he belonged on a football poster.

He turned toward her and smiled—kind, easy, unforced. Allie's stomach flipped. She looked away before he could see the blush creeping up her neck.

The bell rang, and the teacher shut the door. "I'm sure you know the drill," he said, cracking open a soda. "Get your Chromebooks out and make sure you can access the class modules."

"Does that mean we all get a soda?" the blonde called, sugar-sweet without even raising her hand.

He didn't miss a beat. "Do you have a soda?"

She blinked, then pouted. "No, but if you're going to drink in front of us, you could at least share. Amiright?" She turned to her friend, who nodded dutifully.

Allie clicked "Syllabus" for the third time. Nothing happened.

"It doesn't work like that," the teacher said, taking another sip. "If you want to eat or drink in my class, fine—I just don't want to see it, hear it, or smell it. Leave trash behind and you lose twenty points. You only get ten a day for attendance, so you can do the math."

Laughter rippled across the room. The blonde rolled her eyes.

He continued, "Since nothing's loading, we'll skip the paperwork and start the first lesson. We'll deal with the tech later."

"So you're actually going to teach on the first day?" the blonde teased. "No icebreakers?"

He grinned. "Of course. Silly me." He leaned against the desk. "I'm Dr. Matthew Gray. PhD in Applied and Computational Math from UW–Madison. I'm originally from California—I did my undergrad at Berkeley. Got my master's at the University of Chicago. Would not recommend unless you like competition disguised as collegiality."

A few chuckles. Then he turned back to his laptop. "Now, open your notebooks. Let's see how much trig you remember."

That was it. No getting-to-know-you games, no syllabus reading marathon. Just straight into functions and angles—the exact place Allie always lost her footing.

Her stomach knotted as the symbols on the board stacked into something she was supposed to recognize but didn't. The boy beside her was already writing, his pencil moving fast and sure. When he shifted his Chromebook slightly, she caught the name on his login screen—**Jackson Moore.**

Allie copied the first line of his notes just to have something on the page, but her hand was shaking.

The more Dr. Gray talked, the less she understood. Every word blurred into the next until she couldn't tell what she was missing or when she'd started falling behind.

She shoved her Chromebook into her bag, trying not to think about how long the year suddenly felt. If this was just day one, she thought, what was the rest of the year going to look like?

* * *

Her head was pounding when she stepped into the hallway. Every number from the last hour clung to her like static—angles, functions, formulas that might as well have been written in another language. The noise outside the classroom made it worse: lockers slamming, sneakers squeaking, everyone around her somehow lighter, freer.

She shifted her backpack higher on her shoulder and followed the tide of students through the hall. The air in the history wing was warm and stale, faintly metallic from the hum of projectors and too many screens running at once.

A stack of syllabi sat on the counter near the door. She grabbed one on instinct, tucking it under her arm as she found a seat halfway back. The page was dense with text —a neat grid of dates, readings, and acronyms — that made her throat tighten. DBQs. LEQs. Weekly essays. Unit projects. Her dad had fought the school to let her take five AP classes, and now, looking at the schedule, she wondered what exactly he thought she was proving.

Students trickled in, loud and confident, tossing jokes across the room. At the front of the room, the teacher stood near the smartboard, reviewing notes on his tablet, his expression unreadable. He didn't need to speak to command attention; even the loudest students dropped their voices when they saw him there.

Allie straightened in her chair and smoothed the edge of her syllabus. He didn't look like someone you could charm or coast with. You either kept up—or you didn't.

She glanced up as someone walked in— the curly-haired boy from Bio and Lit & Comp. He nodded when he saw her, offering the smallest smile before sliding into a seat on the opposite side of the room. For a moment, she thought he might say something after class, maybe even just a quick Hey, how's your day going? But he didn't look over again.

When the bell rang, he turned to face them. "Good afternoon, everyone. I'm Mr. Tracy, and I'm not going to waste your time with introductions or icebreakers. This is a college-level class, and I treat it like one."

He dimmed the lights and queued up a video before anyone could respond. The title card—The Economics of Early Colonization—flashed across the screen, and a narrator launched into a lecture about mercantilism.

Allie opened her notebook, trying to take notes, but the words slipped away faster than she could write. The voice on the video spoke too quickly, stacking dates and policies into a blur of names and numbers. Her brain felt like it was buffering, seconds behind everything.

The video ended, the lights came back on, and Mr. Tracy clicked through a few slides. "You'll find the syllabus on the counter by the door," he said, nodding toward the stack she'd already taken. "Read it carefully tonight. There's a quiz tomorrow on this video."

Someone groaned softly. He ignored it. "This class isn't meant to be easy. AP stands for Advanced Placement, not Average Performance. I don't hand-hold, but I will meet you where you are if you put in the work. Think of this as the boot camp of your academic career."

A few polite chuckles broke the silence, but Allie didn't join in. Her hand still hovered over her notes, unsure whether to underline something or just close the notebook entirely.

The bell rang, sudden and jarring. Students gathered their things in a rush, voices overlapping as they made plans for after school. Allie waited until the room cleared before sliding her syllabus into the front pocket of her binder.

She adjusted her backpack again and stepped into the hall. The noise hit immediately—hundreds of conversations, the static of a thousand tiny distractions. Her pulse ticked in time with it. She was so far behind already, and the year had barely started.

She felt like she'd been run over by a truck by the time she reached the cafeteria for study hall. Her bag felt heavier with every step. The plan had been to spread out her papers and start mapping her workload, but one glance at the chaos inside told her that wasn't happening.

This year, every student who'd requested a study hall was lumped together for the last period of the day. The noise was unbelievable—music, laughter, a football arcing dangerously close to the ceiling. Teachers lined the walls, looking like they'd already given up.

Allie scanned her ID at the door, then froze. She was about to turn around and find an empty hallway when she spotted Miss Lindstrom standing near the back, arms crossed, amusement tugging at her mouth.

"I'm guessing the powers that be are going to rethink this decision very quickly," Miss Lindstrom said when Allie reached her.

"Can I go to the library instead?" Allie asked, hesitant.

Miss Lindstrom shrugged. "You can go home and study if you want. Think anyone would notice?" She nodded toward the football sailing dangerously close to a teacher's head.

"I guess not," Allie said, uneasy. "But that would be... wrong. Could you give me a pass?"

"I'll do you one better. Come on."

Allie followed her into the hallway, relief flooding through her shoulders as the cafeteria noise faded behind them.

"That's crazy," she said. "How is anyone supposed to study in there?"

"They're not," Miss Lindstrom replied. "But at least now you don't have to pretend."

She led Allie into the main office, explained the situation to the aide at the desk, and within a minute, Allie's schedule was updated.

"Scan your card in the library from now on," the aide told her.

"You'll be fine there."

As Miss Lindstrom waved goodbye, Allie realized her chest had loosened for the first time all afternoon.

The library was quiet, almost empty. She slid into a seat by the window and opened her planner, staring at the mess of deadlines and assignments she'd scribbled throughout the day.

She should've felt productive, but instead her head ached. Kenzie's voice from that morning echoed in her mind: *It's going to be a great year.*

Allie rubbed her temples. After today, she wasn't so sure.

CHAPTER 6- WHAT A WEEK

The rest of the week didn't get much better. Not even a whole week in school, and she was already drowning. Thank god it was finally Thursday.

And seriously, who thought it was a good idea to start school the week before Labor Day? Four days of school, four-day weekend, then another four-day school week. Dumb.

She was mentally rehearsing what she would say to her father to convince him to let her drop AP French and AP Psych as she made her way to the cafeteria. Technically, she could take the AP French exam even if she dropped the class- that wasn't an issue. The hard part would be convincing him she could still do well enough on it to get college credit, which was really all he cared about.

She was a little rusty, sure, but she was still fluent. Just a week with Mme Lowell, and she was already back to speaking and understanding everything in class. She'd been to France multiple times — she already knew a lot about French culture…

She froze. Kenzie was not sitting at their table.
Instead, a boy was in her seat, and his backpack was in Kenzie's.
Allie's pulse pounded in her ears.
He was sitting in *her* seat.
He didn't even have a lunch, he was just reading a book with his headphones in. He could do that in the library. He should do that in the library.

Where was Kenzie? Her chest tightened. Her vision blurred. She realized she was taking short, shallow breaths.
Where. Was. Kenzie?

"Allie! Earth to Allie! Over here!" Kenzie was waving at her from a table in the middle of the cafeteria… a table that was full.
Allie looked back at her usual spot, where the boy with shaggy hair and ratty clothes still sat in her chair. She turned back to Kenzie, who was smiling and walking towards her.

"We talked about this," Kenzie quietly reminded her, her smile a little too bright. "I told you yesterday that Teagan was going to save us seats." She gestured back to the table where Tea, Allie's AP Psych partner, and the curly-haired boy from her classes were both smiling and waving.

"See?" Kenzie encouraged her. "It's fine."

She steered Allie toward the table, and Teagan slid her chair over to make room..

Across from them, the football player from Trig grinned. "Hey! I know you!"

Allie relaxed a little— she already sort of knew most of the people at the table.

"What's your name again?" he asked her as she sat down.

"Allie, right?" Trent added.

"Yeah, Allie! I'm Jackson," said the football player. "And this is Trent and Teagan, but you apparently already know them. This is my best friend, Eric."

Eric looked up from his phone, gave a short nod, and went back to scrolling.

Teagan motioned to the seat next to her, and Allie dropped into it, still unsure how she felt.

"I can't believe I didn't put it together that *you're* Kenzie's Allie!" Teagan said. "I've been hearing stories about you all summer."

"Yeah, Kenzie talks about you all the time, too." Allie turned to her best friend, "You could've mentioned the red hair, though. I probably would have figured out way earlier that Tea from Bio and Psych was Teagan from work."

Teagan grunted. "Umm, yeah… don't call me Tea, please. Only one person calls me that and…"

Allie felt the shift in the air a split second before Teagan stopped speaking.

"Why is she sitting in my chair?" Said a voice behind her.

Allie didn't need to look to know. It was the blonde.

Whatever brief feeling of belonging she'd had evaporated.

The blonde leaned in between Kenzie and Jackson and set her tray down, shoving Kenzie's to the side.

Allie blinked. Twins? Not twins, but close. And they were wearing the same outfit. It would have been cute if they were little kids. But in high school? Weird.

The other blonde- the twin- circled the table, pulled up a chair, and squeezed herself in, shoving Allie's lunch aside.

"Rude, Sophie," Eric muttered, not even looking up from his phone.

"What's rude is sitting at a table where you aren't welcome," she snapped back.

"I invited them," said Teagan. "This is Kenzie, the girl I've been telling you about from Vibe. And this is her best friend, Allie."

Sophie bumped Allie's chair with her legs and wedged herself between Allie and Teagan.

Allie and Kenzie exchanged a look, then shifted their chairs until they were sitting next to each other. Teagan glared at Sophie for a moment, then continued.

"Allie's in AP Bio with Trent and me, and AP Psych with Darcy and me. She's my partner on the brain project." She finished.

"Wait a sec," said Trent. "I have three AP classes with you, *and* you're in AP Psych? Four AP classes?"

"She can't be," said Darcy at the same time Kenzie said proudly, "Five actually. She's in AP French, too!"

Everyone turned to stare at Allie, who flushed the color of Teagan's Coke can.

"Yeah, no," Darcy finally said. "I was going to register for five AP classes, and they told me I wasn't allowed to. It's illegal."

Before anyone could respond, Eric said flatly, "So, you wanted to take five AP classes, they told you no, and your solution was... to just take one? And you chose AP Psych? The easiest one they offered." He looked at her a beat longer, then looked back at his phone.

"God, you're a dick," Darcy muttered, then turned to Kenzie with a dazzling smile. "I know you! You're in Spanish 4 and history with me. How fun!"

The conversation picked back up around her, but Allie wasn't part of it anymore.

Her eyes drifted to the messy boy sitting at her table.

Still alone, still reading, still not eating. In her seat.

She felt simultaneously annoyed and jealous. He looked so peaceful reading his book in his own little bubble. No.

Her bubble, she thought angrily, and then checked herself. At least someone was enjoying the solitude of the little table in the back corner of the cafeteria.

She flinched when Kenzie tugged on her lunch bag.

"Sorry," she said, pushing the bag over. "You can have whatever you want. I'm not really hungry."

Kenzie pulled out the pasta salad and the little cucumber sandwiches. "You need to eat. Do you want the apples and peanut butter?"

Allie shook her head.

"Don't throw them out," Eric said, holding out his hand. "I'll eat them."

Kenzie narrowed her eyes. "Who said I was going to throw them away?"

Jackson leaned toward Allie. "Do you have to go to your locker, or do you want to walk to Trig with us?"

Darcy jumped in before she could answer. "Actually, I need to go to my locker, so she can just go to class by herself."

Allie saw her roll her eyes, but no one else seemed to notice-everyone was back to their conversations.

Kenzie slid the apples to Eric, who accepted them with a grateful nod.

Allie started packing up her lunch. She was going to tell Eric to just bring the container back on Monday, but he'd already finished them and pushed the clean container back across the table.

"I love crunchy peanut butter," he said simply.

As she was walking away from the table, she heard Darcy say, "No way she's taking five AP classes."

CHAPTER 7- FIRST CRACKS

Jackson found her sitting on the curb, waiting for her mom. Allie had texted multiple times, but there was no response. If the roles were reversed, SWAT would already be here. Her mom knew all of the secretaries at the high school, though, so they were probably keeping an eye on her, *just to be safe.*

"Do you need a ride?" He asked.
Allie nearly jumped out of her skin.
"Whoa, sorry! I didn't mean to scare you."
"Oh, hey," she said, trying to sound friendly and failing miserably.

He sat down beside her. "The good news is, it's a four-day weekend," he offered, trying to lighten the mood.
"Yeah," she said flatly. "That's great news."
"What's wrong?" He finally asked, seeing she either couldn't— or wouldn't— say more.
It all came out in a flood. The three papers she had due on Tuesday. The mountain of reading she had to do for every class.
"And whatever Dr Matt is putting up on the smartboard just looks like modern art. It's squiggly lines and circles, and I don't know what he's talking about." She didn't even try to stop the tears.

Jackson stared, openmouthed. "I can't believe you're taking five AP classes. That would kill anyone."
"I guess," She wiped her nose with her sleeve, then scoffed and fished a pack of tissues out of her backpack. "That was gross. Sorry."

"Are you and Teagan getting together this weekend to start on the Psych project?"
Allie shook her head. "She works all weekend. They just got in a huge shipment of exclusives, and the holiday sales are crazy … Kenzie is there almost open to close all weekend." She hiccuped. "I told her I'd get everything outlined and broken out between us so we can work on it this week."

She shifted uncomfortably under Jackson's incredulous gaze.
"What? She has to work, and I don't."
"Yeah, but your schedule is a full-time job. And then some."

* * *

She opened her mouth, but he held up a hand.

"I can help with Trig, though. Not this weekend— we're going up north to close the cabin. But Tuesday? After school?"

"That would be great," she said, thinking of the packet due Tuesday. Maybe if he helped her on Tuesday, it wouldn't matter if she bombed this one. As long as she did okay on the rest of them.

"Oh," Jackson said, remembering. "What if I FaceTime you over the weekend and help you with it? I finished it during English, so I already know what I'm doing."

"You did the trig homework during English? How does even that work?"

"I'm in regular English, and it's way too easy. I don't care about it. I like computers, coding, and stuff like that. I've already read To Kill a Mockingbird three times. I've got the paper written."

"You'd do that? FaceTime me this weekend and help me with the packet?"

"Sure. We'll relax once we get up there tomorrow. Saturday, we'll take the boat and jet skis out to run most of the fuel down, but after that... not so much. We've gotta pull the dock in and clean everything. I used to think my mom was being super OCD about it, but one year, we rushed through everything, and it was disgusting when we opened it in the spring. My dad didn't clean the toilets after he drained them, and I swear to god, the mold made it look like fuzzy animals were living inside them."

Allie's phone buzzed.

Mom: 5 minutes out. Sorry. Lost track of time.
Allie: okay.

"It'll be okay," Jackson told her. "I got you- at least in Trig."
Allie gave him the first real smile she'd felt all day.
"Want me to wait with you?" He asked.
"I'm okay. She's almost here." Allie tossed the tissues back in her backpack and stood.
A few more pleasantries, and she watched him walk off. Her mom showed up 20 minutes later.

CHAPTER 8- TUESDAY TUTORING

By Tuesday afternoon, the long weekend already felt like a distant memory. It was actually a blessing in disguise that Kenzie had worked all weekend. Allie had finished all her work and organized her planner so she could clearly see what was due when, even breaking down the big assignments and plugging in those mini-deadlines. She felt as prepared as she could be, especially considering her father had not only doubled down on her taking all five AP classes, but also made it known that he expected at least B+s in all of them and 4s and 5s on the spring tests. Allie had been stoic as he delivered his verdict, but had had a good cry after.

She'd even understood Dr Matt as he waved his arms and used words like radians and hypotenuse, but now it all looked like modern art again.

Jackson paused, then tried to explain it again.

"Picasso?" It was the best Allie could come up with.

"How about if I do it a step at a time, then you do it and explain it to me, however it makes sense to you?" Jackson offered. "Yeah, eventually you'll have to use the right words, but maybe if you just get used to how it feels to work through the problem, it'll click?"

"I'm supposed to be feeling things other than rage while doing these problems?" She asked sincerely.

He laughed. Then they worked through the problem with Allie walking him through how she saw what they'd done. He'd laughed a couple of times when she'd said, "And these aren't mistakes, we'll make them birds." But at the end of it, she worked the problem from start to finish by herself.

Jackson high-fived her just as Mrs Ellis came in to tell them that dinner was ready.

Mr Ellis came home halfway through dinner and stared at the stranger sitting at his table.

Allie introduced them, and immediately Mr Ellis started grilling Jackson like he was cross-examining a defendant.

Jackson held his own, though… No, despite his size, he didn't play football. Yes, he was taking one AP Class— AP Computer Science. Yes, he was planning on going to college. No, not Madison or the Ivies.

UW Stout was well known for its computer science and engineering technology programs, and he could graduate debt-free— unlike at Madison or the Ivies… Eventually, Mr Ellis gave up and went down the hall to his office.

Jackson helped clear the plates and left so Allie could finish her homework. He texted her later.

Jackson: Look at it one more time to make sure it still makes sense. We'll probably have a quiz tomorrow.

Allie was sound asleep by the time he sent it, but when she looked over everything the next morning, it all still made sense. Maybe she would pass Trig after all.

CHAPTER 9- VICTORY

Despite the chaos of the cafeteria, Allie was zoned out.

94. No. Way.

She exited the Trig grade book and clicked the quiz grade again. It still said 94.

Kenzie had already distributed the contents of Allie's lunch, including the extra apples and peanut butter she'd asked her mom to pack— technically for her in case she got hungry during study hall, but really for Eric— and they were chattering away.

Jackson turned to her, smiling, phone in hand, but paused when he saw the expression on her face. "Uh, how did it go?"

Speechless, she handed him her phone.

"Yes!" He exclaimed, stopping the conversation at their table. "Allie got a 94 on the trig quiz!" He told the table.

Darcy scrambled for her phone, a gleeful, boasting smile on her face. "Hundred," she said proudly, flashing Allie a sweet smile.

Sophie whooped and jumped up from the table to hug her.

Not to be outdone in the best-friend department, Kenzie jumped up too and wrapped Allie in a hug. She whispered in her ear, "I knew you could do it. See? This is going to be a great year!"

"Why didn't you get a hundred?" Eric asked, chomping on an apple.

In just the short time she'd known him, Allie had already figured out that when Eric asked questions like that, he wasn't trying to be rude. He just said whatever was in his head, apparently without a filter.

"I suck at math," Allie admitted. "I'm usually lucky to pass with a B."

"You don't suck," Jackson and Kenzie said in unison.

* * *

"That's awesome," said Teagan, nodding to both Darcy and Allie. "Did Jackson help you study?" she asked Allie, tilting her head at a grinning Jackson.

Allie smiled, still shocked, "He did. He had me keep reworking the problem until I could explain how I did it. And then it finally clicked!"

"Awesome!" Teagan smiled.

"It's not like it's hard," Darcy cut in, then took a drink of her Diet Coke.

Teagan rolled her eyes. "Ignore her."

"I feel like this calls for pints for supper!" Kenzie exclaimed.

"Of beer? There's no way you've got a fake ID." Sophie said skeptically. The table turned to look at her.

"What?" Sophie asked, shrugging.

"Of ice cream," Allie clarified. She nodded at Kenzie. "Culver's it is!" Then she turned to Jackson, inspiration dawning. "What's your favorite flavor? I definitely owe you for helping me not just pass, but get an A."

"We all have plans tonight," Darcy jumped in, "but thanks anyway, *Ellie*." She checked her watch and turned to Jackson, "We'd better get going. I have to do that thing before class."

"Mint chocolate chip," Teagan said casually, once Darcy was out of earshot. "It's his favorite."

Kenzie: Did u tell J we didn't want to go to the football game with them tonight?

Allie: Why?

Kenzie: Everyone's making plans during yearbook and J said you said we didn't want to go.

Allie: We've already got plans tonight

Kenzie: We talked about this. We can go to the game first and then come home and watch a movie.

Allie: I don't like football.

Kenzie: U don't have to. We're just going to hang out.

…

Kenzie: We said we would go to the game

Allie: no. you said we would go to the game. I said I didn't want to.

Kenzie: I want to go

Allie: so go

Kenzie: Okay. I'll come over after

…

Kenzie: It won't be late and I'll pay to rent that rom-com you wanted to watch

…

Allie stared down at her phone and was too exhausted to argue.

Kenzie: Hello?

Allie: I actually have a lot of homework. Why don't we just skip this week?

Kenzie: I can't tell if ur mad

Allie: I'm not mad. Its fine

Kenzie: If ur sure

Allie: I'm sure. Have fun.

Kenzie: Tell ur mom I said hi.

Allie: K

"What time is Kenzie coming over?" Her mom asked as Allie sank into the passenger seat. "I don't want to put the pizzas in too early, but I want the oven off before we leave."

* * *

"I have a lot of homework, so we decided to skip this week." Allie kept her gaze fixed out the window so her mom couldn't see how close she was to crying.

"Well, she can still come for dinner," her mom insisted. "And is her mom working tonight? She'll still need to come over if her mom is working."

"It's okay. She's gonna stay at another friend's house tonight."

"Allie, honey. You and Kenzie have been friends for a long time. You can't just push her away because your classes are harder this year. When you make plans with someone, you don't just break them like this."

Allie wished she could say it was Kenzie who broke their plans—but Kenzie White was like a second child to Angela, and she defended her fiercely.

"Listen to me," her mom continued, "She has stuck by you all of these years, been like a sister to you. You can't just abandon her because her classes aren't as hard as yours."

Sometimes my mom is so absolutely clueless, Allie thought, and let her mind drift.

She was startled awake as they pulled into the driveway. Her mom was still talking, not even noticing that Allie had fallen asleep, much less stopped listening.

"Okay," she said as she shut the car off. "I got a notification that the ACT review materials we ordered for you arrived today, so you can break those open and get started on them this weekend."

Allie wished the ground would just swallow her up. She didn't have time to do ACT review stuff on top of her homework. *I did fine on the language parts; I only bombed the math. I'd never taken Trig before, so obviously my score is going to go up.*

She heard her mom's reply in her head immediately: *There's no guarantee, and you have to bring that score up if you want to get into Madison and get a scholarship. These review materials will not only help you with the content; they'll help you with timing, strategy, and the rigor of the test.*

Have you seen my schedule this year? Did you actually read anything on any syllabus before you signed them? Allie continued the argument in her head. *Every class is all about rigor, timing, and strategies. Did you count how many essays we have to write in Lit & Comp?*

Her mother's imaginary answer came instantly: *Your father expects at least a 32. You'll never get that unless you buckle down and do the work. If you want to go to Madison, you've got to bring your score up.*

But I don't want to go to Madison, Allie mentally replied.

"Allie? Allie, are you listening?" Her mom's real voice replaced the one in her head, and Allie turned to look at her. "The box is on the front steps. You can bring that in while I heat dinner up."

"Yes, mom," Allie replied dutifully.

Later, as Allie drifted off to sleep, her phone buzzed twice in quick succession. She groggily reached for it but nearly set it back down when she saw it was a text from Kenzie. It buzzed again before she could let go, so she sighed and swiped it open.

A picture of a smiling Kenzie, face painted with school colors, arms thrown around Teagan and Trent, stared back at her. The first text below it read:

"Miss you! Wish you were here."

Followed by another "Seriously, Allie. It's not the same without you."

Allie exhaled and set the phone facedown beside her. She'd been bone-tired just seconds ago, but now her mind wouldn't stop spinning. It didn't matter how long they'd been friends; they were going in different directions this year. Kenzie made it look so easy —walking into a room full of people and finding a place like she belonged there.

Allie wanted to be that brave, but even the idea of it made her chest tighten. And even if she could make herself go —stand in the bleachers, pretend she wasn't counting the minutes —her parents wouldn't let her. There was always a test, a practice exam, something more important.

I miss you, too, Kenz. She thought, as sleep finally pulled her under.

CHAPTER 11- RUNNING A MARATHON

Allie hadn't done anything except study and write papers all weekend, but she felt like she'd run a marathon.. She and Kenzie had texted a little, but Kenzie was at work, and Allie was trying to memorize flashcards on early Spanish colonization, so they didn't say much.

The ride to school this morning had been just as awkward. Allie'd been quiet, and Kenzie'd filled the void with stories about customers and clothes. When they'd parted at their lockers and Kenzie'd said, "See you at lunch," Allie only hesitated for a second. But it was a second too long, and Kenzie saw it.

"C'mon, Allie, don't be like this. You're already friends with Teagan and Jackson, and you've got a ton of classes with Trent…"

Before she could say anything else, Allie interrupted, "And Sophie and Darcy hate me, and I liked it better when it was just us in the back corner."

"I'll make sure you sit between me and Teagan, and we won't let Darcy talk to you." Kenzie gave her a quick hug and then ran off.

Allie *wanted* to want to sit with them. To fall back into that easy rhythm she and Kenzie used to have. That had to count for something. Didn't it?

Now, she was staring at the prompt Miss Lindstrom had put up on the board, while the timer counted down next to it.

"Choose someone who made an impact on your life without realizing it. What did they do and why did it matter? How has your perspective changed?"

The list the class had brainstormed did nothing for her.

Definitely not her parents, unless you counted making a negative impact. She knew it was harsh to think that way, but really.

Not her grandparents. Her dad's parents had died when he was a teenager, and her mom's parents were just as overprotective as her mom was. Sometimes, Allie felt depressed when she watched her grandmother follow behind her mom, questioning every decision and making "little changes" that would make things "so much better." Her mom didn't even realize that she said those *exact* words to Allie on a regular basis.

A teacher? She'd loved her first-grade teacher— the one who spoke French on the phone and made Allie fall in love with the language. But her hands moved on their own.

"Kenzie White walked up to me in kindergarten and announced to me and the world that we were now best friends." Allie began. Once she started writing, the words just flowed. She wrote about her parents buying a trundle bed for Allie's room when the girls were in first grade, and Kenzie and her mom moved in with them. She wrote about vacations, and the times Kenzie had defended her when kids picked on her because she was smaller and younger than the rest of the class. She was writing about how different things felt this year when the bell rang. Startled, Allie looked around the room to see everyone else packing their bags. She hastily finished, "She's been my best friend and the sister I never had since kindergarten, and I don't think she has any idea how much she means to me. If she did, she wouldn't be trying so hard to run away from me." She hit submit, wiped the tear from the corner of her eye, and followed the rest of the class out into the hall.

When Allie opened her computer in APUSH that afternoon, there was already a notification from Miss Lindstrom.

"She sounds like a keeper. I hope she knows that.

Your essay packs an emotional punch, but it needs more structure. Try anchoring your timeline or connecting your stories to a central theme.

Also, revisit your conclusion. It trails off, which might have been intentional, or you just ran out of time. The point is, I can't tell, so you need to clean it up. Even if you feel like your friendship is transitioning this year, you still need a strong conclusion.

The prompt gives you the full word count— use it. There's a powerful essay here if you give it space to breathe."

Transitioning? Allie thought, then quickly clicked out of Miss Lindstrom's comments and opened the review guide for her first APUSH exam.

CHAPTER 12- LIAR LIAR

"So let me get this straight," said Teagan, shoveling another bite of the pasta dish into her mouth. "Your parents go out every Wednesday night, and your mom makes dinner for you and Kenzie and leaves it in the fridge?"

Allie nodded, watching her new friend with fascination.

"And you texted her today to tell her I was coming over, so she came home at lunch and made a completely different dinner so there would be enough for all of us?"

Allie nodded again, and Kenzie jumped in, mouth full. "The crazy thing is, Allie is a great cook— she totally could have made this for us — but her mom will only let her use the microwave when they aren't home. So every week we get dinner in individual reheatable containers. There's dessert in the fridge, too."

"You get this every week?" Teagan moaned, "Can I please be invited? I'll do all of the work on the project if I get dinner like this." Allie blushed and carried her plate to the sink.

"Wait," said Teagan, catching on to something Kenzie'd said, "you aren't allowed to use the stove when your parents aren't home?" Kenzie and Allie shook their heads. "Or the toaster?" More head shaking. "What about the oven? The air fryer?" She paused and then finally came up with, "What about the blender?"

"Her parents are so overprotective," said Kenzie. "I kind of get it, but it's so over the top. They might as well wrap her in bubble wrap."

"My mom is overprotective," muttered Allie, "my dad would have to be around."

During the awkward silence that followed, Kenzie finished loading the dishwasher as Teagan pulled out her Chromebook and the notes they'd been compiling for the last week.

Teagan's phone buzzed.

"Trent wants to know if you two are going to the bonfire? He's trying to figure out how many pizzas to get."

The girls answered simultaneously. Allie asked, "Bonfire?" And Kenzie enthusiastically responded, "Yes!"

"That's right, we talked about it at the game, and you weren't there," said Teagan. She continued, "There's a bonfire and Barn Party this Friday off of Allen Rd. Josh's parents— " she paused at Allie's bewildered expression, "— you might not know him since you're not on yearbook— anyway, they'll be out of town and his brother's band is playing. They go to Madison and play at the bars and frats there. They're awesome." She turned to Kenzie. "I thought you were going to talk to her?"

"I was. I am. I just didn't get a chance yet," said Kenzie, a defensive edge in her voice. "We've both been busy."

Allie opened her mouth, but Teagan steamrolled ahead, "You have to come. It's so much fun. I know your parents would probably say no, but that's fine… You can just stay at Kenzie's. What they don't know won't hurt them."

Allie and Kenzie turned to each other, blurting out at the same time:

"But we're supposed to stay at my house because your mom is working all weekend," said Allie.

"We can just tell your parents her schedule changed and we're staying at our apartment this weekend," Kenzie offered.

Allie's stomach flipped. "Lie to my parents?" She whispered, looking straight at Kenzie, who suddenly wouldn't meet her eyes.

A beat of silence.

"You've never lied to your parents?" Teagan asked, wide-eyed.

Allie glared at Kenzie, waiting. Finally, Kenzie mumbled, "Allie's never lied to anyone." Then, she perked up and turned back to Allie with a hopeful smile, "Technically, it's not really lying. My mom's schedule did change. We just…. don't have to explain every detail for them. That's not a big deal, right?"

"Lying by omission?" Allie interrupted.

"Wait… you really don't lie to your parents? Like ever?" She paused as they both stared at her. "Oh, Allie… you need this barn party. You two can stay the night with me. My dad and stepmom will totally vouch for us. They'll totally say they'll be home all night and we're all going to pop popcorn and sing Kumbaya."

"That won't work," said Kenzie and Allie. Allie continued, "My mom doesn't know your parents. She won't let me spend the night at your house." Kenzie nodded.

"She does know that in two years she's not going to have any say in where you go and what you do, right? You're going to be on a college campus far, far, away, and she's not going to have a clue who you're spending the night with?" Teagan asked in disbelief. Allie flushed a deep crimson.

"The plan is for her to go to Madison and commute," said Kenzie quietly.

Teagan started to answer, but couldn't say anything in response to that.

"Why would they pay for a dorm and meal plan when we live less than 30 minutes from the campus?" Allie parroted the words her father seemed to have on repeat now. Teagan stared at her, dumbfounded.

"Let's just work on the project," Allie said, her voice wavering, not missing the look that passed between Kenzie and Teagan.

CHAPTER 13- THE BONFIRE

"Would you stop?" Kenzie laughed. "It's fine."

Allie fidgeted in her seat, craning her head around Teagan to see out the window.

"You don't know that," she said, voice tight. "What if it doesn't work? What if they call your mom?"

"They're not going to call my mom," Kenzie replied with confidence. "And if they do, she'll text me. She's not going to answer and get stuck on the phone while your mom tells her every thought she's ever had. Allie, chill. It's fine."

"It should be up here on the left somewhere," Eric said from the front seat, then turned to Allie. "Besides, we put that app on your phone. If your parents check your location, it'll show you're safe and sound at Kenzie's. We all use it, and we've never gotten busted. I seriously can't believe you've never lied to your parents before."

Eric turned back around and squinted into the setting sun. "Here! Turn right here!"

Jackson hit the brakes. "I thought you said left?"

"That's what I said. Turn left right here!" Eric pointed toward a barely visible driveway, half-hidden by overgrown brush.

Jackson turned onto the dirt road, the little Accord bouncing over ruts as they rolled into a field packed with cars. The five of them tumbled out as laughter and music drifted from the barn ahead.

"That's the band? The one everyone's been talking about?" Teagan asked, suspicious. "I don't get it."

Allie silently agreed, but kept her mouth shut. She felt overwhelmed and completely out of her element.

Eric laughed, popped the trunk, and pulled out a cooler. When he offered her a beer, she flinched.

"No, thank you." She said quietly,

Jackson handed her a Coke without saying anything, and she took it gratefully.

Kenzie and Teagan clinked their beers and chugged them like they'd done it a hundred times. Allie stared, stunned.

What was Kenzie doing?

They weren't drinkers. Or at least not before this year.

What am I doing here?

Teagan and Kenzie threw their arms around her and turned her towards the barn.

"I'm so glad you came," Kenzie told Allie as they walked through the field. "Please don't worry about everything tonight. Just have fun with us. I promise it's all going to be fine."

Everything will be fine, Allie repeated to herself, trying to believe her best friend.

A loud squeal rang out behind them, and Allie lurched forward as Sophie and Darcy crashed into her, laughing.

"Kenzie! Teagan!"

Darcy and Sophie wrapped them in a group hug, barely noticing that Allie was pressed between them.

To make matters worse, Kenzie squealed back, "Oh my god, you look so good! I told you that shirt would look amazing on you!"

Allie stepped back, heat prickling at her cheeks as no one looked her way.

The four girls launched into a chorus of outfit compliments, falling into synch like they did this every weekend.

Darcy pulled out her phone. Instantly, they all looked up and smiled.

"Say Besties!"

Allie hesitated awkwardly, not sure what to say or do. The other four girls were dressed in trendy outfits from Vibe. She was dressed for being outside in September in Wisconsin. Jeans, a flannel shirt, puffy vest, and hiking boots. She even had her gloves tucked in her pocket in case it got really cold. Kenzie had told her to wear her new jeans, but Allie had summarily rejected that idea. They were ripped and full of holes— totally impractical.

She took a step forward to join the group, and Darcy shifted— without seeming to notice she was there — and blocked her. Without a backwards glance, the four walked off together, leaving Allie standing disconsolate.

She wanted to go home. They hadn't even been there five minutes, and Kenzie had already abandoned her.

"Look who we found!" Jackson smiled as he, Trent, and Eric

caught up and set the coolers down next to her.

She tried to smile back, but her heart was racing, and she knew she was close to crying.

Eric threw his arm around her shoulders, filling the void Kenzie had left.

"We're more fun than they are, anyway," he said, then launched into gossip about the people they passed on their way to the barn.

The boys dropped the coolers near the makeshift stage and started passing out beers.

Allie wrinkled her nose and declined. Beer smelled gross. She had no desire to taste it.

"Yeah. Me, too," laughed Trent, opening the other cooler. He fished around and then handed her a slim can. "Tequila seltzer. Tastes so much better."

She took it to be polite and surveyed the crowd, looking for Kenzie.

"Did you want to go with the girls?" Trent asked, "I'm pretty sure they're out back. Darcy brought shots for everyone."

Eric groaned. "They're taking shots? Darcy's supposed to drive her and Sophie home, and Sophie never paces herself. We'll be lucky to get through the first set."

Without a word, Jackson handed his beer to Eric and grabbed a Coke from the cooler. He handed one to Allie and put the seltzer back.

"It's fine," Trent said. "Darcy swore she'd be the DD tonight, and Teagan's not drinking. She can drive them home if Darcy pulls a Darcy and gets slammed."

"Teagan's supposed to be our driver," Jackson said.

Trent sighed. "Awesome."

Allie's breath hitched. She immediately flashed back to Kenzie and Teagan clinking their beers and chugging.

Eric laughed when he saw the panic on her face.

"Oh my god, Allie. It's fine. She had one beer. She won't have any more. I promise. " He paused, tilting his head. "Wait... is this your first party? Like, first party with alcohol ever?"

* * *

Before she could reply, a shrill squeal echoed through the barn.

She snuck a glance at her watch. How was it possible they'd only been here for half an hour?

From the makeshift stage, a boy wearing a cowboy hat, motorcycle leathers, and fuzzy slippers tapped the mic.

Once the crowd quieted, he shouted, "We are the Grainbelt Saints — and we are ready to party!"

A cheer erupted.

The guitarist slammed into a power chord as the lead singer screamed something completely unintelligible.

Like moths to a flame, the boys automatically moved closer to the stage.

Allie, on the other hand, thought her head might explode. She scanned the barn for an escape route.

Instead, Kenzie pounced.

She threw her arms around Allie and pulled her into a sloppy hug. "Aren't they awesome?" she gushed. The alcohol on her breath made Allie pull away.

Oblivious, Kenzie leaned in again, shouting over the noise, "Where'd you go? I couldn't find you! You missed the shots! Don't worry, we'll get more when the band takes a break."

Allie shouted back— partly to be heard, partly out of anger.

"What do you mean, where did *I* go? *You* left *me*. Darcy showed up, and you turned into this shrieking Barbie doll and didn't even look back."

Kenzie blinked, genuinely confused. "Nuh uh. You were with us, but when it was time for shots, you weren't."

Allie couldn't take it anymore. She turned to leave— and ran straight into Darcy.

Red punch sloshed out of Darcy's cup and all over Allie.

"Watch it," Darcy snapped, loud enough for Allie to hear but not enough to draw attention. Her smile stayed fixed, and her tone was razor sharp — an illusion of control— but her glassy eyes told a different story. How many shots had they done that they were all this drunk already?

Allie opened her mouth to respond, but before she could, Sophie leaned in behind Darcy, close enough for only Allie to hear.

"Stupid bitch," she said, then dumped her drink onto Allie's boots.

Allie's breath caught. She looked around, but Jackson, Eric, and Trent were still up by the stage, focused on the band.

She turned to Kenzie, eyes wide.

They locked eyes briefly… until Darcy leaned in and whispered something.

Kenzie hesitated for just a moment, then turned away, following Darcy towards the boys.

Allie ducked her head and slipped out the side door of the barn, wiping at her shirt and her tears with shaking hands.

She had no idea how long she'd been outside when the hay bale tilted as someone sat down beside her. Allie wiped her nose with her sleeve and refused to look up.

If it was Kenzie, she didn't want to talk to her. If it was Jackson, she didn't want him to see her like this.

"I'm not exactly sure what happened earlier," a voice said, "but it looked pretty brutal."

The voice was unfamiliar, and Allie startled, nearly falling off the hay bale. Strong hands steadied her, then passed her a towel and a bottle of water.

Curious now, she glanced up —and blinked.

The boy from the cafeteria. The one who stole her table.

"I wouldn't dump the water on your shoes, " he said, "and I can't promise the towel is clean, but it's not covered in shit and it's better than being covered in red Kool-Aid."

"Thanks," she said quietly. "Um, do I know you, or are you just being nice because you saw me get humiliated?"

"I'm Andrew." He gave a small nod. "We don't know each other, but that was rough to watch, and I figured you could use some company."

"You're the one that stole my table," she said flatly, turning her attention back to the barn.

"Huh?"

* * *

She started wiping her boots. "Kenzie and I have been sitting at that table for the last three years." She didn't look at him when she spoke. "You stole it."

"No, I didn't," he protested. "You sit at a table in the middle with the Barbies and the redhead."

She turned to look at him, stunned.

"What?" He said, shrugging defensively.

Allie wasn't even sure what she wanted to say. Andrew seemed nice enough, but she didn't want to be here, on a hay bale, in the dark, on the edge of a party where her best friend had just chosen someone else.

She turned away, but not before Andrew saw a tear roll down her cheek.

"That bad, huh?" He said gently. He cracked open a beer and passed it to her.

"I don't drink," she said, then hesitated. "Fuck it. Maybe tonight I do."

She took a sip, gagged, and coughed. "God. That's gross!"

Andrew laughed, "Have you ever even said the F-word before? That sounded like it hurt on the way out." He opened another beer and took a drink.

She finally laughed, too. "Thanks for coming out here. It was really nice of you." She took another sip of her beer and made a face.

"You really don't have to finish that," he told her. "I figured a cup of whapatuli might be a little inappropriate after what just happened."

"Whapa what?"

"Whapatuli. That's the punch. Haven't you been to a party before?"

Her smile vanished, and regret flashed across his face.

"Well, hey," he said, trying to recover. "Everybody's gotta break their cherry sometime. I'm glad I was here when you did."

Allie stiffened. "What did you just say?"

He blinked. "Your first time? Your first party? I didn't mean... I wasn't..."

"I know what you meant." She wasn't totally sure what he meant, but she didn't want to ask.

He raised his beer. "To firsts, then. Even the crappy ones."

She hesitated, then tapped his beer with hers. They both drank, and she sputtered again.

"Still gross," she choked.

They sat in companionable silence, Andrew tapping his foot to the music, Allie wiping her shirt with the rag and trying unsuccessfully to sip her beer.

"You're funny," he said with a grin, bumping her shoulder. "Not what I expected at all."

"What do you mean?"

"I dunno. I figured you'd be shallow… like your friends. But they're not really your friends, are they? Why do you hang out with them?"

He reached for the water bottle she'd dropped. "Can I?"

She nodded. "Darcy and Sophie— the ones you called the Barbies — are definitely not my friends. Darcy hates me even though I've never done anything to her. I think Teagan is my friend, but I'm not sure. And Kenzie's been my best friend since kindergarten."

She looked down at her boots.

"If I want to hang out with Kenzie, I have to hang out with Darcy and Sophie because she's friends with them now."

"Which one's Kenzie?" he asked. "The other Barbie?"

Allie started to protest, then stopped.

The other Barbie?

How had she not seen it?

The clothes. The hair. The makeup… The way she'd acted tonight.

A sob escaped before she could stop it.

"I'm sorry," said Andrew quickly. "I didn't mean to make it worse. I was just trying to…"

Voices shouted from the barn.

"Later, later, Allie-gator??? We gotta go. Sophie's puking. Allie-Gator????" Kenzie yelled, slurring her words.

Someone was bent over in the grass, retching.

"That's your name?" Andrew smiled. "Allie?"

"Or Allie-gater if you've been my best friend since kindergarten." She said softly.

She stood— or tried to. Her knees wobbled, and she dropped back onto the hay bale with a thud. Am I drunk? She thought, panicked. I didn't even finish my beer.

Andrew reached out to steady her. "You okay?"

"Yeah," she lied. "I just stood up too fast."

"I can get you home if you don't want to go home with them," Andrew offered, standing to help her. "If you don't want to go with them, I mean."

"I'm spending the night at Kenzie's. I have to go with them."

More voices called her name.

"Offer stands," he said, steadying her as she rose. His hands felt hot on her shoulders, or maybe her shoulders were hot because of her hands?

"Thanks again," she said, giving him a wobbly smile, ignoring what was happening to her heart rate. "I guess I'll see you around?"

Andrew nodded, and she felt his eyes on her as she joined her friends at the barn.

"Wait, Teagan. Where are you going?" Slurred Darcy. "You're supposed to be with us."

Teagan stopped, took a deep breath, and turned to Darcy, visibly annoyed. "I'm driving Allie and Kenzie home. We're crashing at Kenzie's tonight. Jackson is driving you and Sophie back to your place since you got drunk and can't drive yourself home."

"What the hell, Tea? Whose side are you on?" Darcy demanded.

"Yeah," said Sophie, "whose side are you on?"

Trent stepped up next to Teagan, offering a silent show of support.

"There are no sides, Darcy. Jackson is sober and driving you home. I am sober and driving them home. End of story."

"Allie can drive herself home, and you and Kenzie can stay the night at my place," Darcy argued, waving her hand wildly towards Allie. "She's such a little goodie goodie, I bet she's never even tasted a beer."

Allie blushed, thinking of the beer she chugged with Andrew, and then, in a psychosomatic response, let out a huge burp.

"That is so gross," Darcy sneered— then jumped as Sophie turned and heaved again. The group scattered.

"So gross," Sophie agreed as she wiped her mouth with her sleeve.

"Just give her the keys and let's go. We're taking the party back to my place."

Allie froze, wondering if Teagan would actually listen to Darcy. Yes, she was sober, but no, she didn't have her driver's license yet. Her birthday wasn't until the end of the month. Allie had always been the youngest in her class, but that was something she didn't want to talk about in front of Darcy. Not tonight.

Thankfully, Jackson spoke up, "C'mon, Darce. Let's get going before Eric falls asleep standing here. Everyone's coming over to your house after the game next week, remember?"

She drunkenly turned to him and smiled like he'd just given her the best gift ever. "That's right! Everyone is coming over to my house next weekend." She turned and glared at Allie, "Except you. You're not invited."

That seemed to snap Eric out of his haze. "Don't be such a bitch, Darcy. She probably wouldn't come anyway." With that, he threw his arm over her shoulder and half-dragged her away from the group.

"You guys okay?" asked Trent, watching them walk away.

"We're good," Teagan replied, then added, "This would be so much easier if we had another DD…"

She smirked at his grimace., "I know, I know. You don't want your license. You don't need your license. Whatever, Cuz."

He gave her a quick hug and jogged after them.

Before the group was fully out of sight, though, Darcy called back over her shoulder to Allie, "Just remember who he's going home with tonight. Me. Not. You."

Kenzie, who had been leaning sleepily against a car, picked her head up and said confidently to Allie, "He's only driving her home because she's drunk. Everyone knows he wants you, Allie. You're just too naive to see it for yourself."

Allie froze, Darcy's words echoing long after she'd disappeared into the dark. She knew Kenzie meant to make her feel better, but the heat in her chest said otherwise.

Allie volunteered to take the back seat as Teagan got Kenzie settled in the front. "Oh my god, please stop," Teagan muttered as Kenzie launched into another round of "Allie and Jackson sitting in a tree." As soon as the door was closed, Kenzie leaned against it and fell asleep.

"Hey," Teagan caught Allie's eyes in the rear-view mirror. "Just ignore Darcy. She's jealous of you." Allie's eyes widened. Darcy was beautiful and popular. There was no way someone like that would be jealous of her. The overhead light turned off, and Teagan started to drive slowly out of the makeshift parking lot.

"She's had a crush on Jackson since freshman year, but Jackson's never even looked at her the way he looks at you. Annoying rhymes aside, Kenzie's right. Jackson's crushing on you hard."

Allie tried to process what Teagan was saying. Cute boys didn't crush on her. They teased her her whole life for being flat-chested. For being too smart. For being a prude. No one crushed on Allie Ellis.

Before she could say anything in response, Kenzie murmured sleepily, "See, Allie? I told you. This is our year," she sighed heavily. "Parties. Friends. Boys… Everything we've always wanted." Allie could hear her best friend's sleepy smile and fought the tear that was threatening to spill.

This isn't what I want, she thought. I want things to stay the way they were. Why isn't that enough? Why am I not enough?

"Allie? Allie? Wake Up. I'm leaving."

"What? Huh?" Allie opened her eyes to the full brightness of Kenzie's bedroom. Apparently, they hadn't closed the blinds before they fell asleep. "Oh my god. I'm late for school." She shot upright, barely avoiding a head-to-head collision with Teagan, who was leaning over her.

Teagan laughed as Allie scrambled to find her clothes. "Chill out. God, you're wound tight."

She laughed again at Allie's bewildered look.

"It's Saturday. There is no school today." Teagan handed her the sports bra from the end of the bed.

Allie took a deep breath and shook her head to clear it. "Saturday. Right." And then she remembered the night before and spied her hiking boots with dismay.

Teagan watched her face fall and said, "Do not let Darcy get to you. Once you get to know her, you'll see it's all bark and no bite. She's just trying to establish herself as the alpha."

"Uh-huh," Allie said absently, wondering how she was going to explain her now-pink boots to her mom. She was definitely going to get caught for lying to her parents. She should just come clean.

"Hey," Teagan said, interrupting her spiral. "Do you know if they have coffee here? I don't have time to stop and get one on the way to work."

Allie nodded and led her to the kitchen, grabbed a travel mug for her, and showed her the selection of flavored pods. "There's flavored creamer in the fridge, too." She added. Teagan nodded, but her attention was fixed on the cabinet full of coffee mugs and travel tumblers in all shapes and sizes.

"Jesus," she whispered. "I've never seen this many not in a store." Allie blushed, embarrassed that there were three shelves full of mugs and nothing but creamer, butter, and takeout leftovers in the fridge.

"Yeah," she said, recovering. "Kenzie's mom is a nurse— the drug reps drop off stuff all the time to promote their meds." Allie swept her hand across the kitchen, and Teagan realized that the calendar on the wall, all of the magnets on the fridge, even the pens strewn on the table, were all labeled with various drug company logos on them.

She turned her attention back to the cabinet, "Yeah, but those aren't all drug companies? What's this one?" She looked at the logo on the mug in her hand, "Saban and Bryant?"

"That's my dad's law firm. He gets a new one every Christmas."

Teagan looked impressed. "Your dad's a lawyer?"

Allie blushed again. She used to love bragging about her dad being a lawyer, but she was starting to question whether his constant assertions that the "next case" would be the one to finally make him a managing partner were nothing more than blind optimism bordering on delusion. Over the summer, her parents had hosted a casual get-together for the firm, and Allie had overheard two younger associates laughing and calling him a try-hard.

She forced a smile and gave the same line her father always did, "Yeah, he's a trial attorney, that's the toughest kind there is."

Teagan turned her attention back to the cabinet and grabbed a mug. "Young Voices Matter. Wisconsin Scholastic Region?" Allie shifted uncomfortably as Teagan grabbed another. "Fact Attack- Knowledge Bowl @ UW- Milwaukee?" She turned to Allie, eyes wide. "What *are* all of these?"

"I used to do a lot of academic competitions. Those are the ones we didn't have room for, but Stacy wouldn't let me throw them out."

"You little McBraniac. I totally lucked out getting you for a Psych partner." Teagan laughed, then panicked, "Oh shit! I'm gonna be late!"

"C'mon, Kenzie. If we don't get to the library soon, it's going to be Saturday Story Time, and we're not going to get a parking spot, and it's going to be loud, and you're not going to get a computer because all of the older siblings are going to be playing Minecraft." Allie took a breath and leaned over Kenzie, shaking her gently.

"God. Stop. The room is spinning, and you're making it worse." Kenzie snapped and pulled the blanket back up over her shoulders. Allie took a step back, trying to understand this new person that had taken over her best friend's body.

"I'm sorry," she said quietly. "We don't have to go to the library. You can come over and use our printer."

Kenzie groaned.

"I'll work on my APUSH essay in the living room. Whenever you're feeling better, we'll just go to my house," she said, stepping away from Kenzie's bed.

"No," said Kenzie, but it came out more like a moan. "Your dad always acts like I'm mooching off of you guys. I'm not using your printer again. Especially not for all of the color prints I have to do."

"You're not mooching. You know that anything I have, you have," Allie said, but she was thinking about the other night at dinner when her dad asked how much longer they would be "sponsoring" Kenzie.

"I'm not using your printer." Kenzie burrowed deeper into her blankets and sighed sleepily. "Just go to the library without me. That way, you can get your favorite table in the back, away from Saturday Story Time. By the time you're done with your paper, I'll be there. It won't take me long just to print out that stuff for yearbook."

Allie wanted to argue with her. Allie didn't need to be at the library to do her paper. That's why she had her Chromebook with her now— she could write and submit her paper from anywhere. She shifted her weight between her feet and tried to find the right words.

"But," she started.

Kenzie interrupted immediately. "For the love of God, Allie. I cannot go to the library right now, and you know as well as I do that if you stay here, you will not let me sleep this off. You're going to hover and fret just like your mom does. Please. Just let me sleep. I promise you I will meet you at the library."

Allie froze. She was *not* like her mom. Her mom freaked out over everything. Allie didn't freak out. She just made sure everyone was okay.

Stunned, Allie backed out of the bedroom and closed the door behind her.

It didn't occur to her until she was already outside, backpack slung over one shoulder, that she had no way to get to the library.

She eyed Kenzie's Jeep, but she still had two weeks until her 16th birthday, and her mom still hadn't committed to a date for her to get her license. When they'd been younger and rode their bikes to the library, it hadn't seemed far, but walking almost two miles in her now-pink, still-damp hiking boots, carrying her backpack, did not sound appealing at all.

As she was weighing her options, a small, beat-up pickup truck pulled into the lot. Its engine sputtered, rough even to her ears. It parked right next to Jackson's Accord— which she hadn't even noticed until now. She squinted at it as the driver and passenger both jumped out, doors creaking loudly.

"Allie?" She realized it was Eric waving at her, and Jackson was crossing the lot towards her. She hadn't noticed Jackson's car until now. Oh yeah— they'd brought his car back to Kenzie's last night.

"Hey," she said tentatively.

Jackson reached the steps first and gave her a friendly hug. Eric was moving much more slowly, and Allie remembered he had barely been standing at the end of the night. The end of the night, when Darcy had yelled at her and Kenzie had gushed about how much fun they'd had. Between Kenzie and Eric, Allie was sure she never wanted to drink again.

"Where's Kenzie?" Asked Eric, squinting against the sun.

"Still sleeping. She's not feeling so hot," Allie told them.

"Are you waiting for your ride?" Jackson asked her. "We can wait with you if you want."

"No, we can't," said Eric. "*You* can wait. I have to get to work. Some of us work for a living."

"Again. Carrying rich people's clubs does *not* count as work."

"Tell that to my back. Those bags are heavy. You try carrying three at once."

Allie looked so forlorn, Eric finally had to laugh. "Nah, I'm just kidding," he said, and she looked relieved.

"I've been forecaddying for these same dudes all summer. I don't have to carry their bags at all. I just walk ahead and tell them stuff about the hole. They're loaded, and they want me to go to college so they tip really, really well. Same with the group this afternoon. They're only playing 9, but I could still make $500-$600 today."

Allie's jaw dropped.

Eric gave her a playful salute. "As much as I'd love to stay and shoot the shit, I gotta bail."

They watched him drive away, then Jackson turned to her, "Want me to wait with you? I don't have to be anywhere until later."

Allie faltered, then said, "That's okay, I'm actually not waiting for anyone. Kenzie and I were supposed to go to the library, but she's not ready yet. I'm just gonna go and grab our table, and she'll meet me later."

Jackson scanned the parking lot. "So… was she your ride?"

"Um, yeah," she hesitated. "But I can walk. It's not that far." That was a total lie. Two miles in damp boots was really far.

"That's so far away!" Jackson exclaimed. "I can drive you if you want," he offered.

Allie paused, weighing her options. On the one hand, she did *not* want to walk to the library. But on the other hand, Darcy had made it very clear that she didn't want Allie anywhere near Jackson, and Allie was a little afraid of Darcy now- regardless of what Teagan said.

"The fact that you're even thinking about this hurts my feelings," he joked. He pitched his voice into a high falsetto, *"Should I walk two miles with a heavy backpack or get in the car with this total loser?"*

Allie laughed.

"You're not a loser," she said. "It's not really *that* far. You probably have stuff to do anyway… Besides, I haven't paid you back for all of the tutoring yet, I'm not gonna ask for another favor."

Jackson smacked his hand to his chest and staggered backwards. "You're killing me, Smalls." Allie laughed. "No, seriously," he laughed with her, "you don't owe me anything for the tutoring. That's what friends are for.. Besides," he said, "I don't have anything to do until later, and the library is on my way home. It's not a big deal, I promise."

When she still hesitated, he laughed, "Are you serious? I actually took a shower this morning."

"Shut up!" She laughed, "Fine. I'll take a ride to the library. But you … are a total dork."

Jackson let out a yelp when he turned the car on, and the radio screamed at them. When he'd turned it down, Allie said sheepishly, "Sorry. Teagan was sleepy, and she needed the music to stay awake."

"Yeah, I can see that," he said, pulling out of the parking lot. "Is she at work already?"

Allie confirmed that she was, and the two chatted amiably until Allie's stomach let out a growl that Kenzie could have heard back in her bedroom.

"Don't you eat?" Jackson asked, incredulous.

Allie blushed, then answered, "Yes, but..." She paused while her stomach bellowed angrily again, "We didn't really eat dinner last night, and there wasn't really anything for breakfast at Kenzie's this morning." She dug around her backpack, "It's fine though. I'm pretty sure there's a protein bar in here..."

Jackson abruptly turned the car into a parking lot and pulled into a recently vacated spot in front of The Corner Deli.

Allie froze. She didn't have any money. No cash, no card, no Venmo. Or any way to pay for anything that wasn't a free protein bar of questionable age she'd just dug out of the bottom of her backpack.

"Thank you, Allie. You have no idea how happy I am that you haven't eaten in a day, and there's no way I can possibly take you to the library when you're clearly starving." The words tumbled from his mouth as he fought to get out of his seatbelt. "My mom is on this crazy health kick, and I swear she's trying to starve all of us. Do you want to know what my choices were for breakfast this morning?" Allie was frozen in her seat, but Jackson continued, oblivious. " A fruit cup with cottage cheese, yogurt with weird seeds in it, or a smoothie that's the same color as my baby cousin's poop." He struggled with his seatbelt, then finally unbuckled it.

"I will buy you anything you want if you promise to say this was your idea and that I ordered a salad." He took three steps away from the car, then turned abruptly to wait for her. She was still frozen in the passenger seat. He threw his arms out dramatically, then pointed at the door. Allie could practically hear the unspoken words, "You're killing me, Smalls."

She smiled despite herself and scrambled out of the car after him.

By the time they'd left the deli, Allie had forgotten to be nervous. Jackson was as funny as he was smart, and he'd kept the conversation going the entire time.

* * *

She pulled out her phone as Jackson pulled into the library parking lot. There was nothing from Kenzie after the "K" she'd sent after Allie told her they were stopping to eat.

Allie: Just getting here. Are you in the back? Sorry if I'm late.

She waited, but nothing happened. Jackson pulled up and stopped in front of the doors.

"Hey, thanks for being my excuse to stop for breakfast." Jackson laughed and rubbed his belly, satisfied.

Allie looked up from her phone, startled.

"Anytime!" She smiled. "But next time, remind me that I *can't* eat the whole Badger Breakfast and I should just get scrambled eggs and toast." She glanced at the phone, then put it back in her backpack.

"Why would I do that? Now I have second breakfast— technically third if yogurt and weird seeds even counts." He gestured at the take-out container in the back seat. Allie laughed.

"Thanks again," she said and sucked in a breath as the unseasonal heat hit her.

"It's supposed to snow later this week," Jackson said seriously.

"What???" Allie's stomach sank. She'd lived in Wisconsin her whole life, but she still hated the cold. She'd never tell her parents, but *her* dream school list didn't include a single campus where it snowed.

Jackson burst out laughing. "You're so gullible! No snow in the forecast."

She punched him in the arm. "Jerk. Don't even joke about that."

"At least until next week," he said with a grin.

"Have fun aerating the yard," she said dryly as she climbed out of the car. "And wear your safety glasses this year." She laughed, thinking about the story he'd told her about aerating the yard last year.

He laughed, too. "See you Monday."

"See you Monday," she said, then shut the car door behind her.

CHAPTER 15- STILL NOT A DATE

Allie watched Jackson drive away, then circled to the back of the library. Huh. Kenzie wasn't in their spot. She set her bag down next to her usual spot and checked her phone. Nothing since the "K" earlier. *Did Kenzie go back to sleep? What if she was sick? What if she had alcohol poisoning?* She shouldn't have left her there by herself.

Allie: You okay?
Allie: You still coming to the library? I'm in our usual spot.
Allie: I have to tell you about breakfast with Jackson.

She flipped to the spoofing app that Eric had installed and breathed a sigh of relief … it still showed she was safe and sound at Kenzie's.

Allie pulled her Chromebook out and reread the prompt:
"How did the systems of trade, labor, and resistance reflect power structures in the early British colonies. Use at least two regions in your analysis."

What if Kenzie was dead?
Allie: Hey, I'm getting worried. Can you at least text me back?

There was no way Allie was going to be able to write this paper until she knew whether or not Kenzie was okay.

"Hey, Allie-gator! You look a lot better this morning than you did last night."

Allie jumped, dropping her phone before looking up. "Andrew?"

"In the flesh!" He sat down next to her and pulled a book out of his backpack.

"But what are you doing here?" Allie asked.

Andrew laughed, "I come here every Saturday. I help set up StoryTime."

Allie couldn't believe she'd never noticed him at the library before, but she was impressed that he volunteered here.

"How's your friend doing? I'm guessing she wasn't up bright and early this morning." He laughed and checked his phone. "Is it okay if I crash your study sesh? I have to kill some time before I need to be back home."

She hesitated for a second, considering. Kenzie would be there any minute. *But maybe if Andrew was here when she showed up, she'd be happy about it, right? It might not be Jackson, but at least she was talking to a boy. And Kenzie was all about this being the year of boys. Besides, Andrew was cute.*

"Of course," she smiled. "But I have to get this paper done, so no talking."

He held up three fingers on his right hand, "Scouts honor."

She pulled her notebook out and settled into the chair.

"So what's the paper about?" he asked, leaning over to look at her notebook.

She shot him a look, and he leaned back into his seat.

"Sorry, sorry!" he grinned sheepishly. "Just going to sit here and read and not bother you."

She checked her phone, sighed, and put it back in her bag.

"You look upset. Is someone else coming? Do you want me to leave?"

He'd been such a good listener last night. Maybe if she talked to him about Kenzie, she'd be able to focus on her paper.

She finally turned to him and said, "Kenzie is supposed to be here, but she was so hungover she didn't come."

Before he could reply, Allie launched into the whole story, forgetting that he'd been there last night. By the time she finally admitted she was worried Kenzie was dead, Andrew had set his book down and leaned in, listening intently.

Allie stared at him expectantly. "Oh," he said, startled, realizing she was waiting for him to say something. "Sorry."

"Honestly?" he asked, and she nodded. "I think the way she treated you was shitty, but she's not dying. She's just hungover."

Allie felt like someone had taken a 200-pound weighted blanket off her. "Thank you! You are such a good listener."

"No problem," he said and picked his book back up. "Okay, in all seriousness, though," he said, turning to her, "You have an essay to write and this book is not going to read itself."

* * *

She smiled, relaxing for the first time since Kenzie had told her they were going to the party. It was nice to have someone listen to her for a change.

The two worked in comfortable silence. Allie bounced between typing furiously and flipping between the pages of her notebook. Andrew leisurely flipped the pages of his book.

Finally, Andrew checked his phone and sighed. "Hey... I know you're not done, but I gotta go." He stood. "Do you want to text Kenzie before I leave to see if she's coming? If not, I can drive you home."

Allie had been lost in the complexities of the early British colonies and looked up blankly. "Oh," she said when she realized he was waiting for an answer. She sent a quick text to Kenzie, and they waited for her response.

"You can go," Allie said, half-smiling. "You've already spent your whole afternoon babysitting me."

Andrew slung his bag over his shoulder but didn't move. "I didn't mind. Honestly, I'm kind of glad Kenzie bailed. I had fun today."

She blinked, surprised by how sincere he sounded. "You did?"

"Yeah," he said, grinning. "You're easy to hang out with. Quiet, but not in a bad way. It's... nice."

Her chest warmed, even as guilt twisted through her. Kenzie still hadn't texted back.

Andrew noticed. "Still nothing?"

She shook her head.

He leaned back against the table, thoughtful. "She'll come around. People do their own thing sometimes. It doesn't mean they stop caring."

Allie sighed. "It just sucks. One day we're fine, and the next she's ghosting me for her new 'bestie' Darcy."

"The mean Barbie?" he repeated with mock horror. "That's rough."

Despite herself, Allie laughed. "Exactly!"

* * *

"There you go," he said, smiling. "You'll talk it out. Probably laugh about all of this by Monday."

"Maybe."

"Maybe," he echoed. "But you handled today on your own. That's something."

She hadn't thought of it like that. She'd gotten through the afternoon, even had fun.

"See?" he said. "Told you. You'll be fine."

She checked her phone —still nothing from Kenzie. But, she felt lighter somehow. "Maybe I should tell her what a great day I had with you and Jackson. Make her jealous."

"Jackson?" His eyebrows lifted. "Is he your boyfriend?"

"What? No." She laughed, shaking her head. "He's just—he's Jackson."

Andrew smiled but didn't say anything else.

Allie gathered her things, still a little breathless from the turn her mood had taken. "Seriously, thank you. I didn't realize how much I needed today."

"Anytime," he said quietly.

She gave him a quick hug before she could overthink it. "Now I'm the one who has to go."She rushed to leave, but stopped and turned around. "Hey, maybe you could sit with us at lunch?"

"Yeah, no," he said immediately and made a face.

Confused, Allie asked, "But why? You said we had a great time today."

"Exactly. *We* had a great time. Your 'friends' wouldn't like me any more than I like them. I'd love to hang out with you again, but hard pass on hanging out with people who treated you the way they did last night."

Allie was tempted to argue with him, but her phone buzzed. *Kenzie!*

Her heart leapt— until she saw the name on the screen: **Mom**.

She looked up to tell Andrew, but he was already gone.

* * *

Mom: We're meeting one of the partners for brunch tomorrow. Any chance Stacy can bring you home?

Shit. They think I'm still at Kenzie's. I need to get back there before I get in trouble.

Allie: She's currently unavailable. I'll ask her though.

Mom: Unavailable? What does that mean?

Why had she lied to her parents? She mentally calculated how long it would take to get back to Kenzie's and considered the chance that Kenzie's mom would get sent home from work before the next morning.

She fought the urge to confess everything to her mom and left the library without answering the text.

The lights were off and the door was locked when Allie finally got to the apartment. Her feet and back ached- she definitely wasn't wearing the right shoes to walk that far.

She'd been looking forward to hanging out with Kenzie and telling her how much fun she'd had without her. But the second she opened the door, she knew that no one had been there all day. She took the fact that Kenzie's Jeep was missing as a sign that she wasn't dead— she just went somewhere.

She dropped her backpack by the front door and checked her phone.

Mom: Hello? Are you there?

Allie: Sorry. Stacy just got called into work. She can't bring me home.

Mom: Work? Why didn't she tell me? How long have you been there by yourself?

How does she know I'm alone? Then Allie remembered that she'd told her mom Stacy didn't have to work at all this weekend, so she'd be staying with Kenzie. *Think! How to explain that I'm alone and probably will be all night...*

Allie: Just a little while. Kenzie had to go to work, too.

Mom: So you're there ALONE?????

Allie: Yes. And the doors are locked and I'm fine. But Kenzie has to close and she's going to stay at Teagan's tonight. They said I can stay here or you can come get me.

* * *

Where is all of this coming from? Allie had no idea where Kenzie was, but she was lying about it like she'd been doing it all her life.

Mom: I'm on the way. I can't believe they just left you there by yourself. I'm calling Stacy.

Allie: NO!

Allie: She feels terrible. One of the other nurses was sick and they were already short staffed bc a different one got married. And all of the beds are full. She felt like she couldn't say no.

Mom: I understand that. She should've called me instead of leaving you by yourself.

Allie: If you call her and make her feel bad, I'm never speaking to you again. Her boss basically begged her to come in right away. She would've called you if she had time.

Mom: Poor Stacy.

Allie: It definitely sucks to be her. Don't make it worse.

Mom: I'll talk to her about it next week

Allie: Okay

If Allie knew one thing about her mother, it was that there was zero chance her mom would remember this by tomorrow, much less next week.

Mom: See you in a few

Allie: 👍

CHAPTER 16- DELIVERED

Allie: Where are you? My mom's coming to get me bc there's no one here.

Allie: Are you okay? Do you need us to come get you?

Allie: My mom was freaking out so I told her you had to work and staying the night at Teagans

Allie: Seriously, though… where are you? I'm getting worried.

Allie: Hey… Are you mad at me? I don't think you are, but if you are just tell me and I'll stop texting you.

Allie: Okay, it's 2am. Whatever I did, I'm sorry. Please just text me and tell me you're alive.

Allie: I know your moms shift ends at 8. Please text me back or I'm going to call her.

Allie: Are you with your mom? Her phone went straight to voicemail.

Allie: don't be mad.

Allie: I asked her to call me.

Allie: I just got off the phone with your mom and she said that you went to Darcy's to work on your yearbook project and that you spent the night there and you'll call me when you get home tonight.

Allie: ?

Allie: You know I had to walk home from the library?

Allie: Why are you mad at me? What did I do?

Both Allie and her mom had moved through the morning like zombies, still half-asleep as they rushed out the door. Mondays were always rough, but this one… was something else.

Angela Ellis shrieked and slammed on the brakes.

"Mom!" Allie cried, grabbing for her coffee before it tipped. She looked around, heart racing, trying to see what had spooked her — then spotted Kenzie's Jeep right behind them, Kenzie mirroring Angela's wide-eyed panic.

"I thought you said she wasn't coming this morning," her mom's voice was as shaky as her hands.

Allie had no idea what to say, then finally, "I didn't think she was."

Then Kenzie was standing outside her door, bent down, waiting for Allie to roll her window down. In the two seconds between Kenzie tapping on the window and her mom sliding it down, Allie's brain went into overdrive.

Anger that Kenzie had ditched her and made her walk home from the library.

Worry that Kenzie had had too much to drink on Friday, was too sick to call, and needed to go to the hospital.

Anger that Kenzie had ditched her.

Worry that she was sick or in trouble.

Confusion. Betrayal. Misery. Rage.

She finally settled on relief. *Kenzie was okay.* And deep down, Allie had been more scared than mad.

"Hey, Allie!" Kenzie said, sounding confused. "You didn't tell me you were riding with your mom. Don't you need a ride to school today?"

Before Allie had a chance to respond, Mrs Ellis chastised Kenzie, "Kenzie, sweetheart! You should *never* pull behind a car that's backing up. That's just irresponsible. I knew you weren't ready for Allie to ride with you."

"Mom!" exclaimed Allie, who couldn't help defending Kenzie, even under the current circumstances.

"But Angie!" Kenzie protested, "I've been sitting here the whole time. Well, not the whole time, I didn't realize Allie was in the car. I thought she was coming out right behind you. I thought you saw me. You waved at me."

"I waved at the neighbor," Angela Ellis corrected, then paused and addressed her daughter. "We'll have to discuss this whole thing tonight, but for now, I suppose it's okay for you to ride with Kenzie today."

Allie froze. She wasn't sure she wanted to ride with Kenzie, but like before, Allie's mom jumped in before she could say anything and unlocked the door. Kenzie threw it open and grabbed Allie's backpack. "Thanks, Angie. I promise I'm a safe driver and I would never let anything happen to Allie. You know that."

Allie mechanically undid her seatbelt and followed Kenzie to the Jeep.

"Have a good day, girls!" Her mom called. They waved at her, and Kenzie backed out of the driveway before Allie had a chance to even buckle her seatbelt, like nothing had happened at all.

Kenzie chattered non-stop all the way to school— about the layout, Eric's new camera, how Sophie was actually good at captions. She didn't notice that Allie hadn't said a word.

"What's wrong?" She asked, "Do you have a test today? You always get so stressed, but you always do great. Don't worry, Allie. You've got this!"

Allie shifted away from her and continued to stare out the window.

"Allie?" Kenzie reached across and put her hand on Allie's arm. Allie jerked her arm away like she'd been burned. Her heart pounded in her ears, and everything she'd been feeling exploded out of her.

"*What's wrong?*" Kenzie flinched— Allie never yelled. "You ditched me on Saturday, and I had to walk two miles back to your empty apartment because you were at *Darcy's* house having fun." Allie choked back an angry sob. "Your mom said you would call me when you got home, but you couldn't even do that, then you show up this morning and act like nothing's wrong, and you just keep talking about how much fun you had. *I. Thought. You. Were. Dead.*" She glared at Kenzie, then turned back towards the window.

* * *

Kenzie searched for something to say, but couldn't find anything that made sense.

She pulled into the parking spot and immediately hit the child lock so Allie couldn't run away.

She turned toward Allie, who was yanking the door handle and finally screamed in frustration. "Let me out of here. I don't want to talk to you. Go have fun with Darcy."

"Stop acting crazy," Kenzie said, "You aren't making any sense. How are you even mad at me?" She reached for Allie again and then pulled back when Allie swatted at her. "You're the one that ditched me. You decided to hang out with Jackson, which is totally awesome and I wasn't mad at all— but you don't get to be mad at me for hanging out with Darcy when you were hanging out with Jackson."

"What are you even talking about?" Allie turned to face her. "He drove me to the library because you were too hungover to get up and go with me like we planned. We stopped for breakfast because I was hungry, and then he dropped me off at the library. I waited for you *all day*." She turned and yanked on the door handle again. "You didn't even bother to text me and tell me you weren't coming."

"Yes I did. Well, Darcy did while I was brushing my teeth."

"No, you didn't. The last thing you texted me was 'okay' when I told you we were going to breakfast. I texted you for two days, and you didn't respond. At all."

Kenzie started swiping through messages on her phone. "You did not. The last thing you texted me was that you were hanging out with Jackson. See? Here."

Allie shoved her phone into Kenzie's hands. "No. You see what I see."

They stared at each other's screens, confused.

"Okay," Kenzie conceded, "I can see them here, but I never got any of these."

"There's no message on here saying that you were going to Darcy's," Allie said, handing her the phone back smugly. "Why was Darcy there when you were brushing your teeth?" She asked, realizing what Kenzie had said.

"Apparently, drunk-me forgot you and I were supposed to go to the library, and I asked Darcy if I could work on the project at her house. Drunk-me also told her where the key was, I guess. I don't really remember… I don't even remember you texting to tell me you were going to breakfast." She was swiping through her phone as she talked to Allie and gasped. "Oh no!"

"What?" Allie asked, her voice quieter now.

"Allie… I'm so sorry. I blocked you. I don't remember doing it at all, but I remember you being all up in my face about getting up, and I remember being frustrated when my phone kept buzzing." The color drained from Kenzie's face. "Oh shit."

"What?" Asked Allie, curiosity piqued.

"I blocked my mom, too. What if she's been trying to get in touch with me? She must be frantic." Kenzie shot a quick text to her mom.

Kenzie: Just wanted to say good morning and tell you I love you.

"Don't panic," Allie reassured her. "If your mom was worried, she would've called my mom. Oh shit."

"What?"

"If your mom had called my mom, she would've told her that she worked all weekend. My mom would've known I lied to her."

"Shit." They sat and let that sink in.

"I'm sorry I yelled at you," Allie finally said.

"I'm sorry I blocked you and made you think I was dead."

Kenzie's phone buzzed.

Mom: Nice to finally hear from you. Love you, too. See you tonight?

Kenzie: I work til close.

Mom: Okay. There's food in the fridge for dinner. I love you.

Kenzie: Love you too

"Yeah," Kenzie sighed, "she wasn't even worried."

Allie shrugged, trying to reassure her friend, "You two always go days without talking."

Kenzie leaned back against the seat. "I know. That's pretty depressing, isn't it?"

The noise in Allie's head seemed that much louder compared to the quiet of the library during study hall.

She was completely zoned out; something didn't make sense.

She replayed the conversation at lunch over in her head, but still couldn't make the pieces fit together. Darcy said the "work group" was Kenzie's idea, even though no one else remembered talking about it Saturday night, and everyone agreed Darcy was the one doing all the texting. And then there was the key—Darcy *swore* Kenzie let her in, and Kenzie swore Darcy let herself in.

Either way, Darcy had gotten in—and Allie had been left out.

A hand waved in front of her face.
"Allie?"
She blinked and jumped in her seat.
"Sorry," Andrew said in a stage whisper when she finally focused on him. "Can I sit by you and read again? I promise I won't interfere with your daydreaming."
Wordlessly, Allie moved her backpack to the floor and gestured for him to sit down. He smiled and dropped into the chair. Almost like he belonged there…
"What are you working on? You were totally out of it. Lots of deep thoughts?" He asked casually. She shook her head, trying to clear the jumble of thoughts.

"I'm supposed to be working on this reading response for Lit & Comp, but I can't focus."
"What's going on? Maybe if you say it all out loud, it will make sense, and then you'll be able to focus?" He leaned in, his undivided attention on her. Allie glanced around the library, hoping they weren't bothering anyone.
"That's okay," she said barely above a whisper. "We're not supposed to talk in here. I'm okay."
He nodded and settled into the chair. A moment later, he leaned over to her, "You haven't typed anything yet."
"And you haven't turned a page," she whispered back and smiled. "Let me work."

He returned to his book and didn't look up again until the bell rang, finally signaling the end of a day that had felt endless —heavy and endless in ways Allie couldn't even name.
"Did you finish whatever it is you were working on?"
"Sort of," she said, "I got my notes done, so now it's just

organizing them and actually writing the response." She crammed her Chromebook into her bag.

"Same place, same time tomorrow?" He asked.

"As long as you let me work."

"Then it's a date," he said with a smile.

CHAPTER 18- BUSTED

Thursday. Somehow it was already Thursday, though the days between Monday and now had crawled by in slow motion. She'd gone through the motions—classes, homework, lunch—but her mind hadn't really been there for any of it. Now she sat in the library for study hall, notebook open, staring at the same blank page she'd started ten minutes ago.

"You're still staring off into the void," Andrew said in a stage whisper.

When she didn't reply, Andrew bumped Allie with his knee.

Startled, she turned to him and struggled to focus. "I'm sorry, what?"

"What's wrong?" He asked. "You've been zoned out all week. Something's up."

Allie blushed. She hadn't meant to be so obvious, but she cared more about what had gone down at lunch today than writing about narrative voice. "Nothing. Everything's fine," she reassured him.

"The same nothing that was wrong on Monday, Tuesday, and yesterday?" He asked, leaning in to look her in the eye.

Allie sighed. Kenzie was oblivious to what was going on, and her mom was caught up in trying to find long-term subs for two teachers who had gone out on maternity leave early, while barely pretending to listen when Allie tried to talk to her. "Do you seriously want to know?" Allie asked him as she closed her Chromebook.

"I wouldn't have asked if I didn't want to know," he reassured her.

Another sigh.

"I don't understand why she hates me. Darcy, I mean," Allie implored, "I've never done anything bad to her. Why is she so mean to me?"

The librarian walked by and shushed a warning. Allie flushed with embarrassment.

"She's jealous," Andrew replied, not bothering to lower his voice.

"Shhhh," said Allie.

* * *

Andrew looked around and shrugged. He lowered his voice enough to show effort, but not enough to really make a difference, "You need to talk about this. Let's get out of here." He grabbed his book and stood.

Allie thought she might faint. "I can't leave!" She whispered fiercely.

"Why not?" He held out his hand to her. "We don't have to scan out when we leave, only when we get here. No one will ever know we left."

She sat, frozen in her chair.

"Gusto's is a five-minute walk from here," he said, leaning down to pack her backpack. "We'll go, talk this out, you'll feel better, and then you'll write your paper and get an A."

She shook her head, but could feel her resolve weakening. In the short time they'd been hanging out, it *had* been nice to talk to him about everything that was going on with Kenzie and Darcy.

"You look like a Rocky Road girl," he smiled, grabbing her bag like the decision had already been made. We'll be back before anyone knows we're gone."

She stared at his outstretched hand. Her stomach fluttered with nerves — and not the good kind. Allie Ellis didn't skip school. She didn't disappear, not after what happened when she was little.

Andrew smiled and softened his voice. "No one will know," he said, as if he'd read her mind. "Promise."

Just this once, she promised herself.

She hesitated just a minute more, then let him pull her up from the chair. By the time they reached Gusto's, her nerves were buzzing almost as loudly as the espresso machine.

Allie was shocked at how many kids were there. Did everyone skip last period?

"We need to leave," she tugged at his hand, "We're going to get in big trouble.

He gave her the crooked grin she was beginning to recognize as a sign he was amused by her. "Seriously?" He put her backpack on the bench and helped her slide into the booth. "Who's going to tell on you? This is honor among thieves. No one can snitch without busting themselves."

Allie shrank into the booth as he walked to the counter to order. She watched the kids laughing and joking with each other. Andrew was right; no one was even looking at her.

He slid onto the bench opposite her and handed her the cone with the Rocky Road. For a moment, she thought to tell him that she actually liked plain vanilla in a cup, but then smiled and thanked him anyway.

"Okay, so what's up with Darcy now?" He asked, working around the outside of his cone.

"What flavor is that?" Allie eyed his cone suspiciously. The orange wasn't quite right for blood orange or mango.

"Cheddar cheese," he said with a grin, taking a huge bite.

Allie almost choked. "Cheese-flavored gelato?"

"Want a taste?" He held it towards her.

Her eyes widened. Allie shook her head slowly.

Andrew hesitated, then burst out laughing. "You should see your face!"

Heat rushed up her neck. She hated being teased. After weeks of Darcy and Sophie "just kidding" about her grades, her clothes, her chest, she couldn't take it from him, too.

His smile vanished. "Allie?" He moved to sit beside her. "I'm sorry. I was kidding —it was a test. I wanted to see how adventurous you are."

God. She was every bit the baby Darcy said she was. "It's fine," she whispered, voice shaking.

He slid an arm around her shoulders. "No, it's not. I'm supposed to be making things better, not worse." His voice softened, fingers smoothing her hair.

"It's not you," she sniffed, "Darcy and Sophie are awful, and everyone just laughs like it's funny. Even Kenzie. " The words broke loose with a sob. "She's supposed to be my best friend."

Andrew just held her until she finally stopped crying.

"I'm sorry," she said, glancing at the puddle of melted gelato.

"No, I'm sorry," he sighed, "I shouldn't have teased you. You have a tender heart, and I was wrong."

"You think I have a tender heart?" She asked. "Everyone else says I'm oversensitive."

"Well, everyone else is wrong," he said, his voice low and sure. "You're perfect the way you are, and they suck for teasing you."

She stared at the table, lost in thought.

"I have an idea," he said, perking up. "Let's go get some real food. Let me make this up to you!"

Allie panicked, "What time is it?" She hadn't noticed that the shop had emptied during her meltdown." She leapt up from the booth, slinging her bag over her shoulder. "I have to meet Jackson out front of school. He tutors me in Trig on Thursdays." She hastily grabbed the pile of napkins and swiped at the mess on the table. The woman behind the counter assured her she'd take care of it, and Allie bolted.

Andrew easily kept up with her short strides. "He's one of your problems," he said, taking her backpack from her.

"What?"

"He's the main reason Darcy's so mean to you. She's jealous of your brain and your grades, but she wants him, and he wants you. If you want her to leave you alone, you need to leave him alone."

"That's crazy," Allie huffed. God, she was out of shape.

"You asked for my opinion. But it's not even an opinion. You're the only one who doesn't see it."

"But he's the only one that makes Trig make sense. What am I supposed to do, just not talk to him?" She stopped at the corner of the building. Sure enough, Jackson was leaning against his car, talking to Darcy and Sophie. Darcy reached up and brushed his bangs out of his eyes.

"See?" Andrew said.

"Yeah, but he doesn't like me like that. We're just friends. He tutors me. That's all."

Andrew looked at her intently, clearly skeptical of her assessment of the situation.

"Okay, well maybe he does," she sighed. "Kenzie and Teagan have said that, but I don't think he does."

"Has he ever asked you out? Other than tutoring?"

Allie felt the color rise to her face again, thinking about Jackson telling her about homecoming. But he hadn't exactly asked her. He'd told her they were all going as a group, and he wanted to make sure she knew she was invited. That's not asking someone out on a date.

"Do you like him back?" Andrew asked softly and kicked a rock.

"No!" Allie answered quickly. Maybe a little too quickly.

"Well," he shrugged, "it's your choice. As long as you continue to hang around him, she's going to hate you."

"I have to go," Allie said regretfully, watching Jackson scan the kids leaving the building. She really didn't walk up to his car with Sophie and Darcy there. She turned to go back to the side door.

"It's up to you," Andrew reiterated, still walking with her. "Is Jackson really the only person who can tutor you? Or is he just convenient? If you don't like him back, it's kind of mean of you to use him like that."

Allie gasped. She opened her mouth to argue, but the words got stuck behind a lump of guilt she didn't understand. "I'm not using him," she finally said, but even as she said it, she wondered if it was true.

"So what do you want more?" He asked her, "Darcy to leave you alone, or to keep stringing Jackson along so you can get a good grade in Trig?"

He pulled his phone out of his pocket and frowned. "I gotta go, too." He texted something then said, "I probably won't be in school tomorrow or Monday. Family stuff."

He gave her a quick hug, then walked off, just as her phone buzzed.

Jackson: Are we still on for our Thursday Trig date or did you stand me up?

Why did he call it a date?

Allie: Running late. Totally understand if you don't have time and need to bail. I don't want to take advantage of your kindness.

Jackson: I always have time for you.

Shit.

Allie breathed a sigh of relief when the side door was unlocked.

She made a quick pass by her locker, then headed to catch up with Jackson.

There was no sign of Darcy and Sophie as Allie exited the front of the building. Jackson's face lit up when he saw her, and her heart sank.

"What's wrong?" He asked, opening the door for her. She threw her bag in the back and sank into the passenger seat.

"Long day, lots of homework," she sighed.

Her phone buzzed in her lap, and her body went cold when she saw the text from her mom.

Mom: Did you leave school during study hall?

Jackson started the car and adjusted the radio, oblivious to her distress.

Mom: FindUs said you were at the shopping center instead of at school.

Mom: I'm waiting for an explanation.

A bead of sweat rolled down Allie's forehead.

"Are you hot?" Jackson asked, sliding the windows closed and turning on the air. "It's still really warm for this late in September," he chatted casually, but Allie's mind was on the texts from her mom.

She stared at her phone. She should just tell the truth and take whatever punishment came with it. But then she'd have to tell her mom about Andrew, and she wasn't ready for her mom to say she couldn't see him anymore.

Allie: Kenzie had my phone. I put it in her bag at lunch and forgot to get it out until after school.

Mom: So Kenzie left school?

Allie's stomach clenched.

Allie: Maybe? She was complaining about cramps during lunch. She might have walked over to the drug store.

Mom: Did she ask Stacy? I better text her.

Allie: Don't.

Allie was afraid she was going to get sick. She should just come clean, promise to never do it again, and take her punishment. But her mom wouldn't stop there. Not once she got going.

Mom: Excuse me?

Allie took a deep breath and made a decision. She typed, then deleted, then typed again. If she didn't shut her down now, who knew how far she would take it?

Allie: Don't you think it's between Stacy and Kenzie? Remember the last time you put yourself in the middle?

Allie: Stacy called the police and then they didn't talk to us for months because everything was fine and you interfered.

She realized Jackson was trying to get her attention and turned to him. "I'm sorry, my mom is having an existential crisis."

"Your mom is funny," he laughed.

Mom: This time.

Mom: If those kids that Kenzie works with are bad influences on her, then maybe it's time for her to rethink their friendship.

Oh shit. Now she'd gotten Kenzie, Teagan, and everyone else in trouble, too.

Allie: She's fine mom. She probably just couldn't wait any longer for Advil and tampons.

Mom: I'll pack some in your bag to keep in your locker. She shouldn't be leaving school grounds.

Allie: K thanks. You're the best.

She turned her attention back to Jackson, who was already talking about the worksheet they were supposed to do that night.

When Allie sat down at the lunch table, Eric and Trent were in a heated discussion about who the backup quarterback should be for that night's football game.

"They benched the JV starter so he could play tonight," Eric said, "He sucks, but that's who's going to start."

"They're not going to start a freshman over an experienced senior," Jackson insisted, "Just because he lost the starting job doesn't mean they won't start him tonight."

As soon as Allie sat down, Eric had his hands out, smiling.

"Patience, grasshopper," Allie laughed, pulling out the extra container of apples and peanut butter and handing it to him. Kenzie reached in and helped herself to the other container of apples, the veggies, and the dip.

"Jesus," Trent laughed, "You two are like Pavlov's dogs. As soon as Allie sits down and opens her lunch box, you start salivating." The whole table laughed.

Eric shrugged, "Guilty as charged."

"Lunch wouldn't be the same without the apple-peanut butter handoff. I kinda like it," Jackson observed.

"I think it's creepy," said Sophie, "Like seriously, who brings the *exact same thing* for lunch every day?"

Allie kept her eyes on the floor, cheeks burning, praying someone —anyone— would change the subject. But Kenzie was in full-on performance mode, clearly enjoying the spotlight.

"It's not the same thing every day!" Kenzie insisted, defending one of her favorite quirks. "On test days— which feels like every day this year— it's all about the protein… Turkey in a protein tortilla, Greek yogurt… stuff like that." When she saw she had their full attention, Kenzie continued. "There's a schedule when it's not test days. Mondays are Meatless Mondays.. Caprese salad is my favorite, but there's also mini charcuterie boxes with hard-boiled eggs, fruit, cheese, nuts.. Just wait until she brings one of those. It will blow your mind."

* * *

Eric was fully invested in what Kenzie was saying.

"Tuesdays are 'Tea Sandwich' Tuesday. When we were in… third grade? I think? We went to 'high tea' and fell in love with the little sandwiches."

"The cucumber and cream cheese are my favorite," Allie mumbled miserably.

Kenzie nodded and continued, " Wednesdays are Wrap Wednesdays. Spinach is her favorite, if you're curious, but she always has 2-3 different kinds in the freezer, and it doesn't actually matter what's in the wrap… just that the main course starts with a wrap."

She took a deep breath and smiled at her rapt audience. "Thursday is three-cheese Thursday," Kenzie chuckled. "There's a whole story behind that."

When she saw they were still listening, she wrapped it up, "Friday is 'Free-For-All Friday' which is basically whatever is left in the fridge that she can make into a lunch."

Kenzie smiled, completely missing the embarrassed flush creeping up her friend's neck and face as everyone turned to stare at her.

The table was silent. And then it erupted.

"Please make me a little charcuterie box."- Eric.
"I love tea sandwiches!"- Teagan.
"Genius!"- Trent.
"I should've been taking notes."- Jackson.
"What the hell?"- Sophie.
Allie looked up, surprised that almost everyone seemed genuinely enthusiastic.

For the first time since the beginning of school, she felt like maybe —just maybe— she belonged.

Darcy took a drink of Diet Coke and said flatly, "I'm with Sophie. Totally giving serial killer." Everyone turned to look at her. *Was she joking?* One look at her expression made it clear she was not.

* * *

"No, for real. Most of them have rituals just like this. Color-coded sock drawers, strict meal plans. It's totally a control thing. If any of you ever goes missing, I'm going to tell the FBI to check her locker first."

If Allie could've melted into the floor, she would have.

"Yeah," Sophie chimed in, "We watched this KillerCast series last year and, like, *all* of them had rituals like *that.*"
Allie started to object, "It's not a ritual…"
Darcy interrupted, "It's all about control. I mean, weren't we just saying that Kenzie and Eric are like Pavlov's dogs whenever she brings her lunchbox out?"

She took another sip of her Diet Coke, waiting for someone to challenge her. Everyone shifted uncomfortably and looked around the table, but no one spoke. Allie's soul left her body.

"I'm just saying," Darcy continued, "It starts with triangle sandwiches and ends with a KillerCast documentary."

Allie prayed that God would strike her dead. When he didn't, she grabbed her lunchbox and fled.

The library was becoming her favorite place to hide.

Kenzie: I'm really sry. I didn't kno the convo would go off the rails like that
Kenzie: It's cute how you always do things the same way
Kenzie: C'mon Allie don't b like this

Allie: I don't feel well. Can you come get me?
Mom: What's wrong? Dad and I have dinner with the McCormack's tonight
Allie: You don't have to miss dinner, you can just drop me at home
Mom: What's wrong? It's almost the end of the day
Allie: Yes but I need to go home now.

She tried not to think about the way Darcy whispered and laughed throughout Trig, but it was hard to forget. Dr Grey had even stopped the lesson at one point to scold Darcy and the group around her. Allie burned again just thinking about it

Mom: I'm sorry, but you'll have to take the bus home. I just can't.
Allie: I started my period and bled through my pants.
This time, she didn't even feel guilty for the lie.

Mom: I'm on the way.

She scrolled through her phone until she found the only number without a contact assigned to it. Her parents reserved the right to check her phone at any time, and even though they'd never even asked to see it, Allie couldn't risk having Andrew as a contact.

Allie: I'm not going to be in study hall. Going home sick
Unknown: U ok?
Allie: I'll be fine. Just need to get out of here.
Unknown: Something happen or ru actually sick?
Allie: How do you know me so well?
Unknown: Want me to slash her tires?
Allie: You're the best but no.
Unknown: I'll miss you
Allie: Miss you, too

"I'm sorry I can't stay with you. You need to soak your pants and panties in peroxide before you wash them." Allie's mom pulled the peroxide out of the cabinet, along with the Motrin. "Are you feeling especially stressed? Your period isn't due for another week." She set two tablets on the counter and turned to get a glass.

Allie obediently reached for the pills and went to sit on the stool to wait for the glass of water her mom was getting.

"Don't sit down!" Her mom exclaimed, and Allie jumped back to her feet, confused. *What did I do now?*

"Sorry for yelling." She apologized immediately. "I know that you didn't get anything on the papers we put down in the car, but your father will kill me if we get a stain on the new barstools."

Allie rolled her eyes. No matter how her dad tried to spin it, getting barstools with the firm's logo on the seats wasn't the same as getting a cash bonus.

"I know you're not feeling great," her mom said, either missing the eye roll or ignoring it, "but try to take advantage of this quiet time and don't waste the opportunity to study and get ahead."

"I've already got the ACT prep course up on my Chromebook," Allie said, turning it towards her mom. "An exciting night of…" she glanced at the screen, "reading passages about the agricultural revolution in Mesopotamia!"

Her mom kissed her on the head. "I'm so proud of you. Please don't ever doubt that."

Allie couldn't help but think of her Mom nodding her head last spring when her dad dressed her down for only getting a four on the AP Spanish exam, but chose to let it go.

"I love you. Thanks for bringing me home." She wanted to say more, but her mom was already gone. She sighed and turned her Chromebook back around. Mesopotamian agricultural revolution…

She was knee-deep in her analysis of the agriculture passage when she realized the noise in the background was the doorbell. She glanced at the clock and paused. Kenzie was at the football game with Darcy and the rest of the group. Besides, she had a key and didn't need to ring the doorbell.

She cautiously got up and peeked out the front window. Allie could almost hear the brakes screeching as her heart, lungs, and brain all stopped when she realized Andrew was on her front step. What was he doing here?

Her mouth went dry. Her face flushed hot. Her brain completely short-circuited when he turned, met her eyes, and grinned.

"Are you gonna let me in or what?" He yelled.

That jump-started her body into action. She rushed to open the front door before the neighbors saw him out there. Someone would definitely tell her parents she'd had someone other than Kenzie over when they weren't home.

"What are you doing here? Quick, come inside before someone sees you!" She waved her hands frantically, trying to usher him inside.

He looked bewildered but stepped inside as she slammed the door.

"Are you okay? You didn't text me back, so I came to check on you." He studied her, smiling as she fumbled to get her phone out of her pocket.

Her cheeks turned pink as she swiped and saw the texts from her mom, Andrew, and Kenzie— all sitting unread, waiting for her to take her phone out of focus mode.

"I'm so sorry!" She exclaimed. "I didn't realize you texted. I'm working on ACT prep." Her face grew even hotter, which only made her more flustered.

"As long as you're okay. I was worried, and you didn't tell me what happened today." He looked around and then back at Allie, who was frowning at her phone.

"Uh, okay," he said, stepping back. "Sorry I just came by. I'll go."

"Wait!" She blurted, louder than she meant to. Her face was on fire.

"I mean, just give me a second to text my mom back. I guess my dad is talking about staying downtown instead of coming home tonight." She typed quickly, then exhaled as she put her phone away.

They stared at each other, awkward and uncertain.

"I'm not allowed to have anyone but Kenzie over when my parents aren't home," Allie finally admitted. "But thank you for coming by to check on me. That was so sweet of you." Her brain scrambled to find words that made sense.

"Hold on." Andrew shook his head like he'd misheard her.

"You're a junior in high school, and you can't have *anyone* but Kenzie over? Overprotective much?" He leaned casually against the doorframe and smiled at her.

Her heart hammered so loudly she was sure he could hear it.

Was he always this cute? She'd never noticed how perfectly his hair fell over his eyes. Or how blue his eyes were. Or how hard it was to decide whether to look at his lips or his eyes.

As if he knew what she was thinking, he smiled again. "I'm sure they have their reasons, he said, "but they're not here. And what they don't know won't hurt them."

He reached for her hand and gently pulled her down the hall. "This has been a shit week, and you deserve to relax. Not do whatever it is you're doing."

Like an animal hearing an unfamiliar noise, Allie snapped back to reality and froze. What was she doing? This was not okay. Her pulse was still racing, but now for a different reason.

Andrew turned back, eyebrows raised.

"I love the idea, Andrew," she said, fighting to keep her voice steady, "but I can't. I will be grounded until I die if my parents ever found out."

He took a step towards her, voice low. "How are they going to find out? Are there cameras in your house? I didn't see any on the front porch, and I don't see any in here."

He tugged her hand gently. "I'm parked around the corner, so your neighbors won't say anything. Seriously, Allie, don't you think you deserve a night to relax, eat popcorn, and watch movies?"

Her eyes widened. "How did you know that that's my favorite

Friday night?"

"You and I," he said, slipping one arm around her waist and leading her down the hall again, "are more alike than you want to admit. So, let's pop some popcorn, put on a movie, and talk shit about Darcy for the next two hours."

It was hard to argue with his logic... especially when he was looking at her like that. And she loved that he was always on her side.

Allie let out a nervous giggle and followed him into the kitchen, ignoring the electrical current running through her body where Andrew was touching her.

Andrew moved through the kitchen like he lived there. He grabbed glasses from the cabinet and filled them with ice, then grabbed Cokes from the pantry. Allie sat on the stool and watched as he grabbed the large pot and began pouring oil into it.

"No, wait!" Allie exclaimed, "I'm not allowed to make popcorn on the stove when no one else is here. The microwave popcorn is in the pantry." She pointed to a door behind him.

"Seriously? Why do your parents treat you like you're still ten?" He sighed as he put the pot back.

"My mom just doesn't want anything to happen to me," said Allie. "And even though she's overprotective, I try not to get mad about it. After all, we both almost died while she was pregnant with me, and then she couldn't have any more kids. I'm a 'one and done,' according to my father."

Andrew started the microwave and leaned in, "For real? What happened?"

"You remember learning about Rh factor in biology?" She took a drink of Coke as he shrugged. "Well, it's a protein on red blood cells. Some people have it and some don't. When a pregnant mom doesn't have it and the baby does, it can cause problems. My mom had a bunch of miscarriages because of this before they figured out what was going on. Then, when they got pregnant with me, she had to quit work to go on bed rest. Not just because of that— there was other stuff going on, too. Anyway, they ended up having to do an emergency C-section, and I spent a month in the NICU. The doctors told my mom no more kids."

"Wow. That's a lot of pressure on you. It's not your fault they couldn't have more kids."

Allie couldn't help but think of all of the fights she'd overheard throughout the years. According to her dad, if they'd stopped trying to have kids, they wouldn't have to be so tight with money. Her mom screaming back that they'd agreed they wanted a big family before they got married, and she didn't feel complete after just one child.

"You can't blame her, though," Allie said, then stood as the microwave beeped.

Andrew hesitated, then followed her into the living room.

"I won't bring it up again," he told her softly.

"Thanks," she said, settling on the opposite end of the couch from him.

He stayed still for a beat, then dramatically sniffed his armpits, "It's not me. I showered today. And I know you don't stink because I followed you in here."

She laughed and rolled her eyes, then reluctantly scooted closer to him, her heart rate increasing the closer she got to him.

He grabbed the remote and turned on the TV.

"You only have ReWatch?" He asked, grinning as he pulled her a little closer. She was afraid he would feel her heart pounding in her chest, and shifted to keep some space between them.

"My dad won't pay for Netflix or Hulu," she explained. "Besides, I'd rather just watch things I already know and love." As soon as the words left her mouth, she flashed back to the lunch room and Darcy and Sophie making fun of her routines and laughing at her. Her breath caught, and she knew her feelings were showing all over her face.

"C'mere," he pulled her into his chest, "I'm sorry. I didn't mean to upset you."

"It's not you," she said quietly. "I'm so stupid. I'm sorry for being upset. It's just that Darcy's so mean. She called me a serial killer today."

She managed to get the whole story out while Andrew listened patiently. "I can't believe Kenzie did that to you," he finally said, smoothing her hair down.

She lifted her head from his chest, confused. "What do you mean?

No one stood up to her. Everyone just let her call me a serial killer." She fidgeted with her hands.

"Yeah, but Kenzie's the one that started the whole thing. If she hadn't been trying to impress everyone at your expense..." he said confidently.

Allie glanced up, then hesitated. Andrew was shifting positions and was patting the couch for her to lie down with him.

"I promise I don't bite," he said, scooting back further into the cushions. "But you've had a crappy week and you deserve to be cuddled while we watch *You've Got Mail*."

Allie whipped her toward the TV. It was paused on the opening credits.

"That's my favorite movie! How did you know?"

He smiled mischievously. "It's my superpower."

She awkwardly dropped onto the couch in front of him, then slowly relaxed into him. He shifted behind her, wrapping an arm around her waist.

"Seriously," Allie said, "How did you know this was my favorite movie?"

He laughed, leaned over her, and grabbed the remote. With a few clicks, he backed to the home screen. Right in the center, with a glowing "Most Watched" banner, was the link for *You've Got Mail*.

Allie blushed and laughed at herself.

She sighed contentedly in response as he hit play.

"See?" He put the remote back on the coffee table and settled in behind her. "It's better already, isn't it?"

Two hours later, Allie had forgotten about everything —Darcy, Kenzie, the scene at lunch. The movie played on, and Andrew's arm stayed loosely wrapped around her, steady and warm.

Allie wasn't even aware she was mouthing the words along with Meg Ryan, "I wanted it to be you," as a tear slid down her cheek.

"Are you crying?" Andrew whispered, gently squeezing her.

"No," she said, then corrected herself, "Yes. I always cry at the end."

"I love that about you," he said softly, pressing a light kiss to the back of her neck.

Allie stiffened, shocked by how that made her body feel.

Andrew stiffened, too. "Sorry," he said quickly, pulling back to give her space.

"I'm just going to get the remote," he told her as he shifted his weight to reach across her. He lost his balance, and she squeaked as his full weight landed on top of her.

"Oh my god," he apologized quickly, but hesitated as he lifted himself off her. He stopped, his face just inches from hers.

Allie stared up into his eyes, then flicked her eyes to his lips.

He's going to kiss me! Right here, right now. Just like Tom Hanks kissed Meg Ryan! Her head spun as he slowly lowered his face toward hers.

He hesitated for a moment…

And then her phone buzzed in an all-too-familiar pattern.

Allie jumped, slamming her forehead into Andrew's nose.

"Shit!" He hissed, holding his face as Allie pushed herself out from under him, scrambling for her phone.

Eyes wide, she turned and put a finger over her lips. Andrew nodded, eyes watering as he pinched the bridge of his nose.

She took a deep breath and answered the call.

"Hey Mom, what's up?" She prayed her mom wouldn't hear the panic in her voice.

"What's wrong?" Her mom asked immediately.

"Nothing," she said, trying to steady her voice and control her breathing. Andrew stared at her from the couch, still rubbing his nose.

"You sound out of breath. What were you doing?"

"I didn't realize I left my phone in the kitchen, so I had to run and get it before it went to voicemail. I know you hate that, and I didn't want to make you worry about why I didn't answer the phone."

Her words were tumbled out. Her mom was definitely going to know something was up.

"That's very considerate of you," said her mom.

Allie stepped toward Andrew, trying to make sure he was okay.

"Your dad and I decided not to stay downtown," her mother said, "and I didn't want you to get scared when the garage door goes up."

Allie's eyes snapped open. "So when will you be home?" She asked, heart racing.

"We're just getting off the highway, so we'll be home in about ten minutes," her mom said. "Also," she dropped her voice, barely above a whisper, "your dad is not in a good mood, so if you could make sure your dishes and books and everything are all put away, that would be great. And if you're in your room when we get home, I promise I'll come say goodnight."

Allie gestured wildly for Andrew to get up and put on his shoes. He didn't hesitate.

"Okay, Mom," Allie said, sure her voice sounded as panicked as she felt, "I understand. Everything will be good before you get home, and I'll be in my room."

"Love you, sweetie," her mom said before disconnecting.

Allie was going to faint. There was someone at her house besides Kenzie, and her parents were going to be home in ten minutes. To top it off, her dad was already in a bad mood, so she was sure she was going to be grounded for life.

"Allie? Are you okay?" Andrew said, gently shaking her. "Going out on a limb here, but I'm guessing your parents are going to be here soon? Yes?"

Allie nodded her head dumbly. There was a boy in her house, and her parents were going to find out.

Andrew shook her again, then leaned in and kissed her gently.

Her body lit up, breath catching in her throat.

"There she is," said Andrew, grinning.

"This isn't funny," Allie cried. "In ten minutes, we're both going to be dead. My dad is going to kill us."

Andrew collected the glasses and popcorn bowl, grabbed her hand, and headed to the kitchen.

"In ten minutes," he reassured her, "I'm going to be long gone, you're going to be in bed, and your parents are going to be none the wiser — as long as you keep it together."

"I can't lie to my parents," she wailed, "I'm the worst liar ever."

"Not true," he said, dumping the popcorn in the trash and loading the dishwasher. "We've been at Gusto's instead of study hall all week. Plus, you lied to them about going to the bonfire, and then you lied to cover up everything that happened after. You can do this."

He helped her pack her homework and Chromebook in her backpack.

"But," she started.

"No buts," he interrupted, "If you can't keep it together, I can't come back. If you're going to have a secret boyfriend, you need a poker face and you have to get better at lying."

Allie froze. Her brain caught on those two words: *secret boyfriend.*

Andrew pressed her back against the front door, eyes locked on hers. Gently— almost lovingly— he lifted her head with two fingers.

"You can do this," he promised, voice low.

He waited, watching, until she gave the faintest nod. Then he kissed her- firmer this time, like a period at the end of a sentence.

Before she could even process the fact that he'd kissed her not once, but twice, he was gone.

CHAPTER 21- ANTICIPATION

Allie took a deep breath as she approached the Jeep. Kenzie stared straight ahead, both hands gripping the steering wheel. When Allie opened the door and slid into the passenger seat, she offered a quiet, "Hey."

Kenzie backed out of the driveway without a word.

They rode in silence until Allie finally turned and said, "I don't know why you're mad at me."

Kenzie glanced at her, then turned up the radio.

Allie reached over and turned it off. "Seriously, why are you mad at me? You ignored me all weekend, and now you're not talking to me." She'd been so excited to tell Kenzie about Andrew, but obviously that wasn't going to happen this morning.

"I didn't ignore you," Kenzie snapped. "I texted you a bunch of times on Friday. You never answered."

"I texted you back," Allie's voice cracked. "On Saturday."

"Right." Kenzie flicked the radio back on. "And you never even acknowledged my apology. I didn't mean to embarrass you, but you didn't need to make it such a big deal."

"Everyone was laughing at me. Including you." Allie turned toward the window.

"Everyone laughs at everyone," Kenzie said stiffly, "no one else stomps off."

Allie reached over and cranked the volume.

"Darcy's right. You *are* a baby," Kenzie muttered.

When they pulled into the school lot, Allie opened her door without a word. She was halfway out when Kenzie spoke again.

"Yeah, so…I can't drive you the rest of the week."

Allie froze. "You can't drive me home?"

"Or to school. I picked up extra shifts so I can be off this weekend."

"You don't have to take off work just because I'm staying with you. I'm fine at your place while you're gone."

* * *

Kenzie hesitated. "Uh… yeah, about that. Darcy invited me to go camping. I guess I forgot you were supposed to come over."

Allie stared. "Are you serious? My parents are going to be out of town. Where am I supposed to stay?"

"You can still stay at my place, if you want," Kenzie offered. "My mom's working all weekend, or… I don't know, maybe just stay at your place? Most people would kill to have the house to themselves."

"My parents won't let me stay by myself. You *know* that."

"Then just tell them you're staying with me. It's not a big deal."

Kenzie adjusted her bag on her shoulder. "Seriously, Allie, we're juniors now. It's time to grow up."

She walked up the sidewalk without looking back.

The rest of the day was a haze. French, AP Lit, Bio- they all blurred together, background noise against Kenzie's voice calling her a baby. The word echoed long after, twisting everything that followed. Trent and Teagan hadn't waited for her after the Bio quiz. Darcy and Teagan whispering during Psych —it all felt like proof that the rest of them agreed with Kenzie. When she reached the cafeteria and saw there wasn't even a chair for her, she didn't bother to look for one. She turned and headed straight to the library, hiding there until the final bell.

When the buses lined up after school, she slipped into a seat near the back and pressed her forehead against the window. Not seeing Kenzie, she slumped lower in her seat, pulled out her phone, and finally checked her messages.

Jackson: Hey, is everything okay? Where were you today?

Mom: Can you make sure everything is picked up? Bad day for dad.

Teagan: The slides look good. You okay to practice tonight?

Dad: Looking at your grades. Why are there only scores in AP Lit?

She sighed, feeling the weariness throughout her body. Without replying, she dropped her phone back in her bag.

Teagan had texted twice more before she got home. Her stomach tightened when she thought about Teagan and Darcy whispering during class.

Her phone buzzed as she emptied the dishwasher. She couldn't avoid Teagan any longer.

Teagan: Is everything ok? We present on Wednesday and we need to practice.
Allie: Sorry. I didn't realize my phone died. Can you FaceTime later?
Teagan: Sure. What time?
Allie: After dinner? Around 7?
Teagan: That works. I'll call you then.

Allie scanned the kitchen and living room. Everything was clean, nothing left that would trigger her dad. Her parents wouldn't be home for at least an hour.

Still nothing from Kenzie. Just more texts from Jackson and her mom.

Jackson: Just checking on you.
Jackson: If I did something, please tell me. I thought we were friends.

Mom: We've got two kids that are getting picked up late. Call Nonna's and just get the usual. I'll pick it up on the way home. I should still be home before your dad so it will be fine.

Allie opened the app and hit "reorder."

Allie: Done. I said you'd pick it up at 5:30. I have five minutes to change that time if you need me to.
Mom: 5:30 is fine.
Allie: Lakeford Mutual didn't sign?
Mom: They've been ghosting him…
Allie: Ouch.

Mom: It gets worse.
Mom: They signed with McNamara..
Allie: The one that just made partner?
Mom: Yes. Apparently he went to school with their new chief legal counsel.
Allie: Can I eat in my room?
Mom: Good plan.

Then the guilt gnawed at her, and she opened Jackson's texts.

Allie: Just stuff at home. Didn't mean to make you worry.
He replied almost immediately.
Jackson: Do you need to talk?
Did she? Part of her wanted to say yes- but he'd laughed at her just like everyone else.
Allie: I'm good, thanks.
Jackson: Okay. See you tomorrow at lunch?
She thought of her missing chair.
Allie: Prob not. Big week with papers and projects.
Jackson: Ok. I'll meet you at my car after school then.
Her stomach twisted. *Was* she using him just to pass Trig?
Allie: You don't have to tutor me anymore. I think I've got it.
Jackson: So you are mad at me?
Allie: No, I just feel bad about taking up so much of your time.
Jackson: All good. Even if it's easy, going over it helps me too. Tutoring for you. teacher training for me.
Allie: ? I thought you wanted to do computers and stuff.
Jackson: Do you know how much tutors can make in college?
She smiled in spite of herself.
Allie: You're a great tutor.
Jackson: So I'll meet you at my car tomorrow after school?
Allie: "Of course!"
She immediately panicked. What would Andrew say?
Too late now.

Allie's phone buzzed just as her mom came through the door.
Unknown: Missed you at study hall.
Allie: ?
Unknown: I was craving Gusto's
Allie: Andrew? Did you get a new number?

Unknown: Maybe. Or maybe I'm a secret admirer.

Allie slid the phone in her pocket.

Her mom's phone was on the counter, open to the FindUs app. Her dad's icon was blinking red, speeding down the highway at 92 miles per hour.

"How bad is it?" Allie asked, grabbing plates.

In response, her mom took a swig from the wine bottle she'd just pulled from the fridge.

Allie divided the salad into bowls with practiced ease.

"He was so sure he was going to land Lakeshore Mutual," her mom dumped the container of chicken Alfredo onto a plate and passed it to Allie. "He's been wooing them for over a year. And instead they signed on with McNamara, who's only been a partner for a year. Everyone already calls him 'The Future of the Firm' and now this. He's landing clients in a week that your dad couldn't land for an entire year. And it's just been so long since your dad brought in any new clients."

She leaned against the counter with both hands, put her head down, and took a deep breath.

Allie's heart rate picked up, almost in synch with her mom's rapid babbling. Each rushed sentence made her chest feel tighter. She hated seeing her mom like this. It wasn't just disappointment. The emotional preparation for her father's mood took a toll on both of them.

She slid the wine glass to her mom, who poured a glass and put the bottle away.

Allie carried her parents' salads to the table.

When she came back, her mom was leaning against the counter, wine glass held tightly against her chest, looking at the ceiling. Allie saw the tears in the corner of her eyes. Her mom stood like a statue, then, as if someone had flipped a switch, she turned to Allie and smiled.

"The good news is that there are plenty of other potential clients out there," she said brightly, "In fact, he has a meeting scheduled next week with Summit Insurance. If he can just land a few more clients, the partners won't have a choice. He'll make managing partner by next month- he has to."

Allie carried her dad's veal parm to the table and checked the place settings.

The garage door rumbled.

Allie met her mother's eyes— wide, tense, a little desperate.

"Dad will land Summit next month and prove he's still capable of bringing in business," Allie said softly. "He'll make managing partner."

Her mom nodded quickly, regaining her composure. "Of course he will," she said, carrying her own plate to the table. She kissed Allie's head and said softly, "I've got this. Go upstairs before he gets in."

Allie hesitated… but only for a moment. Then she grabbed her plate, salad, and drink and bolted for her room.

As soon as she put her food down on her desk, Allie pulled out her phone.

Unknown: Maybe. Or maybe I'm a secret admirer.

Allie: I don't have a secret admirer.

Unknown: But you do have a secret boyfriend

Allie smiled. The words sent a warm feeling through her whole body.

Allie: So how do you know about him then?

As soon as she hit send, she panicked. *What if that didn't come across the way she wanted it to?*

She watched the three dots as they appeared, disappeared, appeared, and vanished again.

She tried to eat her dinner, but when the three dots didn't reappear, she set her fork down.

Of course she blew it. She pushed her dinner aside and pulled out her Chromebook.

At 7:02, FaceTime rang. She sighed and answered it, smiling like her mother had done.

Teagan's smiling face filled her screen.

* * *

"I thought you were bailing on me!" Teagan laughed.

"Sorry," Allie offered, "Just pulling up the slides."

"No problem. Is everything okay? We missed you at lunch."

No, you didn't, Allie thought automatically. Then: *Well, maybe you did, but only because you all didn't have anyone to pick on.*

"Everything's fine," she said.

Teagan didn't look convinced. "Okay. I fixed the font on some of them. Did you notice?"

"I did," said Allie, adjusting her phone. "I cleaned up the chart on slide four. Are you okay with how it looks?"

They spent the next hour tweaking slides and practicing their presentation. At one point, Allie heard shouting from downstairs, but worked to keep her focus on the project.

Finally, Teagan said, "I feel good about it. How're you feeling?"

"Honestly?" Allie hesitated. "I'm afraid I'll freeze or lose my voice. Or..." She froze.

"Or what?"

Allie blurted, "What if I pee myself?"

Teagan cracked up. "Oh my god, I thought I was the only one who was afraid of that happening. What if we both pee ourselves?"

Allie laughed too, relieved at how easy it felt.

"Seriously, though," said Teagan. "Here's a trick. Just look above everyone's heads. No one can tell. And if you start to panic, find Trent. He's my secret weapon."

"Is he your boyfriend?" Allie asked before she could stop herself.

Teagan laughed so loud that Allie instinctively turned the volume down on her phone.

"God, no." She shook her head, and her curls flew around her face. "He's my cousin. Well, sort of- it's by marriage. We've been best friends since we were little."

That explained the easiness they had around each other, Allie thought.

"Speaking of boyfriends," Teagan's eyes lit up. "What's up with you and Jackson?"

Allie flushed. "Nothing."

"You like him!" Teagan grinned. "He likes you too, you know."

"I don't!" Allie insisted. "And neither does he."

"Methinks the lady doth protest too much," Teagan laughed.

"I don't. I swear," Allie insisted, "But even if I did like him, I'm not allowed to date. And… Darcy likes him. She already hates me enough."

Teagan softened. "Darcy's liked him for forever. He's never shown any interest. But *you*? He *likes* you. A lot. And you two look so cute together."

A new text slid across the top of Allie's phone:

Unknown: Your secret boyfriend says he's kidnapping you tomorrow. You have a date with Rocky Road.

Allie blinked, reread it, and smiled. She felt a different kind of warmth bloom across her cheeks.

"I knew it!" Teagan gasped. "See you tomorrow, Allie!"

She hung up before Allie could correct her.

Allie grabbed her phone.

Allie: Is that so?

Unknown: Only if you want it to be.

Allie: I want it to be.

Unknown: Then it's a date. See you in study hall.

Heart racing, Allie reread the last message. She packed her school bag and got ready for bed. Before she turned out the light, she opened her contacts and changed the name:

SB 🩶

Goodnight, Secret Boyfriend, thought Allie as she drifted off to sleep.

CHAPTER 22- STOOD UP

Allie glanced nervously at the clock. 7:08 pm.

Was she really doing this?

Andrew would be there in 22 minutes.

She felt like she might be sick.

What had possessed her to invite him over, knowing her parents would be gone for the weekend?

They'd been sitting under the stairs during study hall today, and she'd been venting to him about the fight with Kenzie and how she'd "forgotten" Allie needed to stay there because her parents were going out of town. But it wasn't just that. Kenzie had forgotten about Birthday Friday altogether.

That's what stung the most.

She hadn't told Andrew she was scared to be alone, but somehow he'd known. *He'd* offered to stay with *her*. Right?

She couldn't even remember now.

Had she actually invited him? Or had he just decided to come?

Either way, if they got caught, her dad would kill her.

He wouldn't care who invited who— if Andrew was in the house, they'd both be dead.

She promised herself she wouldn't check her phone. She didn't care if Kenzie was having fun with Darcy. The phone stared back at her from the counter. *One quick peek.*

It wasn't bad enough that Kenzie bailed on their Friday night ritual again. She'd bailed on her to hang out with Darcy. And the icing on the cake? She'd bailed on birthday Friday.

No popcorn. No blanket fort. No Ten Things I Hate About You for the hundredth time.

As soon as she opened PicSee, she regretted it.

Since she didn't really follow anyone but Kenzie, the first and only thing she saw was the picture of Darcy, Kenzie, Teagan, and Sophie in front of the tent, arms around each other, cups in the air, toasting the camera. The caption, "Say BESTIE!" was like a knife in her gut.

* * *

At least she and Kenzie were speaking again. Thanks to Andrew, they'd finally talked— just long enough to get their stories straight for their moms. As checked out as Kenzie's mom could be, she'd still get in trouble for ditching Allie when she was supposed to be staying there.

Allie hadn't even bothered to remind her it was Birthday Friday.

What was the point? She'd tried so many times to tell Kenzie about Andrew, but it was like Kenzie had zero interest in Allie's life anymore. So Allie stopped trying to tell her about the most exciting thing that had happened to her in, well, ever. She didn't know what hurt more: that her former best friend forgot birthday Friday or that she no longer had a best friend to share her most exciting moments with.

She didn't put her phone down. Couldn't put her phone down was more like it.

She swiped to the photo Darcy posted and tagged Kenzie in. The four girls, now in a circle, heads back, tiny red cups at their mouths. "FIREBALL!"

The next picture was the worst. Kenzie and Eric. Darcy and Jackson. Sitting close together. Laughing. Very much looking like they were on a double date. Darcy had captioned this one, "MY HEART IS HAPPY 🤍"

I don't care if Jackson's there with Darcy. He can be with anyone he wants, and I don't care. We're just friends. She knew she was lying to herself, though. It hurt that the people who were supposed to be her friends were having fun with someone that was so *mean* to her. She put the phone back on the counter and snuck a glance out the front window. Cars in all of her neighbors' driveways. *Please let Andrew be super careful.*

She paced around the kitchen. Everything was put away. Everything was clean. The house was inviting.

She double checked that the back door was unlocked. Even though the sun had already set, it wasn't completely dark out. She couldn't risk the neighbors seeing him at the front door.

7:25 pm. Allie's stomach flipped. Five minutes and he would be there.

7:48 pm *Was he standing her up? Blowing her off? But he'd texted her earlier that day about how much he was looking forward to this.*

She watched the clock for another twelve minutes, her heart sinking with each passing minute. Her stomach twisted into a tighter knot until she couldn't take it anymore.

At 8:30, Allie gave up.
She put the dinner containers back in the fridge, turned off the kitchen lights, and went upstairs to get ready for bed.

She wanted to just crawl into bed and forget the night ever happened— but couldn't let go of her routine.

Vitamins. Teeth. Skin care. Check, check, and check.

The routine helped, but even when she was done in the bathroom and back in her room, she wasn't sure what felt worse— being alone or the sinking feeling that Andrew blew her off.

She dropped her clothes in the hamper and reached for her pajamas.

Then she saw the figure in her mirror and screamed.

Andrew screamed too and dropped the bags he was holding.

"What are you doing here?" Allie shrieked, ducking behind her bed.

"You invited me!" he shouted back and bent to pick up his bags.

"Turn around," she yelled at him. "Don't look at me."

"You're on the floor. I can't even see you!"

"I need to put my pajamas on. Turn around," Allie said again, sharper this time. Then, quieter, "Why are you even here?"

As her heart rate came down from the stratosphere, her confusion turned back to disbelief.

He was supposed to be here an hour ago.

"I came in through the back door like you said, but no one was there," he said, finally facing the opposite wall. "So I came up here looking for you."

He glanced back at her. "Did you forget I was coming?"

Allie was trying to get her body to cooperate. She was bright red from head to toe. He'd just seen her in her underwear.

Her heart was pounding, chest still heaving, from the scare.

But now, mixed in with everything else, was a wave of shaky relief.

He'd come.

"Of course I didn't forget," she said, voice shaking. "You were supposed to be here an hour ago."

"I texted you and told you I was stopping to get something special. And then I texted again to tell you your neighbor was sitting on her front porch, and I couldn't get to your backyard without her seeing me." He glanced around her room. "Where's your phone? I'll show you."

Allie dropped her head. She hadn't looked at her phone since the picture of Darcy and Jackson, and it was set so it only notified her if her Mom or Kenzie called or texted.

"I'm sorry," she whispered, unable to meet his eyes.

He crossed the room and pulled her into a hug. "Sorry about what?"

"My phone's downstairs and I didn't think to check it," she admitted. "I thought you blew me off."

"Never," he whispered in her ear, then pulled back and gave her a mirthful grin. "That's Kenzie's job."

"She didn't blow me off," Allie said quickly. "She just… forgot."

"You are such a sweet, trusting girl." He pulled her to his chest again and rested his chin on the top of her head. "But next time, don't give up on me. Have I ever let you down?"

She sighed, the tension in her shoulders melting a little as he squeezed her tighter… but then he suddenly jumped back.

"You scared me and I almost forgot!" He thrust the bigger gift bag at her, "Your surprise!" He grinned and nodded for her to open it. "Happy birthday."

She dug through the tissue paper until her fingers brushed something soft. She gently pulled out an adorable stuffed panda. She gasped and buried her face in its soft fur.

"My mom got me one almost like that before she left," his voice caught. He looked up to the ceiling, working to keep his emotions under control.

"She told me that she'd always be close to me and that if I ever got sad or scared, I could whisper my secrets to it and everything would be okay."

He paused, then added softly, "She used to call me Andy Panda."

Allie blinked, startled. "Your mom left you?"

The question seemed to snap him out of it. "She did," he said, voice tightening. "But it was a long time ago."

He recovered himself and gently set the panda on her bed.

"I don't want you to be scared or lonely. So… if I can't be here, Andy Panda will be." He smiled, then reached for her hand.

When she looked back at him, he was staring intently at her.

"Can I kiss you?" He asked, and then leaned in and gently pressed his lips to hers before she could answer.

This is what swooning is. I'm going to faint. Allie felt Andrew's soft lips against hers and unconsciously leaned into him. It felt like the kiss lasted forever before Andrew finally broke away.

"We should go downstairs," he said and turned away from her.

Allie went from feeling faint to feeling rejected, and couldn't keep the hurt expression from her face. This time, a tear did escape and roll down her cheek. "Okay," she choked out.

Andrew turned back to her quickly. "Why are you crying?" He asked, confused.

"I don't understand," she stammered, "what did I do wrong?"

"Wrong?" He smiled, "Oh, Allie. You did everything right."

She stared at him, still confused. Why was he rejecting her, then?

"Allie, do you have any idea what it does to me to be around you? Just to be near you?" He shifted his weight and looked at the ceiling as a flush crept up his neck. Finally, he met her eyes and, embarrassed, gestured to the bulge in his pants.

"If you keep kissing me like that, here, in your bedroom…. I can't promise I'll be able to control myself." He blushed.

Her jaw dropped. She'd done that to him?

"C'mon," he said, taking her hand. "Let's go downstairs before I forget how to be a gentleman."

He rubbed the back of his neck and glanced from her to the bed, a shy grin tugging at his mouth. "You make it really hard to think straight."

Her cheeks flushed, and his expression softened. Still holding her hand, he brushed his thumb over her knuckles and led her gently toward the door.

Allie inhaled deeply as she entered the kitchen. "What is that delicious smell?"

"Surprise number two!" Andrew grinned from ear to ear and gestured at the matte black bags on the table.

Allie instantly recognized the logo and gasped. "My parents have eaten at Velluto before, but I've only had dessert from there. My mom brought home the tiramisu. It was *heaven.*" Her eyes were wide as saucers as Andrew pulled a small black box out of one of the bags. He lit up, unmistakably proud of himself, like he knew he'd just won the big prize.

When he flipped the box open, Allie squealed. "After that reaction," said Andrew, "I vote we skip dinner and eat dessert first. I also happen to love their tiramisu."

"You can't eat dessert first!" Allie insisted. "Did you actually bring dinner? I told you I would have food here."

"You told me you'd have food your mom made earlier to reheat. I'm sure her dinner is delicious, but I wanted to impress you." He shrugged, turned back to the bags and started pulling more black boxes out and spreading them out on the table.

Allie went cold. *Oh no. I hurt his feelings.*
Look at all of this. He did all of this for me.
"I am very impressed," she said, gently squeezing his arm. "I'm sorry if I hurt your feelings." He turned to meet her eyes for a beat, but Allie couldn't read his expression. He turned back to the bags, so Allie reached into a smaller bag and pulled out two sets of silverware, each neatly rolled in what she assumed were cloth napkins.
Cloth napkins for a takeout meal? No wonder her parents only ate here when the firm was paying the bill.

It wasn't until she unwrapped one that she realized both the napkins and utensils were actually disposable. The forks and knives were heavy-duty plastic with a metallic sheen, and the napkins, though soft and thick like linen, were actually high-end paper... definitely fancier than anything she'd ever used before.

While Allie ogled the silverware packets, Andrew had opened the meals and was waiting nervously for Allie to notice them.

"I wasn't sure which one you would like, so you pick." The words tumbled out of his mouth, then he pulled out a chair and gestured for her to sit.

When she did, he cut a bite of the first meal and held it up. "Chicken Marsala with garlic mashed potatoes and roasted green beans." Allie tried to hide her panic. She liked chicken Alfredo. That's what she always got from Nonna's. What even was Marsala? Was there a way to not eat this without hurting his feelings?

Oblivious to her hesitation, he carefully fed her the first bite, making sure none of the Marsala sauce dripped on her, and then waited for her reaction.

She hesitated for a moment, then exclaimed, "Oh my god, that is so good." She reached for the fork. "I pick this one."

Andrew laughed and handed her the fork. "Not so fast! You can have another bite while I cut the second dish. You have to try them both."

She finished the second bite of the chicken Marsala and waited eagerly for Andrew to finish cutting the next entree.

"Short rib ravioli in brown butter sage sauce. Also with garlic mashed potatoes and roasted green beans." He carefully fed her the second bite, and almost immediately she rolled her eyes and moaned.

"How am I supposed to choose?" She whined.

Andrew's smile spread slowly, and he let out a huge breath. "I knew you'd love them. Well, I hoped you'd love them." He reached back into the bag and pulled out a bottle of white wine.

Allie flinched— just slightly— and made a face she hoped he didn't catch.

"I was so nervous," he continued, not noticing Allie's reaction to the wine. "I want this to be such a special night for you. I want to spoil you!"

He froze.

"I am so stupid," he muttered under his breath. "Please, eat whichever one you want. I left something up in your room. I'll be right back."

Allie watched him leave, then reached for the bottle of wine. She'd never had wine, so she had no idea if she would like a Moscato. She shifted uncomfortably in her chair, then turned the bottle to read the label.

Maybe the wine was pushing it too far?

Andrew being here again without her parents wasn't as scary as it was last time. He'd been so careful to wait while the neighbors were outside. This was going to be fine.

She thought of the picture of Kenzie and Darcy and their little red shooter cups and made a decision. She was a junior now, and kids in high school drank all the time. If her best friend could ditch her on her birthday to go drink and party, she could have wine with dinner. She jumped and thudded the bottle down on the counter when Andrew rushed back into the kitchen.

"That's for dessert," he said quickly. "Don't worry, I have one for dinner, but I can't believe I forgot to give you this." He set a small gift bag on the table in front of her.

"What is this?" Allie hesitated. "Andrew, all of this is too much." She gestured at the spread in front of them.

"No, it's not," he insisted. He searched for the words. "I know that we haven't known each other long, but I've never felt this way about anyone." He exhaled as a blush slowly crept up his neck.

"You're so smart and so kind and so beautiful. When I'm around you, you make me feel smart and strong. You make me want to take care of you." He took a breath and met her gaze. "You make me want to spoil you."

"That's the nicest thing anyone's ever said to me," Allie said softly.

Andrew's smile was back. "Then open it!" He slid it closer to her.

She reached in and pulled out a small, velvet box. Inside was a delicate gold chain with a charm dangling from it. "Is that a lock?"

"As soon as I saw it, I thought of you," he said excitedly and sat down next to her. "When I was little, my dad and my stepmom took me to Paris with them, and I remember there was this bridge. The whole thing was covered in locks. It was crazy how many locks— and how many different kinds of locks— there were." He pulled a bottle of red wine and a corkscrew out of the bag.

"My stepmom put one through the fence, and my dad locked it. They kissed, and then my dad threw the key into the river. I was little, but I totally understood it was a promise. A love promise that you don't take back."

He worked the cork out easily and set the bottle back on the table. "I don't know, Allie. That's how I feel now. About you." Allie's mind was reeling. Was Andrew saying he *loved* her?

No way. Her parents had been married for twenty years, and her dad never talked to her mom like that. She'd never heard her dad say such nice things to her mom.

Realizing Allie had set the box back on the table, he turned his attention to the smaller bag and pulled out two disposable stemless wine glasses.

"Wow," he said quietly, "I completely misread this situation, didn't I?" He lifted the wine to pour it, then hesitated. "Maybe I should just go? This is really awkward."

"Don't go," she said quickly. "It's just. A lot." *I've never even had a boyfriend. Can you fall in love that quickly?*

"I'm sorry," he said, "I shouldn't have gone so overboard. I just…I don't know what to do with all of these feelings."

Allie didn't know what to do with all of the thoughts in her head. She tried to force the picture of Darcy and Jackson out of her head, but it was there, front and center. How long could she have a secret boyfriend before she messed up and her parents found out?

Was it too soon to be in love? What does it even feel like to be in love?

She wished she could talk to Kenzie about this, but Kenzie was too busy drinking and partying with Darcy. And then she heard Kenzie's voice in her head. *"Darcy's right. You are a baby. Grow up, Allie."*

She turned to him and smiled, "Help me put it on?"

He was on his feet in a flash, box already in hand. He gently fastened the necklace around her neck, his fingers brushing her collarbone.

"Je t'aime," he whispered.

Allie's heart stuttered. Her mouth opened before her brain could catch up.

"Moi aussi," she whispered back.

* * *

Still beaming, Andrew reached for the red wine and poured them both a small amount.

"Chianti?" She asked.

"Have you ever had it?" He asked and handed her the cup. "Don't drink it yet. Tell me what you smell."

"Umm, wine?" She floundered, "What am I supposed to smell?"

He grinned. "Chianti is a dry, acidic, earthy red wine. It's bold and tannic, which means it goes well with anything meaty or rich."

He took a sip, then nodded for her to do the same.

She took the smallest sip humanly possible. It tasted just as bitter and weird as it smelled, and she flinched. Andrew laughed.

"Just wait," he said, eyes gleaming. He lifted a forkful of ravioli. "Eat this, wait a second, and then take another sip. But a real one this time. It doesn't count if it doesn't actually go in your mouth."

She started to protest, but he fed her the bite anyway. She couldn't help the moan that escaped as she chewed. This might be the best thing she'd ever tasted.

She hesitated, still not thrilled about the wine… but the way he was looking at her… he looked so happy. He was happy because of her. She smiled at him and took another sip.

This time, with the taste of the ravioli in her mouth, her eyes went wide. How was this the same bitter drink as before? It actually tasted *good*.

She met Andrew's gaze. He was already smiling.

"Told you."

He added more wine to each of their glasses and then pushed the ravioli in front of her.

"Are you sure you don't want the ravioli? I liked the chicken dish, too. Actually, I loved the chicken dish *and* the ravioli, so I'll eat whichever one you don't want." She took a small sip of the wine, and it still tasted good, so she took an actual drink of it.

"We could share?" He suggested.

"That's a great idea," she stood. "I'll get us plates."

He put his hand on her arm to stop her. "Nothing that we have to wash or put away," he told her. "What if your parents come home early again?"

She nodded her head in understanding and said, "You're good at being sneaky, aren't you?"

Instead of answering, he pulled her chair next to his and then put the food containers side by side. "Not sneaky," he corrected her. "Just careful." He took a bite of the chicken Marsala.

The two laughed and talked through dinner. Allie told him about how Kenzie had 'adopted' her in kindergarten.

Andrew told her about places that he'd traveled with his dad and stepmom before she left, too.

He'd been right about the wine— she really did like it. It was sweeter than she expected, and every time she glanced down, she was surprised her glass was still full.

"That's so sad," Allie sniffed.

"I was sad at the time, but it turned out okay," Andrew assured her, "It was just me and my dad, so I got to go everywhere with him. We got stuck in Spain during Covid and ended up staying over there for a while."

"Wait," Allie interrupted, "you got stuck in Spain???" *Her words sounded funny. Why did she sound funny?*

If Andrew noticed she sounded funny, he didn't say anything. He just kept on with his story. "I got to go to this big formal dinner with him, and *Messi* was there. I got to meet him, and he signed the menu. It's framed on my wall with the picture of us."

"Who's Messi?" The words felt funny in her mouth. She didn't notice the flicker of irritation that crossed his face before he covered it with a smile.

"What am I going to do with you?" He laughed and poured the rest of the wine into her glass, "he's only the best football player in the world."

"Gotcha," she said, "I'll remember that. That's cool you got to meet him." He started to reply, but she interrupted. "Time for dessert?" She asked hopefully, glancing at the fridge.

"I suppose," he teased her, "but the Chianti was for dinner, so no dessert until you finish your wine."

Allie drank the rest of her wine as he pulled the Moscato and tiramisu out and brought them to the table.

"I don't think I need any more wine," she told him, shaking her head. "I feel spinny and giggly already." As if to prove her point, she started giggling and then hiccuped.

"I already opened it," he said, taking their cups and rinsing them in the sink.

He came back to the table and poured a little bit into each of their cups.

Allie reached for hers, but he stopped her.

"Patience, grasshopper," he said, handing her the other cup. "To us,"

"To us," she repeated dreamily.

Dessert lingered, the minutes slipping by in easy laughter until she couldn't remember why she'd even been nervous.

"That wine was really good," Allie giggled, "but the tiramisu was better." She patted her stomach in an exaggerated motion.

"You are adorable," Andrew kissed her on the head and cleared the food containers, wine bottles, and the rest of the stuff from dinner into the Velluto bags and set them by the back door.

"And you are so *careful!*" She said, with a dramatic emphasis on the last word. "You're right. If my parents came home right now, you could just run right out the back door," she gestured wildly, "and you would grab all of the... *evidence*," she dropped her voice to a whisper.

He laughed and put his hand out to help her up. She giggled and stumbled into him.

"I like this," she said softly, resting her head on his chest.

"I do, too," he said, pulling her closer and resting his chin on her head. "I like it a lot."

"I'm sleepy," Allie finally said, "would you be mad if we skip the movie?"

"Of course not," he stepped back and turned towards the door.

"What are you doing?" *Why am I talking so loud?*

"I don't want to keep you up," he leaned in and kissed her softly, "if you need to go to sleep, I can make sure everything's good down here. Don't worry, I can take care of this." He assured her.

"But," she wasn't even sure what she wanted to say, but she was sure she didn't want him to go. "But… maybe you could tuck me in?"

He melted when he saw her exaggerated expression.

"As you wish," he said, grabbing her hand and leading her upstairs.

"You could stay," Allie said as she turned her covers down.

"I don't think that would be a good idea," Andrew said, shifting uncomfortably.

She turned to face him, "Why not?" *Why didn't he want to stay? They could cuddle until she fell asleep.*

"Well, umm," he stuttered and looked at the ground.

"Never mind," she said and turned away from him. *She should have known. He didn't love her. He didn't think she was beautiful.* A tear slid down her cheek.

"Allie," he pleaded softly, "Don't be like that."

"Just go away," she said, curling under the covers. "But leave the light on. Please."

He sighed and sat down on the bed. "Do you remember what happened earlier when we were kissing?" She didn't say anything, but he continued, "All I had to do was think about being in bed with you, and it happened again."

He reached under the covers and pressed her hand to his chest, right over his heart. "See what you do to me?"

Her curiosity got the best of her. "Why is your heart going crazy?"

"Allie, that's not the only thing going crazy." He let go of her hand. "If I stayed, I'm not sure I could… You have no idea how much I want to stay with you, but I …" He sighed.

She watched him struggle for the words, and then she understood.

"You could stay," she said again.

"Allie…"

"Andrew," she answered.

She could hear her heart pounding in the silence of that moment. *He loved her. He wanted her.*

"Kiss me," she whispered.

"Allie, I don't think it will stop at one kiss, and…"

"I don't want it to stop at one kiss," she said confidently, in spite of the sudden spike in her own heart rate. What was she thinking? Her brain was fuzzy, but she was thinking about how electric her body felt every time he touched her. She was thinking about locks and bridges and love promises. She was thinking about how Allie Ellis, flat-chested, nerdy, Allie Ellis, was driving Andrew to the point where he was afraid he couldn't stop.

He hesitated. "What did you say?" He asked breathlessly.

"I don't want it to stop at one kiss," she said, lowering her voice. "I want… what you want." Her voice shook just slightly.

"You don't have any idea how much I want this, Allie. How much I want you. Are you sure?"

"I'm sure," she whispered, then pulled the covers back as an invitation.

"Say it again," he said, untucking his shirt.

She blinked, startled, as he took his shirt off in one fluid motion.

"I'm sure," she said again, quieter this time.

And in that moment, she was sure.

Looking back, though, it was the wine. It was his words.

It was so many things she didn't know she needed.

He stood, unbuttoned his jeans, dropped them to the floor, and slid into the bed next to her. "I need to hear you say it, Allie. What do you want?"

"This. You," her voice was still shaky, but now there was an undercurrent of something more. "I want you," she cupped his face with her hands and smiled, soft and certain. In that moment, there was nothing she wanted more than to make him happy.

"I'm falling in love with you, Allie," he said and kissed her.

CHAPTER 24- THE MORNING AFTER

Allie groaned and covered her face with both hands. *What was wrong with her? Why was the room spinning? Why did it feel like her skull might split open?*

She rolled over, reaching blindly for her phone… then froze.

Why was she naked?

Her gaze dropped to the floor, where her pajamas lay in a crumpled heap. She yanked her covers up to her chin and quickly scanned the room.

She was alone. *But it didn't feel like it.*

And then the memories.

Andrew's bare chest against hers. Their shared breaths in the inches between their mouths. His tenderness. His voice in her ear when it was over:

"I'm yours now, and you're mine."

Some of it was still a blur. Other pieces were painfully sharp.

"I want what you want."

"I'm sure."

What had she done?
Where was Andrew?

"I love you." Had she imagined him whispering it over and over, like he was reassuring them both? And maybe he had been.

Allie's heart broke when he'd talked about the revolving door of women his dad had kept while they lived in Spain; some of them had been half his dad's age, and none of them were remotely interested in being a stepmother.

Her phone buzzed on her nightstand, but she grabbed her clothes first, like somehow the person texting her would *know* she was naked.

A stream of texts lit up the screen.

Dad: Text your mom before she has a nervous breakdown. You're ruining the weekend.

Teagan: OMG! Check ClassLink.

Mom: I'm very concerned. Please text me back.
Jackson: Do you want to study together tmrw night?
Mom: Hello?
Kenzie: Im sry.
Mom: Are you sleeping in?
Mom: I thought you and Kenzie were going to the library this morning? Is everything okay?

Nothing from Andrew.
Except for the necklace around her neck… and the small stain on her sheets… there was no sign he'd been there at all.
But her body *knew*. She didn't exactly hurt, but she was sore in a way she'd never been before.

Her phone buzzed again. She jumped, dropped it, scrambled to pick it up. Only three people could bypass her Do Not Disturb settings now: Kenzie, her mom…. and Andrew.

But it wasn't Andrew.

Mom: Dad and I are coming home

A wave of panic crashed over her.
That was the worst possible thing that could happen. Not only would she have to pretend everything was fine… that she wasn't sore and nauseous and completely wrecked… but her mom would see right through her. And her dad? He'd be furious they cut the weekend short over "nothing." He'd blame *her* for making her mom spiral.
She had to stop this.

Allie: No mom. I'm sorry. We actually slept in this morning
Mom: You have no idea how worried I was.
Allie: It's only 9am. The library isn't even open yet

Her stomach turned. She wasn't sure if it was nerves, wine, or… something else.
She gingerly got up, praying she could talk her mom down.

Mom: That's still no excuse for not answering
Allie: ?

Mom: I was worried
Allie: Mom. Im fine

But she wasn't.
Her head throbbed. Her body ached. Her stomach was roiling. And where was Andrew?

She scrolled through her phone as she padded downstairs, slow and sore.
Aside from the necklace—and the way she *felt*— it was like he'd never been there.
If it weren't for those things, she might have convinced herself it had all been a dream.

She texted her mom first.
Allie: Tell Dad I got a 110/100 on my AP Psych project.

Then, to Teagan…
Allie: That's awesome!
She hesitated and then added, "It was fun working with you," and hit send.
The three bubbles appeared almost instantly
Teagan: Loved working with you too McBraniac. Be so happy you aren't here. This is a shit show
Allie: ?

Another buzz. Her mom again.
Mom: We are so proud of you.
Mom: I'm sorry if I overreacted. You deserve to sleep in.
Allie: It's okay. Really, I'm fine.
Mom: I know. I am really proud of you.
Allie: So you're staying?
Mom: Yes.
Allie: …

Allie let out a shaky breath. Some of the tension left her body.
She poured herself a glass of water and went back upstairs. As she pulled her covers back to crawl into bed, her eyes landed on the small

stain again.

More proof that last night had happened.

Shouldn't she feel different? Happier? More grown up?

Instead, she felt sick, sore, and confused.

And maybe even… betrayed?

Where *was* Andrew?

She stripped the bed and threw her sheets in the wash. Once she'd remade it, she curled up with her phone.

Despite knowing better, she opened PicSee.

The first photo stopped her cold.

A group selfie. Darcy, Sophie, Teagan, Kenzie, Jackson, Eric, and Trent.

Jackson had taken it, but Darcy had posted it and tagged everyone. They were all smiling, arms draped over one another.

The caption read, "What happens on the camping trip… stays in the group chat."

Group chat?

It was too much. She closed the app and finally let the tears come. All the confusion, the aching, the shame… *everything* broke loose at once.

She was still crying when she heard the footsteps.

She didn't register them at first. Not until Andrew walked into her bedroom holding two coffees and a bag of bagels.

"Allie?" He rushed to her, nearly spilling the drinks as he dropped down beside her. "What's wrong? Shhhh… Don't cry, baby. Talk to me."

She stared at him through her tears. "Where.. were.. you? I woke up… and you… were *gone*… I thought…"

"I'm so sorry," he said quickly. "You were sleeping so peacefully, I didn't want to wake you. I thought I'd only be gone ten minutes, but the bagel shop was insane. I should've texted"

He pulled her into a hug,

"But why are you crying? Did you really think I'd *leave*— after last night?"

She sobbed harder.

"Allie," he murmured, brushing her hair from her face, "last night was a *promise.* I'm yours until you decide you don't want me."

He gently cupped her chin, tilting her face to his. "I pray that never happens. But you *do* know I'm falling for you, right? After last night? Didn't I show you how much I care about you?"

Her body tensed. That flicker of something… *off.*

Allie sniffled. Her mind was spinning, her body aching, but his voice was soft and full of certainty. Maybe…. she *had* overreacted.

She finally nodded and whispered into his chest, "I'm falling in love with you, too. I'm sorry I doubted you."

Allie's phone buzzed in her bag. Her mom had gotten better about not texting during class, so she knew it had to be important.

They hadn't talked much since yesterday. Her parents had come home from their trip already mid-fight, barely even noticing she was there. She'd apologized again for not answering her mom's texts, but her mom had just waved her off, distracted.

And this morning? Nothing… No good morning, no have a good day, no *happy birthday*.

That must be why she was texting.

Mom: Are you at school?
Allie: Of course. Why?

The dots appeared and disappeared.

Allie glanced up and saw Teagan and Trent at their lab table, heads bent together, laughing at something on his phone.

She hadn't wanted to go camping with them, but still. She wanted to be in that picture. She wanted to be included. Or maybe she wanted Kenzie back, and for things to go back to the way they used to be.

Mom: I can't figure out how to take a picture of it, but FindUs says you're at Kenzie's house. Don't lie to me, Allison Catherine.

Oh *shit*. AltLoc was still running.

Allie: Weird. It says you're still at Lake Geneva. Maybe the app is glitching?

Mom: Your dad is at work, where he's supposed to be. The app is working fine.

Allie: Maybe it's my phone? Hang on a sec and let me restart it.

Heart pounding, she opened the fake calculator, typed in her passcode, and disabled the spoof.

The Bio teacher was in the front of the room, and she knew she needed to put her phone away, but she had to fix this with her mom first.

Allie checked FindUs, saw that her parents were both at work, and texted her mom.

Allie: What do you see now? I see you and Dad both at work.
Mom: I see you're at school.
Allie: Okay, I have to go. Class is starting.
Mom: Why did your phone do that?
Allie: IDK. I have to go. We can talk tonight.

She threw her phone in her bag and stared at the smartboard. Her mom *still* hadn't said happy birthday.

Teagan and Trent were waiting for her outside the lab.

"We're figuring out a time to study for the Bio test," Teagan said, falling into step beside her. "Kenzie's working, but I can drive you if you want to join us."

Allie blinked. "Sorry. I guess I zoned out. What day?"

"Wednesday after school. Library, or maybe your place if it's easier?"

Allie hesitated. She liked the idea of studying with them, of being included.

"Let me know at lunch," Trent said, and peeled off to go to class.

Allie hesitated at the door to their class.

"Darcy's probably not even here today," Teagan reassured her. "Oh my god, I totally forgot to tell you about this weekend."

Did Allie really want to hear this? It didn't really matter, because that was when Mr Grant flicked off the lights and started a video.

Allie let herself sink into the dark. She still wasn't sure how she felt about what happened with Andrew. When they were together, it felt so right. But apart... it felt... confusing.

He'd stayed the whole weekend. They'd had sex again, which she thought would make her feel closer to him, but instead she felt.... off. She wished she could talk to Kenzie about this, and she'd tried. But

Kenzie had been in a terrible mood this morning and had barely talked to her on the ride to school.

AP Psych was almost over when the intercom buzzed.

"Mr Grant?"

"Yes?" He answered, as if speaking to God herself.

"Can you please send Allie Ellis to the office?"

Allie's heart dropped. Her mouth went dry.

Mr Grant chuckled at her panicked expression. "Settle down, Miss Ellis. If there's anyone in this class that I don't worry about being in trouble, it's you."

But she was in trouble. She knew it.

They'd figured it out— that she'd skipped study hall to be with Andrew.

Allie thought she might faint. Her parents were going to kill her. What if they found out about the rest of it? That he'd stayed the weekend, that she'd lied? A good girl wouldn't have done any of that, but she had. And now she had to face the consequences.

She moved like she was walking underwater. Her legs felt like they might give out. She didn't even notice the familiar voice until she was already in the office.

"Allie?" Her mom's smile disappeared as she took in her daughter's expression. She crossed the office in two strides and pulled Allie into a hug, then leaned back and looked her over like she was checking for visible wounds.

"What happened? Are you okay? Did someone hurt you?"

"What?" Allie shook her head, not understanding what was going on. "No, I just...Why are you here?"

"I'm so sorry." Her mom hugged her again, then turned her around.

The secretaries burst into a chorus of *Happy Birthday*, and her mom lifted the lid on a pink box from Sweet Treats.

"Your favorite," she said, and Allie smiled at the box of vanilla mini cupcakes. "I meant to say it this morning. I really did," her mom said, "I just... one of our subs quit and everything spiraled. But that's no excuse. I'm sorry. I thought maybe you'd want to share these with your new friends."

Allie forced a smile. *So she wasn't in trouble?*

Her mom pulled her into another hug. "I already told your dad we're having a special dinner tonight, so don't make study plans, okay?"

Allie nodded, still stunned, trying to find her voice.

"Thanks, Mom," she finally said. "They're perfect."

Lunch had been… complicated. Kenzie's face had gone pale as soon as she'd seen the pink box, clearly realizing what day it was. They sang happy birthday and were devouring the cupcakes when Darcy arrived late, with a new haircut and the same attitude. First, complaining that Allie was in her chair, and then wrinkling her nose at the box… "Ugh. Who picks vanilla?"

For once, though, the others ignored her. Sophie pulled in a chair from another table, and Darcy did not dominate the conversation. Allie, half-mortified and half-grateful, managed to stay through the entire lunch.

"Thanks for the ride," Allie said as she pulled her backpack from the Jeep.

She paused, wondering how to bridge the divide between them. She so wanted to tell Kenzie about Andrew. "You could come in, you know." She said quietly. "For old time's sake?"

"I'd like to," Kenzie sighed, "but…"

"It's okay," Allie said, closing the door. She leaned back in the window, "See you tomorrow morning?" It had never been a question before this year, but now Allie was afraid of the answer.

Kenzie turned the Jeep off and smiled at her. "How can I say no to an Angela Ellis birthday dinner special?"

After dinner—just Allie, her mom, and Kenzie, as usual—the girls headed upstairs. It felt easy, almost normal.

"So what really happened to Darcy?" Allie asked, once they were settled in her room..

"What do you mean? You heard what she said at lunch. I was drunk and swinging my marshmallow around like a sparkler. I caught her hair on fire. End of story."

Allie raised an eyebrow. "You can lie to our moms, but not to me. What *really* happened?"

Kenzie groaned. "It was so scary, Allie. One minute I was flaming my marshmallow, the next, Sophie tried to dip Darcy —like they were on Dancing with the Stars or something— and she dropped her. Right onto my stick. And then- boom. Her whole head was on fire."

Allie's eyes widened, "Wait, *what*?"

"She was screaming. We all were. Well, everyone except Trent. He just grabbed his jacket and smothered the flames. It was over in, like, ten seconds. But still… her head was literally on fire."

Allie leaned in, wide-eyed.

"Darcy and Sophie were hysterical," Kenzie continued. "Sophie kept apologizing, and Darcy… just lost it. She was screaming at Sophie, and then she was screaming at me. Like it was my fault because I was sitting there flaming my marshmallow."

"But she looked totally fine today," Allie said. "Her hair didn't even look damaged."

"Trent said that it was all of her hair products. They caught fire fast, but it didn't spread. She's totally fine. Except that she just spent almost $400 at the salon this morning fixing it."

"Four hundred dollars?" Allie exclaimed, "That's crazy. How do you know how much it cost?"

"She sent me a PingPay. Since it was my fault, I owe her."

"But it wasn't your fault. Sophie dropped her on your stick."

"Well, that's not the way Darcy and Sophie are telling it now. And of course, no one else saw what actually happened. Jackson and Eric were peeing in the woods, and Teagan and Trent were building s'mores."

"I can give you the money," Allie said without hesitation, and reached for her phone. "Or at least some of it. Both my grandparents sent money for my birthday. It's supposed to go towards a car, but two hundred dollars isn't going to do me any good. Done." She said, smiling at her best friend.

Kenzie didn't reach for her phone. Her voice went quiet. "I'm sorry I forgot your birthday."

"You're here now," Allie said simply. "We had fun tonight. It's like old times."

"You're the best," Kenzie hugged her. "Not sure where the rest is coming from, but maybe she'll let me pay in installments?"

Allie was about to reply when Kenzie gasped.

"What's wrong?" Allie sat up, alert.

Kenzie laughed it off. "It's nothing. Sorry I scared you."

"It's not nothing," Allie said firmly. "Tell me."

Kenzie hesitated, then tucked her phone away like she'd made a decision. "It's not something you'd like or approve of."

"What's that supposed to mean?"

"It's just… well… " Kenzie struggled to find the words she wanted. Then they tumbled out, "I love you, Allie, I really do. You're basically my sister. But you're kind of a goody goody."

Allie opened her mouth to object, but Kenzie rushed on. "There's this super cool new app, but you would hate it."

"I'm not a goody goody," Allie insisted.

Kenzie laughed. "You went to one party and you didn't even drink a whole beer. It's fine, though. I told you— I love you and all of your goody-two-shoes self."

Allie didn't respond right away.

She thought about the weekend… the sweetness of the Moscato, Andrew's hands on her skin, the way he held her after…

She *wasn't* a goody-goody. Not anymore.

Kenzie misunderstood her silence. "Fine. I'll show you. But don't say I didn't warn you."

They stared at each other, and then Kenzie reached for Allie's phone.

"What are you doing?" Allie asked uncertainly.

"It's part of it," Kenzie explained, "if you want to be on Burn Book, you have to be *all in*. First rule of fight club?"

"I hate that movie," Allie replied.

"What's the *first rule* of fight club?"

"You do not talk about fight club," Allie sighed.

"Same rule for BurnBook. I'm sharing with you because I trust you. But you can't talk about it to anyone." She handed Allie her phone back.

"Now- click on the calendar app. That's the door in. I'll walk you through the rest."

Allie followed the steps, watching, as animated flames danced across her screen.

Then, three lines of text slammed up in stark white, glowing against the black.

"No Names. No Filters. No Mercy."
That didn't feel like a welcome. It felt like a warning.
"Kenzie, what is this?"

"Rule one- *No Names.* You can tag who's in the picture, that's fine. And you can trash-talk them, the party, or whatever. Also fine. But things like, 'Don't be mean to my best friend?' Instant delete. It stays anonymous."

"Rule two," she continued. *"No Filters.* No edits, no airbrushing. Pics go up raw, exactly how they are."

Allie's eyes were like saucers.

"And rule three- *No Mercy.* Even you know what that means."

She looked at Kenzie uncertainly. Kenzie's eyes twinkled with amusement.

"Don't you remember the Burn Book from *Mean Girls?*"

"I hate that movie, too," Allie said, exasperated.

"Well, it's like the digital version of that," Kenzie continued, ignoring Allie's comment. "Think of a screen name— the app is completely anonymous. You have to pick something no one will guess is you."

"Book lover?" Allie asked.

"Oh my god, Allie! You know what anonymous means."

"Well, yeah, but I don't know what name to pick. What's yours?"

Kenzie let out an exasperated sigh.

"Okay, fine," said Allie, and started typing.

"Not *The Sixth Bennet Sister.* That's your WritePad name." Allie side-eyed her. "And your Roblox and Minecraft name. Pick something

I've never heard and wouldn't guess was you."

"This seems like a lot. I'm fine not doing this," said Allie.

"Yeah, no." Kenzie said, "That's not the way it works. I had to use my login to put the app on your phone. If you don't finish with this, I'll get kicked out. Maybe worse."

"We're juniors in high school, Kenzie, not spies fighting the KGB. Nothing bad is going to happen if I don't finish making an account."

"I'll lose my account!" Kenzie threw her hands in the air. "I get that you don't care, but I care. You have to get *invited* to this, Allie."

Things had been going so well, and now Kenzie was getting mad at her again. She quickly picked up her phone and stared at the screen. Kenzie knew everything about her. There was nothing Allie could pick that Kenzie wouldn't guess.

Unless....

Kenzie didn't know about Andrew.

"Can I see what kinds of names other people picked?" She asked.

Relieved, Kenzie opened the app to a discussion thread.

Wow. The first name she saw was HungLikeAHorse. Followed by 42Y7XR, JoeyTribbiani, SuperSwiftie, and CarlaHorne. *Who was Carla Horne?*

She could pick a name like that. Not pop culture, not gross... just a name.

But not Andrew. When Kenzie finally met him, she'd guess right away. But his middle name was James.

She chose James for her name, and the app rejected it. She read through the requirements and thought for a moment. CatherineJames. Her middle name and his.

She typed it in, and it went through. "I'm in."

Kenzie squealed. "Click on the HotHotHot button!"

Allie added her note cards to the stack on the table. Teagan laughed. "Did you make a study question for every sentence in your section?" Allie blushed when she realized she had twice as many study cards as both Teagan and Trent.

"I wasn't sure how detailed you wanted the questions," she admitted as Trent shuffled their deck.

He grabbed the card off the top and read aloud, "What's the main function of the rough endoplasmic reticulum?"

Teagan answered before Allie even blinked, "Protein synthesis. The ribosomes give it the rough texture.

Trent smirked, "Show off."

Teagan shrugged. "You picked from my section."

Allie's phone buzzed.
SB: Where are you?
Allie: Studying. Why?

Trent read the next question, and Teagan answered again before Allie could refocus on what they were saying.
SB: I thought that Wednesdays were for us since Kenzie decided she'd rather work than hang out with you.
Allie blinked. *What? Had they made plans?* She didn't think so, but she felt like she was forgetting so much lately.
Teagan answered another question, and Allie texted quickly:
Allie: We only have a little bit more to study. Do you want to meet after?
SB: Or I could pick you up and we can hang out now.
Allie: I need to study. We have a big test.
SB: Of course. I can wait.
"Rough makes proteins, smooth makes lipids," Allie said, then blushed at how loudly she'd responded.
Allie: We should be done in about 30 minutes.
SB: Okay. LMK when you're leaving and I can have dinner ready when you get home.
Allie: ?

SB: I still have the key you gave me. I can either heat up what your mom left or I can bring something else. Anything you want.

Trent was talking. "The sodium-potassium pump uses ATP to move ions against their gradient—three sodium out, two potassium in. Active transport. You got that?"

Allie tried to focus on Trent, but her brain was spinning from Andrew's last message. Allie blinked. "Three out and two in. Got it."

"Because that's how they maintain their charge, right?" Teagan clarified.

SB: What time will your parents be home? I brought wine but don't want to open it if it'll be a problem.

Trent continued, "Exactly! It's like cellular boundaries. Keeps the outside different from the inside."

Cellular boundaries? What? Allie thought in a panic.

SB: ?

…

…

SB: If you're too busy, I understand. We can do this another time.

Allie was struggling, trying to keep up with the flashcards, the conversation, and the constant ping of her phone.

Trent was saying something, but Allie was reading between the lines of Andrew's texts. Even after a quick re-read of the entire thread, she wasn't entirely sure what they were talking about. *Did they have plans tonight?* She replied quickly, trying to focus on what Trent was saying.

Allie: my dad is presenting tonight. They'll be late. Whatever you want is good with me.

"You good, Allie?" Teagan asked her. "We said an hour and a half, and we're just about there."

Allie's heart rate soared and her body went cold. Was she good?

SB: Can't wait. See you in a little while.

Was she good? She didn't feel good. She smiled anyway. She guessed she had to be.

Allie eyed her house warily as Teagan pulled into her driveway. Even from the street, she could see there were too many lights on. Her dad would have a fit if he came home and the downstairs looked like that, so Allie was sure her mom hadn't left it that way.

* * *

Her parents had only come home early from the Roundtable a couple of times, and it was never a good thing.

She turned back to ask Teagan if she'd come in with her, just to make sure everything was okay.

"See you tomorrow!" Teagan put her car in reverse and waved.

Allie forced a smile and waved back. Everything would be fine.

She braced herself and opened the front door.

Her body reacted immediately, switching from high alert to relief, to something that felt dangerously close to longing —her pulse still racing but for an entirely different reason.

The smell hit her first. Velluto's.

Then the music.

Iris. From City of Angels- her second-favorite movie of all time.

She stepped out of her shoes as John Rzeźnik belted out, "I just want you to know who I am," on repeat. She felt it like a warm hug… the quiet, startling realization that Andrew knew her. Maybe even better than Kenzie did.

She smiled, half-expecting to hear Peter Gabriel next— if Andrew actually was playing The City of Angels soundtrack. Instead, the tenth track started: Eric Clapton's bluesy "Further on Up the Road."

Andrew rounded he corner, shuffling and snapping his fingers. Without a word, he took her hand and danced her straight into the kitchen, where wine and dinner from Velluto were already waiting.

Dinner felt like a new, comfortable habit, and she could imagine this in ten, twenty, even fifty years from now. By the time they finished, the soundtrack had looped through, and Paula Cole was feeling love again.

Allie and Andrew cleared the table as the music transitioned to U2.

As she drained her wine glass, Allie had to admit that there was a certain appeal to having the soundtrack on shuffle. She normally preferred listening to it the way it was produced, but this was nice tonight.

Andrew pulled her into him and whispered in her ear, along with Bono, "It's just you and me and the rain." Her pulse raced and her stomach fluttered as she leaned into him. He tipped her chin and kissed her softly.

"We could go upstairs…"

"You are so beautiful," he whispered, kissing her bare collarbone.
"I wish we could stay like this," he sighed.
Allie nodded dreamily, warm from the wine and the quiet weight of his skin against hers.

Her phone buzzed on the nightstand.
"Can I just ignore it?" She asked him, not wanting to lose this perfect moment.
He nuzzled her neck. "I would love to say yes," he nibbled at her ear and reached for her phone. "But your parents have a way of ruining things. You should make sure it's not them."
Allie's eyes flew open. *Her parents? What was she doing?*

Andrew kissed his way across her neck, from one ear to the other, whispering quiet promises that made her forget her momentary panic.
"So who is it?" He finally asked, rolling off of her when he realized she hadn't checked her phone yet.
She arched into him, pulling him back to her, then blushed again. She checked her phone.
"Oh," she said quietly.

He pulled up on one elbow, watching curiously as she stared at the phone and typed back.
"And?" He prompted.
Allie hesitated, "Did you know this weekend is homecoming?"
"And?"
"Well, I guess everyone is going as a group. I mean, I knew they were going, but they're figuring out the plan."

He shifted, putting a millimeter and a mile between them at the same time. "Kenzie's at work."

"Well, yeah," Allie said, uncertainly. "Do you want to go with everyone?"
"Who's texting you about homecoming?" Andrew sat up, then reached for his boxers on the floor.
Allie wasn't sure if it was the wine making her feel uneasy or the tone of his voice.

Jackson was just a friend, but Allie could not find the words to tell Andrew that Jackson was texting her.

He pulled his jeans up over his hips and stared at her. Then, without a word, he took her phone.

Jackson: So did you decide about homecoming? I promise you'll have fun.

Andrew's face contorted into something Allie couldn't interpret. "This says nothing about the group going to homecoming. This is Jackson asking you. And not for the first time, apparently."

Allie froze. When Jackson had talked to her about homecoming, it was very clear he meant to invite her as part of the group. Right?

Andrew stood perfectly still, waiting for her to respond.

"He's not asking me, I swear," Allie said, pulling herself up to her knees, reaching for him, then grabbing for the sheet to cover herself, embarrassed.

"Why don't we go together? You and me?" The words tumbled out, desperate.

Andrew paused, then said quietly, in a voice Allie had never heard before, "Don't pretend you want to go with me when you obviously want to go with him." His face was expressionless as he grabbed his shirt and turned to leave.

"Wait," Allie cried, jumping off the bed. She grabbed him and turned him around so she could plead with him.

He looked her up and down, and she cringed at her nakedness.

"I don't want to go with him. With them," she pleaded. Her voice dropped to a whisper. "I want you. I want to be with you. At homecoming. Or here. Or wherever you want to be with me." She pulled him into her. "Please don't leave."

He didn't move as she wrapped herself around him. Allie clung to him, praying he would believe her. "Please," she whispered.

* * *

"We talked about this," he said to the ceiling, his voice almost unrecognizable- a heartbreaking mix of anger and pain. "Why are you still spending so much time with him when you know he wants you? Why? Am I not enough?"

"Of course you are," Allie cupped his face, turning it down to her. "You are everything," she said, her voice thick with a desperation even she didn't understand.

"No, Allie," he said, locking eyes with her. "You are everything." He finally put his arms around her. "Jackson, Kenzie... that whole group. They tolerate you, but I love you."

She barely registered the intensity of his words; she was so focused on needing him not to be upset with her.

She just wanted to go back to right before her phone buzzed— when her body was still electric from what they'd done and her heart was quiet with the certainty that he was in love with her.

Then, without a word, he pulled her in and kissed her hungrily. He pushed her onto the bed, grabbing at her, desperately.

There was a moment when Allie was unsure.

How many times would she look back on that moment and wonder what if?

She wanted to ask him to slow down. To look at her tenderly the way he had before.

Instead, she kissed him back.

Hard.

He needed proof, and she needed to give it to him.

Allie said a silent prayer of thanks that her parents had already left for work as she hurried to the waiting Jeep. It was unseasonably warm, and Kenzie had taken the soft doors off. Her music was blaring. Allie cringed, imagining her neighbors on the phone with the police.

She winced as she gingerly lowered herself into the seat and reached to turn it down, "Jeez, Kenz. You know Mrs Campbell will call the police."

Everything hurt this morning.

Last night had been so… Intense? Desperate? Unsettling?

Allie wasn't even sure what she was trying to name— the feeling of giving herself so fully to Andrew — the feeling of being needed that much — or the strange, quiet feeling of knowing she'd taken his pain and made it her own?

Seeing Andrew so raw, so vulnerable, and then feeling him collapse into her…

He had given himself to her just as much as she'd given herself to him.

Powerful?

Last night had been intense and desperate, it was true. But there was still something else.

It changed something between them. She couldn't name it, but she could feel it.

It was beautiful.

And it was worth not being able to sit properly today.

Kenzie checked the rearview mirror, turned the radio up a little, and pulled out of the driveway. "You *have* to hear this song!" Allie couldn't think of the last time she'd seen Kenzie so excited.

The wind whipped through the Jeep as the music blasted.

"Oh my god, I wish you'd been there last night!" Shouted Kenzie. "Vibe Society hosted an after party, and we all got to stay and hang out."

Allie shifted uncomfortably as Kenzie took a turn way too fast.

"I hung out with the merch girl all night," Kenzie continued, oblivious. "She gave me her number and invited me to stay with them in Chicago next weekend! Can you *believe* it?"

Allie couldn't.

When they pulled into the parking lot, Kenzie was still talking about the band and the music and how cool everything had been. As annoyed as Allie felt, she was grateful for the distraction.

Both girls reached into the backseat to grab their backpacks when Kenzie froze.

"Allison Catherine Ellis," her tone was ice, and her eyes blazed. She grabbed Allie's hand, careful to avoid the bruises on her wrist.

Eyes wide, Allie tried to pull her hand away, but Kenzie was already pushing her sleeve up.

"Was your dad drunk when he came home last night?" She asked, barely controlling her rage.

Allie froze in her panic. She'd seen the bruises this morning, but they hadn't looked *that* bad. Bad enough to wear long sleeves when it was supposed to be 80 degrees today, but…

"I'm calling the cops," said Kenzie, letting go and grabbing her cell phone.

Allie snapped out of her frozen stupor.

"No, don't!" she insisted, "it's not like that."

Kenzie's finger hesitated, waiting for Allie to explain.

"If you can't keep it together, I can't come back. If you're going to have a secret boyfriend, you need a poker face and you have to get better at lying." Andrew's words echoed.

"Okay, so it's sort of like that," Allie admitted. "But please put the phone away."

"The hell I will," said Kenzie.

"Seriously," Allie insisted. She desperately wanted to tell Kenzie about Andrew. But not now. Not like this. "You have to listen to me. You can't call the police, Kenz, you can't."

Allie took a steadying breath. So much depended on her

convincing Kenzie not to make that call. "It looks bad, I know. But he stopped *himself*. I left my stuff all over the living room." Now, Allie reached for Kenzie's hand. "You know how he is about that. I was sleeping and I didn't move fast enough. Once we got back downstairs, he let go, and that was it. I put my stuff away and I went back to bed."

The best friends were locked in a stare-down, waiting to see who would blink first.

"That was it," Allie repeated, "nothing else. We can go to the locker room, and you can check."

Allie held her breath, knowing that this would go from bad to worse if Kenzie decided to do a full-body check.

"Where was your mom?"

"She was there," Allie said quietly, realizing how enormously wrong this would go if Kenzie did call the police.

"And?"

"And she's fine. I swear," Allie slowly pulled her sleeves up to show Kenzie. "I promise this is all there is. There's this huge case at work. And he's been working really hard to bring in more clients. He hasn't been pulling his weight for a while now, and he's under so much pressure."

"That's not an excuse, and you know it," said Kenzie, voice softening.

"I know," said Allie.

"He's never going to make managing partner."

"I *know*," Allie repeated.

"If I even think he's stepping out of line again, they'll never find the body." A small smile crept across Kenzie's lips.

"Because I'll have helped you get rid of it," added Allie, smiling at their familiar joke.

Allie was reviewing her answers on the AP Bio test when she first heard the buzzing.

Reviewing her answers was just a formality. She knew she'd aced the test thanks to Trent and Teagan.

But what was that noise?

Phones. People's phones were buzzing in their backpacks.

When the bell rang, Allie hit submit and closed her Chromebook. There was a weird energy in the room, subtle but unmistakable, as the rest of the class packed up to leave. Most kids were whispering on their way out, probably comparing answers. But a few, including Trent, hadn't moved.

He was still in his seat, eyes locked on his phone, swiping like he couldn't look away.

He squirmed, cheeks flushing deeper by the minute, eyes flicking around the room — furtive, uneasy— trying to read everyone else's reaction without giving away his own.

Allie glanced between the handful of boys still in the room, all of them red-faced and squirming in their seats, and decided that she really didn't want to know.

Her AP Psych class hummed with that same strange energy, most of it orbiting around Darcy, who was preening in the middle of the room.

Allie slipped into her usual chair in the back and watched as one of the boys walked over and held out his phone.

Darcy casually flipped her hair over her shoulder, arched her back, and stood to whisper in his ear— slow, deliberate, and clearly for show.

Almost without realizing it, Allie leaned forward, trying to see what she said.

Lip-reading was admittedly one of her weirder quirks. Back in fifth grade, she'd been obsessed with *Undercover Allie*, a Disney show about a teenage spy who always figured things out before everyone else. She'd spent hours practicing in the mirror, pretending to be Allie the Spy.

That ended after she witnessed a particularly vicious fight between her parents.

But it came back easily now.

Darcy's face was smiling, but everything else — rigid posture, clenched hands, and that hard, flat look in her eyes that Allie recognized and was a little afraid of— made it clear she was pissed.

She leaned into the boy and whispered sharp and low, "What is the first rule of Fight Club?"

"Aw, c'mon," he laughed nervously, taking a step back.

Before he could say anything else, Darcy grabbed a fistful of his shirt and yanked him closer, their faces just inches apart.

If Allie hadn't seen the last thirty seconds, she would've sworn they were about to kiss.

Darcy pressed their cheeks together like they were posing for a picture… like it was a moment meant to be seen.

Allie leaned in farther, trying to catch the rest of what she said.

Whatever it was, it made the boy go pale.

Allie flinched and sank back into her seat.

She was pretty sure Darcy had said, "…and then bad things happen."

If Allie had been unsettled before, she was completely unnerved by the time she got to the cafeteria.

As soon as she got within earshot, her friends stopped talking. She scanned their faces, trying to read the mood, but it was all over the place.

Darcy and Sophie looked smug and triumphant.

Teagan looked furious.

Kenzie looked guilty.

Eric looked vaguely bored.

And Jackson and Trent looked like they might die of embarrassment.

She pulled out the chair next to Kenzie, but Darcy cut in before she could sit.

"Could you eat somewhere else today, Allie?" She said sweetly. "We're making plans for homecoming tomorrow night, and since you're not coming with us, it'll just be awkward having you here."

Allie froze, mid-sit, quietly hoping someone would jump in and defend her like they had on Monday.

No one did.

"God, you're a bitch," Eric muttered. For once, he wasn't on his phone.

None of them were. Which somehow made it worse.

"Um, okay?" Allie stood back up and turned to go.

"I'll come with you," Teagan said, grabbing her tray and stalking off.

Allie had to scramble to keep up, but Teagan was already gone.

She held it together until she got on the bus.

The rest of the day had been off. At first, she'd thought it was something about Darcy, but when Jackson wouldn't even look at her after Trig, it felt personal.

Had Kenzie told them about her dad?

She wouldn't.... Would she?

All of that had been years ago, before Allie was old enough to read her dad's moods. He hadn't laid a hand on her since eighth grade. Well, maybe freshman year, but still.

The thought of Kenzie sharing something so personal, so humiliating, was devastating. She'd hoped to talk about it with Andrew, but he hadn't been in study hall and wasn't texting back.

Neither were Kenzie or Jackson.

She managed not to cry until she stepped off the bus, but then the tears flowed freely.

She screamed when Andrew opened the front door.

He stuck his head out, checking for any neighbors who might've heard, then quickly pulled her inside.

Before she could catch her breath, he pinned her against the door and leaned in with a smile.

"I've missed you." He kissed her, but pulled back when he realized she wasn't kissing him back.

"What's wrong?" He stepped back and studied her, one hand over her heart, as she tried to breathe.

"You just scared me to death!" She said, half laughing. "What are you doing here? What if my parents had been home? What if my mom had driven me home, and *she* was the one that opened the door?"

Andrew grinned and kissed her again. "They're going out to dinner tonight, remember? We have the house all to ourselves." He slipped her backpack off her shoulder and led her upstairs.

"But Andrew," Allie insisted, "you haven't been answering my texts. You have no idea if that's still the plan. Just because it *was* the plan yesterday doesn't mean you can count on it now."

He set her bag by the door, closed it, and led her to the bed.
"My dad will *kill* us both if they ever catch you here."

She winced as they sat on the bed. Her body had felt better throughout the day, but she was still tender when she sat.

Andrew noticed. He leaned in immediately. "What's wrong?"
"It's nothing," she smiled and let out a slow breath.
"We have to be honest with each other, Allie."
She looked down. "I'm a little…sore. From last night."
He went still. "I hurt you?"
She pushed away the image of her bruised wrists. "Not hurt, exactly."
When she looked up, he was staring at his shoes. "It was just a little more… intense… than the other times."
"Why didn't you tell me to stop?"
She knew she had to answer carefully. He already looked upset.
She'd replayed it over and over. She *thought* she'd told him to stop. More than once. But he'd been upset about Jackson, and she'd wanted to prove how she felt about him. Maybe he hadn't heard her. Maybe

she hadn't actually said it out loud.

"Why?" he asked again, softer this time.

"Because I didn't want you to," she said. It felt like the right answer. The one he needed.

She pulled him toward her, kissed him, and didn't resist when he gently laid her back on the bed.

He gazed down at her, his brow creasing again.

"Were you crying?" Guilt flashed across his face, and he sat up, backing away.

She blinked, confused. "I'm sore, not in pain," she said quickly, trying not to think about how she'd felt after he left last night.

"When you came home?" He clarified. "I know I scared you, but it looked like you'd already been crying."

"Oh. That." How had she forgotten about Kenzie already?

She told him how weird everyone had been acting and that she was sure Kenzie had told them about the "dark period" her dad went through.

"Your dad hits you?" Andrew's voice was low and dangerous.

"Not anymore," she said quickly. "It was a really hard time, and I wasn't good at reading his moods and staying out of the way yet."

"If I ever see a mark on you, I'll kill him."

Allie flinched.

The movement snapped him out of whatever place he'd gone to in his head.

"Figuratively," he added, then pulled her into his arms.

He looked down at her. "Kenzie is not your friend."

"Yes, she is..."

"She's not," Andrew interrupted. "A real friend wouldn't do that. Ever. And remember when she used your lunch routine to 'entertain' Darcy? Or left you stranded because she wanted to go camping with her instead?" Allie's face fell.

"Did she stand up to Darcy when she and Sophie dumped their drinks all over you in the barn?"

Allie shook her head. "No."

* * *

Andrew kissed her neck and whispered, "I would never treat you like that."

She tensed as his hand slid to her thigh.

"What's wrong?" He asked, inching toward the waistband of her jeans.

"I'm… It's just that… " Allie's body hurt just thinking about it.

Realization dawned. He pulled back and stood up.

"I wasn't thinking. I'm so sorry. I just get near you and I want to be with you. I want to hold you…" He trailed off, rambling, unable to stop.

"I want all of that, too," she said, trying to soothe him. "Just maybe not right now. Besides, I've got a huge paper due on Monday."

She stood and wrapped her arms around his waist.

He kissed the top of the head, then gently pulled away.

"I'll let you work, then." He handed her the backpack.

"Wait, what?" Allie hadn't expected him to leave. "You don't have to go yet. My parents *did* go out. They won't be back until after ten. You can read while I write, it's fine." She smiled.

"I didn't even bring my book," he shrugged. "I thought we'd just hang out. I don't want to be a distraction and, no offense, as much as I love looking at you, I don't want to sit and watch you write your paper for the rest of the night."

Allie laughed. "I love you!" She turned to open the door. "I got more birthday money from my aunt. How about I treat at Gusto's tomorrow?"

Andrew looked puzzled. "I love an independent woman, but I'm not going to be in school tomorrow. I told you that yesterday. My dad's meeting with a board of directors in LA, and I get to go."

She nodded slowly, forcing a smile, but the words hit harder than they should've.

Another high. Another crash.

"So I won't see you until Monday? I thought we were doing something for homecoming?"

Andrew shook his head, "We won't be back until Wednesday. I won't be in school, but I can still come over that night if you want."

She tried to process it.

"Couldn't you stay a little longer tonight then?" She asked. "That feels so far away. I can work on my paper this weekend since you'll be gone."

"I'm not gonna be that guy, Allie," he said sincerely, "I know how much school matters to you. I respect that. I don't want to be a distraction."

She remembered how she'd begged for him to stay last night. And he had.

"What if I *want* a distraction?"

please stay please stay please stay

He hesitated. "You said you wanted to write your paper."

She smiled and took a step back towards the bed. "I don't want to write my paper."

please stay please stay please stay

"But, you said…"

"And now I'm saying different." Another backwards step to the bed.

please stay please stay please stay

Andrew wavered. "But what if your parents come home? Your dad…"

"They won't be back until after ten," she said, easing onto the bed. She fought the urge to flinch. "Lock the door."

please please please

He did. And then he just stared at her.

Allie held her breath.

He crossed the room and knelt in front of her.

"I don't want to hurt you," he whispered.

"You'll be gentle," she said, lifting his chin, guiding him beside her.

"I'll be gentle," he echoed, pulling her shirt over her head.
If he saw the bruises, he didn't say a word.

CHAPTER 29- ANONYMOUS

Allie bolted upright, heart pounding. Her phone lit up on the nightstand, buzzing with an incoming call.

She grabbed it. "Are you okay?"

"Shit, I'm sorry," shouted Kenzie over the wind. "I didn't realize how late it was."

"Put your earbuds in," Allie said, whispering as loudly as she dared. "I can't hear you."

She reached for her own and waited.

"Can you hear me now?" Kenzie asked. It wasn't much better, but it would have to do.

"Yes. What's wrong?" Allie's voice rose with panic.

"Nothing, nothing," Kenzie was still yelling. "I'm sorry it's so late. I just got off work, and I need to talk to you before tomorrow."

"It is tomorrow. Why are you just now getting off work?"

"Stephan hosted a party for some of the fashion— excuse me, Textiles and Fashion Design— students tonight, and I got to stay." She sipped something noisily. "Allie, it was amazing. I want to go to Madison with you now!"

Allie shook her head. *What? Since when did Kenzie want to go to college?*

"But that's not why I called," she went on. Allie wished she would just pull over, but then again, she didn't want her best friend parked on a country road in the middle of the night with no doors or locks on her Jeep.

"Thank you so much for not saying anything in the cafeteria today," Kenzie added.

Allie blinked. *What?*

Then she remembered— Kenzie had told them about her dad.

"I mean, I love Darcy and all, but I can't believe she did that. She denies it, of course."

Kenzie gulped more liquid. Allie tried to focus, picking through the chaos of Kenzie's words for meaning.

Gravel crunched. Finally, Kenzie turned off the Jeep.

* * *

Kenzie, still shouting, said, "The whole thing is anonymous, but come on… There is no way she's not QueenDee. Puhleeze."

"Shhhh. You're going to wake the whole building," Allie hissed.

"Oh, shit. Sorry."

Allie heard her fumbling for her key to the main door and imagined a giant in a ski mask crouched behind a car, waiting to pounce. She exhaled when she heard the door click and squeak open.

"Pull it closed behind you," she said automatically..

"Yes, Mom," Kenzie teased, their old rhythm returning. Allie waited while Kenzie fumbled with her keys again and didn't say anything until she heard all three deadbolts click behind her friend.

"What are you talking about?"

"The *Homecoming Hot or Not*. Like anyone else would make that post. Darcy looks like a porn star, and everyone else looks like they've got the troll filter on."

Allie sighed. She was supposed to be mad at Kenzie right now.

"It's late and I'm tired. I don't understand."

"Burn Book," Kenzie said like that explained everything.

Allie rubbed her eyes.

"Ohmygod, Allie. Please tell me you've been logging in every day. We *talked* about this."

"I've been busy," Allie protested, "Bio test, Trig quiz, plus papers in French and APUSH."

"You have to log in now," Kenzie breathed. "Bad things will happen if you don't."

"You don't seriously believe…."

"Please just do it,"

Allie swiped and clicked until she reached the spot where Kenzie had hidden the BB icon.

"Kenzie is not your friend." She heard Andrew's voice, but clicked anyway.

The flames lit up the screen like before, then suddenly — a skull and crossbones filled it.

"WELCOME ALLIE ELLIS" the letters danced across the screen. "IT'S BEEN 2 DAYS SINCE YOUR LAST LOGIN."

The skull faded, and a new banner appeared.

"PLEASE REMEMBER TO LOG IN EVERY DAY."

She stared at it until the screen cleared., "I thought you said this was anonymous."

"It knows your user name, Allie, it's fine. It's totally anonymous."

Something crashed in the background, and Allie wondered if Stacy was home.

"Just go to the CheckIn thread and type 'here.' Don't argue with me, please," Kenzie preempted Allie's objection. When Allie did, the red background turned black.

"You heard that Justin Davis was in a wreck over the weekend?" Kenzie whispered.

"No. Why would I have heard that?"

Allie flushed, remembering last weekend with Andrew. Her skin was suddenly way too warm. She actually had to fan herself, like that would do anything to cool her down. Thank god Kenzie hadn't CamCalled.

"He *deleted* the app last week." Kenzie said breathlessly, "And he wrecked on the way to school Monday. Totaled. His. Car."

Allie started to object, pointing out how it obviously could have been a coincidence. Except the app knew who she was. Kenzie's assurances be damned, it had put her name on the screen.

"I checked in," Allie told her.

"Thank you," Kenzie said, crunching on something. And thank you for just playing along at lunch and not telling everyone you're on BurnBook.".

"What does BurnBook have to do with you telling everyone about my dad? I don't understand."

"What are you talking about? No one as old as your dad is on BB. I told you, Allie, it's invite only, and if anyone invites their parents, I promise bad things will happen."

Allie turned her bedside light on so she could see the screen better. "Did you put it on this app that my dad…" She paused. It hurt to think about, much less say. "Did you tell all of them what my dad was like before? Is that why they were all being so weird to me?"

Her voice cracked. She hated how whiny she sounded.

"What?" Kenzie protested, "I have never and will never talk about that unless you or your mom tells me I can. I love you, Allie."

"Then I don't understand," said Allie.

"Click on the Hot or Not button and then click on Homecoming."

Allie did. Her breath caught.

A photo of Darcy in a string bikini filled the screen. She was sprawled across a lounge chair, fingers tugging the side tie of her bottoms like she was trying to undo them for the camera.

"Right?" Said Kenzie. "And she's been strutting around all day like it's not totally photoshopped."

Allie was silent. She felt gross looking at it and closed the app.

"The rest of the pictures are just as bad," Kenzie went on. "All edited to make them look as awful as possible. Jenny Jones is literally rolling in the mud. Based on likes, though, Darcy's a lock for Queen tomorrow."

"Queen?" Allie wasn't keeping up. This was about Darcy trying to be homecoming queen?

"Anyway," Kenzie continued, unfazed. "Thanks for not saying anything about me giving you my invite. When you walked up, everyone was fighting about what Darcy did, but you can't talk about Fight Club with someone who's not in Fight Club. That's why Darcy made you leave— and none of us said anything."

Allie was starting to understand. "But it's supposed to be anonymous. How would they even know I'm not on it? And why are you so sure it was Darcy that posted the pictures? Other than her looking great and everyone else looking terrible?"

Water ran in the background.

"I told you, we each only get one invite to start, and Darcy wanted me to give mine to someone else. Everyone else already used theirs, and you don't know anyone but us. So how could you have gotten in?"

Toothbrush sounds.

"And *obviously* it was Darcy. 'Queen Dee' posted the pictures. She's about as subtle as a glitter bomb."

More toothbrush sounds. Then the toilet flushed.

Gross.

"Anyway, I told Teagan I invited you, so she's going to tell Darcy that she earned an extra invite and that's why you're in. I'm sorry she kicked you out today, but she won't again once she knows you have Burn Book."

"Okay, I guess?" Allie said, still not sure she completely followed what Kenzie had said.

"Love you Allie-gator."

Click.

CHAPTER 30- HOMECOMING

Jackson: Sorry I bailed on tutoring yesterday. But did you think about Homecoming? You can ride with me since Kenzie's riding with Darcy.

Her phone was lit up on the nightstand. She grabbed it, blinked. 6:00 am. *What?*

Jackson was already texting.

As her brain tried to catch up, she reread the message. She definitely couldn't go with him… not like that.

She really liked hanging out with Jackson. It was so fun and easy— lately the only time she ever felt completely relaxed. Which was totally ironic, considering most of that time they were working on math.

Jackson: I promise Darcy will behave herself. And if you don't want to go over to her house before the dance, we can get dinner by ourselves and meet everyone there.

Allie went cold.
Before she could stop herself, she typed back:

Allie: That almost sounds like a date.
He replied immediately.
Jackson: It can be if you want.

Her first thought— *I have to delete this so Andrew never sees it.*
Her second— *Andrew was right.*
Her third wasn't a thought at all— just a slow, aching kind of sadness.

Allie: I can't. My parents won't let me date anyone. And I can't go to the game or the dance. I have too much homework.

* * *

Technically, that was true.

But if she'd learned anything this year, it was that if there was a will, there's a way. And a small part of her—one she was actively trying to ignore—*did* want to go.

She shoved the thought aside.

Andrew would never forgive her. He already thought Jackson liked her, and here was the proof.

The three bubbles appeared and disappeared.

Maybe she'd misread Jackson's text… maybe he was joking.

When her real alarm went off, Jackson still hadn't replied.

His read receipt was still there when Kenzie pulled into the driveway.

Kenzie barely said a word on the way to school, which was fine with Allie. She stared at the window, letting Jackson's "I can be if you want," loop through her brain until it hurt.

Allie zombie-walked through the morning, dreading seeing Jackson in the cafeteria. Trent and Teagan were friendly in class, and a pop quiz in AP Psych created a buffer against Darcy. But now that class was over…

As she walked to the table, she could see that Darcy was already holding court. She slipped into the seat next to Kenzie as Darcy said, "And after they make the announcement at the pep rally, I expect you all to *stand* and cheer." She surveyed the group, and when her eyes fell on Allie, she made a face.

"Why are you even here if you're not going to the game or the dance?

"God, Darcy," Eric looked up from his phone. "What is your problem?

She flicked her eyes to him, then focused back on Allie and fixed a smile on her face. "He's right, Allie. That was really rude, and I'm sorry." She glanced around the table, ensuring everyone noted her apology. "Jackson told me this morning that you weren't going with us, so what I meant was it's probably going to be really boring for you to listen to us make plans."

Allie glanced at Jackson, who was intently studying his lunch, then back to Darcy. "It's fine."

She set the extra food containers on the table.

"I mean, you can come, I guess," Darcy shrugged and grabbed the bag of cookies. "Just… try not to make it weird."

"Thanks," Allie said again, quieter this time.

Darcy had already moved on.

"So, yeah. Make sure you stand and cheer loudly. It's been years since a junior was crowned homecoming queen, so let's make this pep rally memorable." She smiled magnanimously.

The group glanced at each other, but no one dared speak.

"Great!" Darcy clapped her hands. "So moving on to tomorrow night." She took a small bite of the cookie, then inhaled deeply and rolled her eyes, "Oh my god, these are good."

Allie just pushed her food around in the lunch container.

"So, obviously, I'll ride with Jackson. Everyone else can fit in Teagan's SUV."

She turned to Teagan. "Make sure you get it detailed before tomorrow night so their dresses don't get dirty."

Trent started to object, but Kenzie beat him to it. "I thought you were riding with me? I thought the girls were all riding together in the Jeep?"

Darcy inhaled, then let it out sharply. "That was before we knew I was going to be queen. Obviously, I can't show up in a Jeep with a bunch of girls. Besides, Teagan doesn't mind being the DD, do you?"

Teagan didn't even look up, just waved her hand in assent.

"Perfect, Darcy said, smiling as if everything was going exactly as planned. "Remember, we're dressing up now. Casual was fine before. Boys, that means coats and ties. Ladies, I know I can count on you to represent."

Allie knew she had no right to be jealous that Darcy and Jackson were clearly going as a couple, but it stung.

She picked at her food until the bell rang.

She stood at her locker, deciding.

There wouldn't be another quiz in Trig— they'd just had one.

The bike path behind the school led straight home. Half a mile, maybe less.

The only times she'd ever skipped before were because Andrew pushed her.

But honestly? She liked it. She'd pick Gusto's over study hall every time.

But today wasn't about Andrew. He was in LA with his dad.

She was going home because she could.
Because she didn't want to sit in the gym and watch Darcy get crowned Homecoming Queen while their friends fake-clapped.

She was going home because she could—
And because, for once, she *wanted* to.

Allie tried to relax, but after a full day of her mom hovering, she was wired and exhausted all at once.

Her mom "checked in" on her ACT prep.
And "gently reminded" her about Ms Lindstrom's policy of early feedback.
She only asked "a few" questions about her grades (or lack thereof) on ClassLink.

Her head hurt.

Allie wasn't behind. Not yet.
But it still felt like she was one assignment away from everything unraveling.

She'd ignored her phone until after dinner.
She already knew what she'd see.

Once her parents were in bed and she could finally breathe, she finally opened PicSee.

And there they were.
Darcy in her crown.

Jackson, smiling as he held her.

Kenzie in the middle of the group, laughing at something Allie wasn't a part of.

None of them even caring she wasn't there.

It felt like a gut punch.

She plugged in her phone and turned off the light, praying sleep would come quickly.

Instead, her chest tightened as soon as her head hit the pillow.

Had she checked in this morning?
Just to be safe, she opened the app and checked in again.
"See you tomorrow," the app promised.

CHAPTER 31- CONFESSIONS

Allie stared at the library doors and sighed. "I don't understand why I have to be at the library today. I have everything I need to study at home."

Her mom exhaled and looked at the car's ceiling. "Please just do this for me. Go into one of the study rooms and take a practice test. Your dad needs to see that your score is improving. He's upset about all of your missing and incomplete assignments, and you need to show him that you're serious."

Allie felt a flash of anger. Yes, she had missing assignments, but she was taking five AP classes that she didn't want to take. She'd told them her schedule was too hard. And she hated those stupid practice tests.

She saw the resignation on her mom's face and tamped down her anger. She still didn't want to be at the library today, though. "But I can take the practice test in my room. And most of those assignments are turned in, just not graded." Her mom turned away and looked out the window. "Please?" Allie hated how her voice cracked. She felt like a baby.

"I'll pick you up at five when the library closes," her mom said, refusing to meet her eyes.

Without another word, Allie exited the car.

She stared at ClassLink and felt the panic rise in her chest.

Two papers for AP Lit, a lab write-up, a practice Long Essay for APUSH, and a worksheet for French. That's what she'd gotten extensions on… she didn't want to think about the assignments that were actually due this week on top of those.

She needed to talk to Andrew and explain to him that she couldn't keep skipping study hall; that if he wanted to keep coming over on Wednesdays, she had to work after supper, not do what they'd been doing.

Thinking of Andrew made her mood even worse.

She hadn't expected to get a Sweetest Day bouquet at school on Friday, but it stung that he hadn't even acknowledged it. It was fine. It was just a stupid, made-up holiday that only people in the Midwest celebrated anyway.

She pulled up her notes for one of the AP Lit papers. She'd done a thorough outline and only had to make minor adjustments and fill in the body of the work. She hit submit and said aloud, "God, I hate the narrative voice."

"Totally," a voice beside her agreed. "That narrative voice sucks." She squeaked and almost dropped her Chromebook as Andrew laughed.

She clutched at her chest and tried not to hyperventilate. He grabbed her hand and moved around the chair, kneeling in front of her.

"You are so beautiful when you concentrate, and you are so cute when you're scared." He pulled her to him and kissed her.

She pulled away quickly and glanced around.

"What are you doing here? We can't do that here. What if someone sees? What if they tell my parents?" She was so shocked, she forgot she was upset about Sweetest Day.

Unfazed, he cupped her cheek and smiled. "I missed you." He kissed her again, and she pushed him away.

"Andrew, stop. I'm serious."

"I am, too. I haven't seen you in two days. Are you actually surprised that I can't get enough of you?"

She stared at him until he got up and sat in the chair next to her. "I thought you'd be happy to see me. Don't you want to hear about my trip?"

Trip?

"I brought you a present," he told her, not giving her a chance to respond. "But it's at my house. How much time do we have?" He was already zipping her Chromebook into her backpack.

She shook her head and found her voice. "I can't, Andrew. I have to get caught up. I wanted to talk to you about this anyway. I can't skip study hall anymore."

* * *

He froze, halfway to standing up, and his face fell.

"You're breaking up with me?"

"What?"

She didn't even know what to say.

Andrew spoke first, his voice husky, barely above a whisper, "I should've known."

Allie struggled to process what had just happened. She hadn't said anything about breaking up, and now Andrew was turning to walk away.

She grabbed his hand and tugged him back down to her.

"Why would you say that? I just said I need to get caught up on my school work. My dad is so mad right now."

He stared at the floor.

"Talk to me," she pressed. "I don't understand."

"Can we talk somewhere else? I just want to get out of here." He stood and turned to leave.

She followed him out, not allowing herself to think of all the work she still needed to do.

"Where are we going?" She finally asked. They'd been driving in silence, and she had no idea where she was.

"Do you love me?" He asked instead of answering her question.

Did she? "You know I do. I don't understand what this is about."

"Allie, I've never felt like this before. You are the first thought in my head in the morning and the last before I fall asleep. If something makes me laugh, I want to tell you about it right away." He stared straight ahead, knuckles turning white on the steering wheel. "I wish we didn't have to sneak around. I only get a little time with you because everything is so secret, and now you're telling me we can't even spend that time together. What am I supposed to think?"

He turned onto a gravel road that seemed to disappear into the woods.

"I didn't say we couldn't spend any time together. I said I needed to get caught up on my work. And Andrew, I am not allowed to have a boyfriend. If my parents find out I've been skipping study hall... that you're coming over on Wednesdays instead of Kenzie? I'll be lucky if

I'm allowed out of the house to even go to school."

He started to say something, and she held up a hand to stop him.

"No. I'm serious. I had to start kindergarten early because my parents didn't want me in daycare, and my mom wanted me in the same school with her so she could keep an eye on me. From kindergarten until middle school, I rode to and from school with my mom. Every single day because she was afraid of what might happen if I made a mistake and talked to the wrong person." Allie knew she was getting worked up, but couldn't stop the words tumbling out of her mouth. "Kenzie and her mom are the only people I'm allowed to be alone with. Do you understand what will happen if they find out about us? About what I've been doing?"

Andrew stopped and turned to her. "What happened? Why are they like that?"

She shook her head. "It was a long time ago. We went out to dinner, and I needed to go to the bathroom. I got lost and asked someone for help. I was so little, I don't remember this, but the police found me in the back of his car before anything physical happened to me, but he wasn't fully dressed when they pulled him out of the car. My mom has never forgiven herself, and my dad has never forgiven me."

He stared at her, wide-eyed. "Wait, this was before you were in kindergarten?"
Allie nodded, ashamed.

"What do you mean your dad has never forgiven you? I guess I get why your mom is the way she is, but I don't understand your dad's reaction at all."
"I was supposed to go straight to the bathroom and come right back. Instead, I went with that man. And I guess things happened. Like I said, I don't remember."

They sat in silence until Andrew finally said, "You know it wasn't your fault, though, right?"
"Yeah, mostly. I know what you're going to say. My parents

shouldn't have sent me off by myself. I was too young to understand that he wasn't a good person, that just because I went with him didn't mean I wanted it to happen. I get all that." She waved her hand in the air to make a point. "So *now* do you get it? Why I'm not allowed to date? How bad this will be if my dad finds out? I love you, but that can't happen."

"I promise you," he said, leaning across and pulling her to him until they were nose to nose, "I promise you that I will never let anyone, including your dad, hurt you again."

He kissed her gently, then opened his door. She was shocked to see they were parked in front of a beautiful cabin. As he walked around to open her door, she took it all in. The lake behind the house was perfectly still, reflecting the trees like glass. The landscaping was beautiful —a mix of flowers and perfectly manicured hedges. She could imagine Elizabeth and Mr Darcy strolling through them, arm in arm.

Andrew opened her door and reached in for her. "Where are we?" She asked in awe. "Is this your house?"

"It's our lake house," he shrugged, but he couldn't hide his grin. "I can't wait to show you what I got you," he said excitedly.

"Your lake house?" She repeated, letting him pull her inside.

As soon as they stepped inside, Allie froze.
The cabin was stunning.

Straight ahead, the floor-to-ceiling windows looked out over the lake- still and serene, like something out of a movie.

The massive stone fireplace was beautiful and inviting, even without a fire.

Everything about the lake house was cozy and welcoming.

She turned to Andrew, eyes wide.
"Right?" He grinned.

"This is an awesome picture," she said, studying the photograph of a bald eagle in the snow.

"So is this one," she said. "Wait, is that the lake behind your house?"

Andrew grinned. The walls were covered with photographs... of the lake, of animals in the woods, of covered bridges.

Allie gasped, "You took all of these?" She studied them, fascinated. "You're amazing! Is this what you want to do? Be a photographer?"

"Nah," he replied. "It's just a hobby. I'm gonna end up taking over my dad's company someday.

"*How* did you get this shot?" She said, examining a picture of a fox mid-pounce in the snow.

"I always keep at least one camera and a couple of lenses in the car. You never know when you're going to get the money shot."

He reached over and flicked on the lights in the entry, then led her into the living room. She sank into the couch, eyes closed, temporarily forgetting the angst of earlier.

When she opened them, Andrew was sitting on the ground in front of her, holding a small velvet box, looking up at her like he might burst with excitement.

Her heart jumped.

She knew how crazy it was- she was sixteen, and they'd only been together for a month.
But for one wild, irrational second, her brain went there.

When there's a boy looking up at you holding a velvet box, it doesn't matter how old you are or how long you've been dating; your brain short-circuits. Velvet box = ring.

She caught herself before that thought went any further.
"What's this?" She smiled.

"I meant what I said earlier," he said, opening the box to reveal a pair of diamond stud earrings. "I know it's only been a month, but this has been the best month of my life."

Allie gaped. They were so sparkly. "Are they real?" She whispered.

"Of course."

"Andrew, I can't. It's too much- and I couldn't wear them. People would ask."

"Just tell people they're fake and you won them in a contest. No one's going to get a jeweler's loop and inspect them. But you'll know and I'll know." He pulled himself up so they were face-to-face. He smiled and kissed her. Slowly at first, but then hungrily.

Allie felt a moment of panic. What time was it?

Almost as if he read her mind, he whispered, "It's only a little after two. I'll have you back in plenty of time."

For a second, Allie wanted to tell him to take her back now. That she needed to get her work done. But then she told herself that even if she'd stayed and worked the whole time, she still wouldn't have been able to catch up. And this was so much better.

CHAPTER 32- WASH, RINSE, REPEAT

After Homecoming, it was like everything took a hard reset— same classes, same people, but the vibe had shifted. She knew that things had changed, even if she didn't fully understand the new rules.

Eric and Kenzie were a couple now. Her PicSee feed was full of pictures of them— selfies, quotes, inside jokes... They even had nicknames for each other.

And something was going on with Jackson and Darcy. She acted like they *were* a couple, and Jackson didn't act like they *weren't*.

Whatever it was, there was a clearly unspoken rule that Jackson couldn't tutor her anymore. It hurt, even though she knew it shouldn't. *I'm not allowed to date.* She'd been the one to draw that line. Somewhere along the way, though, the basic Trig concepts had clicked and she was holding her own. Even though she missed him, she was doing okay without him.

And... even though Andrew had said he understood she needed to study and catch up, he'd quietly taken over the time Jackson used to fill.

Any time her parents weren't home, Andrew was there... and they weren't studying anything she'd be tested on in class.

She told herself everything was fine. Kenzie, Teagan, and Trent were still there; they hung out when they could. But there was a divide that wasn't there before.

She had never worked out how to tell Kenzie about Andrew, and now, with too much time having passed, it felt weird to bring it up and have to explain why she had kept it secret for so long.

And Andrew... he was her steady presence, her constant cheerleader, the one who held her when it all felt like it was all too much.

Allie paused in the doorway, trying to adjust to the chaos of the cafeteria- voices bouncing, trays clattering, chairs scraping. She took a breath, forced herself to smile, then walked to the table.

She wasn't sure how much longer she could pretend this was okay. It wasn't as bad as it was at the beginning, when Darcy and Sophie had been so mean. But somehow this was... worse?

She sat down, everyone greeted her, then went back to their conversations.

Eric always thanked her for whatever extra food she'd packed for him. Teagan and Trent talked to her about lectures and assignments.

Sometimes Kenzie pulled her into whatever story she was telling.

Mostly, though, she sat in their orbit while they existed without her. They weren't unkind —just complete in a way that didn't leave space for her.

She wished she'd never sat at this table with them.

Wasn't it Robin Williams that said the worst thing in life isn't being alone, but being surrounded by people who make you feel that way?

Yeah. She totally got it now.

How was this even her life? Barely hanging on to her grades, a group of people that were more mannequins than friends...

They all had their phones out today, looking at the latest posts on BurnBook. Allie hated that app; tried not to resent Kenzie for putting it on her phone.

They were block voting on the HotOrNot Halloween pictures.

The first rule of Fight Club?
Irrelevant when everyone at the table was in Fight Club,
    Allie voted for Eric and Kenzie as cutest couple.
    Jackson and Darcy as hottest.
    Best group costume.
    She felt a twinge of... jealousy? regret? ...that she wasn't in the pictures with them.

True, she'd been sort of invited.

Kenzie had said, "You can come, but it might be weird with Jackson and Darcy."

Then Andrew had said, "My dad is gone, and we can have the lake house all weekend."

It wasn't a difficult decision.

She watched them, in their circle but on the outside, and thought that maybe this ache in her heart and her bones wasn't worth it.

She opened ClassLink on her phone, and blood went cold.
She reread Miss Lindstrom's feedback, focusing on the last line.
"Please come see me during study hall. I have concerns."

Allie knew she was spiraling, but didn't know how to stop it. The chaos of the bus added to the chaos in her head, leaving her shaky and out of sorts.

She'd met with Miss Lindstrom during study hall, and it could have been much worse.

Miss Lindstrom hadn't yelled like her father would have. Didn't guilt-trip her like her mother would have.

"I've noticed you're not as focused in class, and your current submissions certainly don't match the quality of your work at the beginning of the year. Is everything okay?"

Everything was fine.
Her life was imploding.
She just needed time to get caught up.
Everything would be fine.

She tried to take a deep breath in like the therapist had taught her, but the bus smelled so bad, she gagged midway.

Her phone buzzed, and Allie automatically read the text on her screen.

Mom: Stacy and Kenzie aren't coming for Thanksgiving?

* * *

Allie scrunched her face, pretending she hadn't just read that. Pretending that Stacy and Kenzie were coming to Thanksgiving like they had every year since Kindergarten.

Nurses had to work on Thanksgiving.

Black Friday wasn't just Friday anymore. When you worked in the hottest boutique… it started when they told you it started.

Allie: They both have to work.

Miss Lindstrom had had all of her essays on her desk. Allie knew the quality of her work had slipped, but seeing it in red pen across four months' worth of work was awful.

"You know you can talk to me, right?" Allie had believed Miss Lindstrom, but couldn't find anything to say.

The buzzing never stopped.

Kenzie: No pressure.

Kenzie: Do you want to come to Kurt's party this weekend? It's been forever and you can crash at my place.

SB: Dad is gone again so the lake house is ours all weekend if you can make it work.

SB: I have a surprise for you.

A single, frustrated tear slid down Allie's cheek. She had to rewrite two papers for Miss Lindstrom, and she had at least five assignments overdue in her other classes.

SB: Remember that thing we did…

The problem was that Allie did. And her body flushed hot with the memory.

She replied to Andrew: Is that you asking for an encore?

She didn't feel awkward flirting with Andrew anymore. She knew what he was asking for. She knew that if she pressed her body a certain way… breathed on his skin a certain way… arched her body a certain way… she wouldn't be the only one flushing hot.

* * *

Her mom didn't reply, and she left Kenzie on read.

It had been Miss Lindstrom's idea for Allie to work in the classroom during lunch.

"Seriously, I eat at my desk and scroll social media. There are a couple of other kids who eat in here who are catching up on some papers. If they have questions, I answer, but for the most part it's just a quiet, focused place to work."

No one texted to ask where she was the first day she skipped lunch with them.

By the bell, she'd finished and turned in one of the revised ACT essays. For the first time in weeks, it felt like she could breathe.

She asked Dr Matt if she could work in his room during lunch, too. Even better— he had a tutoring session then. He admitted he'd thought about asking if she wanted to join at the beginning of the year, but she'd seemed to turn things around on her own, so he never did.

She was holding her own in AP French, Bio, and Psych, so she vowed to use study hall to focus on APUSH. Mr Tracy didn't invite students to his room during lunch, but offered her two study hall days a week.. Allie hesitated, thinking of Andrew.

Mr Tracy didn't.

"This is a college-level class, Miss Ellis, and you are dangerously close to failing. Without the district's late work policy, you'd already have an F. My job is not to fail you, it's to teach you. If you're willing to work, you can use my room during study hall, and I will be available to you."

She signed up for Mondays and Tuesdays, when Andrew was more likely to be out of town.

He wasn't thrilled at first- two afternoons without her. But when she framed it as a way to protect their Wednesday nights, he'd called her his "smart girl" and dropped it.

* * *

This new plan should have been a win:
- No lunch with Darcy.
- Real progress in her classes.
- Andrew… mostly happy.

Except she didn't seem to be catching up. She wasn't falling behind anymore, but she wasn't getting ahead.

And now her dad was calling the school to complain about her teachers not updating her grades in ClassLink.

And Andrew complained that she should be caught up enough to spend more time with him.

Allie felt like no matter what she did, she couldn't win.

CHAPTER 34- GIRLS' WEEKEND

Andrew: It's Friday night. Why are your parents even home? I wanted to introduce you to one of MY favorite movies.

Allie: Not exactly sure. I think my dad lost a client

Allie: What movie?

SB: Nope. No Googling and forming opinions ahead of time.

Allie: ☺

SB: Will they be home all weekend?

Allie: Not Monday. My dad is supposed to do something with the parade and my mom goes with.

SB: is he a vet?

Allie: No. It's through work.

SB: Cool. But we leave for Nashville Monday morning, so I guess I won't see you.

Allie: Boo. I was hoping we could spend the day together.

SB: Me too but when my dad says go, I go

Allie: I'll miss you.

SB: Promise?

Allie: 🤍

She set the phone on her nightstand and picked it back up.
She hated this, but she'd convinced herself it wasn't *that* bad.
Open the app, check in, log out.
Her thumbs moved without thinking.

She'd just settled back into her bed when raised voices cut through the quiet.

He had lost another potential client. She didn't know the details, only what she'd overheard from her mom's hushed call with Aunt Rachel. Her dad's drinking was getting bad again, and her mom was worried.

Not like she's going to do anything about it.

Allie closed her eyes and listed the things she loved about Andrew until she finally fell asleep.

When Allie opened her eyes, her mom's face was inches from her own.

"Are you awake?" Angela whispered.

Allie flinched. "Creepy, Mom. What are you doing?"

"You were talking. I thought you were awake, but then you didn't answer me so I had to check."

A spike of panic- *talking? Please, please, please not about Andrew.*

Her mom moved to sit on her bed, and Allie rubbed her eyes and scooted to accommodate her.

"You've been working so hard," she brushed hair off of Allie's forehead. "So much you're talking about Manifest Destiny in your sleep." Angela chuckled, and Allie exhaled.

"So I was thinking we could do a girls' weekend in Madison," her mom continued. "We can watch the parade there, do some shopping… catch the new John Clear movie. One of the new teachers used to be a student tour guide at Madison and volunteered to give us a personalized tour tomorrow." She gave Allie a hopeful smile.

Since when did they do girls' weekends? Short answer… they didn't.

"What's going on?" Allie asked carefully.

Something flickered across her mom's face. "We've all been so busy." She picked at imaginary lint on Allie's comforter. "And since your dad has a bunch of work he needs to do this weekend, I thought we could have fun together somewhere else. You know, get out of his hair so he can prep for the Ashford trial."

And there it was. It wasn't so much that Angela wanted a weekend with Allie; she wanted them out of the house, away from her dad.

Still… after what she'd heard last night, maybe she didn't want to be here either,

"Sounds good," Allie said, aiming for a genuine smile. "Maybe on the way home, we can stop at Vibe and buy something from Kenzie? She works on commission."

"We'll see, but that sounds fun," her mom said, standing. "I miss Kenzie."

"I do, too," Allie admitted, though the words sat heavy in her chest.

"Can you be ready in thirty? We can grab breakfast on the way there?"

Allie nodded and threw back the covers.

As soon as her mom closed the door, Allie grabbed her phone.
Allie: Headed to Madison with my mom for a "girls' weekend"
Three dots appeared, then disappeared. He finally responded:
SB: Sounds fun?
SB: Just don't have so much fun you forget about me.
Allie: Not possible 🤍

CHAPTER 35- CRAFTING THE STORY

Her phone died at some point on Sunday, but she didn't realize it until she tried to check in on Burn Book that night.

Neither she nor her mom had brought a charger. *Who does that?*
She'd been distracted on Monday morning at the Wisconsin Veterans Museum — *what if Andrew was trying to text her? What if she got in trouble for missing check-in?*

By midafternoon, her mom gave up on sightseeing and agreed to go see Kenzie at Vibe.
The store was packed with people there for the holiday sale, and Kenzie barely had time to acknowledge them. Teagan came over, introduced herself to Angela, and helped them pick out matching jewelry sets.

Back in the car, her mom said, "So, just put this in the bag with the stuff from the Bookstore and put it in your closet until tomorrow. Your dad's got enough going on... He doesn't need to worry about how much we spent." Angela smiled, but Allie could tell she was worried.

When they got home Monday night, they sat silently in the driveway; they knew what awaited them inside the house. Allie forced herself to smile, but her eyes kept flicking to her bag. Every second her phone stayed dead was another second she couldn't see if Andrew had texted— or if BurnBook had noticed.

"I had fun," her mom smiled at her. "You've grown up so fast, and I miss spending time with you."
Allie tried to hide her surprise. She didn't remember doing much together except riding to and from school. But maybe that's what her mom meant.
"Me, too," she said, hoping it was the right answer. "Thank you. For everything."
"So, why don't I go in first? I'll fill your dad in on how much fun we had." Her mom's smile widened. "I know you need to charge your phone, so grab the bags and go straight upstairs."

Allie watched as her mom crafted the story they would tell her dad. Had her mom always done this?

As soon as her screen lit up, she opened her messages.

A string of texts from Andrew on Sunday. Their plans changed—he wasn't leaving until Tuesday. Could she come home early?

But only one today-

SB: Okay. I get it.

Her stomach dropped.

She texted back furiously, thumbs flying across her phone.

Allie: I'm so sorry. My phone died.

Allie: We're home now. I missed you so much. I thought about you the whole time.

Nothing.

Then her dad yelled at her to come help with dinner.

He was drunk. The chicken was dry. Her mom chattered about their "fun girls' weekend," weaving a version of events Allie barely recognized. She excused herself as soon as she could and bolted upstairs.

Still nothing from Andrew.

Allie: I'm not sure I can go a whole week without you.

She sighed, knowing she had to check BurnBook. Not because she was afraid of "bad things" happening, but because Kenzie was.

The familiar flames danced across her screen, then another pop-up.

The rules are that you check in every day, Allie.
New rule for you: You have to start a thread or comment on three threads. Every day.
Play by the rules or bad things happen.

Her chest tightened.

She had no idea what to post, and she'd never looked at any of the threads except the check-in thread. She started there. "Present." Send.

* * *

Then she opened a thread called "Hot or Not." Pictures of her classmates. Most comments were just "hot" or "not." Others made her skin crawl.

Not but I'd still bang her as long as I didn't have to look at that face

Hotter when she's riding me in the locker room while I'm supposed to be practicing.

People did that? In the locker rooms?

She clicked out and opened "Who wore it better?"

Some of the posts were tame. Two girls in similar homecoming dresses. Others were vicious.

One post had pictures of two football players with the same cheerleader. Allie read the first comment and closed the thread.

How was she supposed to comment on any of this? It was all disgusting.

She tried "Fit Check Friday". It was full of screenshots pulled from people's social media, with comments ranging from snarky to obscene.

A picture of Darcy in her crown made her pulse spike.

Boys joked about getting her out of her dress. Then:

SuzeeQ: *Easy to win when you're the one rigging the votes, Queen Dee.* (50 likes)

User90210: *So obvious. So pathetic.* (35 likes)

Before she could stop herself, she typed: *Totally giving Pick Me.* Send

Her heart was pounding now.

She opened "Most Likely to..." and typed "Trent Wilson" under "Become President of the US." Send.

She was hyperventilating now.

This was ridiculous. It was a stupid app. Nothing bad was going to happen. She swiped out of it without making a third comment.

She checked her texts again. Still nothing.

Allie: My parents are downstairs arguing. I wish you were here. Nothing.

The argument had started that afternoon and never really ended. From upstairs, she could still hear them — not the angry whispers they normally used- this was louder, sharper. She caught fragments.. *Have to land Lakeshore Mutual. Starting over.* Her dad's voice, already thick from drinking, rose and cut off. Something crashed in the kitchen.

She needed to go to sleep. She hadn't slept well in the hotel room with her mom, and she had an AP French exam the next morning. Normally, that would make her nervous, but the words and conjugations had come back so easily, she barely had to think about them anymore.

Another crash downstairs made her sit up. She hesitated, listening. Voices- low, then sharper- rose then fell beneath her. She reached for the lamp, the soft click spilling light across the room.

Movement at the window made her jump. Her breath caught— until she recognized the grin.

Andrew pressed a finger to his lips, bent over the latch, and with a quiet snap, the lock gave. Three strides and he was beside her, kissing her before she could speak.

"Miss me?" he asked against her mouth.

She blinked at him, breathless. "What are you doing here? My dad will kill us both."

"Not if he doesn't know." He crossed the room to lock her door, then came back with that wolfish grin that made her pulse stumble.

Her heart thudded. "Andrew, I'm serious. They're right downstairs."

He tipped his head, listening to the muffled argument below them. "They're not coming up anytime soon." His tone was certain, almost amused. "And when they're done?" He leaned in, brushing his lips against her ear. "They'll be too busy to even think about you."

"What does that mean?" she whispered, but he was already pressing a kiss to her neck.

* * *

"It means," he said, his voice low, "I don't want to waste this. Not after the way you've been ignoring me."

"My phone died," she insisted.

"Mmhmm." His thumb traced lazy circles at her waist, sending her pulse skittering. "You're not as innocent as you pretend."

Before she could argue, he added, "You know what's even better than getting along? Making up."

She frowned. "We weren't fighting."

He smirked. "Maybe you don't know what you've been missing. Make-up sex—it's taking all that tension, all those things you didn't say, and turning it into something you can't stop thinking about."

He said it like a fact, carved in stone. Then, almost casually, "My dad does it all the time—picks fights with his girlfriends just so they can make up. It's better that way."

She froze for half a beat. That didn't sound normal. Not even close. But before she could say anything, his mouth was back on her skin and her thoughts scattered.

"Andrew—"

"Nothing else matters right now," he murmured. "Just you. Just me."

He let the silence stretch until she met his eyes, then brushed his thumb along her jaw. "Admit it. You ignored me to get me here."

"I didn't—"

He touched a finger to her lips. "Say it."

She shook her head.

"Say it," he repeated, softer now, "and I'll show you."

The way he said it made her stomach twist in knots—nerves, anticipation, something she couldn't name.

"Fine," she whispered. "I did."

"And now?"

Her voice was barely audible. "Now I want you here."

His smile said he'd won something important.

And that was the tipping point—the second she stopped thinking about the argument downstairs, or the exam tomorrow, or what would happen if her parents came up the stairs. All that was left was him and the heat in his eyes when he kissed her again, pulling her closer until the rest of the world disappeared.

Time blurred. When she finally caught her breath, the room was quiet again, and his hand was tracing the chain at her collarbone.

"You are so beautiful," he whispered, gazing down on her. He fanned her hair out on her pillow, then adjusted her necklace on her chest. "Perfect."

He leaned to get something from the floor, and when he came up holding his phone, Allie panicked.

"What are you doing?" She hissed, pulling the covers up over her.

"Don't you trust me?" He asked, working the sheet back down. "I need something to keep with me for the next time you decide to ignore me.

He arranged her hair again, settled the necklace between her breasts, and told her to close her eyes and think about what they'd just done.

She was going to protest again until he said that last part. She involuntarily thought about his hands... his mouth. Her eyes flew open when she heard the telltale click of the camera.

"You have to delete that," she begged.

"You trust me or you don't," he said, handing her the phone. "Look at it. You are so beautiful. And when I look at this picture, I will know that I'm the one that put that smile on your face."

"Maybe you could crop it? I don't want a picture out there of me with no top on." Her thumb hovered above the trash can, and she waited for him to give her permission.

"You can delete it if you want," he smiled. "You're the most beautiful photograph in my brain."

"Thank you," she said. She clicked the trash can and handed him the phone back.

"Promise me you'll think about me this week?"

He kissed her, "I won't stop thinking about you." A pause, then: "So... was it better?"

She didn't hesitate. "Absolutely."

She smiled as she watched him slip back out the window. She was still smiling when sleep finally came.

She woke hours later—heart racing, chest tight—and reached for her phone. It was too close to her alarm to go back to sleep, but the house was too quiet to get up and start getting ready.

Against her better judgment, she clicked on the fake calendar app.

In the dark, the dancing flames of Burn Book lit up her room. She exhaled when the tagline appeared.

No Names. No Filters. No mercy.

Before she could relax, a pop-up appeared:

Not good, Allie Ellis. The rules are the rules, and when you break them, bad things happen.
Here's a second chance for you.
New rule: start two threads or comment on 6. Every. Day.
PS - you should check out Someone's Got a Secret. You might recognize someone…

She panicked, wondering what rule she'd broken now..

Her thumb hovered before she clicked through. She finally screwed up the courage to click on the thread.

The pinned photo stopped her cold. She'd never seen it before, but she knew it was recent- the sweater she was wearing was new.

In the picture, her head was bowed, hair tumbling over one shoulder. Her eyes looked up through her lashes at something off camera, and she was grinning, tapping her lips with her pen. She tried to remember where she'd been —what she'd been thinking that had made her smile like that— but nothing came. Just the feeling that she should know.

The caption read: *Makes you wonder who she's studying, right?*

She forced herself to open the comments.
BaiGuy: new phone, who dat?
ILv2Vape: Does she even go to our school?
SuzeeQ: I care why?

* * *

The relief was sharp and shaky- they didn't know.

She clicked on the check-in thread. 6:00 am and there were already 75 check-ins.

She typed "here" and then scrolled until she found something low risk- FitCheck Friday.

Darcy's picture was pinned, and she saw her "Pick Me" comment had over a hundred likes. The most of any comments there.

She added six quick, empty replies on other photos.

"Ouch"

"Not wrong"

"So cute."

Finished, she tossed her phone onto the bed and got ready for school, no idea what would be waiting when she walked through the doors.

CHAPTER 37- I'M WAITING

No one acted differently after the *Someone's Got a Secret* thread. Not in class, not at lunch, not even online. By Tuesday afternoon, it wasn't even the pinned pic anymore.

She texted Andrew. He didn't answer.

The old Allie would've been in tears. The new Allie knew it was a game… and she was ready to play.

Allie: It's been 12 hours since you climbed out my window. Miss me?

During study hall, she tried again:

Allie: Just checking. POL pic?

She sent a picture of Mr Tracy at his desk

Allie: I bet you're having more fun than me.

Andrew didn't reply, but she knew he wouldn't.

She heard his voice in her head and her body responded. *Make-up sex—it's taking all that tension, all those things you didn't say, and turning it into something you can't stop thinking about.*

She couldn't stop thinking about it.

After she finished on BurnBook, she sent one last text:

Allie: I feel like you're ignoring me. Are we fighting? Does that mean make-up sex when you get home?

She thought he would reply to that —she hoped he would— but when she finally fell asleep, it was still unread.

Her texts Wednesday went unanswered.

This was *a game, right?*

Thursday morning, she broke.

Allie: Hey… are you actually ignoring me? I'm fr freaking out. Nothing.

She should have been excited that her mom let her go to dinner with Teagan and Trent before their study session. Instead, she checked her phone every five minutes.

Nothing from him since he'd blown a kiss on the way out of her window Monday night.

Had she completely misread the situation?

The librarian had let the three of them have a private conference room to study.

"Mitosis!" Teagan answered, and Trent high-fived her.

"Do you know the stages, Allie?" Trent asked her.

"Interphase, prophase, metaphase, anaphase, telophase," she answered automatically, eyes still flicking to her phone.

Teagan studied her. "You okay, Allie? Is this about the thread on Burn Book?"

Teagan had her full attention.

"It's really not a big deal," said Trent. "It was only pinned for a couple of hours, and now it's buried."

"It was so mild," agreed Teagan.

Allie felt her face heat. She was embarrassed they'd seen the thread, even more embarrassed that Teagan had noticed her distraction.

"Honestly?" Teagan grinned, "I was hoping your secret was you were actually a math whiz and the whole tutoring thing was just a way to get Jackson to ask you out."

Allie froze.

"Kinda same," Trent admitted..

"How is he with Darcy?" Teagan turned to Trent. "He managed to avoid her claws since middle school and now…"

"He's like a semi-willing hostage?" Trent finished. "It's weird, right?"

"You two would have been perfect together," Teagan said wistfully.

"I'm not sure I understand the epinephrine pathway," Allie blurted, desperate for a subject change.

It worked. Teagan and Trent launched into rapid-fire explanation, trading sentences without missing a beat.

Her phone buzzed.
SB: I'm outside.

She did a double-take.
Allie: ?
SB: Of the library. Are we making up or not?

Teagan and Trent were still mid-explanation, oblivious.

Allie: I thought you weren't coming back until Sunday?
SB: You called. I came.
What?

A screenshot popped up before she could respond —every message she'd sent since Tuesday night stacked one after the other. She hadn't sounded desperate at first, but looking at them all together? It was obvious where she'd ended up.

Allie: Hey… are you actually ignoring me? I'm fr freaking out.
Allie: If this is you trying to get me worked up…it's working.
Allie: If we're fighting, I can't wait to make up.
Allie: Are you thinking the same thing I'm thinking?
She'd sent that one a couple of hours ago during dinner.

SB: I'm waiting
Allie: Coming.

Teagan stopped mid-sentence when Allie put her Chromebook in her backpack.

"Ummm, I have to go," said Allie, "it's a family thing. I don't need a ride home."

She felt them staring as she bolted.

* * *

She hadn't planned to leave with him, and definitely hadn't planned what came after. She was still flushed and sweaty when Andrew turned onto her street to drop her off.

Who even was she now?

If someone had told her back in August that she'd be the type of girl to do *that-* in the backseat of a car, pulled over on the side of the road where anyone could've seen- Allie would've said they were crazy. And yet, that's what she'd just done.

"I could come in," Andrew said, interrupting her thoughts. "I just need to be back before my dad gets up in the morning."

"I don't know," Allie hesitated. "I feel like that might be pushing our luck."

"But that's what makes it exciting," he said, grinning. "Besides, with your parents out schmoozing the Lakeshore Mutual people, you know they won't be home anytime soon. If it's going well, they'll stay out late. If it's not... well, you know your dad—he'll just keep drinking." He pulled into her driveway and turned the car off.

"You can't park in the driveway. We'll get caught for sure." Allie said, knowing that he was coming in no matter what she said.

"Gotcha. I'll meet you upstairs in five." He pulled her in for a quick kiss and started the car, headlights washing over the quiet street as he drove off.

Allie couldn't remember a worse Thanksgiving. Even when Stacy had cooked and ruined the entire dinner.

"Allie, honey, don't look so glum." Angela put her dishes in the dishwasher. "It wasn't so bad, was it?"
Allie looked at her mom, then loaded her own dishes and closed the door.
"I'm going upstairs to study."

Her mom touched her arm. "I know this isn't the Thanksgiving you wanted, but we can still watch Snoopy?" She smiled, hopefully.

"This is the first Thanksgiving that I can remember without Kenzie. Dinner came in aluminum trays. Dad's drunk in his office. Snoopy's not going to fix it." She turned toward the stairs. "I'm going to work on my APUSH paper."

Her mom's smile faltered. "We're proud of you, even if we don't say it enough."

"Yeah, that's exactly what it felt like when Dad called me a slacker." The words slipped out before Allie could stop them. Her mom flinched, and Allie almost regretted it —almost.

By Sunday, the holiday already felt like a blur. She'd hidden in her room after the disaster on Thursday, avoiding her father's drunken anger and her mom's constant fake smiles and reassurances.

The calendar said December first, but that didn't feel possible. Midterms were only two weeks away.

She was caught up in Trig, Biology, French, and Psych. Two late papers still hung over her in Lit, and APUSH needed a paper plus a critical analysis. She'd salvaged a failing semester into A's and B's, not that her dad cared. He only saw the missing work. Whatever.

* * *

There was a soft knock at the door. Her mom poked her head in, looking exhausted.

"Don't stay up too late. You need your rest for school tomorrow."

Allie hesitated. Part of her wanted to snap back, still raw from the "slacker" comment her mom hadn't defended her against.

Then she thought about the argument earlier. Her parents were leaving her alone for a whole weekend to go away with the partners from the law firm. Her mom had fought against it now that Stacy and Kenzie worked all the time. Her dad said it was his last chance with the partners, and they better not ruin it for him. Her mom obviously cared- even if she babied her too much. Her dad? Not so much. He only cared about his job.

He'd won, of course. And even though Allie was excited to stay home by herself, it still stung that he saw her as a burden.

"Okay, Mom," she finally said. "I love you."
"Love you, too, sweetheart."

The door clicked shut, and her mom's footsteps retreated down the hall.

Allie closed her laptop and reached for her phone.

Allie: I have a surprise for you
SB: You have my attention
Allie: My parents are going away the weekend after midterms and I get to stay by myself.
SB: That sounds lonely…
Allie: Very lonely
SB: How am I supposed to make it through the next two weeks?
Allie: Well… it's not like they're not going to be gone on Wednesday night
SB: Yeah, but you just said I get you for a whole weekend. I can spoil you rotten. I'm going to make you breakfast in bed.
Allie: Promise?
SB: That's only the beginning…
Allie: 🤍

* * *

She checked in on Burn Book, thankful that the app seemed to be satisfied with her comments. No more popups, and her picture was buried deep in the "Secrets" thread.

Thank god November was over.

CHAPTER 39- UNWELL

Trent and Teagan were waiting for her after the AP Bio midterm.

"Did it really take you the whole time?" Trent asked, adjusting his backpack. "You seemed so confident when we reviewed.

"It's this thing..." she hesitated, embarrassed. "I can't turn the test in early, no matter how quickly I finish. I tried once and had a panic attack. So now I just wait until the clock runs out, even if I'm finished."

"It's not easy being you, is it, McBrainy?" Teagan teased, bumping her shoulder. "Are you done for the day? Do you want a ride home?"

Allie smiled, "I'm done. Can I text my mom quick?"

They walked toward Trent's locker, conversation drifting from exam to winter break plans. As he spun the lock, Trent glanced at her. "Hey, I know you haven't had time to hang out with us except to study, but my birthday party is Saturday night. You should come."

"Kenzie and I are both off work," Teagan added. "It'll be so much fun!"

By the time they reached her street, they'd circled through tests, party talk, and who still had finals left.

"So will you come?" Asked Trent.

"I'd love to, but I need to check with my parents."

"You can just tell them you're spending the night at Kenzie's. I'll pick you up at 6." Teagan grinned, waving her hands like the problem was solved. If only it were that easy.

Four exams down, two to go. She should probably be studying, but she was going to lose her Wednesday nights with Andrew once winter break started, so she wasn't going to skip this for anything.

Allie rolled over onto her side, hair spilling over her shoulder. "There's a party Saturday night. We could go."

"How would that work if I'm supposed to be your secret boyfriend?" He brushed the strands back with a smile. "You are so beautiful."

"You just have to be a secret from my parents," Allie said, thinking maybe this would be the perfect way to finally tell Kenzie about Andrew. She'd figure something out to explain why she hadn't said anything sooner. "Kenzie and Teagan won't say anything."

"They won't —as long as there's something in it for them." His tone sharpened. "They're not your friends, Allie."

That stung. She wanted to protest, to remind him that Kenzie had been her best friend forever, but the truth was they barely talked anymore. Teagan, too- most of their conversations took place during study sessions. Still, she forced the words out. "Yes they are."

"So who else is going to be at this party?"

"Trent, Eric, Sophie…" she exhaled. "Darcy and Jackson.

His look said it all.

"They're a couple. How are you still mad about him?"

"I'm not mad about him, I just don't like that you won't admit he wants you."

"He and Darcy have been dating since homecoming. He doesn't want me."

Andrew rolled out of bed and yanked on his jeans.

"Where are you going?" Allie scrambled to find her own clothes, heart racing.

"You need to choose, Allie."

"Choose?" Her throat tightened. "I only asked if you wanted to go. I thought it would be fun. To be together in public."

He wheeled around. "This was supposed to be our special weekend, and you want to spend it with everyone but me." She winced at the menace in his voice.

She trailed him down the stairs, protesting. "It is our special weekend. Please stay."

He stopped at the back door, shoulders slumping, voice suddenly soft. "Why am I not enough for you?"

Her chest caved. "You are. You're everything to me. I'm sorry I brought it up. We won't go to the party. We'll stay here all weekend. I'll spoil you."

"I wish I believed you," he slammed the door behind him.

* * *

Allie leaned against the door, trembling. The fight had turned so quickly, she could hardly catch her breath. One second, imagining the two of them hanging out with her friends, the next apologizing and begging him to stay.

A dull ache pulsed in her lower back, spreading wider with each breath. Just great. On top of Andrew and midterms, she was about to start her period.

Allie shifted uncomfortably throughout her Trig midterm, the pain gnawing up her spine. Cramps weren't new, but this felt sharper, heavier —like something pressing from the inside. Her stomach rolled. She forced herself to focus, finished the test, and texted Teagan on the way out.

Allie: if you're done, can I get a ride?
Teagan responded immediately.
Teagan: Sure. Waiting for Trent. Did you turn your test in early?
Allie: Should I meet you at your locker?
Teagan: Nah. Come out to the car. I've got snacks.

When she opened the car door, Teagan pulled back, surprised. "You look like shit. Are you okay?"

"Cramps," Allie muttered, easing into the seat. "Really, really bad."

Teagan passed her a bag of potato chips. Allie passed them back, nausea rising.

"My period is so irregular that the cramps are terrible when it finally comes. This is the worst ever, though. I feel like I'm dying."

Trent slid into the backseat a moment later. "How did you get out here before me? Didn't you have Trig today? Whoa, you look terrible. You okay?"

Before she could answer, Teagan jumped in, "She's cramping. Bad. Might be dying."

Allie blushed, tried to laugh, then groaned. "God, this sucks."

"My monthly reminder to be grateful I'm not a girl," Trent muttered as they pulled out of the parking lot.

At home, Allie settled into her bed with her Chromebook and the heating pad. She skimmed her notes for her next exam, but struggled to get comfortable enough to focus.

She texted Andrew:
Allie: If we're going to make up, we need to do it soon. The Wicked Witch is coming soon.
He didn't reply.

Her mom knocked. "You're home early. Is everything okay?" She noted the heating pad and Allie's pajamas.

"I only had Trig today, and Teagan gave me a ride home. I'm about to start my period and the cramps are really, really bad." It slipped out before Allie could stop it.

"It's AP Lit & Comp tomorrow, right? It's Friday, the last day before break; I can take a half day and bring you home. I'll tell your dad I can't go this weekend."

"No!" Allie exclaimed, then winced. "Please don't do that. He'll be so mad." And so would Andrew if her mom stayed home and he didn't get to come over.

"Yes, he will, but you're the priority, Allie. He can still go and schmooze the managing partners by himself."

"Mom, please don't. I heard you two arguing. About me." She said quietly. Her mom blanched. "I'll be fine. It's just a lot worse than usual."

"I'll decide tomorrow," her mom said, brows furrowed in concern. She checked Allie's forehead with the back of her hand.

"I'm not sick," Allie reassured her.

Her mom hesitated. "I know you and your dad both think I baby you too much. And I try not to Allie, I promise." Her mom kissed her temple. "We'll see how you're feeling tomorrow." Her mom lingered a moment —like she had something else to say— then sighed, kissed Allie's temple again, and left.

The Lit & Comp midterm was torture.
A bead of sweat trickled down Allie's cheek as she re-read her essay and hit submit.

"Hey, Allie," Miss Lindstrom called as she headed toward the door. "Is everything okay? You don't look well."

Allie glanced around the room, then leaned in and whispered, "It's just cramps. But they're really bad right now."

Miss Lindstrom lowered her voice, "How do you feel like you did on the exam? If you're sick, I can let you redo it after the break. You've worked so hard to pull your grade up, I'd hate for you to blow it."

"It's okay," Allie assured her. "I was ready for this prompt."

"Well, have a good break," Miss Lindstrom smiled, then turned to address another student.

Jackson was waiting at her locker. Allie's gaze flicked up and down the hall, waiting for Darcy to pounce.

"She went home already," Jackson assured her. "The Spanish midterm was easy, I guess." Relief and dread tangled. She scanned the hallway again, half-way expecting Andrew to appear. He was still ignoring her texts, and it would be her luck if he showed up while she was here with Jackson.

"Are you okay? You don't look good," Jackson helped her into her parka.

"I'm fine," she reassured him through gritted teeth. "It's a girl thing."

He flushed, awkward. "So, um, Teagan said you're coming to Trent's party. That's great —I've missed hanging out with you. I promise I won't let Darcy say anything to you."

"I'm not going."

His face fell, "Because of Darcy or because you're sick?"

"I'm not sick," she snapped, instantly regretting it. "Sorry. I'm not sick, but I do feel like I'm dying."

"How are you getting home? Not the bus?"

"Why? Are you offering to drive me?" She winced again. "Sorry, sorry. God, this sucks."

"Stupid question," he admitted. They both knew he couldn't drive her home. "I just hate to think about you on the bus like this."

"My mom's waiting. Can you tell Trent I'm not coming? I'll forget ."

"Yeah, sure. So, I guess I'll see you next year, then, huh?"

The words jolted her. He was right. Unless she went to the party, she wouldn't see any of them until January. "Yeah, I guess so."

He hesitated like he wanted to say more. She looked up at him, waiting, then finally said, "Well, have a good Christmas. And Happy New Year, Jackson."

He stood and watched her walk away.

CHAPTER 40- PLEASE COME HOME

Allie's phone buzzed on the nightstand. Four new texts from her mom. None from Kenzie. None from Teagan. None from Trent. Still nothing from Andrew.

She groaned, curling in on herself. These cramps weren't normal —sharp, twisting everywhere.

Maybe she should have told her mom to stay home last night.

Hungry but nauseous, she forced herself downstairs, only to find that even the thought of food turned her stomach. She settled on a glass of water, but even that was too much. She only managed to drink half of it before she knew it was coming back up. She barely made it to the bathroom and then collapsed on the floor, letting the cool tiles steady her..

Her phone buzzed. She didn't even have the energy to sit up.

Mom: How did you sleep? Do you need us to come home?
Allie: I'm fine mom. Stop talking about coming home. If dad sees, he'll be mad.
Mom: I love you
Allie: Love you too

She pressed the phone to her chest. She wanted her mom.

She opened PicSee to distract herself and tapped through on autopilot. Liked Kenzie's newest pictures of her and Eric. Clicked on Teagan- nothing new. Trent- nothing new. She messaged him a quick *happy birthday sorry I can't come tonight* before dropping the phone back on the tiles.

Allie: please stop being like this. Andrew, I need you.

The message status changed to read immediately. Finally.
Allie's heart leapt when the bubbles appeared.

But then they disappeared. Reappeared. Disappeared again.

When the text finally came through, though, it wasn't words. It was a picture.

Allie's blood went cold. Yesterday. The hallway. Jackson helping her with her parka.

Except that's not what this looked like. At all.

Jackson, holding her coat, looked as if he were pulling her into his arms.

Jackson, smiling down at her, looked like he was about to kiss her.

And worst of all… Allie looking up at him, *looked like she wanted him to.*

Allie: This isn't what it looks like.
SB: This is exactly what it looks like. I knew it.

Allie's chest tightened. She couldn't get air, couldn't get her thoughts to line up.

Allie: Please come over so we can talk about this.
SB: There's nothing to talk about. I knew he wanted you. I just didn't know you wanted him back.
Allie: I don't want him. I want YOU.
SB: God. Don't lie. It's right there in the picture Allie
Allie: It wasn't like that at all.
SB: Except it was.
Allie: I LOVE YOU. I want YOU.
SB: We're done Allie.
Allie: Andrew, no. Please listen to me.

She sent a string of pleading messages with no reply. She finally called him, only to get a recording that the call could not be completed.

She threw up again.

It was dark when she finally woke up. How long had she been

asleep?

Maybe she should just die here on the bathroom floor.

She couldn't do this. She sent two messages: *Mom, I need you. Please come home.*

Mom, this is so bad. Something's really wrong. Then she called, but went straight to voicemail.

Shaking, she left a broken message, "Mom, please come home. I need to go to the hospital," and ended the call before she started sobbing again.

She wanted her mom, but the thought of worrying her made everything worse. Should she call 911? Could she even go to the hospital without her parents?

She was about to call her mom again when the phone rang- none of the familiar ringtones for her parents or Kenzie. Through the haze of pain, she answered, remembering she'd turned the focus off on her phone in case Andrew called from a different number.

"Mom," she sobbed, "please come home. I need you. I need to go to the hospital."

"Allie? What's wrong? Where is your mom? Do you need me to take you to the hospital? I can leave right now." The questions came at her like a flood.

It wasn't her mom. It was Jackson- his voice tight with panic.

"Allie?" He pressed.

She broke down completely.

"I'm coming, Allie. Stay on the phone."

CHAPTER 41- I'M DYING

He helped her gently into the backseat of his car, using his coat as a pillow for her.

"I don't understand," she sobbed, "Why did you call? How did you know?"

"You sent those texts to me, not your mom."

"I think I'm dying," she admitted. "Did you grab my phone? I need to call my mom. Am I even allowed to go to the hospital without her?"

"Here," he reached over the seat to hand it to her.

She tried her mom's number… straight to voicemail. Shaking, she left a message, voice breaking. "Mom, Jackson's taking me to the hospital. Please come home right away."

In the backseat, she lay curled against his coat, barely conscious.

At the hospital, nurses helped get Allie out of his car and into a wheelchair.

They tried to stop Jackson in the lobby, but Allie clung to his arm, sobbing until they relented.

"Hi, Allie, I'm Joe." The intake nurse said quietly. "You're sixteen, right? We'll get you checked in and try to get the pain under control." He snapped a bracelet on her wrist and handed her a clipboard. "Can you just fill out the top part with your parents' information? We'll do our best to reach them. Do you know where they are?"

"Lake Geneva. For a work thing for my dad." Her breath hitched as the blood pressure cuff tightened on her arm. The sharp squeeze was almost a relief- a different kind of pain than the deep ache ripping through her.

"You're dehydrated," Joe explained. "We'll start fluids and then get you some pain meds." The IV slipped in with a sting. Allie flinched but kept her eyes on Jackson, steady beside her until Joe was finished.

When Joe stepped out, Allie whispered, "Thank you for being here."

Jackson's smile faltered. "That's what friends are for."

"I'm sorry you had to leave the party."

"I'm sorry you're sick." His voice was low. "Besides, the party was lame. Darcy and Sophie were trashed before they even got there. You saved me from having to babysit them all night."

"So you're stuck babysitting me instead, I guess."

Another nurse came in. "Okay, Allie. I'm Trish. I'm taking over for Joe. We haven't gotten through to your parents yet, but we're going to go ahead and start ruling some things out, okay?"

Allie nodded solemnly.

She turned to Jackson, "I just need to ask Miss Ellis some questions. There are vending machines in the lobby if you're hungry or thirsty. We'll come get you as soon as we're done."

Jackson stood to leave, but Allie grabbed his hand.

"Please stay," she whispered. A single tear slid down her cheek.

The nurse hesitated, then nodded.

The blood pressure cuff hissed and tightened around her arm.

"When was your last menstrual period?"

Allie hesitated, trying to remember. "I don't know. It's not regular. Definitely since school started."

"Is there any chance you're pregnant?"

It was just a question. One the nurse would've asked anyone.

But Allie's breath caught—and Jackson saw it.

Saw the shift.

Saw the realization.

Heat rushed to her cheeks. He must hate her.

The nurse scribbled something and moved on, but the damage was done. Jackson couldn't … wouldn't look at her.

Allie reeled with the reality of her situation. It wasn't just that this could be true…it was that she'd let herself believe it couldn't be.

They'd never talked about birth control.

No condoms. No pills. Not even pulling out.

She'd known they needed to have the conversation, and yet she'd let it happen again and again.

So yes—there was a chance.

A very real, terrifying chance.

Once the pregnancy test came back negative, everything blurred. More labs, an ultrasound, the words "kidney stones." Pain meds dulled her body, but not the weight of Jackson's silence.

By discharge, she could barely stay upright.

"Your mom is on her way home," one of the nurses told her. "Your friend has your meds and discharge instructions." Allie hardly registered it.

Jackson drove her back to her house and helped her out of the car when she stumbled.

"Don't be mad at me," she whispered.
"We just need to get you to bed," he said evenly.

Inside, he gave up trying to help her walk and picked her up.
She nestled against him, half-asleep. "You're so strong."

He pulled the blankets up around her, and she grabbed his hand.
"Please don't be mad," she said again.
"I'm not mad. I just don't understand why you lied. If you'd said you didn't like me the way I like you, I could have handled that. But, I thought that maybe if I waited until…"
"But you didn't wait," she yawned, the meds pulling her under. "You're dating Darcy."
"It's complicated." He tucked the covers in around her.
She was already asleep by the time he sat down again.

Allie surfaced slowly, her head pounding. The room was dim, her mouth dry, her body stiff and aching. Her first thought, muddled through the haze of painkillers: *Did I check in last night?*

Her hand drifted toward her phone- then froze as fragments of the night slowly flickered back: the hospital, Jackson's steady presence, her mom clutching him, thanking him again and again. It felt too strange to be true. Maybe she'd imagined it.

Her mom was there now, in the chair where Jackson had been.

"You're awake," she said quietly. She stood, crossed to the bed, and held out a glass of water with two pills. "Drink the whole glass. You have to flush the stones."

"Stones?"

"Kidney stones. At least two, maybe three. One's moving now- that's what all the pain is."

"I thought I was dying," Allie whispered.

Her mom's lips trembled. She turned away, but not before the tears slipped free.

"I'm sorry, Mom. I shouldn't have called. I didn't know it wasn't serious. How mad is Dad?"

Her mom sat on the edge of her bed, taking her hands. Her voice shook.

"No, Allie. I'm sorry. For leaving when I knew something was wrong. For raising you to think you always have to be fine. And most of all, for not being here when you needed me."

Her mom broke then, shoulders shaking.

* * *

Allie wanted to comfort her, but the weight of the meds dragged her down. She squeezed her mom's hand as the darkness pulled her back under.

Shouting jolted her awake. Her mom had left her door open, and she could hear every word, sharp as glass.

"… you were embarrassing me!" Her father thundered. "Texting her all night, right in front of the managing partners. I took your phone because you were being rude."

Her mom's voice was higher, raw. "You didn't just take it- you turned it off! The hospital called for *hours* while our daughter was there alone. Do you understand that?"

"She wasn't alone," he shot back. "Some boy took her- some boy that she shouldn't have even been with. Where the hell was Kenzie?"

Allie pressed her hands over her ears, but her parents kept increasing the volume.

Her dad continued, "She shouldn't have even gone. She overreacts because you coddle her. They sent her home, didn't they? And now we're stuck with the bill."

"*That's* what you're worried about?" Angela's voice shook with fury. "She was doubled over in pain, thinking she was dying, and *that's* what you're worried about? Our daughter needed *us*, and you made sure I wasn't there."

"And you just made sure I'll never make managing partner." His voice rose, matching her fury. "I've worked my ass off for this, and you blew it in one weekend."

A door slammed hard enough to rattle the walls. Silence collapsed around her.

Allie curled tighter under the blanket, the ache in her body nothing compared to the hollow in her chest. She closed her eyes, willing herself back to sleep.

But her phone buzzed. And buzzed again.

She groaned and reached for it, blinking at the screen. Three new messages: Kenzie, Teagan, and a number she didn't recognize.

She hesitated at the strange number, then opened Kenzie's first.
Kenzie: Is this true? Tell me it isn't true.

CHAPTER 43- BURNED

While Allie tried to make sense of the cryptic text, Kenzie texted again.

Kenzie: It won't let me screenshot. Check your CALENDAR. NOW

A new notification shoved it down before she could reply.
Teagan: I thought we were friends.
Teagan: I guess not. Who even are you?

Allie's stomach turned, and her pulse pounded. What were they talking about? Even after she re-read Teagan's message, it didn't make sense.

The third message sat unopened. Her finger hovered, frozen. Finally, trembling, she swiped.

One text
080625011013: You promised. When you break your promise, bad things happen.

She fumbled Burn Book open. What was happening? A cramp pressed hard against her spine.

The app opened with a jolt of black and flames, with the dreaded pop-up in the center.

Pick your poison:
* Somebody's got a secret
* Sneaky links

A burning ache spread across her entire body.
She tapped the first.

The library picture was pinned to the top again— now next to the picture of her and Jackson in the hallway. The implication was clear.

* * *

She needed to know.

She scrolled the comments, pain pressing sharper with each line.

She froze when she saw QueenDee's comment. *She acts like she's so perfect, but she's really just a cheating slut.*

SoFull replied: Totally

The comments continued:

Bad-ger53713: She's in my AP Lit class. She's so arrogant and condescending.

SuperSwiftie: She totally acts like she's better than anyone else.

And on and on. 125 comments. Did she even know 125 people?

Her back throbbed.

She swiped out when she couldn't stand it anymore, but the Sneaky Links thread opened automatically.

Again, her pictures were pinned, now in a rapid-fire slideshow of her and Jackson.

A shot of her and Jackson at lunch, the whole group in frame, but the angle made it look like the two of them were leaning in, sharing something intimate.

Another in the hallway, hands brushing as they laughed… caught at the perfect second to look like flirting.

The parka picture again, zoomed in tight on her expression. She'd been so miserable, but the close crop turned it into something else… soft, almost adoring.

Her skin crawled. Whoever took these had been right there. Watching.

Allie reeled when she saw the next picture, then doubled over in pain.

Jackson was helping her into the car to go to the hospital. But the photo froze everything at the worst possible moment. Allie, half in the car, head back, legs spread, bracing with her hands. Jackson, bent over her, shirt untucked, grabbing her hips.

Her stomach turned, and she retched into her trash can.

* * *

She couldn't stop watching the pictures scroll by.

Jackson "embracing her" on the front step while he struggled to get the key in the lock.

But then the last picture… the most damning of all… had been taken in front of her house, camera aimed directly at her bedroom window.

Jackson, carrying her like a bride to the wedding bed. Allie, looking up at him with love and admiration. How could someone make the worst night of her life look like a love story?

She was sweating now, breaths shallow and uneven. Her whole body shook. Someone had been stalking her. For months. Collecting these moments and then using them as proof.

The caption, though.

Nothing stays secret forever. They've been lying since the beginning. She's been pretending to be the good girl, the loyal friend. He's been using the Queen to cover their secret. Fake news. Both of them.

A pop-up announced a new thread had been started by QueenDee in "Who Wore It Better?"

Allie clicked the X, but it directed her to the thread anyway.

Three pictures.
The picture of Darcy in a bikini, draped across the chair.
Jackson. Smiling. Confident.
Allie. Hair in a messy bun, eyes crossed, sticking her tongue out.

The pain was getting harder to ignore.
15 thumbs up for Darcy. Zero for her.
30.
90.
180. Still zero for Allie.

She stared at her picture. Birthday Friday last year. On her nightstand, two pictures Kenzie had given her were clearly visible. One held a photo of the two of them at Myrtle Beach in fifth grade, arms slung around each other, matching grins, and peeling sunburns.

The other held a line from *Pride and Prejudice*, the Keira Knightley version she'd forced Kenzie to watch a hundred times. *We are all fools in love.* Allie knew it was only in the movie, not in the book — and it wasn't even her favorite quote— but she loved it anyway because Kenzie had made it for her.

Kenzie had taken this picture. Kenzie gave this picture to Darcy so they could mock her on Burn Book.
The humiliation was one thing. The betrayal was worse.

A pain like nothing Allie had ever felt before ripped through her. She leaned her head back and let out a raw, guttural scream.

Her mom's footsteps pounded up the stairs at the sound of her cry.

"Allie?" She was at the doorway in a second, then beside her, catching her under the arm.

"It hurts," Allie whimpered, barely able to breathe through the stabbing pain.

"I know, baby. I've got you. Just breathe."

Her mom stayed through the worst — holding her hair when she vomited, murmuring reassurances, guiding her through the pain until hours later, the stone finally passed.

Allie collapsed against the pillow, wrung out and trembling. Her mom handed her water and pills. "The doctor said you have to stay ahead of the pain."

She swallowed them down, refusing to look at her phone, ignoring the comments that were probably piling higher every minute. As her eyes drifted shut and the medicine pulled her under, it all fell away- the pictures, the comments, the betrayal. All but one. Jackson, holding her like she was his, and her looking at him like it was forever. She clung to that image until sleep took it, too.

Allie had never been so exhausted. Everything hurt, even with the pain meds that either knocked her out or left her brain too fuzzy to think.

How long had she been asleep? Long enough that her phone was at 10%.

It lit up when she plugged it in. No texts. From anyone. She tried reaching out again.

Allie: I don't understand, Kenz. We've been friends forever.
She hit send and added it to the string of unread texts.

Allie: I love you Andrew. Only you.
She should've been embarrassed by the sheer number of unread texts she'd sent, but she didn't care. She needed to talk to him. To make him understand.
She tried to call and got the same recording —her call could not be completed.

She needed to check in. She'd been offline too long, and she'd already learned that lesson. *"Bad things happen."*
 Her first thought was *"How much worse could it get?"* She was afraid the answer was worse than she could ever imagine. She yanked the thought back before it had a chance to manifest.

The pop-up stopped her cold.
New rule. Every new thread about you gets a reply. At least one. No exceptions.
You think it's bad now?

She dropped her phone on her nightstand, took her pills, and asked the universe to end her misery.

By the time she stirred again, whole days seemed to have slipped past. Exhausted and aching, she'd only managed to go from the bed to the bathroom and back, relying on her mom to bring her pills, water, and soup.

Now, though, the water glass was empty, and there were no pills waiting for her.

Her side throbbed as she shuffled to the stairs. Their voices hit her halfway down. Her father's sharp and cutting, her mother's tight and exhausted.

"Maybe if you were timing the turkey instead of timing her pills, we'd be eating Christmas dinner right now. Assuming you even bought a turkey."

"Don't you dare," her mom snapped back. "She's sick."

"Stop coddling her. She's not the first person to have kidney stones, and she won't be the last. You pushed and pushed until we had her - almost bankrupted us in the process- and I haven't stopped paying since."

Allie froze. *Bankrupted us. Because of me.*

Her mom's hiss cut the air. "Don't you put that on her."

The voices trailed into muffled tones as her mom trailed her dad out of the kitchen, refusing to let him walk away.

Allie waited until their voices faded, then slipped into the kitchen, grabbed the pill bottle, and shook two into her palm with shaking fingers. *All because of me,* she thought. She swallowed the pills dry, then pocketed the bottle. One less thing for her mom to deal with.

Back upstairs, she set the bottle next to her phone and wished — again— for the universe to put her out of her misery.

The pain hit harder than before, and by the time it finally broke, she was curled on the bathroom floor, shaking and alone. Her mom had disappeared into the fight with her dad hours ago and never came back. Allie stayed silent as the pain tore through her. She'd already caused enough problems.

* * *

Had it really only been a week since she went to the ER and her life imploded?

She sat awkwardly in the exam room, waiting for the doctor to come back with the results. She didn't quite feel good yet, but she felt better than she had in a week.

"Gramma wants to know your GPA," her mom said, looking up from her phone. "Can you check ClassLink?

"Oh," Allie fumbled. "I don't have it with me. I need a new charger- it's been dead for a couple of days." She didn't even feel guilty about the lie. The phone *was* dead... shoved under the bed where she couldn't see it.

Just then, the door opened, and without preamble, the doctor launched into her ultrasound results.

"So the good news is, two stones have already passed," he said, scrolling the laptop.

"Is there bad news?" Allie asked.

"Not necessarily," he said, turning the screen. "That's the third stone," he said, pointing at a dot inside a blob. "It's shifted a little since your ER scan, but it's still sitting in the kidney. As long as it stays there, it may never give you trouble. Even if it moves, it's small enough that we'd expect you to pass it on your own."

Angela frowned. "But why does she even have kidney stones? No one in our families has ever had one."

The doctor nodded. "That's actually pretty common. In kids and teenagers, it's less about family history and more about how their bodies handle things like calcium, salt, and hydration. Once we get the results of the other tests, we may have a better idea why, but often we never find the cause. We'll reach out if there's anything urgent. Otherwise, we'll send the results in the mail, and they're always available in MyChart." He closed the laptop and stood.

"Like I said, the good news is you've already passed two stones, which tells me your body can do the work. This one's small enough that I don't recommend surgery. What I do want is for you to take it easy the rest of your break. Rest, hydrate. Listen to your body. By the time school starts again, you should be in good shape to go back."

Allie twisted her hands in her lap. "Can't you do something to make it go away?"

"Go away?"

"You said no surgery, but isn't there something else? I don't want to go through that again. It... really hurt."

Her mom's sigh came before her words. "Oh, Allie. The second one wasn't bad at all. I didn't even know you'd passed it until we got here."

Allie looked down. Of course she didn't know. She hadn't bothered to ask.

The doctor cleared his throat gently. "Every stone feels different, and your pain is real. If this stone stays put and you don't have any more symptoms, we'll have you come back in about six months for another ultrasound to make sure it isn't growing or blocking anything. If it passes before then- or even if you feel like it might- call us and we'll get you in right away."

On the way out, they picked up a refill of her pain meds from the pharmacy and a charger from the gift shop. Allie stared at the small bag in her lap, already dreading what waited once her phone powered back on. She couldn't ignore Burn Book forever, no matter how much she wanted to.

CHAPTER 45- I WISH YOU KNEW

The sun was down by the time she got home from her appointment, and their house was completely dark. Allie's mom flipped a switch, and a blow-up Santa and Rudolph came to life. They hadn't hired the company to put the outside lights up this year; the inflatables were the only exterior sign of the season. *This is all my fault.*

The inside was just as depressing. A half-decorated Christmas tree glowed weakly in the corner, with whatever was in the one box her dad brought down from the attic.

"Go ahead upstairs, and I'll heat up some soup. The doctor said you should take it easy." Her mom rummaged through the fridge, frowned, and said, "I guess we ate all the soup. How about a Mac-n-cheese cup?"

Allie nodded, then climbed the stairs.

Resigned, she dug her phone out from under her bed and plugged it in. She threw the new charger in her desk drawer, then watched as the screen slowly came to life.

The PicSee notification popped up first. Relieved, Allie clicked then wished she hadn't. PicSee launched into Kenzie's year-in-review slideshow.

Pictures of the two of them flashed to the beat of the music... Fireworks on New Year's Eve... pink cupcakes for Galentines...but things changed as the seasons did. Allie was still in some of the pictures, but now they were filled with Trent and Teagan. Jackson.

Allie and Kenzie on the first day of school. That was the last picture of the two of them. After that, it was all Darcy and Sophie, or the group, or Eric. Kenzie's feed had been mostly pictures of Eric since homecoming.

The final picture was a group shot from Trent's party. Eyes glassy, red solo cups raised. The picture faded into fireworks and "Happy New Year."

* * *

Allie started to swipe out of the app, but stopped.

Something had caught her attention in that last picture. Something in the background.

She took a screenshot and leaned closer.

Then Allie saw it. Saw him. The recognition lit up her nerves before her brain caught up.

Against the wall in the background, staring at the group. The same set of his shoulders, the casual way he leaned against the wall, arms crossed. She could almost hear his voice, feel his breath close to her ear.

The picture was dark and blurry, but she forced herself to find proof it wasn't him. Short hair, preppy shirt. No. It wasn't him.

But for an instant it was, and her body buzzed with shock.

She couldn't do this. Kenzie. Andrew. BurnBook. It was all too much. She eyed the pills on her nightstand.

She wasn't really in physical pain right now, but maybe they would make some of this other hurt go away…

Allie dropped her hand guiltily when her mom came through the door, carrying a tray with Allie's dinner.

"How's the new charger?" she asked, setting the tray on the desk. Without waiting for an answer, she asked, "How are you feeling? Your color looks better."

"Not as bad as before," Allie admitted, trying not to look at the pill bottle. "But everything still hurts, ya know?"

Her mom grabbed it and handed her two pills. "Can I stay and eat with you?"

She'd brought two dinners.

"Um, okay?" She casually closed out of PicSee and set her phone on the nightstand. "Kind of like bedtime picnics in the old house, right?"

Her mom smiled, and Allie's heart sank. She was a shell of her old self. Allie'd noticed the dark circles under her eyes and heard the weariness in her voice, but she hadn't seen the new lines in her forehead, the way her face sank around her cheekbones, the way her watch slid because it was too big now.

* * *

"I'm sorry," Allie said, "I know I'm causing problems between you and Dad."

"You were on the stairs the other day, weren't you?"

The heat rising up Allie's neck was all the confirmation she needed..

Her mom sighed deeply. "Your dad is going through some stuff right now."

"Because he didn't land Lakeshore?"

"That, and he lost the Ashford Case. Now they're talking about leaving."

Allie's jaw dropped. Ashford was supposed to be a cakewalk.

Angela pressed on. "It doesn't excuse his behavior or the way he's treating you…"

Allie interrupted again, "Or the way he's treating you?"

"That's different," she replied, looking away. "I knew who he was when I married him." Then, softer, "I wish you'd known him when I met him. He was so full of confidence, promise." A genuine smile flickered. "He's so smart, he knows the law better than anyone else. But he doesn't have that thing… Whatever it is that makes juries and judges love you, that makes your coworkers want to be your second chair. It's been hard."

Allie took a bite of mac n cheese, trying to process this. Until recently, she'd believed her dad was the best lawyer around… that managing partner was just around the corner. True… she'd noticed that things weren't exactly adding up, but…

Angela drew a breath."That's not why I wanted to talk to you, though."

She waited until she had Allie's attention."You need to understand that *I* wanted to stop. Stop trying to have another baby." Her voice choked. "I didn't think I could take that loss again. We'd tried and lost so many times. Your dad convinced me we could do this. That we would have a baby and she'd be beautiful and brilliant.. the best of both of us."

* * *

She wiped a tear. Allie set her fork down and waited; her mom had never talked to her about this before.

"Before you could leave the hospital, we had to do an overnight trial- to be sure that we would react to the monitors, that we would know what to do if you stopped breathing or if your heart rate dropped."

Angela paused to collect herself, but her voice still shook when she continued.

"He stayed awake that whole night so we wouldn't fail. I don't think he slept until your second birthday, when your doctor took you off all of the monitors and medicine and said we could come back at your third birthday. You have no idea what it felt like to schedule an appointment a whole year away."

Allie sat frozen, barely breathing.

Angela looked away, embarrassed. "The point is... I know you heard what he said the other night. That's him being afraid, Allie. It's not right, but when he's scared, he lashes out. He loves you. He wanted you. He's so afraid he's going to let you down, he can't do anything except pretend like it's everyone's fault but his own."

Allie had so many questions, but when the door slammed and her mom jumped up, she knew the moment had passed.

Angela kissed Allie's forehead, gathered the tray, and scooped up the pill bottle with the dishes. "Do you need anything else?"

"I'm good," she replied, though she wasn't sure about that.

Allie opened the calendar app, tapped December 28th, typed "Burning it down," and hit enter.

The screen went black. The logo flared. She held her breath, bracing for the pop-up. Nothing

Instead, the home screen had changed. The logo stayed at the top, but beneath it blazed a flaming **Trending** banner. Five circles filled the center: her picture in the #1 spot, Jackson's at #2, Darcy's at #3, a thread called "Drag the Brag" at #4, and finally, "Hot for Teacher" at the #5 slot.

Allie blinked, unsettled. She checked in and was redirected back to the new home page.

Six comments. She could do this.

She clicked Drag the Brag.

The thread was a feed of screenshots- classmates' PicSee posts, hijacked and reposted by Burn Book users with their own captions.

A bikini shot- she recognized the girl from one of her classes. Scroll.

A football player holding a Green Bay Packers jersey. "Guess who got a jersey AND tickets?"

She laughed at the caption:

Bruh. Do NOT go to the game. They lose EVERY time you go.

The comments followed the same thought:

CarlaHorne: We're in the playoffs, dude. Don't fuck this up for us.

She hesitated, then typed "Bruh." One down.

She scrolled, stunned at what some of her classmates had gotten for Christmas. Why did a high schooler need a Porsche?

She froze. Darcy, in a sports bra, surrounded by leggings, the giant red shopping bag every girl recognized next to her. "Guess Santa loves me 🩶" About $700 worth, by Allie's quick calculation.

The caption: "All that money and she still can't buy a personality."

Allie's jaw dropped. She'd never heard anyone take a shot at Darcy.

SoFull: Jealous much?

SuperSwiftie: SoFull… you sound like you might know her IRL.

BaiGuy: She doesn't need a personality
HungLikeAHorse: Better angle would've been from behind.. bending over
ILv2Vape: If she took her top off I could see the leggings better

Allie swiped quickly. She managed to make five more comments in the FitCheck thread, then hit the X in relief.
But instead of closing, a pop-up appeared.

Remember ALL the rules, Allie. Every new thread about you gets a reply. At least one. No exceptions.

She slumped in resignation. She'd never forgive Kenzie for putting the stupid app on her phone.
She tapped her own circle, then opened the Someone's Got a Secret Thread.

CatherineJames liked SuzeeQ's comment, "I care why?" and replied, "Right?".

There were no comments, only votes, in the "Who wore it better?" thread. Another vote for Darcy.

Then she opened SneakyLinks.

ILv2Vape: You downgraded hard my guy.
JoeyTribbiani: Obv his gf wouldn't let him hit.
BaiGuy: Yeah, but wouldn't that be like hitting a 2x4
SoFull: He pretended it was his gf
IndigoGirl: Anyone else wonder who took these pics? Stalker much?
CatherineJames; Creepy, right?

She squeezed her eyes shut and hurled her phone across the room. What had she ever done to deserve this?

"You sure you're up to going back tomorrow?"
Allie slipped her Chromebook into her backpack. "No, but..." *She needed to see Andrew. To make him believe her.*

Angela pulled her into a hug. "The doctor said to take it easy. If you're not ready, you can wait."

Allie melted into her. She couldn't remember the last time her mom had held her like this.

"I have to go back sometime," she said softly.

Her mom kissed her head and left, closing the door softly.

Allie surveyed her room —the bed where she'd told Andrew she loved him again and again. What had gone so wrong? He'd blocked her, but tomorrow he'd have to talk to her. She'd make him believe her. As long as he hadn't seen the other pictures, she could fix this.

Then she eyed the picture frames on her nightstand. Without a second thought, she dumped them in the trash.

She opened her phone. No new texts. The Happy New Year texts she'd sent out still sat "delivered."

No new threads about her on BurnBook, so she finished quickly.

She eyed the empty spot where the pictures had been, tempted to pull them back out. Instead, she turned off her light.

An hour passed. Then another. Counting sheep, reciting poetry, relaxation exercises- nothing worked. Finally, she gave up and opened PicSee.

Four faces filled her screen. Eric, Kenzie, Darcy, and … Andrew? She blinked. His hair was short —no, pulled back— but it was definitely him.

Her stomach lurched. *Why was he with them?*

Allie swiped, confused, to a selfie of Eric and Kenzie kissing, eyes up to the camera. "Best New Year's ever. Can't wait to see what the next year brings."

In the background, Darcy and Andrew were also kissing.

Allie stared, trying to make sense of it. With his hair pulled back, he looked just like the guy in the photo from Trent's party. Had Andrew been there? Why?

She scrolled again and froze.

Darcy's picture showed the four of them, arms slung around each other like they'd always been that way. Andrew was smiling and gazing into Darcy's eyes. The same way he used to look into hers.

"New Year, New Love. Sometimes the universe breaks you so you're ready for something better. So excited I found my something better."

The picture had hundreds of likes and comments, but it was the first two comments that broke her.

It'sMeKenzie: So happy for you, bestie

DWhite: Couldn't have said it better, my love. So happy we found each other.

Allie bent over the trash can and vomited until her stomach was empty.

Angela started the car as Allie slid into the passenger seat.

"You sure you're okay? Your color looks a little off."

"I'll call you if anything happens," Allie said, trying to keep her voice steady. She needed to go to school, to find Andrew.

Then, the ache she'd been ignoring stabbed so hard she cried out, struggling for breath.

Angela took one look at her and said, "We're going to the hospital."

Allie was in too much pain to argue.

Her mom was already calling ahead as they backed out of the driveway.

By the time they reached the ER, a nurse was waiting with a wheelchair. Bracelet, IV, monitors. Nausea swelled until the meds dulled it into exhaustion.

The CT showed the stone had shifted, wedged in the ureter. They admitted her for observation. Days blurred. Nurses slipped in and out; Dr Markel checked in each morning. Her mom never left her side. Her dad didn't even call.

On Thursday, Dr Markel sat across from them.

"The stone hasn't moved in two days. You're off the pain meds, eating and drinking fine. I think you're ready to go home."

"But it hasn't passed," Angela pressed. "What if she has another attack at school?"

"Surgery isn't necessary yet," he said gently. "There's a medication that can help the passage, but we usually reserve it for adults."

"I'll take it," Allie cut in. "I'm already too far behind."

The house reeked of stale air when they walked in. Empty containers and beer bottles litter the counters, the table, and even the floor.

* * *

"Go on upstairs, sweetheart. I'll take care of this." Allie's stomach turned.

That night, her parents' argument boiled over. Her dad's voice thundered through the walls —30 days to land a new client or he was done at the firm. His words slurred, but the weight underneath was sharp enough to silence the whole house.

The last stone took another week to pass. Relief left Allie weak but lighter. Even so, Dr. Markel ordered her to stay home through the long weekend. Nearly a month had slipped by, her days filled with unanswered texts, Burn Book check-ins, endless scrolling through PicSee, and assignments pushed through ClassLink. She managed to keep up on the work, but the silence from her friends pressed in heavier each day. And every time she saw Darcy post about "Drew," the knot in her stomach tightened. By January 22nd, she wasn't afraid of the stares and whispers; she was desperate to go back and finally figure out what was going on.

CHAPTER 48- HOLLOW

Allie's stomach twisted as they pulled up to school. "It's going to be fine. You've been keeping up with all of your work." Her mom reassured her.

If schoolwork was the only thing to worry about, her mom would have been right.

Allie hesitated at the door. A month gone, and everything still looked the same. Students streamed past —laughing, chattering, like nothing had changed —except everything had.

The full weight of what had happened hit when she opened her locker. All of Kenzie's things were gone. The bottom of her locker was full of things she'd loaned Kenzie over the years. Allie shoved her coat inside and slammed the door.

She'd known it would be hard, but she wasn't ready for the stares. She wasn't even trending on Burn Book anymore - why were they staring? In AP Lit, Trent looked startled, then sat without a word. He left the same way.

In AP Bio, someone finally said something.
She took her regular seat at the table behind Trent and Teagan, bracing for silence.

Teagan turned immediately. "I don't get it, Allie. From the beginning, we wanted you to be with Jackson. But you waited until he was with Darcy?"

Allie started to object. "But nothing happened…"
Trent cut her off. "I asked him flat out, because I didn't believe he'd actually do that. You know what he said? He said, *'I guess you never know what someone is capable of.'*" Trent shook his head. "That sounds like an admission to me. Sorry, Allie."

Her throat tightened. That wasn't an admission. It was a judgment.

He'd trusted her, and she'd lied to him.

The lights went out, and Teagan and Trent turned their backs to her in a way that felt final. A video flickered to life on the smartboard.

So that was it. Burn Book was the truth now. And she had no friends.

She dreaded AP Psych.

Darcy pounced as soon as she walked in the door. "So is today's lesson on lying, narcissistic whores?" Several students snickered.
"Knock it off, Darcy," Teagan said.

Allie sat in the back, ignoring the whispers. Darcy kept at it- liars, cheaters, whores- until Mr Grant finally shut her down.

At lunch, she headed toward Miss Lindstrom's room, then turned. She had to face them, explain what happened.

The cafeteria buzzed as always, but every laugh, every glance felt aimed at her. By the time she reached their table, she was sure everyone was whispering about her.

Eric's smile flickered, then dropped when the others looked up. Kenzie and Sophie stared at her, stone-faced; Teagan and Trent, unreadable. Darcy rose, triumphant.

"Well, you've got balls, I'll give you that." She said.

"Those pictures aren't true," Allie said. "Whoever posted them…"
Kenzie coughed, eyes flicking up for the briefest moment, a tiny shake of her head. Allie heard the silent warning: First rule of fight club.

She tried again. "Someone's spreading lies, and I deserve the chance to defend myself."

"Nobody cares, Allie. It's all so last year." Darcy smiled.

* * *

Movement beside her caught Allie's attention. A preppy boy with a ponytail stood from Jackson's old seat.

"Allie, this is my new boyfriend, Drew." Darcy beamed. "Drew, this is Allie, the one I was telling you about?"

Andrew turned. "The one who was screwing your boyfriend behind your back?" His eyes locked on hers.

"I'd say it's a pleasure to meet you, but I don't tell lies." His expression didn't change, but his eyes narrowed, a flash of menace only she could see. Then he leaned in, brushing Darcy's cheek with a light kiss, like nothing had happened.

"I... I don't understand," Allie stammered.

"What's not to understand?" Darcy said. "You lied, got caught, and now everyone hates you." She kissed Andrew hard, then turned with a dagger-smile. "If you hadn't fucked Jackson, I'd never have met my DrewBear."

"Just stop," Eric finally said.

The queasy feeling in Allie's stomach churned as she tried to meet each of their eyes. Only Darcy and Andrew stared back— Darcy smug, Andrew taunting, daring her to speak. Kenzie dropped her gaze the instant their eyes met. The others kept their eyes fixed anywhere but on her.

Allie's head fell. Her arms wrapped around her middle, trying to hold herself together. Her voice cracked, "You know none of this is true."

"You should go," said Kenzie, her voice unsteady.

Allie turned to leave. Behind her, Andrew's voice carried low but clear: "She's every bit the desperate liar you said she was."

She quickened her steps, barely making it to the bathroom before the nausea overwhelmed her.

The rest of the day dragged. Jackson ignored her in Trig, sitting apart from Darcy while Darcy whispered barbs throughout the whole class.

By the final bell, Allie was numb.

She'd lost the group, but she'd never wanted a group. Never wanted a boyfriend, so she told herself Andrew's betrayal shouldn't hurt so much. The real loss, she told herself, was Kenzie, and Allie had lost her months ago.

If she was honest with herself, though, she knew better.

Losing Kenzie hollowed her heart; losing Andrew hollowed everything else.

At home, her mom was on the phone. Allie froze in the foyer.

"No, Rachel, we're not getting divorced. If I couldn't afford to leave him then, I certainly can't afford it now. And what if he does lose his job? We can't afford the house, the cars— college for Allie—on my salary."

Allie tiptoed to the kitchen, grabbed cold leftovers, and ate in silence.

Upstairs, she submitted her French worksheet, went to bed, and tried to pretend life was normal.

When she opened Burn Book, her breath caught.

The pop-up:
You didn't think we'd let you off that easy, did you? Secrets never stay secret, Allie.

She was back in the #1 trending spot.

She checked in and made the required six comments, but what did it matter? Even when she complied, she still got punished.

She didn't even want to know.

She forced herself to click on the trending icon. There was only one thread, but it already had 200 reactions and 75 comments.

Again, a series of three photos.

First: she was bundled in a sweater and a puffy vest the week of exams. The windchill had been -20, and she'd bundled up because she'd known the school would be cold.

Second: Today, jeans and a turtleneck. She was shocked at how thin she looked.

But she didn't understand until she saw the third picture and read the caption. Allie and her mom leaving the hospital. Allie in a wheelchair, looking tired and miserable.
Three pictures, one story. You do the math. Hint… it involves a plus sign. No wonder she's failing Trig.

Her stomach lurched, vision narrowing until the words bled together. For a heartbeat, she thought she might actually faint. Slowly, the blur cleared, and the comments came into focus- line after line stacked under the pictures of her.

QueenDee: The ultimate FAFO. I hope she chokes on the Karma sandwich.
SoFull: Slut's gonna slut.
ILv2Vape: So how soon can she have sex again? Asking for a friend.

The comments, stacked in order —first ones pinned forever. Anyone that opened the thread would see those. Allie let that sink in.

She scrolled, numb, past the ugliest ones until-

IndigoGirl: Or maybe everyone could mind their own body? Just a thought.
OccamsRazor: Tell me you're a misogynist without telling me you're a misogynist.
Anony-mouse: Y'all are gross. She doesn't owe anyone an explanation.

* * *

A new comment appeared.

RandomRando: TBH, I bet she's smarter than 90% of the people here.

Before she could second-guess herself, she typed her comment and hit submit.
CatherineJames: Probably more like 99%

She closed the app immediately, shaking. Had she just made it worse?

But those three comments replayed in her head. Not everyone hated her. And Kenzie had saved her at lunch today —kept her from blurting about Burn Book. Maybe she hadn't lost Kenzie completely.

She texted:
Allie: You know me. You know none of this is true.

She stared at the screen until her eyes blurred. No dots. No reply.
The message still said delivered when she woke the next morning.

CHAPTER 49- WASH, RINSE, REPEAT AGAIN

Allie shut off her alarm before it buzzed a second time. Sleep had been shallow, her brain looping between her dad's closed office door, her mom's sharp tone, and the glowing Burn Book logo she couldn't escape.

She wanted to stay under the covers. Just for today. But she'd already missed so much. Her grades couldn't take another hit—and her dad wouldn't allow another absence. So she dragged herself up, one heavy movement at a time.

Downstairs, the silence was worse than shouting. Her dad's office door was shut tight. Her mom stood at the counter, clutching her coffee mug like it was the only thing keeping her upright.

"You ready?" her mom asked without looking up.

Allie nodded even though the question wasn't really about her.

At school, it was like she'd stepped into a play already in progress, her character written out of the script. Jackson brushed past her without slowing. Kenzie offered a quick smile but nothing else.

Darcy leaned against Andrew's locker, laughing at something he whispered. People stared at Allie as she walked by, then bent their heads together.

In class, a girl's voice carried just enough to catch: *"That's her. The one I was telling you about."*

She kept her head down, moved through classes, scribbled notes she barely absorbed. At lunch, she ignored Miss Lindstrom's questioning gaze. If she hadn't already heard the rumor, she would soon.

By the end of the day, she told herself she'd survived, and maybe that was enough.

She resolved to push down the pain, ignore the chaos, and focus on school. She needed to get that scholarship to Madison —a place that was big enough for her to start fresh and leave all of this behind.

Then it was the same thing, day after day. Wash, rinse, repeat.

By February, the days blurred together into one long stretch of gray.

The snow, once bright and beautiful, was piled into filthy ridges along the streets. Her dad hid in his home office most mornings, too disheveled and hungover to make the drive to Madison. At the Wednesday Roundtable, they'd suggested he get himself together before showing up again. No one wanted to go down with his sinking ship.

Her mom snapped at everything.

School wasn't much better. Whispers followed her from class to class. It didn't feel like this was just Burn Book anymore. Freshmen who would never get an invite whispered and pointed.

Her only saving grace was her schoolwork. She poured herself into assignments, forcing everything else to the edges. Teachers praised her essays, her test scores, the way she always came prepared. It was the only part of her life she could still control.

In spite of that, she still felt like she was spinning out of orbit. She constantly lost and misplaced things- her favorite hoodie, the earbuds she always kept in her backpack, the paperback she'd left on her nightstand. The diamond earrings she'd shoved in the back of her jewelry drawer? Gone. She half-feared her mom or dad found them and were waiting to confront her, or even worse, she'd moved them and completely forgotten she'd done it.

She told herself day after day that she didn't miss him. But just like the earbuds and the hoodie, he was always at the edges of her mind. She poured herself into essays and worksheets, but in the blank spaces —between classes, in the lull of study hall—her thoughts slipped back to him. She found herself wandering instead of working, checking the stairwell where they used to meet, scanning the parking lot for his car. It was like some obsessive Where's Waldo in real life. She just needed to talk to him once, without Darcy. To tell him the truth. Not Burn Book's truth.

Then one day she ran into him—literally. Head down, thumbs flying as she texted her mom, she turned a corner and slammed into someone solid. His hands caught her before she fell. She didn't need to look up. Her body already knew. The way she fit against him, the way he breathed her in—like he hadn't forgotten either.

For a heartbeat, neither of them moved. He kissed her forehead, then pulled back, eyes narrowing.

"How's Jackson?"

Her stomach dropped. "Andrew, please. That's not—none of that's true. If you'd just listen to me, I can explain—"

He gave a soft, bitter laugh. "Explain? Maybe if it had been one time, but it wasn't.The hallway. The car. Your bedroom." His voice cracked. "Your bedroom. There's nothing you can say, Allie. I saw the way you looked at him. Everyone did."

Her breath caught. He'd sent her the hallway pic. As far as she knew, the others were only on Burn Book…

"Andrew, you can't believe what's posted on there. They twist everything just to make it worse. You know that."

He shook his head slowly, as if her denial only proved him right.

"I didn't! I swear—I never—I would never do that to you. Please, you have to believe me." She pressed one hand flat against his chest, desperate, feeling the thud of his heartbeat under her palms. The other cupped his cheek, forcing him to look at her. He looked away.

Her voice broke with urgency. "I don't want Jackson. I want you, Andrew. Come back to me." She slid her other hand up to his cheeks, pulling him closer, forcing his eyes on hers.

For a flicker of a moment, something softened in his face. His jaw flexed beneath her fingertips. She tugged him down and their mouths collided. The kiss was all heat and memory—hungry, familiar, devastating. Her fingers threaded through his hair as his hands slid against her waist, pulling her closer, his body betraying the calm mask he wore for everyone else.

"Like Kevin would actually date someone like her." Darcy's voice rang loud, echoing from the top of the stairwell. Sophie's laugh was even louder, if that was possible.

Andrew tore his mouth from hers, leaving her wanting and breathless.

Then he leaned in, lips brushing her ear like another kiss and said softly, "Darcy isn't you. She never could be."

Her heart leapt—until his tone shifted, colder.

"The problem is, you made your choice. And now you have to live with it." The floor dropped from under her feet.

By the time Darcy and Sophie appeared, he had already stepped back, smooth as if nothing had happened.

"The office is that way. You can't miss it." He gestured down the hall, voice steady, mask in place.

Then he turned, kissed Darcy on the cheek, and walked away with them, leaving Allie frozen, too stunned to defend herself, her body on fire and her heart splintering apart all over again.

Her dad finally landed a mid-level client near the end of the month, enough to buy him another ninety days at the firm. But the relief never reached their kitchen table.

Kenzie was staying back to work during Spring Break—at least that's what Stacy told Angie. It would be the first break they hadn't spent together since kindergarten. The thought of being in the condo with just her parents- no Kenzie to run interference- made her stomach knot.

Spring Break wasn't something to look forward to. Not this year.

By March, the whole school buzzed about the ACT on the eleventh and the break that followed. Teachers reminded them daily. Flyers hung on locker doors. Her mom stacked prep books on the kitchen counter like talismans.

Allie stared at them sometimes, willing herself to believe that if she just nailed the test, it might fix something. But even she knew better.

March first's trending banner on Burn Book hit her like a punch in the gut. For once, she wasn't in the top five. Drew and Darcy had the number one spot: Couple Goals.

She told herself not to click, but she was a moth to the flame.

* * *

Darcy's PicSee caption, "Love looks good on us" had inspired an entire thread of comments about how perfect they looked together.

PatientZero had pulled it from PicSee and posted it here. Allie swiped in and out of threads, chasing the thought tugging at the back of her mind. Patient Zero had posted every thread about her.
And this: The Darcy thread was the only other one.
Was it possible that Darcy had two usernames?

CHAPTER 50- THIRTY

Allie double checked her answers, hit submit, and watched the numbers crawl onto the screen.

Reading- 36.
English- 34.
Science- 28.
Math- 22.
Composite- 30. Again.

Her throat tightened. She heard her father's voice in her head, *"You can get a 32 if you actually try, Allie." "You're not applying yourself." "If you'd just focus on the test instead of Kenzie and those other kids…"* If she couldn't score higher than a 30, it was clearly a lack of effort on her part. Except she really was trying.

She shut the laptop without reviewing a single question. What was the point? Thirty felt like a wall. She pressed her palms to her eyes until stars burst behind them, then let the room go quiet around her.

The next day at school, voices drifted from under the stairwell as she came down the stairs. One familiar, low, and coaxing. The other, unknown, hesitant, and conflicted.

"My dad will kill me," the girl whispered.
"He never has to know," the boy replied.

Allie froze, the metal rail cold under her hand. The words ricocheted through her- the exact same thing Andrew had said to her. She couldn't move until she heard his voice again, his tone firmer: "I'm leaving. You can stay or come with me. It's your choice."

A door slammed.

"AJ, wait!" The girl called.
AJ?

* * *

Allie bolted down the stairs in time to see the girl rush through the exit.

It was true. AJ was Andrew. And Drew? Of course he was.

She didn't understand what was going on, but she knew it wasn't good. For the first time, the urge to tell the truth pressed so hard it hurt.

The next day blurred into a scavenger hunt she couldn't win. She hovered by the stairwell between periods. Loitered outside the cafeteria. Pretended to tie her shoe outside the bathroom door. The girl never appeared.

By the final bell, Allie felt like a ghost clinging to the edges of hallways where she no longer belonged.

That night, she forced herself through another practice test. Thirty. Again. She shut the laptop and lay back, staring at the ceiling, remembering last semester's Wednesday nights—how being with Andrew had felt like oxygen.

On PicSee, Kenzie smiled with Eric, Darcy leaned into Drew, Trent and Teagan bracketed them—six of them together. Six without her. Without Jackson. Their spots erased like they'd never existed. She cried herself to sleep.

The following afternoon, she finally caught the girl by the stairwell.

"Wait. Please. I need to talk to you." Allie huffed, out of breath. "I know you don't know me, but…"

The girl stiffened. "I know who you are," she interrupted. "Everyone does."

Allie shook her head, catching her breath. "People think they know me," Allie said, voice shaking, "but they don't."

"I don't know if you feel like you need to tell me about Darcy because you and I look like sisters or what, but I already know. AJ's told me all about what a nightmare she is." Her tone softened, almost sympathetic. "I understand why Jackson cheated on her with you."

Allie's breath caught. She reached for the girl's arm. "But it *never happened*. I need to tell you about Andrew—"

The girl yanked free, stepping back like she'd been burned. "You are as messed up as everyone says. It's not enough that you broke Jackson and Darcy up; now you're here... doing what? Trying to break AJ and me up?"

She turned, then spun back, jabbing her finger at Allie. "His name is AJ. And you better stay away from him. Do. Not. Ever. Talk. To. Me. Again." Each word a step forward until they were nose to nose.
Allie swallowed hard. The girl glared once more and stalked off.

That night's practice test cratered. Twenty-two. The score pulsed on the screen until her eyes blurred, and she shut the laptop off to ease the ache in her chest.

CHAPTER 51- OPTIONS

Friday morning, Miss Lindstrom asked Allie to come by during lunch.

She was startled that the door was closed, marked with a sign that said, "Lunchtime conference. Please come back later." She hesitated, *was she the lunchtime conference?* Miss Lindstrom opened the door and welcomed her in. "I'm so glad you could make it. I know we don't usually do Fridays." Allie forced a nervous smile.

The classroom felt warmer than the hallway, so Allie shrugged off the cardigan.

"Sit," Miss Lindstrom said gently. "You look wrung out."

"I'm fine," Allie lied.

Miss Lindstrom waited. "I think you would feel better if you talked about it."

Talked about what? That all of her friends hated her? That the whole school thought she was a whore who'd had an abortion? About Andrew or Drew or AJ or whatever his name was? Allie's mouth opened before she could stop it. "I can't get past a thirty. I'm trying—every night I'm trying—but it keeps getting worse. I got a twenty-two last night." The number tasted like failure. "My dad—he wants a number that proves he's not wasting his time and money." *Apparently, we're going to talk about the ACT.*

"*You* are his time and money." Miss Lindstrom said firmly. "With your GPA and a score above thirty, you could be looking at a full ride to Whitewater."

Allie blinked. "What?"

"Don't look so surprised. Half your Common App practice essays mention Whitewater." The smallest smile. "I pay attention."

Allie sat stunned. Miss Lindstrom had just expressed the goal she hadn't let herself acknowledge, the one that had been keeping her sane the past few months. Hearing someone else say it out loud felt so real — and so overwhelming.

"It'll never happen," Allie sighed. "I have to go where my parents tell me."

"You have options." Miss Lindstrom's voice stayed even. "Full scholarships include room and board. You could work for spending money. Tutor English—"

Allie considered this. "I'm not exaggerating about relying on them. I'm not allowed to have a job. I don't even have my driver's license."

Miss Lindstrom's expression softened. She sat back. "Okay. This isn't something you have to decide today. Or even this month. But I need you to hear me: you have options, Allie. You are smart and kind, and you work hard. You'll be successful anywhere you go."

Allie stared at her hands.

"Take your foot off the gas this weekend," Miss Lindstrom added. "Give yourself a chance to breathe. Let your brain settle. You already have the knowledge to rock this test. Don't get in your own way."

The words landed like a blanket she hadn't realized she needed. Allie nodded, not trusting her voice.

Her dad was passed out in his office when she got home, tie loosened, snoring softly. In the kitchen, her mom looked up fast, panic flickering in her eyes. "Another practice test tonight?"

"No." The word surprised them both.

"Oh." Her mom's shoulders loosened. "Are you going out with friends?" There was a hopeful lilt there that stung; it hit Allie then that her mom hadn't noticed—no one had come around or called or texted since before Christmas.

"No."

Her mom hesitated. "Then… popcorn and a movie? For old times' sake?"

Allie nodded.

They laughed through Legally Blonde, their feet under the same throw blanket, the smell of butter clinging to the air. For the first time all week, she let herself breathe.

And then it was test day. The room hummed with the quiet scrape of chairs and the tap of keys. Allie worked the passages, the equations, the bubbles of panic that tried to crowd her vision. When the final screen lit up, she hovered, then clicked submit.

Outside, cold air flushed her cheeks. Her mom was waiting by the curb, hands wrapped around a paper cup.

"How do you feel?" she asked.

"I don't know," Allie said honestly.

Her mom opened the passenger door. "I love you," she said, steady and sure. "And I'm proud of you. No matter what that score says."

Allie slid in, the heat running, the smell of coffee warm and real. For the first time in a long time, she let the words in.

Allie dreaded spring break. Her dad said they couldn't afford it, but her mom refused to stay home. *Even if it's not warm, there's no snow in Myrtle Beach,* she'd said.

The trip wasn't so bad. Her dad sobered up enough to make business calls. She and her mom walked the beach, browsed shops, and wandered museums. By Saturday, things almost felt normal.

Allie packed before bed, turned off the light, and—like brushing her teeth—checked Burn Book. A pop-up froze her in place:

The first rule of Burn Book? We don't talk about Burn Book. But people have been talking. And we know who you are. Bad things happen when you break the rules.

Her skin prickled. She clicked through anyway.

Trending #1: a classmate in handcuffs, being shoved into a police car. Caption: Do you need more proof that bad things happen? Two yes votes. 288 no. She voted no. Unreal.

The second: a group of girls circled a car with four flat tires. Caption: Do you believe we know who's talking? 321 yes votes. Zero no.

Her heart thudded as she checked in, left her required comments, and closed the app. It felt like living in 1984.

She was almost asleep when her phone buzzed in a pattern she hadn't heard in months.

"Allie, I'm so sorry," Kenzie sobbed. "I didn't know who else to call."

Adrenaline jolted her wide awake. "Kenz, slow down. What's wrong?"

"Darcy's party. Too many drinks. I passed out in a guest room—" Her voice cracked. "I woke up with Drew on top of me."

Allie's stomach turned. "What?"

"Then Darcy walked in. Screaming. Fighting. Blood everywhere— her nose. Broken. They shoved me out. No way home."

"Are you drunk?"

"It's a party, Allie. Of course I'm drunk." The snap came quick, followed by a shaky apology.

"Are Trent and Teagan there?"

"No," Kenzie answered quietly.

Allie already had FindUs open, relief flooding when Kenzie's dot blinked by the lake. She kept the call going as her thumbs flew across the screen.

Allie: This is an emergency. Please answer me.

Trent: What's up? How can I help?

Allie: Something happened between Kenzie and Darcy. She's drunk and wandering on a country road. Please get her before something bad happens.

Trent: Send the location.

Teagan: Pick me up on the way?

Trent: Leaving now.

"They're coming, Kenz. Hang on." Only sniffles in response.

Allie stared at the screen, memories shoving in—the deck at Andrew's cabin, the sherpa blanket, the heat from the fireplace. Her body remembered what she wanted to forget.

"I see headlights," Kenzie whispered. "But I'm hiding. What if it's Darcy?"

Allie: I think she can see you. Can you see her?

Teagan: No, but we see the lake house.

Allie: She's hiding. She's afraid you're Darcy.

Through the call, voices called Kenzie's name—then her cry as they reached her. Chaos, yelling, struggling. Finally, Teagan's voice steadied.

"Allie told us a little," she said gently. "Do we need to take you to the hospital? Did he hurt you?"

More shouting.

Trent talking to her, muffled by the way she was holding her phone.

Teagan: She's still fully dressed. But she's so drunk. Are you sure she said Drew did this?

Allie: Positive.

"No hospital," Kenzie cried.

Allie: Don't take her to Memorial. Her mom works there.
Trent: She doesn't want to go. I don't know if we can make her.
Allie: I'm not there. I don't know what to tell you.
The car engine rumbled through the line.
Teagan: She's asleep.
Allie: What are you going to do?
Teagan: Take her home? IDK.
Allie: Please don't leave her alone.
Teagan: We won't.
Teagan spoke softly through Kenzie's phone: "You're a good friend to her. Sorry we were so shitty to you."

Allie swiped her phone closed and cried herself to sleep—not sure if it was for Kenzie, for herself, or because she already knew this was only the beginning.

CHAPTER 53- THIS ISN'T OVER

Monday morning was chaos.

No groceries. No milk. No bread. No granola bars for her backpack. Dad was slumped over his coffee; apparently, sobriety had ended when they pulled into the driveway last night. Mom was on the edge of snapping.

Flustered, Allie ran back upstairs to grab her APUSH packet from her desk, except it wasn't there. This is where she'd left it, right? She remembered finishing it and putting it in the folder. Maybe she'd put it on the kitchen table so she'd remember to put it in her backpack before school. Except it wasn't there either.

Last Sunday had been even more chaotic than this morning. Her mom, with her checklists, her dad —still hungover or already drunk— yelling at them about where they'd put his files. Did her folder get mixed up with his files?

"Allie!" her mom called. "We need to leave. Now."

Her pulse quickened. She hated being late.

The packet wasn't due until Thursday, so she had time to redo it, but still… she was finally ahead on something, and now that was gone.

She slung her backpack over her shoulder, frustrated, and ran out to the car where her mom was waiting impatiently.

"Mom?"

Her mom was white-knuckling the steering wheel, practicing the breathing exercises Allie still did sometimes.

"Mom?"

Angela flinched, then composed herself. "Yes? What's up?"

"I couldn't find my APUSH folder this morning. Could you please look through the stuff Dad brought to the beach? I think it got mixed up with his stuff."

"I can," Angela said, carefully. "But can you just print it out and fill it in again? Your dad's not like us… it could be anywhere…"

Allie knew what her mom meant, but wasn't saying. She didn't want to make things worse for her.

"Yeah, sure. But I think the printer's out of ink. Can you pick some up, or should I try to print it out at school?"

Allie fidgeted in the lunch line. She understood there hadn't been anything for her to pack, but she hated hot lunch this year— hated trying to sneak around Darcy and all of her former friends. She was almost out of the cafeteria when the shouting started.

Kenzie's voice cut through the noise.

"I can't believe you're taking his side! We're supposed to be best friends."

Sophie shot to her feet.

"You are so neurotic. She's my best friend—has always been, always will be. You tried to seduce her boyfriend, got caught, and now you're blaming him? Get the fuck out."

Darcy rose too, bruises around her eyes barely visible, touching Sophie's arm like she had it handled.

"It's okay, Soph. I've got this. Of course I'm taking his side. I saw you with my own eyes."

"Oh my God," Kenzie said, voice climbing. "When you walked in, he was on top of me, trying to get my pants down."

The cafeteria went dead silent. Every head turned.

Darcy's eyes narrowed. "You're just as delusional as that freak you used to hang out with. Why would Drew want you when he has me?"

Kenzie flushed, then found her footing. "I'm sure that's a question you've been asking yourself ever since your last boyfriend dumped you for 'that freak.'"

Darcy visibly recoiled.

"Must've been a blow to your ginormous ego. Maybe Drew's as sick of your shit as Jackson was."

Drew pushed back his chair and stood, bored.

"I'm right here, and I can speak for myself," Voice confident, carrying across the cafeteria, but eyes drilling into Kenzie's. "I get that the 'Me Too' movement dictates everyone should automatically believe you. Never mind you were wasted out of your mind and the one who came on to me." He pulled Darcy closer to him. "I'm blessed to be with someone who sees through your lies." He leaned in, whispered in Darcy's ear, and the only sound was her sharp inhale.

Kenzie's chest rose and fell. Sophie, Darcy, Drew—just the three of them left at their table. Allie wished Teagan or Trent were here to back Kenzie up, but it didn't matter. She had the truth.

Then Darcy's voice rang out, confident and cold. "Well, there you go, Kenzie. I believe him because he's kind and honest, and he loves me. He would never do what you're accusing him of." She turned and offered Drew a beatific smile.

"Fuck all of you." Kenzie's voice shook as she pointed straight at Drew. "This isn't over. You're a lying piece of shit, and I'm going to make sure everyone knows it."

She stormed out, swallowed by the cafeteria's boos and chants of "fight, fight, fight."

Allie slipped out, too. Pride swelled in her chest—Kenzie had stood up to them. Said the words Allie wished she could. But underneath it, the sting lingered. Kenzie really believed she was the kind of girl who would sneak around with Jackson behind Darcy's back.

By the time she reached Miss Lindstrom's room, the seats were nearly full. She scanned for an empty spot and froze. Trent and Teagan sat together at a table in the back.

Her heart sank. There went her safe haven. She turned to leave.

"Allie!" Teagan called and waved her over. "Please. Come sit with us. We need to talk."

Her stomach tightened. For weeks, she'd been invisible to them, erased. Now they were waving her over like nothing had happened.

She slid into the chair, not bothering to set her lunch down. "What?"

Teagan leaned forward, voice low. "We just… wanted to say thank you. For what you did over break."

Allie stared, unblinking.

Trent's jaw tightened. "She was so drunk, Allie. I don't want to think about what might have happened if you'd hung up on her."

"You didn't have to text us when Kenzie called you," Teagan continued, not missing a beat. "We know it's been…." She paused, "Um, awkward? You two haven't really been friends lately. But thank you. Again."

Allie twisted the strap of her bag between her fingers. "Is that all?"

Teagan's voice softened. "I want to believe her. I do. But she was wasted, and… sometimes people misinterpret things when they're that out of it."

Trent's eyes darkened. "Or sometimes they don't." Teagan nodded faintly.

"So you believe Kenzie?" Allie asked.

"Yes," Trent answered definitively. "Maybe?" Teagan's answer was less sure.

Allie stared at them, all of the emotions from the last months threatening to spill over.

Teagan swallowed. Trent looked away.

"Okay, then," said Allie, standing. "Good to know." She hesitated, willing herself to say the words. At the door, she finally found her voice.

"You're welcome," she kept her tone flat. "I'm also glad for Kenzie that you were there to rescue her and make sure she was safe." Her voice hitched. "I'm so happy she has such good friends that believe in her." The sarcasm was obvious, but underneath it was the truth- they hadn't even let her tell her side of the story. She reminded herself that she didn't need or want them. She needed to focus on her classes, her ACT, and getting to Madison, where them choosing Kenzie wouldn't matter.

Neither of them argued. They just watched as she left the room.

The final bell felt like a release. Allie wove through the crowd, head down, her backpack heavy against her shoulders.

Her mom's car was already at the curb. She reached for the handle when she heard it:

"Allie!"

Kenzie's voice.

Her hand froze. For a second, she almost turned. Almost. Instead, she yanked the door open, slid into the seat, and snapped her seat belt.

"Please go," she told her mom, ignoring Kenzie's rapidly approaching figure..

Angela's eyebrows lifted. "Is that—?"

"Please. Just. Go." Allie forced her eyes forward.

Her mom hesitated, then pulled into the pick-up line traffic. Out of the corner of her eye, Allie saw Kenzie standing on the curb, bent over, panting.

Angela glanced between her daughter and the shrinking figure in the rearview mirror, lips pressed together like the pieces were finally falling into place.

CHAPTER 54- TRENDING

Allie was still thinking about Kenzie and everything that had happened that day. Her thoughts wouldn't settle, so she knew she wouldn't fall asleep anytime soon. She picked up her phone to check in on Burn Book, but set it back down.

Teagan and Trent had rushed to Kenzie's side like heroes in some rescue scene, but when it was her—when the lies had been about her—no one had cared. Not even them.

And today in the cafeteria? She still felt stuck between awe and jealousy. Kenzie had stood up to Darcy and Drew today, really stood up. Allie couldn't imagine doing that.

If Teagan and Trent were eating lunch together now, that left Darcy, Sophie, and Andrew at their lunch table. Jackson had been eating in Dr. Grey's room, and on the days she ate there, too, they sat on opposite sides and ignored each other. Eating there every day wouldn't be much different now that Trent and Teagan had taken over Miss Lindstrom's room. But then, where did that leave Eric and Kenzie? Did they break up?

At least one thing had gone right. She hadn't needed to reprint the APUSH packet—she'd finished the assignment and turned it in without it. Still, she was annoyed with herself for losing it in the first place.

Her thoughts circled back, inevitably, to Andrew. His hair pulled back, his shirts sharper, his whole performance—because that's what it had to be—pretending not to know her, pretending to be in love with Darcy. He couldn't really have fallen out of love with her and into Darcy so fast. That wasn't possible. Was it?

She grabbed her phone again, thumb hovering over the Burn Book icon, her pulse quickening.

Like usual, a pop-up blocked the screen.

Welcome back, Allie. Here's your chance to show Kenzie what a shit friend she is. Your comment on her #1 trending thread is:

Kenzie is a cheating slut.

All previous rules still apply.

Allie closed the pop-up, and sure enough, Kenzie's thread was #1. She didn't want to know what the thread was even about, much less say something like that about Kenzie.
She checked in, made her required six comments, and hesitated.

When she finally clicked, her screen filled with a collage of Kenzie and different boys, none of them Eric, in very suggestive positions. This is what Kenzie had been doing at all of those parties she wanted Allie to come to?

Something wasn't right. A lot of these pictures were taken after Kenzie and Eric started dating. However else Kenzie had changed this year, she would never cheat on someone after how her dad's infidelity had destroyed her mom.

She looked more closely at one of the earlier pictures, from this summer. Kenzie in a tiny tank top, arms wrapped around a tall boy with black hair. Except that couldn't be Kenzie. Yes, Allie was sure the face was hers, but the strawberry birthmark that covered her shoulder was missing.

What was going on? Who would bother putting that much work into faking them? Everyone knew BurnBook worked like the paparazzi... lurking until it got dirt on someone. Or could manipulate it to look like dirt, but this was different. Someone had altered those pictures.
What was the second rule of Burn Book? No Filters.

PatientZero started the thread, but pictures like this were usually pulled from other places — mostly PicSee and other socials.
And how was this the #1 trend? It had just been posted and didn't have any comments yet.
She didn't have time to finish that thought before the comments started pouring in.

QueenDee: Drew's lucky he got out of that room. She fr would've given him herpes or something.
SoFull: She probably has herpes

SuzeeQ: I care why?

Allie winced. Then, a different voice cut in.
SuperSwiftie: Wild how If this were a guy, he'd be a stud not a slut.
IndigoGirl: Preach

And then the floodgates opened.
DietCokeLVR: maybe she was with so many bc none of them were any good?
Goin2MadTown: Facts. Justin Glass is awful in bed. Would not recommend.
SuzeeQ: Tim still calls it his "weenie"
LittleDebbie: Peter Kennedy kisses like he's trying to resuscitate you.
53066: Don't bother with Mike Taylor. He always turns in his assignments early. Every. Single.Time.
MKE4Life: Don't even get me started on Noah Brandt's socks

Allie's eyes widened as it spiraled — half the guys in the junior and senior classes, ripped apart in real time. Size, stamina, technique, even hygiene- everything was fair game. Nothing else about Kenzie. Her cheeks burned, but she couldn't stop smiling as she read the comments.

And then, just as suddenly, it was gone. Every picture. Every Comment. Wiped clean.

Relief and disappointment tangled in her chest. Kenzie had been spared the humiliation, but it stung that when the lies were about Allie, no one jumped in to defend her. And the way it all disappeared so fast made Allie's skin prickle.

Allie had her sandwich open on a napkin, but she wasn't eating. Neither was Jackson. As usual, they were the only two in the classroom, sitting on opposite sides of the room, the silence between them louder than the hallway chatter.

Dr. Grey shuffled a stack of essays, then glanced up. "Ellis, your mom just texted me—said to tell you to check your ACT account."

Her stomach flipped. She'd overheard kids bragging about their scores last week. Why were hers taking so long? "Umm, okay?" She dug for her phone before remembering it was dead, the black screen refusing to light up.

Allie opened her Chromebook and logged in with shaky fingers. The page loaded agonizingly slow, and then the numbers appeared.
Reading- 36
English- 36
Science- 32
Math- 30
Composite- 34.

She pressed a hand over her mouth. "Oh my god." All those problem sets with Dr. Grey, weekends buried in prep books, endless practice tests... Miss Lindstrom had been right. She rocked this test.

From his desk, Mr. Grey looked up. "Well? What'd you get?"

"Thirty-four," she whispered, as if saying it too loud might shatter the moment. "I did it."

The world stilled- then she felt him. Jackson. The warmth of him behind her, familiar before her mind even caught up. Muscle memory pulled her to her feet.

When she saw his grin, she launched herself at him. He lifted her off the ground, and for one dizzy second, she let herself melt against him, cheek to his shoulder, heart slamming against his chest. It felt like before.

"Thank you for believing in me," she breathed against his neck.

He let go all at once, like her closeness had burned him- but the pain in his eyes said it wasn't the hug he couldn't hold on to, it was her. It felt like the floor dropped out from under her.

She met his eyes and the air thickened between them- relief that she'd proved herself colliding with the guilt she'd tried to ignore but couldn't shake. For a heartbeat, it felt like before, like they hadn't broken.

Then the weight of everything between them pressed in, reminding her they couldn't go back.

The moment broke first with him.

The smile faded, and the light in his eyes died with it.

"That's great, Allie. I knew you could do it," his voice hitched.

Before she could reply, he grabbed his lunch, tossed it in the trash, and walked out, leaving her rooted in place, still breathless from the contact.

She made it through the rest of the day with her head down, moving on autopilot. The final bell was like a saving grace.

At home, she dropped her dead phone on the nightstand and left it there. The silence was easier than whatever might be waiting for her.

She finally gave up and plugged it in at bedtime. The glow lit up with three unread messages.

Trent: So proud of you! I knew you could do it.
Teagan: 34!!! That's amazing!
Kenzie: I'm so sorry Allie. And I'm so proud of you. Maybe we can do popcorn and movies tomorrow like old times?

* * *

She fought the urge to respond, to celebrate with them the way she would have before. Her thumb hovered, then dropped away. She let the screen dim and set it down without even opening Burn Book. For the first time in months, she skipped the check-in and let the world spin without her.

CHAPTER 56- FORGIVEN

For once, her parents surprised her.

They were going away for the weekend to "reconnect." No networking, no client calls.

More than that, though, she got to skip school. A "mental health recovery day."

She pretended that she hadn't heard them arguing earlier. Her dad insisted that she'd already missed enough school, that UW Madison would frown on her attendance record. Her mom overruled him.

"You deserve a day off," she said before they left.

At first, Allie was excited. Staying home meant she didn't have to face Trent and Teagan. Or Kenzie. Or - god forbid- Jackson.

As soon as they left, she crawled back into bed. When she woke up again, she had ice cream for lunch in her pajamas. She did her homework in bed instead of at her desk. The house was quiet in their absence, and for a few hours, that felt like a gift.

By mid-afternoon, though, the silence was deafening and her thoughts were spiraling. *Maybe she should check in on Burn Book? Should she invite Kenzie over? Why had it felt so good when Jackson hugged her? Could Miss Lindstrom actually help her get into Whitewater without her parents? Was it weird that her parents were "reconnecting?"*

Eventually, she dressed and went downstairs to find something on ReWatch. She'd taken all of her favorite Meg Ryan movies off of the auto-watch queue. They all belonged to Andrew now, and she couldn't watch them anymore. She switched from movies to shows.

She tried Gilmore Girls, but didn't make it through the opening theme song. Friends was out. She and Kenzie had binged the whole series two summers ago. She scrolled until she landed on The Office. Ridiculous humor, nothing she'd ever watched with anyone else. It would do.

* * *

At some point, she'd fallen asleep. She woke up to a dark house, silence, and the TV prompting, "ARE YOU STILL WATCHING?"

Her stomach growled, insisting it was time to get up.

She flicked the lights on as she walked through the house. In her bedroom, she guiltily made the bed she'd abandoned earlier. She grabbed her water glass and headed back downstairs.

Maybe she wasn't paying attention because the day had been so relaxing. Maybe it was because it had been so long since the kitchen had been full of so many wonderful smells. For whatever reason, she didn't realize something had changed until just before she crossed the threshold… her natural momentum carried into the kitchen even as her brain recognized something was wrong.

For a fraction of a second, nothing had changed. Andrew smiled at her and held a glass of wine out to her, and her body relaxed into the familiar scene. As if in slow motion, her heart soared, and she smiled back at him.

Then her brain caught up, and she froze.

Andrew was in her kitchen, with wine and dinner from Velluto.

She watched as he crossed the kitchen with the glass of wine, then felt him kiss her on the forehead. "I've missed you," he whispered.

Was this really happening?

He took her hand and led her to the table. "I'm gonna follow where you lead." She heard the Gilmore Girls' theme song in her head.

Instinctively, she knew she needed to stay calm. To keep him calm. Her heart pounded frantically, not listening to her brain as usual.

"What are you doing here?" She finally found the courage to ask, taking a sip from the glass he held to her lips. He knelt on the floor next to her.

"I was worried. You didn't check in last night, and you weren't in school today. I brought you soup. To make you feel better."

Where was her phone?

* * *

"Thank you, but I don't think Darcy is going to be happy about this." She took the top off of the soup container in front of her. Out of habit, she offered the first taste to him. It was such a natural thing to do.

He smiled, then moved to the seat next to her. "Who cares what she thinks?" He kissed her hand, then brushed her hair behind her ear. "I just wanted to hurt you like you hurt me."

Her blood went cold as she struggled to stay calm. He took the spoon from her and fed her. The soup burned the roof of her mouth.

"But I forgive you," he tipped the wine glass to her mouth again. She swallowed obediently as he forced her to drain the glass. He filled their glasses again and turned his attention back to her.

"I don't understand, but I forgive you," he continued. "Because that's what love is. Hurting. Forgiving. Making up." He slid his chair closer, leaning in to kiss her neck.

Every nerve screamed at her to run, but muscle memory betrayed her —her breath hitched, body leaning into the touch it once craved. She felt the cool of the metal against her skin as he clasped the necklace around her neck again and fought the urge to run.

The weight of it pressed against her collarbone, heavy like the promise they'd made before.
He held the glass to her lips as she finished another glass.

"I love you," he whispered and waited.
"I love you, too," she whispered back. Her brain was still panicking, answering in survival mode, but her body was betraying her. She wanted him.
She froze when his lips met hers. She couldn't do this.
"Baby?" He paused, reacting to her.

"It's just so much," she grasped at straws, "You...here with me again. You've been ignoring me for months." Where was her phone? She struggled to maintain eye contact with him.
Andrew pulled her up from the chair and into him. He nuzzled

into her. "You hurt me so much. I couldn't be around you. But we can make up now."

Heat flared in her body before her mind could catch it, a reflex carved by months of collisions and apologies that had always ended in the same way- tangled in the sheets, breathless. She didn't hesitate when he gave her the glass to finish.

"What did you mean when you said I didn't check in?" She knew she needed to stall, to distract him, even as her body continued to betray her.

He unbuttoned her jeans as she set the glass on the table.

"On Burn Book," he guided her hand to the button on his jeans. "You're so clever, CatherineJames. You picked that so I would know it was you." Her head fell back as he kissed around her neck, breathing heavily.

Across the kitchen, her phone buzzed. The pattern was familiar, but she was distracted by the memories of how many times and how many ways he'd proved he loved her. She didn't resist when he turned her and gently pulled her out of the kitchen.

When the doorbell rang, she startled and pulled away. He pulled her back into him immediately. "We should go upstairs now," he breathed.

"Allie?" Kenzie called hopefully. "I've got the popcorn and Cokes, but my key isn't out here anymore, and you aren't answering my texts."
Allie's head swam, struggling to come out of the haze Andrew had created.

She winced as Andrew crushed her wrist, pulling her towards the stairs. "That fucking bitch," he muttered.
"Kenzie?" Allie shook her head, trying to clear the fog. Andrew whirled on her as she planted her feet, refusing to be dragged to her bedroom. Her breath caught at the look of absolute hatred on his face.
"She's not your friend." Andrew's voice was low and dangerous.

* * *

"Allie??? I have Skittles!" Kenzie sang and pounded on the door. From the landing, Allie could see the lights across the street flick on through the picture window above the front door. She froze.

"Make her go away," Andrew growled. "Now. Before she ruins the night." Allie squirmed, trying to get out of his painful grasp on her wrist.

Her phone buzzed in the kitchen. It buzzed again.

"She should've learned her lesson at the lake house. I'll make sure she learns it now."

"You're hurting me," Allie whimpered, not fully processing what he'd just said.

Andrew leaned in, close enough to kiss her, but instead locked eyes with her and breathed, "It will stop hurting once she's gone." His attention turned back to the picture window, where more lights were flickering on outside.

"Never mind," he hissed. "I'll take care of it."

"Go away," Allie yelled at the front door, panicked. What did he mean he'd take care of it?

The pounding stopped. The pressure on her wrist relaxed.

"Let me in, Allie. I'm so sorry for everything." Kenzie yelled back through the door. "The extra key isn't where it used to be. You have to let me in." Andrew tightened his grip and twisted her arm. She cried out.

"It's too late, Kenzie. You picked Darcy. Now go away." She hoped they couldn't hear the quiver in her voice.

"God, you're sexy when you're angry," Andrew whispered, voice now soft and velvety. Allie fought the bile that was working its way up her throat.

"Allie, I said I'm sorry," Kenzie pleaded and pounded on the door again.

Allie's phone buzzed nonstop in the kitchen.

Andrew leaned, "Make her go away or I will."

"It's too late," she shouted angrily. "You picked her over and over. All year. You gave her that stupid picture and let everyone laugh at me on that stupid app that you put on my phone." Allie gasped for air, all of the hurt and anger since the beginning of the year pouring out. " You promised this was going to be our year, and instead you turned into some dumb Barbie and ditched me." The tears were streaming down Allie's face now. Andrew pulled her into him, and she could feel that he was hard. What the actual?

"Fuck you, then!" Kenzie screamed back. "I've stood up for you, protected you. Dealt with all of your crazy habits and routines. We're done." Kenzie screamed and kicked the door as the neighbor across the street walked hurriedly towards her. Her footsteps retreated heavily off the porch.

"That was beautiful," he whispered, kissing her neck and unhooking her bra.
"I can't," she whispered, pushing him away. He tightened his hold on her and pulled her into a hard kiss.
"I want you." He started working her jeans down. "Here. Now."
Her head reeled, her body was paralyzed with fear- all of the familiar longings forgotten.

"Tell me how much you want me," he whispered, moving her hands to the waist of his jeans.

The doorbell rang again, and they both froze. Her neighbor, Mrs. Campbell, called through the door, "Allie? Are you okay in there?"

Allie almost cried with relief. "For fucks sake," Andrew swore, buttoning up his jeans.

"Allie, honey? Your mom wanted me to come check on you bc you're not answering your phone, and then your friend was kicking the door, and I feel like I should call the police if you don't answer the door."

* * *

Andrew shook her roughly, waking her out of her stupor.

"I'm fine," she called out, buckling under the strength of Andrew's grip on her arm.
"I'll go," he whispered to her. "But this isn't over. We're not over."

"I need to come in and look around so I can tell your mom you're okay."

"Me and you," he promised. He pressed a final, bruising kiss to her lips, then he broke away and was gone — down the stairs in a blur of motion. When she heard the back door click shut, she opened the front door and let Mrs. Campbell in.

Mrs. Campbell sat with her in the front room until she was sure Allie was okay. They called her mom and talked her off the ledge. At that moment, Allie was on autopilot. Being the good girl, keeping the secret.

Whenever she thought about that night, though, she would never fully understand why.
Why didn't she scream for Kenzie to get help?
Why didn't she tell Mrs Campbell or her mom about Andrew right then?
Why didn't she try harder to warn Kenzie and tell her the truth?

If she'd had the courage to speak, maybe it all would've ended differently. But she told herself that staying quiet was the only way to protect Kenzie- and herself.

The weekend dragged on in silence.

She reached out to Kenzie again and again, needing to explain, to warn her. But her texts went unanswered, and calls couldn't be completed.

On PicSee, all of the pictures of Kenzie with Darcey and Drew were gone, and there were no new posts since before Spring Break. Allie was grateful she hadn't been blocked completely, though Kenzie had changed her settings so Allie couldn't comment or message her.

Allie even texted her mom to ask how the weekend was going. Two hours later, the reply came: Fine

By Saturday night, the house was too empty. Andrew's promise- *we're not finished*- hung over her like a cloud. She finally texted Teagan, desperate for noise, for company… for a witness?

Teagan: Hey sorry. At the movies. Maybe another time?

Allie debated going to her room, but decided against it. Andrew knew how to jimmy the lock on her window. At least down here, there were multiple ways out. Still, she brought one of her dad's golf clubs in and fell asleep hugging it like she used to hug Andrew's little panda.

She woke to her parents arguing. Dad's voice slurring and rising. Scrambling, she grabbed her pillow, blanket, and the golf club and bolted upstairs as they came in from the garage.

Her mom caught her on the landing, eyes flicking to the pillow and the club. She gave Allie a questioning glance but didn't press — her dad was yelling too loud for her to answer anyway.

Later, Angela tapped on her door and peeked in.

"Redecorating?" She asked, indicating the stacks of books and figurines Allie had relocated to her desk.

"Sort of?"

Angela crossed the room and sat on Allie's bed, setting her school books aside. Her voice was quiet. "Do you have a minute?"

Allie froze.

"So this weekend didn't go the way I'd hoped," Angela started, gaze dropping to her hands.

"I—I told your dad I can't do it anymore. I asked him to move out." She hesitated. "It's just temporary, though. Just until he gets his drinking under control."

Allie reached for her hand.

Angela squeezed it, then exhaled. "We don't have all of the details worked out, but we're all going to have to make some adjustments. Money's tight. I agreed to do aftercare every day, even after-after care if they need me. So you'll have to ride the bus home and make do by yourself until I get back. Could be six, maybe eight."

Her words blurred together after that. Allie was stuck on *by yourself.*

Angela must've noticed because she gave her daughter's hand another squeeze. "It'll be okay. We'll be okay." She stood, pausing in the doorway. "I couldn't do this if you weren't so responsible, Allie. You've handled every bit of extra freedom we've given you this year without a problem. You're the only steady thing I can count on right now."

The words lingered like both a confirmation and a conviction.

You've handled every bit of extra freedom we've given you this year without a problem.

The words were meant as praise, but they crushed her. She hadn't handled anything. If she told her mom about Andrew now, she'd lose the trust she'd worked so hard to earn, prove she couldn't handle the little bit of freedom she had— and worse, she'd be adding another burden when her mom was already carrying too much.

* * *

She took one of the pictures from her bookcase and balanced it on the window ledge, adding it to the chaos on her desk. If Andrew jimmied the lock, the frame would fall, the piles would crash, and she'd have enough time to be ready for him.

She checked the golf club under her covers, turned off the light, and forced her body through its breathing exercises.

Monday morning came heavy.

Her dad hadn't said goodbye when he'd left; he just slammed the door and was gone. Later, she'd heard her mom crying in the shower. Dinner passed in silence, and afterward they'd packed their lunches on autopilot.

"I know you hate the bus," her mom had said, "but I need to go in early so I can meet with the lawyer after school. I know this will only be temporary, but I need some advice just in case..." The words died in the air.

It wasn't just the bus Allie hated. With her mom working after-after care, she'd be alone until after 8 pm. She checked the piles on her desk, the frame on the window, and decided it had to be good enough.

The bus ride was too quiet, giving her thoughts too much space. She needed Kenzie to listen, to understand what Andrew had said. For a split second, she even considered warning Darcy, then shoved that thought away. Darcy would never believe her.

She was still weighing whether to try to fix things with Teagan and Trent when the bus pulled up and the panic hit. She didn't want to see Andrew.

Deep breath. Warn Kenzie. Keep it together for her mom. One foot in front of the other, she followed the stream of students into school.

To her surprise, Trent waited for her after AP Lit. "Teagan said you texted her?" The conversation flowed from there, the way it had before.

They were still talking when they walked into AP Bio. Teagan waved, and Allie let herself hope that maybe things with them could go back to normal.

Sure enough, Teagan walked with her to AP Psych and chose the seat next to her, instead of across the room.

* * *

Then Darcy sauntered in, flanked by a new orbit of girls ooohing and aaaahing over her earrings.

"Those must be at least a carat," one said, as Darcy tilted her head so the stones caught the light.

"Oh, they are," Darcy said, voice dripping with pride. "And it was so romantic. He said, *'You are the first thought in my head in the morning and the last before I fall asleep. If something makes me laugh, I want to tell you about it right away.'*"

Allie's body reacted before her brain did —head snapping up, heart stuttering, fingers reaching for the necklace she'd taken back off. She knew those words.

"And the box," Darcy gushed, "is gorgeous. Lavender velvet with little gold flowers all over it. He said they were his grandmother's and he'd been saving them to give to the right person. Happy three months to us!"

The girls squealed.

Allie froze, thinking of the velvet box she still hadn't found. She'd believed Andrew when he'd told her the exact same story. God, she was an idiot.

Mr Grant flicked the lights off and started the video, but Allie barely registered it. Her mind replayed images of her and Andrew at Gusto's, at the lake, the closeness they'd shared tangled up together… The stories he'd told— about his mom, about his step mom leaving, crying over it. Lies.. All of it. And she'd been stupid enough to fall for it.

When class ended, Darcy lingered by the door. She flipped her hair so the diamonds caught the light, her voice pitched so everyone would hear.

"Funny how it all worked out, huh, Allie? You ruined things with Jackson, and I ended up with Drew. And now you have… no one."

Her minions snickered on cue.

For one reckless second, Allie almost told her that Andrew had been at her house Friday night and what he'd said. But then she remembered the flash in his eyes, the threat coiled beneath his smile. Her chest tightened, her mouth went dry, and the courage drained out of her.

"Ignore her," Teagan said, oblivious to Allie's distress. They walked to her locker, and Teagan said, "Come eat lunch with us. It's so nice in Miss Lindstrom's room. We can work and talk and eat as long as we're quiet."

"I know," Allie's voice came out sharper than she intended. "I was eating there since last semester until you and Trent hijacked it. Then I had to go someplace else." It felt good to finally say it, even if she hated how she sounded.

They walked in silence until Teagan finally said, "This year has been so messed up. I don't know what's gotten into Darcy, but I'm sorry. I'm sorry none of us listened to you."

Allie shrugged, not sure what to say after all this time.

At Miss Lindstrom's door, Trent looked up and waved. Kenzie, Eric, and Jackson froze when they saw her. Teagan nudged her gently into the room.

"Hey," she said tentatively. Jackson looked down, but Kenzie stood up.

"No." Everyone turned.

"Kenzie, please. I…"

"Just stop, Allie. We said everything there was to say on Friday."

"Please listen to me," Allie reached for her as she brushed by.

"We're done," Kenzie said, shaking her hand off.

The group was silent, then Eric jumped up to follow her out.

"Thanks anyway, Teagan," Allie said, then turned and left the room.

Allie spent the rest of the day in the library, not ready to face Jackson in Trig or Trent in APUSH. More than anything, she wished things could just go back to the way they were before. She bolted for the bus when the final bell rang.

At home, she was still unsettled, unable to focus on anything until her mom finally came in, drained and gray with exhaustion. Allie heated up mac n cheese cups that they ate wordlessly on the couch. Afterward, her mom kissed the top of her head and disappeared to her room.

When Allie went to bed, she was too wound up to sleep. Her thoughts looped between Andrew's threat, Darcy's earrings, and Kenzie's rejection until she finally dozed off.

CHAPTER 59- APRIL FOOL'S

By Tuesday morning, the weight pressing on Allie's chest was so heavy she wondered how she'd make it through the day.

She barely made it through the front doors before chaos erupted.

Darcy and Andrew walked just ahead of her, hands brushing as they laughed and whispered, the kind of casual intimacy that was like a knife to Allie's gut. Across the lobby, Kenzie stood with Eric, his arms around her. When she looked up and met Allie's eyes, hope sparked for the first time since Friday night— maybe Kenzie would finally talk to her. Allie raised a tentative hand in greeting.

Before Kenzie could react, the lobby filled with shouting and a sudden burst of uniforms.

Everyone froze as police officers surrounded Andrew, and then everything happened at once.

"Andrew Mason," one officer announced, voice booming across the tiled space, "you're under arrest for the sexual assault of a minor."
The words slammed into Allie's chest. Her vision tunneled, breath catching in her throat.

Nearly everyone in the lobby had their phones out now, as Andrew leaned in and said something to Darcy. Without even flinching, he held his hands out to the officers, who quickly handcuffed them behind his back.

Gasps rippled through the crowd, followed by nervous laughter. People whispered that this was the best April Fool's Joke they'd ever seen.

Darcy clung to him, sobbing and screaming about Constitutional rights and mistakes and conspiracies. The school resource officer gently pulled her back as they marched him towards the doors. She broke free, ready to chase after him— until her gaze landed on Kenzie.

* * *

"You did this!" Darcy shrieked. The cameras swung instantly, not wanting to miss anything.

Eric pulled Kenzie into him, then stepped in front of her protectively as Darcy took a step forward.

"You couldn't stand that he didn't want you. You tried to seduce him and he blew you off, so this is how you get back at him?" She lunged. "You slut!"

The SRO grabbed her and, with the help of a secretary, dragged her into the office.

Allie turned to Kenzie, desperate to say something, anything, but the look on her best friend's face stopped her cold.

"I told you we're done." Kenzie's voice was flat, final. Eric guided her through the crowd, all eyes following their retreat.

Allie remained rooted in the center of the lobby, as the world moved around her.

Every class that day began with the same warning: *no discussion, no speculation.* The words blurred together, background noise she barely processed.

In AP Lit, Miss Lindstrom asked her to stay after class.

"Are you okay?" She asked gently.

Panic flared— *how could she know?*

"She's been your best friend forever," she continued, "that couldn't have been easy to see."

Relief rushed through Allie, but it was tinged with guilt. "We're not really friends anymore," she admitted, her voice unsteady.

"Sometimes friendships have hiccups. Don't give up on her yet." Miss Lindstrom studied her closely, then continued, "Is there anything else? Talking about it might help."

Allie shook her head, "No, everything's fine."

The look on Miss Lindstrom's face made it clear she didn't believe her, but she only said, "I'm here if you change your mind."

Allie nodded, but the words barely touched the sadness spreading through her.

She drifted through the rest of the day like a ghost, catching fragments of rumors as she passed through the halls.

Darcy had a breakdown and an ambulance took her away…
Kenzie and Darcy got in a fight…
Drew was expelled from his old school for sleeping with a teacher…

The rumors grew as the day wore on, each wilder than the last.

Her phone buzzed constantly.

Mom: Are you okay? I just heard the police were at the high school.
Mom: Allie? Are you okay?
Mom: Why were the police there?
Allie: I'm fine. Yes, they were here. I don't know why.
Mom: I can come get you
Allie: I'm fine
Mom: Text or call if you need me
Allie: 👍

She kept her head down and pretended to take notes, forcing herself to act like she cared about what her teachers were saying.

In APUSH, Trent leaned in and whispered, "I swear she was fully dressed when we found her, Allie. I didn't know."

Allie stared straight ahead but whispered back, "We're not supposed to talk about it."

But Trent wasn't finished. "It's going to be his word against hers, and Darcy will lie to protect him. What I don't understand is why she waited this long to go to the police. She hasn't said a single word about the party since the fight in the cafeteria. We all followed her lead and just let it go. But maybe we should say something? We should talk to the police so it's not her word against theirs."

Allie froze.

He frowned, lowering his voice. "And yesterday- she was acting really weird. I don't get it. Why wouldn't she say something to us?"

Allie's breath caught, blood rushing in her ears.

She was acting really weird yesterday.

Andrew's words flooded back: *She should've learned her lesson at the lake house. I'll make sure she learns it now.*

* * *

What if this wasn't about the lake house at all? What if Andrew left her house Friday night and went to Kenzie's?

A cold shiver ran down her spine.

The loudspeaker crackled to life:
Mr. Tracy, can you send Allie Ellis to the office, please?

Every head turned. Heat flamed her cheeks.

Trent gave her a questioning look, but Allie only shrugged. She packed her things and forced herself to stand.

The office was buzzed with activity, officers carrying crates and briefcases while the secretaries scrambled to keep up with the ringing phones. Allie hesitated in the doorway until she saw Miss Lindstrom talking with one of them.

"Do you know what this is about?" Allie asked her in a small voice.

The secretary slipped away, leaving Miss Lindstrom shaking her head. "No, but I can wait with you if you want."

Before Allie could answer, the principal opened his door and called her name. When she saw the uniforms inside, she stumbled back into Miss Lindstrom.

The principal smiled as if it were all routine. "It's okay, Allie, you're not in trouble. This is Detective Sanders." He gestured toward a petite blonde woman in a sharp suit. "She just has some questions for you."

Allie's voice trembled. "Why are *they* in there?" She pointed at the officers as they unpacked their briefcases.

"They don't need to be," Detective Sanders replied smoothly. "We're just following up on what happened this morning, trying to talk to as many people as we can today." She turned to the principal. "Can you set them up in a conference room somewhere?"

"I can," he replied, "but you need to wait to talk to Allie until I get back."

* * *

"I can sit in, if you'd like," Miss Lindstrom offered.

"Perfect," Sanders agreed. She waited until the officers filed out, then turned back to Allie with a small, practiced smile. "Come on in, I just have a few questions."

Allie's heart hammered as Miss Lindstrom's steady hand pressed against her back, guiding her into the little room.

Allie paused in the doorway, taking in the painted concrete walls, bland conference table, the metal chairs that scraped against the floor. Detective Sanders moved to the head of the table and gestured to the seat beside her. Miss Lindstrom gave her a gentle nudge, and Allie forced herself to move forward.

Detective Sanders settled in, flipping open a notebook as if she were just a teacher taking attendance.

"So, Allie, what grade are you in?"
"I'm a junior."

The detective jotted it down, "Do you play sports? Any clubs?"
"No." Her pulse thudded despite Miss Lindstrom sitting next to her.

"Any college plans?"
"My parents want me to go to Madison, then law school."
"Nice." Sanders smiled, writing again.

Allie let out a breath—until the detective shifted, her smile fading. "I know you saw what happened in the lobby this morning. When one of your classmates was arrested. We're talking to people about Andrew Mason."

"I don't even know him." It was out before Allie had a chance to think about it.

"No, no— no one's saying that." Sanders's tone stayed patient. "We're just trying to get a sense of him. Have you ever heard anything about him? Maybe seen him act in a way that felt aggressive? Anything that made you uneasy about how he treats people? How he treats girls?"

Allie shook her head, unsure if there was a way to take back her original denial without getting in trouble. Miss Lindstrom shifted closer, a quiet reminder that she wasn't alone.

The pen scratched steadily. The detective didn't look up, didn't press, just kept writing.

In the silence, Trent's words echoed loudly in her head: *We should talk to the police so it's not her word against theirs.*

"Darcy and Andrew are lying." Allie blurted. Sanders didn't react, and the words poured out faster: The party at the lake house. How Kenzie had woken up to find Andrew on top of her, tugging at her jeans. Her panicked call to Allie in the middle of the night. How they'd kicked her out, drunk, with no way home. Trent and Teagan finding her. How Kenzie's story had never wavered.

When Allie finally ran out of words, Sanders set her pen down. Her face gave away nothing.

Allie's stomach dropped. She'd wanted to help Kenzie, but what if her story didn't match? What if instead of protecting her, she'd just made it worse?

Even when Sanders offered a calm smile, Allie felt faint. "Thank you for coming in, Allie. I don't have any more questions right now, but we may circle back after we talk to other students. Don't panic if we call you down again, okay?"

Allie nodded, numb. Miss Lindstrom touched her elbow, guiding her up and across the room.

At the door, she hesitated.

She turned back to Detective Sanders and steadied her voice despite her trembling hands, "I've known Kenzie since kindergarten. She's not a liar. If she says it happened, it happened."

CHAPTER 61- FRACTURED

Allie couldn't stop replaying the interview in her head.

Every word, every pause, every time she'd said no too quickly or hesitated too long. What if her answers didn't line up with Kenzie's? What if she'd made things worse? Instead of helping, she might have just given Detective Sanders a reason not to believe her.

By the next morning, the whole school was buzzing. Phones glowed in every corner, kids huddled in clusters, rumors flying about who the police had talked to and why…

The story had made the news. Andrew's name was released because he was eighteen. So was Darcy's face — muted audio but still unmistakable, caught on camera screaming in the hallway. No one else's names were mentioned, but that hardly mattered. Everyone at school already thought they knew. Kenzie had gone home early yesterday and hadn't come back.

At home, it was worse.

Her mom hovered, peppering her with questions.

"Do you know him? Do you have classes with him?"
"They aren't going to let him back in school, are they?"
"Maybe you should stay home? Do your work from home like before?"

Her voice was sharp with fear, the same fear Allie'd heard her whole life whenever she wanted to do something new, but now it had a jagged edge to it. She was bone tired, running on coffee and panic, still double-checking every lock and clinging to FindUs like it was her lifeline.

Allie shook her head until her neck ached. "I don't know anything, Mom." She hated seeing her mom like this, but knew it would be so much worse if her mom knew the whole truth.

* * *

Kenzie came back to school on Thursday and didn't waste any time.

"Who told them? Who told the cops about Spring Break?"

Allie, Trent, and Teagan froze.

Her voice carried, sharp enough to turn heads in the hallway.

Teagan held up her hands, steady, calm. "Kenzie, in my interview, the question was literally, *Have you ever heard of Andrew hurting or trying to hurt someone?* It wasn't about you. They asked me, I answered."

Trent nodded. "Same. That was one of the questions."

Teagan's tone softened. "And honestly? Anyone who was in the cafeteria after Spring Break heard you accuse him. It wasn't exactly private. A lot of people could've told them."

Allie's stomach dropped.

"You—wait." Her voice came out smaller than she meant. "You're not the one who went to the police? They weren't talking about you?"

Kenzie's head snapped around, fury cutting through her expression.

"Well, they are now. Thanks to you three." Her eyes lingered on Allie, hurt threaded beneath the anger, before she spun away.

For a beat, none of them spoke.

"I don't understand," Allie said softly. "If Kenzie didn't go to the cops... why would someone else?"

A shadow crossed Trent's face. He glanced between them, his voice low. "What if this isn't just about Kenzie? What if there's something else going on?"

The words followed Allie the rest of the day, clinging like smoke, refusing to let go.

Friday morning, the air in the halls shifted again.

Andrew was back. His dad had paid bail — everyone said it like a number too big to imagine — and somehow he was allowed to return to school. He walked in like nothing had happened, chin high, Darcy glued to his side.

The school fractured fast. Some sided with Andrew simply because Darcy did —her word carried that kind of weight. Others looked at Andrew himself: the clothes, the confidence, the hot girlfriend, the money... To them, he was exactly the kind of guy the cops said he was.

The lines cut through the school like cracks in glass, and Allie felt the ground tilting beneath her.

She made it through the day on autopilot until AP Psych.

As she was packing up, the secretary stepped into the room. "Allie Ellis? You're wanted in the office."

Her heart stuttered. She slung her bag over her shoulder, head down— but Darcy was waiting in the hallway.

She leaned in, smile sharp as glass, "Keep your mouth shut, you freaky little narc."

The crowd swallowed her up, but her heart still hammered in her ears.

CHAPTER 62- IT'S INTERESTING

This time, Miss Lindstrom was in the office waiting for her. The principal and Detective Sanders were already in the conference room.

The principal said something, but all Allie could hear was Darcy: *Keep your mouth shut, you freaky little narc.* The threat clung to her like static.

Detective Sanders flipped through her notebook as Allie sat in the same uncomfortable chair as before.

"Thanks for coming back, Allie. I just have some follow-up questions, if that's okay."

Allie sat, hands folded in her lap. "Did I... did I do something wrong the first time?" She croaked, mouth and throat completely dry.

Sanders shook her head and handed her a bottle of water from a mini-fridge in the corner. "Not at all. You were very helpful. But sometimes new information comes in, or we hear a different version of the same event, and it helps to check in. To clarify. To see if you might remember something that you didn't before."

Allie's stomach twisted.

Sanders started soft again, asking about classes, routines, how she was managing taking five AP classes.

Allie gave clipped answers, afraid of saying the wrong thing, of making things worse.

Then Sanders asked her why she had study hall in the library instead of the cafeteria with everyone else.

She knows. "It was too loud," Allie fumbled. "I couldn't study."

"You study a lot," Sanders observed. "But I hear it paid off. A 34 on the ACT is impressive."

Allie blushed, still afraid to say anything.

Sanders leaned forward, her tone gentle but focused. "You and Kenzie have been friends for a long time, right?"

Allie shrank into her chair. "I got her in trouble, didn't I?" She asked, voice barely audible. Miss Lindstrom put a comforting arm around Allie's shoulder.

"Why would you say that?" Sanders asked.

"He didn't get arrested because of Kenzie, did he? I told you about the party and now she's mad at me…" She stared at the table. "Again," she whispered.

"She got into a very public argument with Darcy and Andrew in the cafeteria. Almost every student we've talked to so far has told us about it." Allie looked up to find Sanders staring at her. "Kenzie might not be ready to talk to us about what happened, but most of your classmates were."

Allie let that sit.

"I don't understand then," Allie dropped her eyes again. "Someone else got him arrested?" It was as much a statement as a question.

"Yes. Another student reported that he assaulted her." *Assaulted.* The word floated between them, pulling the oxygen out of the room.

"Who?" Allie whispered. Detective Sanders didn't answer.

Allie finally looked up again and met the detective's steely gaze. "This is an active investigation, Allie. I can't tell you that. But I can tell you he hurt her. And another victim came forward after the story hit the news."

Allie flinched, but Detective Sanders continued. "That's two victims that we know of, plus Kenzie." She put her hands on the table and leaned closer, lowering her voice, her words careful and measured. "His father has money, Allie. The kind of money that got a judge to let him come back to school while we investigate. The kind of money that makes things like this disappear so that he can keep on hurting people."

Allie heard her, but the words were echoey, and her peripheral vision was turning black. Miss Lindstrom opened another bottle of water and urged Allie to take a drink.

Detective Sanders sat back in her chair and set her notebook on the table.

"Is there anything you want to tell me, Allie?" Her voice was softer now, almost coaxing.

Allie shook her head immediately. "No." She was afraid to say anything else.

Sanders studied her, calm but relentless, before sliding a business card across the table. "If you remember something later, or if you hear something, call me. Anytime."

Allie nodded, but she knew she wouldn't —she couldn't.

Miss Lindstrom waited at the door for her. Before Allie reached it, Detective Sanders called out to her. "Hey, Allie?"

She froze, then turned around slowly.

"Everyone else at the school calls him Drew," Sanders observed, "But you call him Andrew. Every time. Why is that?"

Allie's stomach dropped, and the blood rushed to her ears. Miss Lindstrom placed a steadying hand on her back.

"I... I'm sorry?" Allie said.

"You're the only person that calls him Andrew. It's interesting." Detective Sanders didn't smile.

Allie forced her hands into balls to stop them from shaking.

"I, uh... I mean, you...You call him Andrew. And that's what the police called him when they arrested him."

"Of course." The practiced smile was back. "That makes sense. Thanks again for coming in."

Allie couldn't muster a matching smile, so she just mumbled something and fled.

CHAPTER 63- SNITCHES

Allie's phone buzzed. She saved the APUSH paper she was working on and saw that Teagan had texted.

Teagan: Check your CALENDAR. We need to talk

She hadn't opened the app in over a week and didn't want to.
Her phone buzzed again— she'd been added to a group chat.

Allie hesitated. She didn't like this. At all. Then her phone buzzed again. And again. Whatever was going on in the group chat, they were busy.

She swiped the calendar app and logged in.
The pop-up was simple, but devastating.

KEEP YOUR MOUTH SHUT, ALLIE

No new assignments. Just five words, pulsing like a heartbeat. Allie's blood went cold.

Another notification from the group chat popped up, and Allie swiped it away without reading it.

She closed the warning and saw only one trending thread.

Snitches Get Stitches.

Her hands shook as she tapped it open.

Rows of photos filled her screen- picture after picture of kids entering and leaving the same conference room where she'd met with Detective Sanders. Trent, Teagan, Jackson, Kenzie… even Darcy. But there were dozens of other faces too, classmates she didn't know, didn't recognize. Detective Sanders had talked to all of these kids last week?

* * *

Her breath caught when she reached her own picture. For a change, there were no likes. No comments.

Her skin prickled.

The comments were eerily absent for the #1 trending thread.

Another notification from the group chat. This time, she clicked on it.

Teagan: It's a threat.
Eric: It's an app.
Jackson: I think Teagan is right. I don't like it.
Trent: So what do you think we should do?
Kenzie: Nothing. Just ignore it.
Teagan: It's not going to go away.
Eric: Seriously, it's an app. Same as a game. If you don't like it, just delete it.
Teagan: We should tell someone about it. This is intimidation. Trying to keep people from talking to the police.
Kenzie: Please just drop this. The trending threads don't stay on top for long. It'll go away the same as the rest of them did.

Allie thought about telling them that the app knew her name, tracked her comments… threatened her.

Kenzie: I'm begging you. Just drop this.

Jackson's dots appeared, then disappeared.

Trent: This affects you more than the rest of us, Kenz. Are you sure?
Kenzie: I just want it to go away.

Teagan's dots appeared, then disappeared.
Eric: I say we let it go for now and see what happens.

Jackson's dots flickered, then vanished.

Nothing happened for a full minute.
Then Jackson gave a thumbs-up emoji. Trent followed. Then Teagan.

* * *

Allie'd missed her chance.

That night, she barely slept. Every time she closed her eyes, the words seared across her mind: *KEEP YOUR MOUTH SHUT, ALLIE.*

By morning, her body was heavy, her mind sluggish. Despite the grogginess, she felt the charge in the air as soon as she walked into school.

Kids clustered in the lobby, frozen in place, phones glowing in their hands. Conversations snapped like live wires.

She caught bits and pieces — enough to piece together that there had been an emergency hearing at the end of the day yesterday, and that the news outlets were reporting the outcome.

"He's got just as much right to be here as we all do."
"She's just white trash trying to cash in on her own drunken mistake."
"Innocent until proven guilty."

Before Allie realized what was happening, a girl shoved her way through the crowd and slammed another student to the ground, shouting about victim's rights.

The SRO burst out of the office, pulled the girl up and away from the group, and barked for everyone else to back away and go to class.

The crowd scattered, but the current didn't fade. The school felt like a powder keg waiting for a spark.

Allie found no comfort in the fact that Andrew wasn't allowed at school. The judge's orders didn't change the fact that he was still out there, free to show up anywhere else.

She thought about the string she'd taped across the back door. It wouldn't keep him out, but she'd know if he'd been there. She needed to convince her mom to change the locks, but her mom was barely keeping it together as it was.

* * *

The stack of papers her dad sent sat on the kitchen counter, edges curled from her mom thumbing through them all weekend. Allie hadn't asked what they said. She was afraid, based on her mom's tears, that she would end up hating her father if she knew.

As Allie walked to first period, the words from her screen echoed louder than the hall fights or her mom's sobs:
KEEP YOUR MOUTH SHUT, ALLIE

CHAPTER 64- I CAN'T

By Wednesday night, Allie was compulsively checking Burn Book, waiting to see what would happen. Kenzie had been right —the Snitches thread had gone silent, replaced by five new ones that trended in its place. But it wasn't the same. Even the trending threads had only a few likes and fewer comments. Nothing like before, when posts and comments came so fast she could barely keep up.

Even Burn Book felt like it was waiting for something. But for what?

Allie kept her head down, moving from class to class, dreading the next blow.

It came Thursday, when a hesitant voice stopped her cold in the hallway.

"Do you remember me?"

Allie turned. It was still like looking in the mirror. "Just because you and I look like sisters," she'd said.

She was paler now, with dark circles under her eyes, but then so was Allie.

"I'm Aubrey," she said softly.

"I remember you," was all Allie could say.

They stared at each other until Aubrey finally spoke again.

"You tried to warn me."

Allie's knees wobbled.

"About AJ," Aubrey continued.

Allie's chest tightened —she needed to get out of there. She couldn't have this conversation.

"You knew something about him, and you tried to warn me. You need to tell the police what you know."

"I.. I can't." Allie's voice was barely a whisper.

"You can't, or you won't?" Aubrey's voice cracked. "Why are you protecting him? You know he did this."

Allie's pulse thundered. "So it was you? That went to the police last weekend?"

Aubrey hung her head and took a deep breath. When she looked back up, her eyes were shining with something fierce and broken all at once.

"He knew my parents were gone for the weekend, and he wanted to stay with me. I told him no. I don't know how he got in, but I woke up in the middle of the night on Friday, and he was in my room." Her voice cracked again, and she took a steadying breath. "He kept telling me he forgave me. Forgave me for what?"

Her voice dropped to a whisper. "He raped me, Allie. Why are you protecting him?"

Allie's mind swirled with images she'd collected over the last nine months; that first night at the barn party, giggling nose to nose in bed, the bruises on her wrists, the stairwell kiss he abandoned for Darcy, the look on his face as Kenzie pounded on the door... her mom in the kitchen, flipping through papers, silent tears streaming down her face... the black screen with the red letters: *KEEP YOUR MOUTH SHUT ALLIE.*

Aubrey searched her face, watching, waiting. When Allie dropped her head, she pleaded, "Please, Allie, it's just my word against his, and the police say we need more."

Allie looked up, "But there's another girl. Detective Sanders said someone else came forward. It's not just your word against his," she said hopefully.

Aubrey's expression fell, hurt giving way to frustration. "Why are you doing this? You *know* something."

"I can't," Allie whispered.

Aubrey's face hardened. She shook her head, hands flying up. "Unbelievable."

She spun on her heel and stormed off, leaving Allie rooted in place, gutted and defeated.

CHAPTER 65- SPIRAL

The words wouldn't let her go.

Allie carried them through the end of Thursday, through the bus ride home, through the dinner she didn't eat. They were louder than the hall fights, louder than her mom's whispered phone calls, louder than the television that stayed on 24 hours a day now to cover the silence.

He raped me, Allie. Why are you protecting him?

She lay in bed, mentally running through a new checklist. The table by the front door was nudged a few inches to the left now so the vase of flowers would topple if the door opened, the string on the back door handle tied to a stack of pots on the counter, the interior deadbolt thrown on the garage door so that even with a key, no one could come in that way now. The picture frame was still on her window ledge, ready to crash at the slightest shift. She'd done all of this, but still didn't feel safe.

Downstairs, her mom moved quietly through the house. Allie prayed she wouldn't notice the improvised defense systems.

Before she slept, Allie opened Burn Book. The Snitches thread had slid off the front page. She closed the app without commenting, her mind too restless to process what she was seeing.

He raped me. Allie didn't believe it. Well, she believed Aubrey believed it, but he couldn't have actually *raped* her. She must've misunderstood the situation.

He had cried when he talked about his mother and stepmother leaving. She'd felt his tender kisses, heard his declarations of love. She fell asleep clinging to a highlight reel of their best moments, willing them to blot out those terrible words.

Friday morning, dread pressed on her chest before she even

opened her eyes. The house was still and silent. No coffee brewing, no clatter from the kitchen. Her heart raced until she remembered there was no school that day, not for her or her mother. Easter Weekend.

Tiptoeing to her mom's room, she sagged at the sight of her mother asleep with the light still on, divorce papers scattered across the bed like leaves.

She wanted to wake her, to pour out everything about Andrew and Aubrey and Darcy and Kenzie and… everything, but looking at her like that, Allie knew she couldn't.

The day dragged like wet concrete. She reset the doors, sat at her desk, tried to study. But couldn't push Aubrey's words far enough away for her assignments to make sense. She did the laundry just to move, restless in her own skin.

Her mom burned dinner, swore, and dumped it in the trash.

"It's fine," Allie reassured her, pulling the cereal down from the cabinet.

Later, they turned on a movie they ignored, each lost in their own thoughts. Allie finally worked up the courage to talk to her mom, but her mom interrupted. "Is it okay if we skip dyeing eggs this year?" Allie hadn't even thought about it. "I'll still make ham on Sunday, but you know your dad won't be here, right?"

"It's fine, Mom. I'm too old for eggs anyway. And maybe we can go out to eat? That would be nice, right?"

Her mom's smile didn't meet her eyes. "That sounds great, but I've already got the ham and green beans. We don't have to change everything just because he's not here."

"Sounds good," Allie lied, though the last thing she wanted was to sit at the table and pretend like everything was fine.

"I'm gonna head upstairs. Sorry about dinner. I promise I won't ruin Easter dinner." She gave Allie a quick, unsettled hug and disappeared.

He raped me. Allie couldn't escape the words. What if Aubrey had been drinking and just didn't remember what actually happened?

* * *

Saturday stretched even longer, slower. They cleaned the house like their lives depended on it. Each lost in their own thoughts, too distracted to enjoy the calm once the work was done.

Another night of pretending to watch a movie. Another night of moving furniture, setting traps after her mom went to bed. Of lying in bed with her golf club, convincing herself everything was fine.

Allie couldn't stop thinking about those words. Even if Aubrey was wrong, nothing was okay right now.

Sunday hurt worse than she'd imagined. No church. No egg hunts or baskets.

When her mom pulled out the ingredients for Easter dinner, she stared at them like the directions were written in a different language. Eventually, she put them away, and they ordered pizza.

Mid-afternoon, Teagan sent a meme to the group chat wishing everyone Happy Easter. Everyone, including Allie, chimed in, and then the chat went silent again.

Later, she curled against her mom on the couch the way she had when she was little.

"I miss him, too," her mom said sadly.
"So can he come back?"
"If he gets his drinking under control. He has before."
"Before?" Allie sat up and studied her mom, the deep lines around her eyes and mouth that made her look sad all the time now.

Her mom's eyes were tired as she explained: how he'd left when Allie was small, come back sober, slipped again. Allie pieced it together—middle school dinners eaten in her room to avoid fights, gauging his mood in the first five minutes, lying to teachers about bruises.

"He didn't really go back to school my freshman year, did he?" She asked as her mom shook her head.
"So this is the third time you've kicked him out?"
Her mom's eyes brimmed with tears. "I knew who he was when I

married him. You don't just give up on someone you love."

They sat in silence. Allie desperately wanted to tell her everything, but one look at the tear sliding down her mom's face, and she knew she couldn't.

"Love isn't easy, but it's not supposed to be like this. It's not supposed to hurt." Her mom said softly, stroking Allie's hair. "Remember that when you get older and fall in love."

Allie inhaled deeply. "What if..." she started, but then her mom's phone rang.

"It's Aunt Rachel," her mom said, kissing Allie on the head and swiping to answer. "Yeah, we're fine," her mom's voice drifted up the stairs. "I never imagined we'd have ham pizza for Easter dinner, but it was fine..."

By Sunday night, setting up her defenses felt routine. She turned off the light and went upstairs. The golf club still lived under Allie's blanket; she hated how the weight of it made her feel both safer and sicker.

She opened the group chat. Nothing.

No one but Darcy had posted on PicSee. Everything about her Easter... Andrew noticeably absent. She'd heard his attorneys had told him to "lay low."

She sighed and opened Burn Book. Another Drag the Brag thread featuring Darcy, but Allie closed out without commenting. Nothing popped up, no warnings, no threats. The app didn't seem to be keeping track of that anymore.

She set her phone down and turned off the light, but silence pressed in. She picked it up again and tried to find Aubrey on social media, but there was nothing. Allie didn't know anyone at school with a smaller digital footprint than hers, but there wasn't a trace of Aubrey at all.

Lying in the dark, she tried not to replay anything, which meant she replayed everything.

Detective Sanders in the conference room —*You're the only person that calls him Andrew. It's interesting.* Her stomach tightened.

Andrew and that final, brutal kiss before he fled that night- *Me and you.* Her chest ached.

Aubrey in the hallway, small and burning at the same time. *He raped me.* The words clanged louder this time. They didn't sound like a misunderstanding. They sounded like the truth.

And underneath them, the memory of the black and red pop up pulsing like a heartbeat- *Keep your mouth shut, Allie.*

Her eyes flew open, unaccustomed to waking to daylight. She was covered in sweat, heart pounding. The dream dissolved in fragments- Andrew, Kenzie, Darcy's earrings, Aubrey. She struggled to hold on to anything about it.

The earrings. The lavender box. Where were her earrings?

She searched her room frantically —dresser, nightstand, bathroom, under her bed —but found nothing except the necklace Andrew had put back around her neck that night. She dropped it back in the dresser drawer and slammed it shut.

Then she froze.

Her gaze locked on the drawer again. She'd worn that lock necklace faithfully until the day she'd confronted Andrew in the stairwell. After that, she'd thrown it in the drawer and tried to forget about it.

Except… how many mornings had she found it on her nightstand instead? She'd told herself it was just some kind of broken-hearted sleepwalking. But she hadn't sleepwalked since she was a kid.

Her ears rang as she gripped the dresser to steady herself.

Andrew had come in through the back door that night.
She'd just come downstairs from her bedroom.
So how did Andrew have her necklace?

The horror dawned slowly, then accelerated like a racecar.

He'd let himself into her house before. How many times had

Andrew come into her house, into her room, while she slept?

Her stomach flipped, and she ran to her bathroom, retching until nothing was left inside her.

Her mom came into her room mid-afternoon to see if she wanted to go shopping. Allie said no, relieved and guilty in the same breath.

"Hey, Mom?" Allie called out, knowing she couldn't keep this to herself anymore.

Andrew had been in their home multiple times. They *had* to change the locks.

"Hang on, Allie, there's someone at the door."

Her mom's voice rose, high and panicked, before the front door slammed. Then came the rushed call to Aunt Rachel.

"There was an accident," she told Allie a moment later, tears streaming down her face. "Your dad is okay, but he hit someone." Allie reached for her jeans on her chair, but her mom held up a hand. "You need to stay here. I don't know what to expect."

"I wanna go see Dad. I'm going to the hospital with you."

"He's not in the hospital, Allie," her mom's voice cracked. "He's in jail. He was drunk."

Allie's heart dropped.

"I promise I'll call you when I know more, but you can't go. Okay?" Her mom looked her in the eye and held her gaze until Allie finally nodded. Her mom gave her a quick hug and kiss, then flew back down the stairs, talking to Rachel again.

"It's all my fault," her mom cried into the phone. "He wanted to come over, and I told him no. He got drunk and tried to drive here anyway. If I'd just said yes, if I'd just told him he could come over, this wouldn't have happened." Her mom's voice disappeared into the garage with the slam of the door.

Allie sat on her bed, stunned, playing her mom's words over in her mind. There was something familiar about them. She struggled until a fragment of her dream broke free to her conscious mind. *"It's all your fault,"* dream Aubrey had said. *"If you had just given him what he wanted, none of this would have happened."*

* * *

Dread spread through her like a stain.

That night. Andrew unbuttoning her jeans, pulling her upstairs. Kissing her neck. Aubrey's voice layering over it. Aubrey in the hallway, recounting her version of that same night. *"I woke up and he was in my room. He kept telling me he forgave me. Forgave me for what? He raped me, Allie. Why are you protecting him?"*

The horror finally landed. Aubrey hadn't misinterpreted anything. Andrew hadn't gotten what he wanted from Allie, so he had taken it from Aubrey.

Her stomach heaved again.

Back in her room, she curled into herself, knees tucked tight, the clock ticking, daylight fading.

At last, she pulled Detective Sanders's card out of her backpack and dialed. The phone rang twice- then her mom called, voice raw, "Allie, come down. I need to talk to you."

She threw the phone on her bed without another thought except for taking care of her mom.

The bus doors folded shut behind her, and Allie stepped down onto the pavement with the rest of the crowd. The sky was washed pale after four days of Easter break, but her stomach stayed heavy, sour from the long weekend at home. She tugged her backpack higher on her shoulder and started toward the front doors.

Each footfall punctuated the mantra that had kept her moving all weekend:
We need to change the locks. We aren't safe.
He's been watching me while I sleep.
I didn't give him what he wanted. This is all my fault.
Mom can't handle this.

She forced her breathing steady. No one knew. Not her mom, not Kenzie, not anyone.

All she had to do was get through the doors, find her locker, and act normal.
But when she pushed inside the building, she saw them.

Miss Lindstrom stood just beyond the glass office wall, posture too careful, expression unreadable. Beside her, Detective Sanders waited with one hand resting lightly on her notebook. They weren't chatting, just… waiting. For her.

Allie's pulse stuttered. Through the glass, Miss Lindstrom lifted a hand in a small, silent beckon. Allie angled away, pretending she hadn't seen. If she kept moving, maybe they'd let her go.
The office door opened wider behind her.
"Allie."

Her name carried out into the hallway — not loud, but clear enough that there was no mistaking it. She froze mid-step, dropped her head in defeat, then turned and retraced her path toward the office.
Miss Lindstrom stepped out into the main space, holding the door open wide, as if to guide Allie inside. When she reached out to rest a

reassuring hand on Allie's shoulder, Allie jerked back, shrugging it off. She'd trusted Miss Lindstrom, and here she was ambushing Allie with Detective Sanders.

Sanders's gaze held steady. "I had a missed call from you."

Allie's eyes darted across the crowded office; no one seemed to be watching. Her throat tightened. *Of course she has caller ID. I never should've called.*

"I—" she faltered, then pushed the words out. "I can't do this right now. I've got stuff going on at home." Her voice tried to sound casual and failed, cracking under the weight of it.

Miss Lindstrom shifted, giving a head nod towards the conference room, recognizing Allie's discomfort. "Maybe we should talk in there."

Sanders didn't move or look away. "I know about your dad. I know this weekend was hard for you and your mom. But you need to understand — it's hard for the girls Andrew hurt, too. And they don't get to pretend it didn't happen."

Miss Lindstrom's shoulders tightened; she flinched at the mention of Allie's dad.

Allie's grip tightened on her backpack strap. Heat crawled up her throat. "I don't know anything."

She turned and fled towards the door before either could answer.

"Allie," Sanders called after her — not sharp, not pleading, but steady. "Silence doesn't protect you. It only protects him."

The words stuck like burrs, following her down the hall no matter how fast she walked. By the time she reached her locker, her hands shook so badly she could barely work the combination.

She hated that the detective's words echoed in her head, merging with the ones already lodged there, until Sanders's voice was just another echo in the noise already filling her.

I didn't give him what he wanted.
This is all my fault.
Silence only protects him.

Her mom picked her up from school that day and gave her the

basic facts in a flat, tired voice- her dad had been drunk, crashed the car, and hurt someone.

A felony, and the bail was set so high it may as well have been the moon. She refused to put their house up as collateral, so he was still in jail. Her shoulders sagged under the weight of it, her exhaustion so heavy that Allie could feel it pressing from the passenger seat.

"I couldn't do it," her mom whispered, "I couldn't trust him not to make us homeless."

They pulled into the driveway just as a Spee-Dee delivery van rolled to the curb. The driver flagged her mom down, barely looking up as she signed the tablet.

The garage door rattled open, and the man carried three cardboard boxes from the van, dropping them against the wall like they were nothing. Then he drove off without a backwards glance, leaving the remains of her dad's career abandoned in their garage.

Her mom muttered something about mac n cheese cups and slipped into the house. Allie stayed behind, staring at the boxes... at the finality of it. Fired. She didn't need her mom to spell it out. An echo of an overheard conversation rose unbidden: *We can't afford the house, the cars —college for Allie —on my salary.*

She closed the garage door and followed her mom into the house, Sanders's words still burning at the edge of her thoughts.

CHAPTER 67- THE ILLUSION OF NORMAL

The days that followed blurred, heavy and airless.

At home, the boxes from her dad's office stayed where the deliveryman had dropped them in the garage. Her mom moved through the house on autopilot — coffee, work, bed — occasionally commenting on Allie's outfits or remembering to ask about Allie's grades. For her part, Allie stayed out of her mom's way, listening outside doors as her mom confided in Aunt Rachel about her dad.

At school, the police were gone by the end of the first week. Promposals, exam countdowns, and senior skip day rumors filled the void they left.

Her days folded in on themselves until one day, when Teagan leaned in during AP Psych, "Come eat lunch with us. We miss you."
Allie shook her head, remembering Kenzie storming off the last time she'd tried to sit with them.
"She misses you, even if she won't say it," Teagan assured her.

Sure enough, when Allie sat with the group in Miss Lindstrom's room, Kenzie offered her a small smile. It wasn't much, but it was enough to make Allie hopeful. Jackson didn't turn away, and Eric immediately put his hand out for her apples and peanut butter as if nothing had changed. For the first time in months, Allie felt some of the weight start to lift.

By Friday, April 25th, Andrew was still suspended, the police were forgotten, and the rest of the school had moved on.
So had Burn Book. The Promposals thread dominated the #1 trending spot, stuffed with blurry photos and over-the-top gestures in the commons. Beneath it, the other trending threads were just as relentless: Finals Freakout, Senior Skip Snitches, Glow up or Burn Out, Summer Bod Watch. The noise felt endless, but at least it wasn't about her.

At lunch, her mom had texted that aftercare was covered and

suggested a budget-friendly girls' night in —nothing fancy, but real time for the two of them to catch up. Allie clung to that all afternoon, though part of her expected her mom to forget or be too tired later. Still, the invitation felt like a small bright spot on the first truly warm spring day of the year.

When the final bell rang, she didn't rush for the bus. Instead, she slipped outside with her backpack slung over one shoulder and the paperback she'd just borrowed from the library tucked in her hands. She found a patch of sun on the low brick wall by the car line and sat to wait.

She shifted on the brick wall, lifting her eyes from the page, and noticed a woman standing off to the side. At first, she thought the woman was just waiting for someone, but the longer she stood there, the clearer it became- her eyes weren't scanning the crowd. They were fixed on Allie.

Before Allie could process what was happening, the woman strode towards her.

"Allie Ellis?"

CHAPTER 68- THE SLIP

"Allie Ellis?"

Allie froze. Recognition prickled—she'd seen this woman before, in news clips her mom always switched off too quickly.

"Do you know who I am?" the woman asked.

"I recognize you from the news, but I don't really remember," Allie admitted.

"I'm Assistant District Attorney Lauren Talley." Her voice was steady, clipped with the kind of formality that carried in a courtroom.

Allie's stomach dropped, and the paperback slid from her lap.

For a moment, Lauren let the words hang there, her title doing the work. This wasn't going to disappear into shadows, not this time. No intimidation. No favors called in. No judge quietly bought off. Then, she softened. "I'm not here as the ADA, though. I'm Aubrey's mom."

Allie's throat tightened. She shook her head hard, words spilling out in a whisper, low and panicked. "I don't know anything. I swear I don't."

Lauren's expression softened, not with pity but with understanding. She crouched to Allie's level, then sat beside her, her voice quiet. "I know why you don't want to be involved. I know it's terrifying. But, Allie—if no one comes forward, he walks. He always has. The charges get dropped, the girls get silenced, and he gets away with it." Her jaw set. "This isn't the first time, and we both know it won't be the last if someone doesn't stop him."

Allie paled, her breath stuttering.

Lauren studied her face for a long moment, then shifted tactics. "When you tried to warn Aubrey… was it because you thought AJ was going to physically hurt her, or just break her heart?"

The question hit before Allie could brace herself. Her reply was automatic, barely more than a whisper. "I didn't think he would physically hurt her."

Lauren tilted her head slightly, as though considering that. Then, evenly: "So you knew he was a player? You were trying to tell her about Darcy?"

"I just wanted her to know he's not a good person. I didn't want him to—"

Realization hit like a punch. Allie's hand flew to her mouth, eyes wide, as if she could shove the words back in.

Lauren didn't move, didn't speak. She let the silence stretch until Allie's pulse roared in her ears.

Then, quietly: "Did he do something to you that you wanted to warn her about?"

Allie shook her head vigorously, the movement sharp, panicked. "I didn't mean any of that."

"But you did, Allie." Lauren's tone held no accusation, only quiet certainty. "You tried to warn her because he's a bad person and you're a good person. You were looking out for my daughter." She paused, reaching out to gently rest her hand on Allie's trembling one. "Thank you for that."

Allie's head kept moving, denial tumbling out in broken whispers. "I don't know him. I don't know anything about anything."

Lauren's voice stayed steady. "I know you're scared, Allie. If he did something to you, or made you do something you're ashamed of, you can make sure he doesn't do that to anyone else." She leaned in, closing the space between them as if to shield her words from the rest of the world. "You have the power here, Allie."

Then she eased back again, giving Allie room to breathe, her tone still gentle but certain. "I can't make you talk to the police, to tell them what he did so they can stop him. But no matter how afraid or how ashamed you feel right now, I know you'll do the right thing—just like you did for Aubrey in the stairwell."

Allie's throat ached. She pressed her lips together, willing the tears back, determined not to let this stranger see her break. For a heartbeat, she wavered, raw and exposed, but then she pulled it all back in — shoving the words, the fear, the truth deep down where no one could reach it.

Lauren gave a small, almost cordial nod, her voice low but even. "I trust you to do the right thing, Allie."

A moment later, the crunch of tires on the curb made Allie's head snap up.
She gathered her book and backpack in one swift motion, like she couldn't get away quickly enough. Angela pulled in, lifting a hand in a curious wave toward the woman before her gaze slid back to her daughter.

Allie yanked the door open and slid into the seat, forcing a light laugh. "She was here to talk about women and the law. She thinks I want to be a lawyer because of Dad."

Angela's eyes lingered on her, suspicion flickering, but after a beat, she smiled and put the car in drive. Allie knew the smile wasn't real, but she loved that her mom was trying. As Angela chattered about their girls' night, Allie resolved to match her energy, to give her the evening they both wanted.
On the surface, it looked like she was invested in the night ahead — but underneath, every word of Lauren's still echoed, hot and unshakable, pressing against the edges of her chest.

Friday night had been their "girls' night in." Both of them smiling too brightly, laughing a little too loudly, pretending the weight of the week could be scrubbed off with some popcorn and an old movie. Allie had been glad for it, glad to feel they were at least moving in the right direction- but it had been work, keeping up the happy facade when she could tell her mom was pretending, too. That energy had stayed through Saturday.

But Sunday night felt different. She'd re-read her APUSH paper, hit submit, and packed her Chromebook away. Clothes for tomorrow, picture in place in the window- check and check. Finished just as her mom called up, "Popcorn's ready."

One glance at the living room told her the truth- no one was pretending tonight. Angela was sunk in the couch, remote in hand, aimlessly flipping through channels.

"I thought we were watching The Secret Garden? I already had it queued on ReWatch." Allie flopped onto the couch, the smell of salt and butter threading through the room.

"I'm tired, Allie." Her mom didn't look away from the screen. "Not sure I'll make it through a movie. The ladies at work were talking about that singing show, Make Me Famous, so I thought we could watch that. I can't figure this stupid thing out, though."

She flipped again and landed on the tail end of a news trailer. Andrew's face flashed across the screen — his school photo — as the voice-over promised more details at ten about pending charges and upcoming court dates.

She accidentally turned the TV off, trying to click away quickly.
Allie sighed and grabbed the remote.

"It's such a terrible thing," her mom sighed. "You don't know him, do you?"

"I told you I didn't," Allie said, heart pounding. "He's just a guy at my school."

"I can't imagine how those girls' mothers feel," Angela murmured, almost to herself.

Allie flipped to Make Me Famous, its catchy theme song providing a welcome distraction as Angela recognized it and started humming along.

Allie tried to force a smile, but couldn't. The words were stuck in her throat. This was her chance to talk to her mom, to open up about Andrew, but she couldn't make herself do it.

Instead, Allie settled on, "Are you going to let Dad come home?"

Her voice came out quiet, like it was trying a different question on for size, unsure how it would fit.

Angela stared at the TV, still as stone. For a moment, Allie wondered if she'd even heard. Then her mom drew in a sharp breath and turned.

"Do you want him to come home?"

The question startled her. What did it matter what she wanted? "Maybe?"

"Same," said Angela, voice low. "It's so complicated, Allie. Your dad is an alcoholic. There's no point pretending he's not anymore."

Allie absorbed the word, heavy and familiar. "But.. he's stopped before, you said so."

"He has." Her mom's mouth tightened. "But it never sticks. He believes he can have *one drink*. But one turns into two, turns into ten." She met Allie's eyes squarely. "I swore I wouldn't take him back after last time. After he hurt you."

Allie's stomach twisted.

"He hurt you, too," she said before she could stop herself.

"He did." The silence that followed wasn't empty; it was crowded, full of memory. Aunt Rachel showing up in the middle of the chaos, bundling them into the car, driving to the ER. Her mom and Aunt Rachel had framed the next weeks as "bonding time," so Allie had played along. Bonding, yes- her mom's bones bonding back together.

"Then why did you let him come back?"

* * *

Angela's answer was clipped, defensive. "It's complicated. He'd done the counseling. He was going to meetings. He missed you."

Allie bit her tongue. She couldn't remember a time her dad missed her, but she let her mom keep going.

Angela exhaled sharply, almost like she'd heard herself. "It's always complicated, Allie. That's the only word that seems to fit."

"I love him," she added softly.

The words landed like a bruise.

Complicated. The word tangled in Allie's chest. It was the same way she'd thought about Andrew —that love explained the knots in her ribs, the bruises on her wrists, the way she swallowed things she should've said aloud. Loving him had meant smoothing over the rough edges, finding ways to make the hurt her fault. Complicated had become the excuse, then the shield, then the trap.

"Are you going to let him come home? If he promises not to drink?"

Angela opened her mouth, but before she could answer, the front door handle jiggled. A soft, deliberate twist, like someone testing it.

Allie's stomach dropped. Andrew. Her gaze flicked to the fireplace poker, the lamp cord, anything she could use as a weapon.

Then came the pounding.

"Open the door, Angela," her father's voice slurred, loud enough to rattle the glass. "My key isn't working."

Their eyes met, wide and wild. Angela recovered first. She stood and headed toward the door.

Allie chased her down, grabbed her arm, and pulled her back. "No, Mom! He's drunk!" The raw fear coursing through her made her palms slick, her voice shrill.

Angela turned, gripping Allie's shoulders. "I promise you, he's not coming in tonight. I'll talk to him. It will be okay."

Allie clung to her mom as they edged closer to the foyer.

"You need to leave," Angela called out, careful to stay away from the narrow, decorative windows on both sides of the door.

He peered in, sneering when he saw them. "You left me in that goddamn cell. I've been there all week." His voice was low and menacing, but still carried through the glass.

Allie and Angela stood frozen.

"Open the fucking door!" He screamed, punctuating it with a kick at the glass.

Allie flinched. Angela instinctively stepped back, pulling Allie with her. "Where's your phone?" She whispered.

Panic shot through Allie. She didn't know.

Another kick. Another roar garbled by alcohol.

"Go!" Angela urged, giving her a small shove.

Allie stumbled back toward the couch, ripping through the blankets, hands shaking so hard she could barely grip the phone when she found it. She frantically wiped her sweaty palms so she could unlock the phone.

"9-1-1. What is your emergency?"

Allie's voice cracked as she stammered out the address, syllables falling over one another in a rush.

She rushed back to the entryway, clutching the phone like a lifeline, her words still tumbling out in a jumbled mess.

The pounding drowned out the operator until another sound began to cut through- distant but certain.

Sirens.

The police arrived without sirens, but the red and blue wash splashed against the houses, pulling neighbors out to their porches.

* * *

At first, the police spoke to her dad like friends. *You seem upset. Why don't you come with us? We'll sort this all out.* But when he resisted, their tones sharpened. Words turned clipped, commands edged with steel. When he shoved one of them, they tackled him to the ground, his curses spilling across the lawn and into the neighborhood.

Allie and her mom stood shoulder to shoulder at the narrow, decorative windows, watching it all unfold.

Eventually, they forced him into the back of the cruiser, still shouting.

"Go upstairs," her mom whispered, "I'll handle this. They don't need to talk to you." She slipped out the front door, smoothing her hair and pajamas into a mask of composure, as if pretending might convince the neighbors clustered on the sidewalks that everything was fine.

Allie stayed in the shadow of the entryway, peeking out the window as her mom spoke calmly to the officers while the neighbors gawked.

What if I'd been brave enough to run for my phone that night? She thought, beginning to spiral.
What if I'd been standing in the yard watching him get put in a cruiser instead of going to Aubrey's house?
What if I'd had the courage to tell Mrs. Campbell the truth?

Then, Aubrey's words: *He raped me. Why are you protecting him?*

Her thoughts echoed until her chest felt raw. She stayed at the window, blaming herself in silence until her mom finally came back in, guided her upstairs, and tucked her in bed.

Allie's alarm finally went off. She'd been awake for what felt like hours, lying still in her bed, just in case her mom had managed to sleep.

She reached for her phone, silenced the alarm, and froze at the sight of a new text waiting. Dread pooled low in her stomach. She'd known people would find out about her dad eventually, but hadn't expected it to be so soon.

She swiped to open it, her breath catching as she saw the text and then the picture that loaded.

080625011013: Keep your mouth shut, Allie.
The photo showed Allie looking down, Lauren leaning in, hand covering Allie's.

It looked like whoever took the picture was standing right in front of them, but there hadn't been anyone else around until her mom pulled up. She was sure of it.

And then an echo surfaced, something Andrew had said months ago at the lake house, when she'd admired the photographs on the wall:
"I always keep at least one camera and a couple of lenses in the car. You never know when you're going to get the money shot."

Allie's blood went cold. Sitting right above the new text was the text she'd gotten after her first trip to the ER.

080625011013: You promised. When you break your promise, bad things happen.

Her chest tightened. She typed back with shaking fingers:
Leave me alone, Andrew. I haven't said anything to anyone.

She waited, but the dots never appeared.

Her mom shuffled into the kitchen like a shadow of herself, dark circles hollowing her eyes. She hadn't slept any better than Allie had.

"I know Kenzie works all the time, but is there any chance she can come home with you after school?" Angela's voice was rough with exhaustion. "I have to meet with the lawyer about last night, and until we get this straightened out, I don't want you here alone."

She set two keys on the table in front of Allie. "Here's your key-the same key works on all three doors. And here's a new one for Kenzie."

A second later, Allie's phone buzzed with the new garage code. She flinched at the vibration, pulse spiking, but Angela had already turned away to stir sugar into her coffee.

The ride to school was silent, each lost in their own thoughts.

Allie knew she needed to tell someone —Sanders, Aubrey's mom, anybody —about Andrew. But how could she? Her mom would never look at her the same way again. If Kenzie still cared, she'd be furious that Allie had kept such a big secret. And everyone else? They'd say what they always did: girls like Darcy were "empowered." Girls like Allie were "sluts."

If only there were a way to tell the truth without anyone else finding out.

"Okay, Allie?" They were parked by the school, and her mom was looking at her expectantly.

"I'm sorry?"

"Please text me when you get home from school. You and Kenzie can order dinner and put it on my card. Just order something for me and I'll eat when I get home, okay?"

Allie gulped, knowing full well Kenzie wasn't coming home with her. But she couldn't say that, so she nodded. "Sure. If Kenzie can't get out of work, is it okay if someone else comes over?"

Angela checked her watch, "I'd prefer Kenzie, but... as long as you're not home alone." She leaned across the console and kissed Allie's cheek. "Thank you for being so strong through this. It's not fair that it's happening right before your AP exams, but you're handling it all like a champ."

Allie's stomach dropped. *She definitely can't find out about Andrew. It would kill her.*

She smiled at her mom. "I love you."

"Love you, too, baby girl," Angela called as Allie shut the door.

The keys weighed heavily in her backpack as she walked inside. She wasn't ready to have that conversation with Kenzie, but knew she needed to convince someone to come home with her today.

The morning passed in a haze of practice tests and review packets.

Teagan's nonstop chatter as they walked between classes was a relief —noise to fill the space where her thoughts might have swallowed her whole.

By lunch, Kenzie, Eric, and Jackson were already at a table in Miss Lindstrom's room. Kenzie flicked her eyes up, offered the faintest smile, and looked back down, about what Allie had expected.

As she unpacked her lunch and handed the apples to Eric, Kenzie asked, "Why did your mom text me this morning? What are those numbers?"

Allie hesitated as everyone's head turned her way. She dug into her bag, pulled out the key, and set it on the table. "It's the new garage code. And here's your new key."

The key sat between them like an olive branch. Everyone's eyes flicked to Kenzie, waiting to see if she'd take it.

She stared for a long moment, her jaw tight. For a second, Allie thought she might reach for it, but then Kenzie shook her head and shrugged. "I think we're probably past that at this point." Her eyes dropped back to her phone.

"Why do you have new keys and a new garage code?" Eric asked, "Did something happen?"

Kenzie's eyes darted up, tension cracking her cool facade.

"Allie?" Her voice was soft and anxious at the same time.

* * *

The dam broke. Tears slid silently down Allie's cheeks as she told them everything- her dad, the police, the locks. "So my mom doesn't want me home by myself until things get sorted out," she finished with a sniff. "He's not allowed to come around."

"I'll come over tonight," Teagan volunteered immediately. "We need to work through the practice packet anyway."

"Wednesdays haven't been the same," Jackson added quietly, "If you're okay with me coming over again."

"I can do tomorrow," Trent offered. "And Teagan and I were going to study Bio at the library on Thursday, so we can just come over to your house instead."

"I guess that leaves Fridays for me and Kenz," said Eric.

Allie choked on a sob. "Really? You'd do that?" She looked between them, desperate and disbelieving.

The group nodded, and Kenzie, without saying a word, slid the key into her pocket.

CHAPTER 71- PROGRESS

Angela came home as Teagan and Allie were finishing the last slices of pepperoni pizza from Nonna's. Teagan had already packed her bag, but instead of ducking out awkwardly, she gave Angela a big hug.
"Don't worry, Mrs. Ellis. We've got your girl."

When the door closed behind her, Allie stayed at the table as her mom reheated a slice. Angela ate slowly, then finally spoke.

"I'm sorry, Allie, but we're going to have to talk about that summer. I had to tell the lawyer about my arm—about lying to the doctors and at work. You're going to have to talk about it, too. Because his name is on the mortgage, the house is in his name…" She trailed off, shaking her head. Then, more firmly: "But I know you can do it. And I'll be right there with you, okay?"

Allie nodded, but her throat stayed tight. *Would her mom really be right there if it was Andrew's name on everyone's lips? Or would she step back, the way she always had before?* She swallowed hard; the words lodged like a stone.

Before she could force them out, her mom broke down—just like Allie had at lunch. The attorney, the bills, being alone and scared… all of it tumbled out. Allie had never seen her like this. Kowtowing to her dad, throwing Allie under the bus to keep the peace, yes. But falling apart? Never.

Angela pulled herself together, embarrassed.

"It'll be okay," Allie reassured, and she told her about the after-school study plans with her friends.

Her mom hugged her tightly. "What would I do without you?"

Allie hesitated, then slid a paper flyer from her backpack. "There's something I wanted to talk to you about. This is the gelato shop right by school—Gusto's. We stopped by on the way home, and I talked to the manager. I can work there after school until you're done with aftercare. That way I'm not home alone, and no one needs to babysit me." She pushed through her nerves and added, "And… I was thinking I should get my license. For the nights you're scheduled late."

Angela stared, stunned. "You've really thought this through, haven't you?"

She shook her head. "It's too much, Allie. You'll be exhausted. You already have school, AP tests, finals…"

"I won't start until after AP exams," Allie countered quickly. "And I'm carrying all As. I'm caught up in my classes. It'll be fine, Mom."

Angela tossed out more obstacles, one after another, but Allie matched each with quiet determination. By the end of the night, she'd submitted her application to Gusto's and booked her driver's test for the next Tuesday.

And then, in a surprising gift from the universe, things actually went as planned. The week passed quietly—no word from Andrew, no sign of her dad. The house felt lighter, their laughter easier. By Sunday night, they had been lulled into a fragile, dangerous sense of comfort.

CHAPTER 72- THE RIGHT THING

The scrape of chairs and shuffle of papers filled the gym as the AP Bio exam ended. Proctors called instructions over the noise, corralling kids toward the doors. Allie slipped her calculator into her backpack and glanced around, but Teagan and Trent were nowhere in sight. That was fine- they'd agreed to meet at the car.

As she moved toward the exit, the proctor pressed a folded slip into her hand. "For you, from Miss Lindstrom. She's waiting for you in the hall."

Allie shoved it into her palm without looking and turned toward the outside doors. She squinted as she stepped out into the bright May sun.

Across the lot, Teagan leaned against her car, waving. Trent stood beside her, tossing his keys in the air. Relief sparked—an exit, something normal. She lifted her hand in return and started toward them.

"Miss Ellis."

Her steps faltered. Detective Sanders stepped out from where she'd been waiting, blocking her path.

Allie's fist clenched tighter around the slip until the paper ground into her skin.

"Please come inside," Sanders said evenly. "We can talk to Miss Lindstrom together."

"No." The word shot out like a blade. Allie shook her head hard. "I told you—I don't have anything else to say." She tried to walk past, but Sanders shifted, cutting her off.

"The other witness recanted," Sanders said, her voice flat but urgent. "We need to know what you know—or he's going to go free."

* * *

Without thinking, Allie blurted, "How can you do this to me *right now*? This is AP week! My whole life depends on these tests!"

For the first time, Sanders cracked. Her voice rose, sharp and raw.
"Your life depends on these tests? A rapist is going to walk free, and you're worried about test scores?"

The words slapped the air. Allie froze, heat rushing to her face, shame and fury colliding in her chest.

Sanders drew a breath, glancing toward the rows of cars as if trying to steady herself, but the effort failed. She turned back, her voice still edged.

"You think a number on a page is going to ruin your life? What about the lives he's already ruined—not just the one who came forward this time, but all the girls his father and his money have silenced? We need you, Allie."

"I told you, I don't know anything," but the denial was unbelievable, even to her own ears.

Sanders didn't apologize. Her glare cut Allie, even as her voice softened. "I know these scores feel like everything. But your GPA, your ACT—you can get a full ride to almost any school you want."
"Not Madison," Allie muttered.
"Do you even *want* to go to Madison?" Sanders asked, too sharp.

Allie's throat closed. She shook her head, unable to answer.

Sanders exhaled, then straightened, slipping fully back into composure as she reached into her jacket. She handed Allie another card.

"I believe you'll do the right thing."

Without another word, she turned and walked back into the building.

* * *

Allie forced her feet toward Teagan's car.

By the time she reached them, her hands were still trembling. Teagan and Trent straightened from where they'd been leaning against the car, almost humming with concern and curiosity.

No one spoke as they climbed in—Trent taking the passenger seat, Teagan sliding behind the wheel, Allie pulling the back door shut a beat later.

Teagan glanced at her in the rearview as she started the engine. "Did something else happen?"

"I don't know," Allie said too quickly, her fingers twisting together in her lap. "I don't know why she wanted to talk to me."

Trent twisted in the passenger seat. "Well… is she gonna talk to all of us again?"

"I said I don't know," Allie snapped, her voice sharp. She pressed back against the seat, shoulders rigid. "Can we just get lunch?"

Teagan shifted into gear, lips pressed tight, while Trent turned back forward. In the narrow space between them, Allie caught the glance they shared- quiet, uneasy, like a judgment passed without words.

Heat pricked the back of her neck. Shame flooded in, sharp and heavy, as if even they could see what she was hiding.

She locked her grip on her backpack strap, the canvas cutting into her fingers, the only solid thing she could hold as the car rolled out of the lot.

Allie sat on her bed with her study guide open but unread, Sanders's words still swirling in her head and scraping raw against her chest.

"I know you'll do the right thing."

Lauren had said the same thing, and Allie knew what they meant, what they wanted.

But how could it be the right thing when the truth of it all would probably destroy her mom?

She flopped back in frustration as her phone buzzed from the nightstand.

She reached for it, then froze mid-swipe. It wasn't Kenzie or Teagan or the group chat.

Her stomach dropped. It was him.

The picture of her and Sanders outside after the AP Bio exam opened below the others. The threat was even more ominous.

Last warning, Allie.

She pulled the blanket tighter, telling herself she was safe here, reminding herself that there were new locks.

I am safe. I am safe. I am safe.

She repeated this until she fell into an uneasy, dreamless sleep.

The next afternoon, she and Angela walked out of the DMV, both grinning ear to ear.

She felt steadier than she would have six months ago—more practiced, more sure. Back then, when her dad told her she couldn't get her license, she hadn't cared; she'd been too afraid of failing. Not now, though.

When the woman at the counter slid the temporary paper license across, the examiner smiled and said, "You passed."

Angela laughed, relief and something like pride shining through. "That's all we needed to hear."

Allie held the thin paper in both hands and grinned as Angela snapped a picture for Aunt Rachel.

"I told you you could do it," Angela said. "You practiced. You earned this." She pressed the keys into Allie's hand with a grin. "Now you're driving us home."

That evening, Gusto himself called to offer her the job, starting the Monday after AP exams finished. He'd been so impressed by their initial conversation that he didn't even want to interview her. A quick conversation about the details, and it was done. She whooped when she hung up her phone, and Angela scooped her into a huge hug.

A license. A job. Despite everything else going on, it felt like things were moving in the right direction.

The rest of the week blurred into review guides and color-coded notes. Miss Lindstrom slid a note across her desk—*You've got this*—and Allie tucked it into her notebook like a small amulet.

The after-school routine fell into place the same as the week before —Trent, Teagan, Jackson, even Kenzie and Eric— and it began to feel less like a protection detail and more like rekindled friendship.

By Friday, the edges of her world felt a little less jagged. Kenzie and Eric sprawled across her couch with burgers on their laps, a movie half-watched and mostly ignored. It wasn't the same as before— silences still pressed heavy—but then Kenzie laughed, a real laugh, and Eric teased them both until Allie couldn't help laughing, too.

Once the girls realized they still needed each other, things slipped back into place. Not whole, but close enough—and beneath it, the things they hadn't dared say hummed like a low static.

Prom came the next night- PicSee and the group chat filled with pictures of Eric and Kenzie. Teagan sent a selfie of her "self-care Saturday night"- complete with a neon green face mask. Trent chimed in from the bowling alley with his brothers. Jackson sent a picture from their cabin up north- *almost ready for the summer!* Allie added a picture of her and Angela curled up on the couch. A small ache pressed in Allie's chest. *Is this what she'd missed all year because of Andrew?*

She curled closer beside her mom, glad—though she'd never say it out loud—that she was with Angela that night.

Allie drove herself to Sweet Treats and grabbed donuts and coffee, then delivered them to her mom in bed. "Happy Mother's Day!"

They spent a lazy morning reading in bed until Allie's stomach growled, and Angela finally declared it was time to get up and be productive. Allie groaned and picked up the tray.

"Why don't you invite Kenzie over? Stacy's probably working today, and I'd love to hear more about prom."

Allie hesitated. Things had gotten easier with Kenzie, but were they at the point where she could just invite her over like old times? But in the old days, Allie wouldn't have had to invite her; Kenzie would have just come on her own.

She sent the text and held her breath. What if it was too much, too soon?

But the dots appeared almost instantly. "I need food. Do you want Culver's?"

Angela collected the wrappers and empty cups from the table. "How's your mom, Kenzie? I feel like it's been forever since I talked to her."

Kenzie gave a quick, crooked smile. "Working all the time, like usual. Between her job and mine, we barely see each other." She let out a small, self-deprecating laugh. "She says I'm basically raising myself."

Angela winced. "That's a lot for you, Kenzie." She looked between the two of them, her expression softening. "Neither of you should have to feel like you're on your own." Her gaze lingered on Allie. "I'm sorry I haven't been there the way you needed me. I'm here now, though. Okay?"

Under the table, Kenzie bumped her knee against Allie's- an old, private habit Allie recognized right away. Except now, Allie wasn't sure what it meant. *Me too, I'm here for you* or just *Join the club*. Either way, she drank in the familiarity of it.

And this time, for once, her mom's promise didn't feel like words that would fade the second the moment passed.

CHAPTER 74- PRESSURE POINT

The second week of exams stretched on, heavy as a rain-soaked coat. Test rooms were too cold, pencils snapped in anxious hands, teachers pacing the aisles as if silence alone could catch cheaters. Every night, Allie carried home more tension than answers, exhaustion piling behind her eyes until even blinking felt like work.

They threw the rotation out the window. Trent, Teagan, and Jackson came over each night. Flashcards, read-alouds, and timed writing exercises... as they each finished their exams, the rigor of the study sessions decreased, until only Allie and Teagan had their AP Psych exam on Friday. Jackson joked that they'd gone over their study packet so much he could probably get a five on the exam, and for a fleeting moment, the laughter around the table felt almost like before.

Midweek, the pressure shifted outside the classroom. Wednesday afternoon, the DA's office went public, formally asking any additional victims to come forward. Within minutes, the school was buzzing again, students retreating to the sides they'd chosen when Andrew was first arrested. Half were convinced the whole thing was a grab for attention or revenge; the other half swore victims would be crawling out of the woodwork any day now.

Allie kept her head down, mouth shut, aware that Kenzie was doing the same. At the end of the day, she texted her a single pink heart. Kenzie sent the matching green heart back immediately.

Thursday night, the four gave up the pretense of studying. They sat around the coffee table, eating leftovers, telling war stories of the exams they'd taken over the last two weeks. They ignored the sitcom on the TV until it cut to a commercial, and the laugh track was replaced by the news anchor's somber voice. A moment later, the image cut to Andrew's attorney, smug and certain, declaring that the DA was panicked and that this was nothing more than a last-ditch Hail Mary before the clock ran out.

The group went silent, exchanging glances.

* * *

"She needs to come forward," Trent finally said.

Teagan's head snapped towards him. "Or maybe," she shot back, "if Kenzie's not ready to talk, no one, especially not someone with a Y chromosome, gets to decide that for her."

Their voices rose, sparring across the plates on the table. Allie sat frozen, guilt rising like a tide, the words she wasn't saying pressing heavier than the ones they were shouting. Relief flickered that the spotlight was on Kenzie and not her, but it twisted fast, curdling when she realized Jackson wasn't arguing. Instead, he was watching her, eyes steady as if he knew everything.

She dropped her gaze, heat crawling up her neck.

Jackson finally cleared his throat, and the cousins quieted. "What matters is she knows we're with her," he said simply. "Whether she talks or not. Whether she was drunk or not. She needs to know we won't turn our backs."

The words landed heavier than any of the arguments before. Trent and Teagan murmured their agreement. Allie mumbled something in return, then rose to start clearing plates as the others packed their bags to go home.

Friday afternoon, she should have felt relieved; the burden of her AP exams finally gone. Instead, the weight of her silence pressed so heavy she could hardly breathe.

Allie slipped out the side doors, scanning the parking lot for Kenzie's jeep.

That was when she saw her—waiting a few yards down the sidewalk, angled just enough to make it clear it wasn't chance. Her first instinct was to flee back into the building, but that wouldn't accomplish anything. Resigned, she crossed the grass to talk to Aubrey's mom.

Lauren turned without a word and guided her around the corner, away from the flow of students. Her expression carried all the control of her profession, but the cracks showed in her eyes.

"I saw the press conference," Allie blurted before Lauren could say anything. "If you're so sure he's what you say he is, someone else will come forward. You don't need me."

"Aubrey needs you," Lauren said quietly. "She needs you to explain why you warned her. What you knew." Her voice hitched. "She's blaming herself. His attorneys have gotten in her head, and now she's doubting herself."

Allie clutched the strap of her bag so tightly her knuckles burned.

"She barely sleeps," Lauren said, words rushing out now. "When she does, it's nightmares. She can't stay in school more than a couple of days before she falls apart. And she thinks—" Her voice broke. She swallowed, tried again. "She thinks he's outside her door at night. That he's waiting for her. She's terrified, Allie. Terrified no one will believe her."

The words tilted the world beneath Allie's feet. Her eyes flicked over her shoulder, skimming the row of parked cars. For one sharp second, she was sure she saw someone sitting behind the glass, a shadowed outline against the light. Her chest squeezed, panic clamping down hard. But when she blinked, the shape was gone. She told herself she was imagining it. She had to be imagining it.

Lauren's eyes pleaded. "If he hurt you too, please—please don't let her think she's the only one."

Allie's throat locked tight. Her thoughts swirled....
She needs to know we won't turn our backs. (Jackson, steady, sure)
I'm here now, though. Okay? (Angela, quiet, sincere)
The answering green heart. (Kenzie's promise that they were still connected)

She drew in a ragged breath. And then one more thought edged its way in- sharp, taunting:
Last chance, Allie.

She shook her head, "I can't," she blurted, a tear escaping, as she turned and ran, desperate to find Kenzie's Jeep- desperate to be anywhere but here.

Angela came home early, the last exam behind them, the house filled with home-cooked smells and, finally, soft with ordinary sounds. Kenzie curled into the corner of the couch, blanket tangled at her ankles. Eric stretched out in the armchair, plate balanced on his knee. For once, it didn't feel like protection duty. It felt like a Friday.

Angela's phone buzzed in her hand. She read the message, frowning.
All three of them turned toward her.

"That was Aunt Rachel. Her basement's flooding again. She needs me tomorrow—pretty much all day." Angela's eyes lingered on Allie. "Sorry, kiddo. I know you were looking forward to a lazy day, but I can't leave you here by yourself. Not until we have an actual restraining order."

The words pressed like a weight against Allie's ribs. She almost argued, but one look at her mom—tired, stretched thin—made her swallow it back.

Kenzie leaned forward, the blanket sliding to the floor. "We can stay," she nodded towards Eric, "We want a lazy day too!"
Eric nodded. "I can take the guest room," he offered, then hesitated at the look on Angela's face, "...or come over first thing if that's easier." He shrugged. "Just so there's, you know... a man in the house."
Relief flickered across Angela's face. "Thank you. The guest room will be fine." She paused, "Do you need a toothbrush or anything? Kenzie's got all of her things here, but I can get you whatever you need."
"It's fine," Eric said, "I've got all of that in my gym bag. I'll go get it."

Something eased in Allie's chest. She looked at Kenzie, already pulling out her phone to text her mom, at Eric heading for the door.

They didn't hesitate. Jackson's voice surfaced: *She needs to know we won't turn our backs.* He'd been talking about Kenzie, but she'd wanted so badly for him to mean her. And now, watching them, it felt like he was.

Angela touched her arm. "You okay?"

Allie nodded too fast. "Yeah. Just tired."

Kenzie tossed her the blanket. "Movie?"

"Sure."

They let the TV pick for them—something loud and ridiculous. Angela reappeared with popcorn, and Eric dimmed the lights. Explosions lit the room while Allie counted cracks in the ceiling until her thoughts let go.

After the credits, they cleaned the kitchen together. It was so normal that Allie's throat tightened. She checked the locks out of habit, fingers pressing hard against the deadbolt. Angela was watching when she turned back, eyes soft with concern.

"You sure you don't mind me going to Aunt Rachel's?"

"I don't," Allie said. And for once, it felt true.

Eric disappeared down the hall to the guest room. Angela set the newly installed alarm, kissed Allie's head, and told them goodnight.

Kenzie followed Allie upstairs without asking, charger in hand. "I'll take the floor if you want," she said lightly.

"Like I'm going to let you sleep on the floor."

They brushed their teeth side by side, then climbed into the same bed they'd been sharing since kindergarten. At first, they lay back to back, but as the house quieted—guest room door closing, Angela's footsteps fading—Kenzie rolled toward her.

"You okay?" she whispered.

"Yeah." Allie's throat tightened. "Thanks for staying."

"Duh. You'd do it for me."

The room went still. Allie let her hand rest against Kenzie's under the blanket, grounding herself in the simple warmth. Sleep came softer than she expected.

And in the pale slice of morning light, when she blinked awake nose to nose with her best friend, she knew the decision she'd only circled last night had settled.

Monday, she would talk to Miss Lindstrom. She would ask for Sanders. Aubrey deserved this kind of circle—someone steady at her side, someone who wouldn't let go.

A quiet knock landed on Allie's door at the exact moment her phone buzzed on the nightstand. She rolled toward it and caught the preview. **Mom**: *At Rachel's. Got here safe. Basement is a mess but we're fine. Love you.* Allie didn't even open it.

Eric slipped inside and went around to Kenzie's side of the bed, crouching low. His hands moved like he was trying to scoop panicked words out of the air without making a sound.
Allie's phone buzzed again—*Mom again.* She ignored it.

Then she saw what Eric was holding—Burn Book open on his screen, the logo like a bruise in the dim light.

Her phone buzzed a third time. She swiped, thumb clumsy.

080625011013: I told you to keep your mouth shut. I hope you're ready for everyone to see exactly what you are.

Her hands went cold. She tapped the app.

A picture filled the screen. Not a picture. **The** picture.

He arranged her hair again, settled the necklace between her breasts, and told her to close her eyes and think about what they'd just done. She was going to protest again until he said that last part. She involuntarily thought about his hands... his mouth. Her eyes flew open when she heard the telltale click of the camera.
"You have to delete that," she begged.
"You trust me or you don't," he said, handing her the phone. "Look at it. You are so beautiful. And when I look at this picture, I will know that I'm the one that put that smile on your face."

Her face was blurred, but there was no doubt. On the nightstand sat the two photos Kenzie had given her. The stack of books. Her nightstand was instantly recognizable to anyone who'd ever been in her room.

* * *

A cry tore out of her throat before she knew she was making it. Kenzie turned and was by her side, pulling her close. The sobs that followed were jagged, animal. Kenzie held her, shushing uselessly, "It'll be okay. It'll be okay."

"I'm calling Jackson," Eric whispered, already backing toward the hall. "Teagan and Trent, too."

"No!" Allie gasped, the word scraping raw. But Eric was already on the phone and heading downstairs.

Allie gagged and grabbed the trash can; when the retching finally stopped, she pressed her forearm to her mouth. Voices gathered on the stairs; shoes hit the hallway hardwood; the bedroom door edged wider.

Jackson came in first, every muscle tight with protective rage, but his eyes swept the room with a soldier's focus, as if he could both shield her and hunt down the person who'd done this in the same breath.

Teagan and Trent followed him in. Teagan went straight to the bed, settling on Allie's other side. With Kenzie tight against one shoulder and Teagan bracing the other, Allie was caught between them, small and shaking, held steady by their quiet presence.

Jackson and Trent moved to Allie's desk, laptops open in one motion. "We need to capture as much as we can," he said, not looking away from the screen. "Trent, Eric—screenshots. Full threads, not just the post. Capture timestamps, handles, and anything tied to PatientZero or Allie. Video your scroll if you have to."

Teagan called out, "Working on damage control. I'm in the comments."

The thread was moving like a stampede—gross jokes, posturing, curiosity doing what it always did when it thought it was safe.

SuzeeQ: WTAF? This is messed up.
DietCokeLVR: If it's who I think it is, she's only 16
BaiGuy: Jail bait HAHAHAHAHAHA

JoeyTribbiani: Wait- what?

Teagan saw the opportunity she was looking for. She typed furiously.

IndigoGirl: *If she's 16 this is CSAM. Report it. Downloading = felony. Look it up.*

That was the crack.

SuzeeQ: *Reporting.*
Goin2MadTown: *Reporting and deleting. This is disgusting..*
JoeyTribbiani: *...oh shit*
42Y7XR: *Delete your downloads. I'm out.*

The copycat replies multiplied until the thread was clogged. *Reporting and deleting. Reporting and deleting.*

The app hiccuped, stuttered, and collapsed into a gray error screen: *Something went wrong. Try again later.*
All six of them froze. It wasn't just the thread- the entire app had gone dark.

Jackson swore and dropped his head in resignation.

"What happened?" Teagan asked quickly, eyes darting between them. "Everything's gone."
Trent and Eric lifted their phones, both showing the same gray screen.

Jackson stared at his laptop, then at them, his hands lifting helplessly. "Somebody shut it down." The focused intensity was gone. He turned to Allie, "I didn't get it. I'm sorry."

Kenzie's grip tightened around Allie, pulling her closer. "We'll figure something out," Teagan whispered.

Eric rubbed his face, "So what- do we call the cops?"

"No cops!" Allie burst out, curling tighter against Kenzie. "I can't. I just can't."

* * *

No one argued. The air filled instead with hushed scraps of thought- Teagan worrying the image would resurface, Trent muttering about colleges, Eric pacing at the foot of the bed… all talking around her, over her.

Jackson closed his laptop softly, like ending a scene. "We still have what we saved," he said. "Someone with more experience and technology can use it. Maybe they can find who did this."

Allie stared at the dimmed phone, at the place where the picture had been, at Kenzie's knuckles pale against the duvet. Something clicked into focus—not bravery, not really. Just the smallest sliver of control she could grab with both hands.

"I know who to call," she said. Her voice shook; she made it keep going. "She can get everything to the right people."
The group sat silently as Allie made the call, explained what happened, what she needed.

Lauren arrived twenty minutes later, coat damp from the drizzle, face composed in the way of someone who has learned to walk into hard rooms without making them worse. Detective Sanders followed, and quickly introduced the two men with her.

The computer forensic analyst went straight to where Jackson had the laptops set up on the table, "Talk me through what you've got."
Detective Sanders and the second man moved to the other end of the table, setting up their own laptops, arranging bags and containers in neat rows.

Lauren took in the bedraggled group of friends. "I can't be part of this officially," she said, eyes steady on Allie. "But once I understood what we were looking at, I told Detective Sanders we needed to move quickly. She and Officer Parker will handle collection and preservation. You don't have to say anything you're not ready to say. Right now, we're making sure what you caught doesn't disappear."

Sanders and Parker spoke with each of them and copied the relevant information from their phones. Took statements.

Except for the questions and answers, and some coordination between Sanders and the other police officers, no one spoke.

As soon as Sanders indicated they had what they needed, Lauren stood. "Can I speak with you privately?" She asked Allie.

Allie followed Lauren until they were out of earshot. Detective Sanders slipped into the room with them. "Do you need a hug?" Lauren asked.

Allie burst into tears again. "What am I going to do about my mom? This is going to kill her. She's going to kill me. I just got a job and my license, and now it turns out I'm just the stupid kid my dad always said I was."

Lauren's voice was soft. "No, you're not. Believing he loved you isn't stupid."

Sanders spoke up, "I have to ask you about the texts on your phone."

Allie choked back a sob, "I don't want to talk about it."

"The person that took that picture is in your phone as SB, Secret Boyfriend, right?" Sanders continued. Allie nodded numbly as Lauren gently squeezed her shoulder. "You call him Andrew."

Allie didn't say anything, just stared at the floor.

"This is going to come out, Allie. At this point, there's nothing we can do to stop it; we can only try to manage the timeline and the narrative. We aren't judging you, but we do need the full picture."

"I can't," Allie squeaked.

"Andrew Mason was your secret boyfriend, right?"
Allie finally nodded.

"You had a sexual relationship with him?" Another nod. "And at some point in the relationship, he took that picture of you?"

"He said he deleted it," Allie blurted, tears falling again. "He promised me."

* * *

Sanders continued to walk Allie through the timeline of her relationship with Andrew- the breakup, the harassment on Burn Book, the threats once he was arrested. Allie just nodded.

Sanders waited until Allie finally looked up. "You didn't do anything wrong here. You're lucky you have friends that were so quick to act. I'm confident we'll get him, Allie, but it's not going to be easy for you. Keep your head up. You're not the first person—not even the first high schooler— that this has happened to. Trust your friends. Trust your mom."

Sanders nodded, then turned to go.

Allie started to follow, but Lauren stopped her. "I wanted to apologize, Allie. This whole time, I thought you were trying to protect him. You were just trying to protect yourself and your mom."

"I can't go back out there and face them," Allie said. "I can't face my mom."

"You can," Lauren reassured her. "It wasn't easy for Aubrey to tell me. She blames herself. She feels the same way you do. But she's not stupid, and it wasn't her fault. You have to believe that, too. Trust them, Allie. They won't let you down."

When Allie and Lauren returned to the living room, Sanders and the officers were packed up and waiting for them.

Sanders thanked them again, said they'd be in touch, and left- the group frozen, trying to process what had just happened.

Then, they all spoke at once,

"Are you okay?"- Teagan and Kenzie asked at the same time.
"I can order pizza." - Eric.
"I'm sorry I didn't get it all, Allie."- Jackson.
"What do you need?"- Trent

Another tear slid down Allie's cheek. She felt like she hadn't stopped crying since she first saw that awful picture.

"No, I'm not okay," she finally answered. "Thank you for being here and helping. I don't know what I need. For this to have never happened? To not talk about it?"

They stared at her, a range of emotions across their faces.

Kenzie's phone buzzed. She looked down and typed a response. "Your mom is staying at Aunt Rachel's tonight," she said, looking at Allie. "Teagan and I are going to stay here with you tonight, and she said to go ahead and get dinner for everyone from Nonna's. It's Aunt Rachel's way of saying thanks."

"My mom knows you're all here?"
"I told her it was an end-of-APs party. She thought it was a great idea."

Kenzie reached out and grabbed her best friend's trembling hand. "You don't have to tell us. We're here for you no matter what."

One by one, they each reiterated the sentiment until Allie was a puddle of tears in the middle of their friendship.

CHAPTER 77- THE LOST WEEK

By Sunday afternoon, the house felt wrong. Too quiet, too clean—like it had swallowed everything that happened yesterday and was pretending nothing was missing.

Teagan stayed through most of the day, then left to go home and shower.

Kenzie and Allie sat on opposite ends of the couch, scrolling through their phones even though there was nothing left to check.

The only sounds were the refrigerator humming too loudly and the washing machine thudding down the hall.

Angela was still at Aunt Rachel's, helping pump water from the flooded basement. Around noon, Allie's phone buzzed.

Mr. Gusto: *I'm going to be out of the store this week. Let's start you next Tuesday instead, okay?*

Relief hit so hard it almost made her dizzy. She texted back a quick *of course* and set the phone facedown. One more reprieve.

Angela pulled into the driveway that evening, headlights washing across the front windows. She came in smelling like rain and disinfectant. "Hey, sweetie," she said, hanging her jacket. "You okay? You look pale."

Allie shrugged. "Just tired."

Kenzie jumped in before Angela could ask more. "She hasn't been sleeping great. Finals stress."

Angela nodded, too worn out to argue. "Maybe stay home tomorrow. Get your feet back under you."

Allie nodded again, eyes burning.

Later, she lay awake listening to the dishwasher hum, the steady rhythm of normal life pressing against everything that wasn't normal at all.

The week drifted by in fragments. Each day folded into the next until even the silence had patterns. Angela stayed home on Monday, then agreed to leave Allie home alone as long as the doors were locked and the alarm was set.

* * *

Her teachers put assignments in ClassLink.

Her friends texted funny memes and came over after school, but now an awkwardness was slowly eroding her sense of belonging with them. She knew they wanted an explanation. She believed she owed them one.

But she couldn't make herself say the words. Couldn't tell them who or why.

Lauren called once to confirm the FBI had everything they needed. Her voice was calm, professional. *We're still working backward*, she said. *Don't worry about school yet. Just take care of yourself.*

Allie promised she would.

Angela hovered at the edges—refilling Allie's water glass, leaving toast outside her door, checking her forehead like it was the flu. Each time Allie said she felt better, her mom's relief looked real enough that lying almost felt kind.

Outside, spring kept moving. The trees thickened, lawns brightened, and graduation banners appeared on fences. The rest of the world felt louder for how still she'd become.

By the time the long weekend came, the neighborhood smelled like charcoal and rain. Angela tried to coax her into coming along to a cookout at a coworker's, but Allie faked a headache and stayed home.

She spent the afternoon scrolling through old pictures — she and Kenzie grinning ear to ear, arms around each other. She didn't recognize that girl anymore.

Mr Gusto called, apologized, explained it was a family emergency, and asked Allie if she could start later in the week. Allie agreed, no longer sure she could even work somewhere where all of the kids from school hung out.

Kenzie called, encouraging her to come back.

Teagan texted.

The group chat swore they would end anyone who even looked at her funny.

* * *

Tuesday came before she was ready.

Allie struggled with what to wear. She settled on jeans and a t-shirt and her mom's old, gray cardigan.

Downstairs, Kenzie waited in the driveway, Jeep idling. The ride to school was a rhythm of Allie starting to panic, Kenzie talking her down. Teagan and Trent were waiting for them in the parking lot, and the four walked in together.

The halls still smelled like floor wax and sweaty teens, the lights too bright after a week in hiding.

The whispers started almost immediately.

Kenzie walked half a step ahead, daring anyone to speak. Allie kept her eyes on the floor.

Darcy started to say something in AP Psych when Teagan leaned in and whispered something. Darcy paled, but flipped her hair and made a comment about how stupid it was to assign papers over a 4-day weekend.

By the time the final bell rang, she felt scraped raw.

"You survived," Kenzie said, looping her arm through Allie's.

"Barely," said Allie. "I just want to go home and sleep for a week."

"Everyone's stopping for snacks and then heading to your house." Kenzie pushed the side door open. "Do you want me to text them and tell them not to come?"

"No," said Allie. "I like having them all come over."

"You mean you like having a group of friends? Like more than just me?" Kenzie pressed a hand to her chest in mock horror.

Allie laughed, then sobered as she remembered Kenzie's goals for their junior year- parties, friends, boys... at least the friends part had finally worked out.

Kenzie unlocked the Jeep, and they threw their bags in the back.

Allie had just started to climb in when she heard her name.

"Allie!"

The voice froze her in place.

She turned to see Aubrey running toward them.

CHAPTER 78- THE TRUTH OF IT

Aubrey's hair was loose, her eyes red-rimmed, her expression raw.

Kenzie had already opened the driver's door, one foot in, but she hesitated, hand still on the handle.

Aubrey stopped a few feet away, breathless. "They're filing a motion to dismiss," she blurted. "The DA lost the hearing on Friday. My mom says the judge doesn't think there's enough to move forward."

Allie's pulse stuttered. "I'm sorry," she managed, her voice paper-thin.
Aubrey's eyes filled. "Sorry? That's all you have to say?"

Allie shook her head, already trembling. "I don't know what you want me to…"

"I want you to tell the truth!" Aubrey cut in, voice breaking. "You warned me. You knew."

"I didn't know," Allie said softly. "I just… he was saying the same things to you that he said to me. I didn't want him to…"
"Didn't want him to what?" Aubrey demanded, taking a step closer.

Allie's throat closed. The parking lot noise blurred around them—the slam of car doors, the faint sounds from the baseball field. Everything else felt miles away.

Aubrey drew a shuddering breath, shoulders shaking. "He *raped* me, Allie."

Kenzie's head snapped up, but Aubrey didn't even notice her.

Allie's voice cracked. "But he didn't rape me. He told me he loved me. I wanted him… wanted it."

"Then why did you warn me? Because of Darcy?" Aubrey demanded.

"No. Because after he started dating her… things seemed clearer. When he wasn't always around —telling me I had to prove I loved him — it was like I could finally think. I didn't want him to make you feel the same way."

"So you *did* know what he was," Aubrey whispered, tears staining her cheeks.

"No," Allie faltered, pressing her hands to her temples. "It's complicated. I didn't know he would do that," Allie's voice dropped to a whisper. "But he made me do things… that I didn't want to do. Things I thought I wanted because he said I should."

Aubrey's voice wavered as she put the pieces together. "The picture? That was him?"

Allie's head bowed. "And other things."

The silence that followed was heavy, alive.

Then Kenzie came around the Jeep, voice trembling. "The bruises? He did that, didn't he?"
Allie nodded.
"Why didn't you tell me?"
"I didn't think there was anything to tell," Allie said, shoulders curling inward. "And we weren't really talking about important things then."

Kenzie's face crumpled. "I'm such a shitty friend. I'm so sorry."

Aubrey finally looked at her. "You're the one from the cafeteria," she said slowly. "You said he tried to rape you, then you wouldn't talk to the police."

Kenzie swallowed hard. "It was my word against his and Darcy's. They made me think no one would believe me. Then those fake pictures on Burn Book made me look like a slut."

* * *

Aubrey took a shaky step forward. "It's not too late. You both have to come forward- before they file the motion. Allie, you're only sixteen. You can't even give consent."

"But I'll have to tell them everything I did," Allie said, shame coloring her cheeks. "Everything I said yes to... and then what happened when I finally said no."

"So tell them," Aubrey whispered fiercely.

Allie shook her head, tears catching in her throat. "You don't understand."

"What don't I understand?" Aubrey pleaded.

"It's my fault." The words were barely audible.

Aubrey froze. "What do you mean?"

The words spilled out in a whisper. "That night... he broke into my house. He acted like everything was fine. Like we were getting back together." Her voice fractured. "But I didn't want to. Be with him like that again. He kept pushing and pushing." Her eyes flicked to Kenzie. "He threatened to hurt you. When you were banging on the door."

Kenzie went absolutely still, her face draining of color.

"So I yelled at you," Allie whispered, tears sliding unchecked, "And told you to go away. Then Mrs. Campbell came over, and he ran. If I had just said yes, he wouldn't have gone to your house. It's my fault he raped you."

For a long, aching moment, none of them spoke. Then Kenzie stepped forward and pulled Allie into a fierce hug.

Aubrey hesitated, then put her arms around them both. "It's not your fault. Or mine. It's his."

When they finally stepped apart, the silence between them was raw, but steadier.

"So you'll come forward?" Aubrey asked, eyes red but hopeful.

Kenzie reached for Allie's hand- the same gesture she'd used a hundred times when they were little, on playgrounds and in hallways, and every other time words had failed. Their eyes met, and Allie gave the slightest nod.

* * *

"I'll call my mom," Aubrey's voice shook.

"Tell her we'll talk to her tomorrow," Allie said, summoning confidence she didn't feel.

Around them, the parking lot came back into focus- the shouts, the car doors, the everyday hum of a world still moving. But the three of them stood in the center of it, the quiet between them the fragile start of something that could finally make them whole again.

The house was bright with late-afternoon light, quiet except for the steady murmur of the TV.
Kenzie had dropped her off and gone home to talk to Stacy—to prepare her for what was coming.

Allie set her keys on the counter and walked toward the living room.

Angela was home early, papers stacked beside her on the coffee table, her jacket draped over the arm of the couch. She looked up when Allie came in.
"I met with the lawyer," she said, her voice steadier than it had been in months. "The judge granted the permanent restraining order this morning."
Allie blinked. "That's good."
Angela nodded once. "Yeah. It's finally over."

But Allie barely heard her. Something on the TV had frozen her in place. Her breath caught, and her body stilled. She felt a chill run down her spine and leaned into the couch to catch her balance.

"Andrew Mason," the anchor said, "appeared at the Dane County Courthouse this afternoon as his attorneys filed a motion to dismiss all charges."

The camera panned wide.

Andrew stood on the courthouse steps, Darcy draped on his arm, his father and the latest girlfriend poised on the other side of the attorneys. He looked untouched—hair trimmed, suit pressed, sunlight glinting off his watch as if he'd earned the right to shine.

For a heartbeat, memory collided with reality: that first day in the cafeteria.
Headphones on. Book open. The way he'd brushed his hair from his eyes and smiled without looking up.

He'd been quiet, thoughtful, invisible.
Now everyone saw him.

Flashes burst from every direction as reporters crowded the steps. The headline across the bottom read:
JUDGE NOT EXPECTED TO MAKE RULING TODAY.

The lead attorney spoke first, calm and certain.
"The district attorney's office made a public plea for additional witnesses and received no response," he said. "We remain confident the case will be dismissed. There is simply no credible evidence."

The noise of cameras and shouting reporters filled the screen.

His father stepped forward, smiling as though the cameras belonged to him.
"My son is a good young man," he said. "This has been a nightmare for our family, and it's time for it to end. These claims were never about truth—they were about money."

Another lawyer leaned in, whispered something to the first. He checked his watch and turned toward the crowd. "We have no comment at this time. We are confident the facts of this case will speak for themselves and that our client will be found not guilty on all counts. It's time to go in," he said. "By this time tomorrow, this will all be over."

The group began climbing the courthouse steps. Andrew turned halfway up, met the camera's gaze, and smiled—confident, deliberate, practiced.

Allie's chest constricted. The light from the TV felt too bright, the air too sharp, the sound too close.

Angela followed her stare, her expression softening as she recognized the name.
"Allie?" she said quietly.

Allie didn't look away.

* * *

The screen stilled on his smile, the same one she'd once believed was just for her.

"Mom," she whispered, not sure her mom would hear her over her pounding heart.
"I need to tell you something."

Epilogue

Federal Charges Filed Against Monona West Teen in Burn Book Case

DANE COUNTY — Federal prosecutors have filed new charges against Andrew Mason, 18, the former Monona West High School student accused of creating the teen social media app *Burn Book*.

Investigators say the app spread quickly among Monona West students last fall before being shut down in May, after an explicit image of a minor was posted and widely reported. The FBI traced the app's servers to a company owned by Mason's father and has since collected evidence from dozens of student devices.

In addition to the federal charges, Mason is now facing a growing number of sexual assault allegations. Earlier this month, two more Monona West students came forward, one of whom reported an attempted assault. Prosecutors say their statements encouraged additional victims to speak out, widening the scope of the case.

Mason faces multiple counts of sexual assault and attempted sexual assault of minors, along with federal charges related to the possession and distribution of child pornography.